SAVE IT FOR SUNDAY

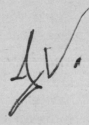

*Look for these exciting Western series from bestselling
authors William W. Johnstone and J.A. Johnstone*

The Mountain Man

Luke Jensen: Bounty Hunter

Brannigan's Land

The Jensen Brand

Preacher and MacCallister

Fort Misery

The Fighting O'Neils

Perley Gates

MacCoole and Boone

Guns of the Vigilantes

Shotgun Johnny

The Chuckwagon Trail

The Jackals

The Slash and Pecos Westerns

The Texas Moonshiners

Stoneface Finnegan Westerns

Ben Savage: Saloon Ranger

The Buck Trammel Westerns

The Death and Texas Westerns

The Hunter Buchanon Westerns

Will Tanner: U.S. Deputy Marshal

WILLIAM W. JOHNSTONE
AND J.A. JOHNSTONE

SAVE IT FOR SUNDAY

PINNACLE BOOKS
KENSINGTON PUBLISHING CORP.
www.kensingtonbooks.com

PINNACLE BOOKS are published by

Kensington Publishing Corp.
119 West 40th Street
New York, NY 10018

PUBLISHER'S NOTE: Following the death of William W. Johnstone, the Johnstone family is working with a carefully selected writer to organize and complete Mr. Johnstone's outlines and many unfinished manuscripts to create additional novels in all of his series like The Last Gunfighter, Mountain Man, and Eagles, among others. This novel was inspired by Mr. Johnstone's superb storytelling.

All Kensington titles, imprints, and distributed lines are available at special quantity discounts for bulk purchases for sales promotion, premiums, fund-raising, and educational or institutional use.

Special book excerpts or customized printings can also be created to fit specific needs. For details, write or phone the office of the Kensington Sales Manager: Kensington Publishing Corp., 119 West 40th Street, New York, NY 10018. Attn. Sales Department. Phone: 1-800-221-2647.

PINNACLE BOOKS, the Pinnacle logo, and the WWJ steer head logo Reg. U.S. Pat. & TM Off.

First Printing: April 2023
ISBN-13: 978-0-7860-4957-8
ISBN-13: 978-0-7860-4958-5 (eBook)

10 9 8 7 6 5 4 3 2 1

Printed in the United States of America

CHAPTER 1

Wyoming Territory, 1876

And it came to pass . . .

It was a stagecoach, moving as though the hounds of Hell were trying to jump into the rear boot. It wasn't a Concord, but one of those Abbott & Downing mud wagons—though the trail wasn't even damp. Boxy-looking, not as big as a Concord and bouncing like it was out of control as the driver serenaded the six mules pulling the coach with every cuss word in his vocabulary. The leather curtains were rolled up. No guard to be seen.

Perhaps he had jumped off or quit.

The horse and rider nearby didn't get a good look at any passengers inside.

It passed Taylor Callahan, riding the slow-footed white gelding he'd named Job, as if horse and man were standing still like wind-blown boulders sprinkled across the rolling plains.

Nary a salutation came from the driver, who spit out a stream of tobacco juice that shot past Callahan's beard stubble like a minié ball.

And it came to pass . . .

Taylor Callahan ran those words through his mind again, nodded, and pulled down the kerchief as the dust kicked up by the mud wagon settled on the grass and rocks on the southeastern side of the trail. Yes, he could use that. It would work fine. *It* being the stagecoach. *Pass* being the verb and . . .

The jangling of traces and more ribald language caused Callahan to turn around. Could that be?

He eased Job farther off the trail, turned the gelding around to see another approaching mud wagon, also with a foul-mouthed driver and no guard. Remembering one of his pappies had always said, "Time brings wisdom to most critters," Callahan had time and wisdom to pull up his bandanna and cover his mouth and nose again.

Once again, the driver paid no attention and made no gesture, friendly or otherwise, to the tall man in black on a white horse. But Callahan got a good look inside the coach. A handsome woman in a fine green dress, her hair in a bun, was holding what might have been a Bible. And she might have smiled at him, or perhaps Job. She even offered a friendly, fleeting wave as the coach rolled past.

Callahan let the dust settle again before he lowered the bandanna and nudged Job back onto the road. He looked behind him a good long while before he felt satisfied no more speeding mud wagons were stampeding north. And he forgot about any puns or wit he would display at his next preaching, as he just let the gelding carry him leisurely north.

However, he did keep looking over his shoulder while plodding across a country that looked like waves on the ocean. He wanted to make sure no other coaches came up behind him. The last thing he wanted was to be greeted by the Major General in the Heavens at Saint Peter's Gate and be told he had been killed after being run over by an Abbott & Downing Company mud wagon.

The sun had started to sink behind the mountains far off to the west. Coming out of Denver, Colorado, Callahan had thought most of the Rocky Mountains would be like the

Front Range just west of Denver. Mountains reaching to the skies, often their tops disappearing behind clouds. But in what Callahan figured had to be Wyoming Territory, the mountains appeared to be a good ride southwest or northwest.

Oh, they weren't flat plains like he had seen in Kansas, or just last year way down in southern Texas. The way the wind blew the tall grass, Callahan almost thought he was in an ocean. Which reminded him: *I still ain't let my eyes feast on an ocean.*

That had been his plan when he was drifting south in Texas. To see the great seas, where the whale had swallowed Jonah, though some blowhard Texan had told him he wouldn't see an ocean, just the Gulf of Mexico, or maybe even nothing more than the Corpus Christi Bay. He had hardly seen anything wet except one of the most vicious flash floods he had ever witnessed. And coming from a childhood in western Missouri, Taylor Callahan had seen many a flood. The Mighty Missouri was no little crick when she flooded. One of the first funerals the Reverend Taylor Callahan had ever preached was for a ten-year-old boy who got caught when the Sni-A-Bar Creek got to raging.

That reminded him of the four Harris boys. If they had not been lynched or shot down like the dogs they were— *May the Major General in the Heavens forgive me for thinking in such an unforgiving kind of way*—they could be after him yet.

He reined in Job and looked down the trail. The dust from the two stages had long settled. No travelers could be seen as far as he could see. And he could see a right far piece in that country. Hills were all around him, popping up here and there, rocks strewn about, and he could even find a tree, usually along the creek beds, even though he'd not seen much in the way of water in those creek beds.

Strange country. Pretty, but different. It looked as though the old Major General in the Heavens had been trying to see what He or She ought to make Wyoming Territory look like. Maybe the General had decided those mountains off to the west were too much like Colorado and the Great Plains had already been perfected when Kansas got created. How about some of these red rocks and boulders and dust to blow? That ain't half bad, but, well . . . Callahan understood. He had seen parts like that when he had left Texas and ridden up through New Mexico Territory, mostly following the Pecos River.

The hills he was riding through weren't consistent, either. Some of them were rolling like the waves, but here and there he found buttes, mostly barren, some with boulders that appeared to have been dropped out of the sky.

Meteorites? Maybe all those shooting stars he had seen, sometimes making wishes on, though rarely, if ever, seeing one of those wishes come true. Those stars had to land somewhere. But the rocks like the two Job was riding between did not look like the moon did when she was close and shining bright, nor had that little piece of hard rock he had paid a three-cent nickel to see at that dog-and-pony show in Trinidad, Colorado, a few months back. The professor swore it was a part of a meteorite that had come past Mars and the moon and landed in Utah back in '69. But he might not have been the most honest person since his assistant was peddling bottles of Doctor Jasper's Patented Soothing Syrup—guaranteed to cure infant colic, consumption, whooping cough, female complaints, malaise, and warts.

Just before darkness fell, Callahan found a muddy bit of water where a little creek made a bend around another boulder, and he stopped there. Loosening the cinch but leaving the saddle on the gelding, he let Job graze and drink. Pulling another bandanna out of the saddlebag, he used it to strain water into a coffeepot. Just enough for two cups of coffee.

He built a fire, stretched his legs, pushed back his hat as the water began to boil, and turned his thoughts to how far he had ridden since Denver.

The carpenter Callahan had been working for in Fort

Collins had said it was about a hundred miles from Denver to Cheyenne, but keeping track of miles traveled came hard for this circuit-riding preacher. The carpenter had hated to let Callahan go, and since they were building a church, he had kept delaying his departure, even though the church already had hired a minister who was coming in from North Platte, Nebraska, if he didn't get scalped by Sioux and Cheyenne. The congregation was decidedly Episcopal, and Callahan had known many a fine Episcopalian, and even had enjoyed a pilsner with one of that cloth—before the War Between the States, anyway.

He had moved on to Poudreville, preached a few days at the livery, and then went through Virginia Dale, preached in a saloon, before lighting out again.

Callahan knew he was in Wyoming by now. The beer jerker at Virginia Dale had said the territory wasn't more than a hop and a skip away. While Job had never been inclined to hop or skip, they had gotten a good start not long after breakfast.

Callahan remembered the conversation.

"Just follow the trail," the beer jerker said, *"and make good time. Indians be on the prod."*

"Most of that's way up Montana way," the faro dealer corrected.

"They's enough injuns between Montana and New Mexico to give us fits."

As he rested and drank the coffee he'd made, Callahan continued thinking about that conversation.

"Best to travel at night," the beer jerker told him. *"Injuns won't attack at night."*

"Who told you that?" the faro dealer barked.

"An old-timer at Fort Lupton."

"That ol' coot? His brain left him before the Pikes Peak crowd showed up in Colorado."

"I read that in the Denver Twice-Weekly Reporter, *too."*

"You can't read."

"Plantin' moon," the beer jerker said.

"Raidin' moon, you moron," the faro dealer countered.

Callahan shook his head. They'd still been going at it when he had pulled on his hat and left the saloon for the stable.

He stood, massaged his thighs and buttocks, emptied bladder and bowels, washed his hands in the muddy stream, and looked at the moon. Since it was full, he figured it would be light enough to follow the road, even if the road was really nothing more than tracks of wagons—like those fool mud wagons he'd encountered—made by flattening the grass.

Callahan was used to traveling at night. Back in Missouri, he'd traveled a lot without even a moon to guide his way. But that's what a lot of Missouri bushwhackers needed to do during the late War Between the States. Carbine Logan's boys made a habit of not being seen. That was a long time ago though, back when Taylor Callahan was younger and impetuous, and a tad bitter and angry.

He was a changed man now.

He was also broke.

The money he had made working for the carpenter in Fort Collins did not amount to much, and while the livery in Poudreville had paid him in coffee and hard tack, the coins collected in the black hat Callahan passed around barely covered the feed bill he had been charged for Job's appetite. He had done a wee bit better in Virginia Dale till that old codger with a wooden leg came in with a story about an ailing wife, all four kids with the croup, and not enough money to hire the barber across the way who sometimes doctored folks up.

"Here's what I can give you, old-timer," Callahan had said, and dumped his change into the man's calloused hands. "As long as you promise me you ain't buying Doctor Jasper's Patented Soothing Syrup."

"Cures warts," the faro dealer had said.

"No, it don't," the beer jerker had argued. "But it works wonders on the grippe."

Callahan wanted to get to Cheyenne so he could maybe get enough tithes to spend at least one night in a hotel with hot bath water and decent linens. Maybe even a shave since he had traded in his straight razor for a bit of ground coffee in Poudreville.

The faro dealer at Virginia Dale had told him not to go to Cheyenne, but make way to Laramie. It was closer and had a lot of sinners.

The beer jerker had said, "No, the real action is to be had farther west, at Fort Steele on the North Platte because nobody sins worser than soldiers that far from the civilized world."

That's why Callahan had picked Cheyenne.

He kicked out the fire, doused the smoke with the remnants of his coffee, and got to work on Job, tying the coffeepot to the bedroll, tightening the cinch, saying a short prayer, and eating the last bit of beef jerky he had been saving. Looking up, he checked the moon, waited for it to rise just a bit higher, and then opened the saddlebags. He pulled out the .45-caliber long-barreled Colt revolver, and checked the loads. He thought about sticking it inside the deep pocket of his black Prince Albert coat, but decided against it.

Indians might have a different color skin than Taylor Callahan, and likely practiced a different religion, but if the faro dealer had been right, Callahan would rely on his faith, and the Major General in the Heavens, to protect him. His will, or Her will, be done.

He returned the Colt to its place, fastened the buckle, moved around Job, keeping his hand on the gelding's hide so not to get kicked, and reached the other saddlebag. Opening it, he touched the Bible, said a brief prayer, and found two corn dodgers. He thought about eating one but figured the salt would just make him thirsty, and took them to Job, letting the horse eat the stale balls of bread.

Callahan led the horse back to the trail, which would be easy to follow on a cloudless night, tightened the cinch again, and eased into the saddle.

Job snorted.

"You'll get a fine stall and a good rubdown in Cheyenne," Callahan told him.

That was a bit of a prayer, he realized. But maybe the Major General in the Heavens was listening and feeling charitable.

Callahan laughed when Job bucked twice, an informal protest, but the preacher was a better horseman than many people—at least those who had never known him as one of Carbine Logan's Irregulars—realized.

"You done?" he said, then kicked the gelding into a slow walk.

"That's what I figured." Callahan shook his head and clucked his tongue. "Two jumps and you're played out. Come on, boy, just follow the trail."

He'd done some figuring while he'd rested and the way he figured, those stagecoaches that had almost run him and his horse over that afternoon would not be traveling at night. Maybe he could be out of their way by the time dawn broke if, by chance, they started making a return trip to whatever burg they had come from.

He grinned, hearing his late ma telling him with some amazement, "You got some brains beneath that hard skull of yourn that I never knowed you had, boy. How come you don't always act like you know somethin'?"

An hour later, he realized he had erred. As the stagecoach barreled toward him, he could hear his late ma's voice again.

"Boy, you ain't got the sense the Lord give a corncob."

CHAPTER 2

Riding horseback at night had its risks. Taylor Callahan understood that. The odds—he remembered a thing or two about such things from his wilder years when he saw nothing sinful about wagering on anything— likely favored a stagecoach over a man on horse. Even with a shining moon. A stagecoach, after all, had headlamps. A stagecoach would not likely be startled by a rattlesnake or a pronghorn. And most stagecoach drivers did not whip six mules into running at a hard gallop over not much of a road up and down a steep hill.

Thank the Major General in the Heavens.

Callahan—and Job—heard the rattling of the coach, the cannonade of hoofbeats, the snapping of a whip, and the reprehensible language of the driver, giving the circuit rider time to turn the white gelding off what Wyoming called a road.

Neither horse nor rider expected the lead and trailing mules to leap into view on the crest of the hill. The stagecoach went airborne. The mules and driver—again, no one rode as a guard—spotted Job, beaming brighter than he actually was because of the big moon. Mules might not be spooked by a rattlesnake or an antelope while galloping hard, but seeing a ghostly figure in black atop a bright white steed led to a totally different reaction.

The mules turned left, away from Job and Callahan on the right. The driver shouted out something lost in the chaos that followed, and Taylor Callahan knew he would never know exactly what happened till that glorious day—many years from now, he prayed—when he stood at the Pearly Gates and heard the story from the Major General in the Heavens.

The mules and driver were not the only ones spooked. Job started bucking.

The top of the stirrups caught Callahan's boots when the gelding kicked out his back legs, right before the seat of the saddle caught the Missourian's crotch when the horse's legs touched ground. Those moves repeated themselves for four or five or fifty more jumps. Well, Callahan would concede later, it probably did not get as high as fifty, but that didn't mean he couldn't use it in a sermon at a camp meeting now and then. In any event, once his right foot lost its hold in the stirrup, and Job's twisting, turning, bending head jerked one rein from Callahan's grip, he knew he was not long for the ride. He kicked his left foot free, let go of the other rein, and propelled himself off his mount on Job's next high kick.

He landed on his left foot, bounced up, twisted around, and fell on his back. His legs landed next while the air rushed out of his lungs, and he felt a sharp pain in the back of his head. Since he had no idea where Job might be bouncing around, Callahan did not wait to wiggle his fingers and toes or turn his head one way or the other. The last thing he wanted was for eight hundred pounds of glue bait to stomp the life out of him.

Rolling over sage and rocks and cheap grass, he realized he had not broken his back or neck. Once he stopped, he shoved his hands flat on the ground and pushed himself upright.

There he stood, breathing in dust. As his lungs worked extra hard, he wet his lips with his tongue, and turned to find Job. The horse had bucked itself out pretty quickly. That came as no shock, but the gelding remained out of sorts, ears flat against its head, staring off to the southwest, and pawing the earth.

"Easy—" Callahan said, surprised that his jaw was not broken.

But he never got to finish saying, "boy," for behind him came a deafening crash, followed by hideous screams of man and beast. The next words that escaped from Callahan's mouth would not please the Major General in the Heavens, but the battered preacher could remember to ask for exception and forgiveness later.

He turned around as dust rose like fog glowing white and tan and ominous in the bath of moonlight and started up the incline toward the path that pretended to be a road. Then, he stopped suddenly, turned around, found his hat, and took one more glance at Job. Satisfied the gelding wasn't going anywhere unless someone dangled a carrot, Callahan pounded some shape back into his Boss of the Plains, rid it of dead grass and some of the dirt, and reached the trail.

More dust rose in separate locations. The thickest cloud was southwest, maybe forty or fifty yards—what was left of the stagecoach and driver. The other dust came from the mules, all six of them, still in their traces and making good time for Virginia Dale, Poudreville, Fort Collins, Denver, Hades, or wherever those animals felt like stopping.

Callahan stopped, bit back another unkind word, and turned around. Job stared at him as he approached, but seemed to have calmed down a mite. The preacher hummed softly. The saddle was leaning far to the right, and the canteen was missing from the horn. He walked to the horse anyway, maybe just to let the animal know he was well thought of, which might not be entirely true. Reaching the horse, he rubbed the white neck, and gently pulled the saddle back into place. He looked around for the canteen, but didn't see it, and didn't want to spend the rest of the night looking for it. Most likely, he would find it or trip over it this evening or tomorrow morning. At the moment, someone else needed his attention.

"Easy, boy. Just eat some Wyoming grass and get some rest. I'll be back directly." Callahan turned, shook his head, sighed, then thought about swearing a bit more, but did not go through with it.

He returned to the trail and moved in the direction of the crumpled heap that once was a mud wagon. He heard the moaning, but ignored it for the time being. Leaping up onto the kindling that passed for a stagecoach, he peered through the opening. Nope. No one was inside. A good thing. He held that thought for a moment when clarity, slow to come, returned. Like the moaning driver, a passenger or passengers could have been thrown clear of the mud wagon.

Callahan backed up and studied the rolling waves of grass, hills, bounders, and one antelope that had come out to see what was going on. No humans appeared or at least none the circuit rider could see, which didn't mean there weren't any.

The driver, loosely defined, started moaning louder, so Callahan walked toward the groans. The man lay on his back, boots crossed at the ankles as though he were being laid out for the undertaker, arms stretched out over his bearded head. His nose was leaking blood, which stained his white mustache, and his lips were busted, but the man still breathed, and his breath reeked of bad whiskey.

His eyelids moved, gray eyes focused, and he spit out blood and saliva before asking timidly, "Are you God?"

"No." Callahan knelt.

The man gasped. "The . . . devil?"

"Not the devil you should be seeing." Callahan ran his right hand over the man's ribs, noticing the man's eyes were wild with fear, but he didn't seem to feel any agony where Callahan applied pressure.

"I could use some whiskey," the driver said.

"You ain't the only one, Brother." Callahan looked at the man's hands and ordered, "Wiggle the fingers on your left hand." He waited. And frowned. "Are you wiggling?"

"Yeah."

Callahan sighed, and turned to look at the man's battered face and broken neck. Something else grabbed his attention, and he fought back that urge to curse again. "Your *left* hand."

The man looked confused, till the fingers on the left hand began to move. Then he just looked stupid.

"Turn your feet, left to right, or right to left. It don't really matter."

That he did without any stupidity.

Callahan let out a sigh. The Major General in the Heavens did look after idiots. He stared down at the driver. "Where all do you hurt?" he asked, knowing the answer.

"All over!"

"Can you stand?"

"I could use some whiskey."

"Do you think you could stand?"

"I said I could use—"

"I heard you the first time, but your breath tells me you've had enough whiskey. Now, can you sit up at least?"

The man whimpered. But he did bring his arms to his side, and used his forearms to push himself up. Callahan reached around and grabbed the driver's shoulders and eased him till he was sitting in the dirt.

Seeing what was left of the Abbott & Downing wagon, he cursed. "What happened to my mules?" he cried out. "Tell me they ain't dead."

"They were lighting a shuck south last I saw," Callahan answered.

"You shouldn't have startled my team so," the man complained. "It's your fault. You'll have to answer to the Poudreville Stagecoach Company."

"Mister," Callahan said, "I wasn't the one drunker than a

bluebelly on payday. Nor the one whipping a team like a maniac uphill and downhill on a road seldom traveled. All like there's no tomorrow."

"There ain't gonna be no tomorrow if I don't get to Poudreville before the Peaceful Valley stagecoach does."

That statement brought back memories from the afternoon. The second mud wagon. The one with the female passenger who had smiled—or at least Callahan had fancied a smile—that was being whipped just as wildly. He looked toward the road and up the hill. He also listened, but just heard the driver's groans, moans, and then, a stinking, rippling, long whiskey fart.

Callahan glanced at the moon and asked the Major General in the Heavens what he had done to deserve such punishment, but stopped quickly, whispered an apology, and looked down at the battered old driver. "My name's Callahan. Taylor Callahan. Circuit-riding preacher bound for Cheyenne."

"Preacher?"

"That's what I said."

"In Wyoming?"

"If this indeed happens to be Wyoming."

The driver blinked and stared, which he followed with a stare and a blink. Then he remembered his manners. "My name's Absalom."

Callahan laughed so hard his ribs almost broke. Tears filled his eyes. Drunk as that driver was, as beaten up as he had to be after that wreck, the man had a wicked wit underneath that raw, rank exterior.

"What's so dad-blasted funny?" the driver wailed.

"Absalom!" Callahan shook his head.

"That's my name."

Callahan laughed again and shook his head. "Your name can't be Absalom?"

"The devil it can't!" the man barked with genuine sincerity and, if Callahan were not mistaken, a good deal of anger. "Why can't it be?"

Perhaps this drunken fool was a thespian to match the talents of Edwin Booth. The preacher might have felt sorry for the old cad, till he heard Job walking toward him and saw the ruins of the mud wagon and remembered trying to ride out a bucking show by the usually lazy gelding. "Because you ain't hanging between two boughs of a big old oak tree, 'between the heaven and the earth,' though your mules sure had the right idea."

"Huh?"

"Second Samuel, Chapter Eighteen. But don't ask me the verse. Not till morning, maybe afternoon, when I ain't so flustered."

"I don't feel so good, Preacher," the man said, and sank back to the ground.

Kneeling quickly, Callahan placed the back of his hand on the man's forehead. The eyes fluttered, but did not open.

"Where do you hurt?" Callahan asked.

"Everything's just spinnin'," the man whispered. "Spinnin' like a top. Feel sicker than a dog."

Could be the whiskey, or a bad combination of whiskey and wreck.

"Don't let me die, Preacher." The man's voice barely carried to Callahan's ears.

"You just rest, Absalom." Callahan lifted his eyes to the moon one more time and began praying for a bit of help, a smidgen of courage, and a whole lot of explaining exactly what all he needed to do.

Like many a Western man, Taylor Callahan had experience in patching himself and other people up. Doctors were mighty scarce on the frontier, and where Callahan and poor drunken Absalom found themselves was beyond *frontier*. They had to be right dab smack in that clichéd but omnipresent Middle Of Nowhere.

For a circuit-riding preacher who had been traveling across the Western states and territories since before the War Between the States had ended, Taylor Callahan was no stranger to injuries and illness. During the unpleasantness between North and South, and, more specifically, Missouri and Kansas, he had been doctor and surgeon as much as parson and priest. He had amputated fingers, toes, feet, arms, and legs. Some of his patients even survived. He had dug out bullets with knives, spoons, and pliers. He had bandaged bloody wounds, and he had cauterized them. And he had held down screaming men while others did the dirty work.

He had also tended to the sick. Measles and mumps. Cholera and bowel complaints. Bad water, bad food, bad whiskey. The grippe, broken arms, broken legs, shot-off ears, rope burns, knife cuts, saber wounds, fevers, chills. He had even helped the wife of one of Carbine Logan's Irregulars birth a baby girl—six pounds and twelve ounces according to the kitchen scales—while six of the boys fought off a Yankee patrol in a cabin deep in the Sni-a-Bar.

But Absalom wasn't pregnant. He wasn't shot or cut. He had no fever or chills. And he wasn't bleeding anywhere except from his lips and nose. Internal injuries? Callahan knew of such things, but he had never had to treat any.

Concussion. That was Callahan's uneducated guess. He knew of concussions. But no one had ever told him how to treat one. No one there was going to, either. He would have to throw the driver over the back of Job and get him to . . . where? And that was the problem.

Go back to Virginia Dale? The town had no doctor, but did have a bartender who sometimes cut hair and had pulled out a few bullets from human beings.

Keep going north to . . . Cheyenne? Wherever and how far away it was.

Or sit where he was with one canteen—if he could find his—and wait till someone passed by? Or until poor Absalom went to hear orders from the Major General in the Heavens.

Callahan listened as the man snored softly. Maybe he passed out from sheer drunkenness? Even so, Callahan knew he had to do something.

He moved to what once had been an Abbott & Downing vehicle of commercial transportation, picked up a broken spoke about eighteen inches long, and used it to prod around the driver's box. Hearing something roll, he reached against the side and found a jug of whiskey. Somehow, the thing had not busted or gotten flung into the scorched grass. He shook the clay jug. Still some left. He hadn't tasted liquor in some time, and it took a lot of conviction not to pull the cork, but he set the jug on the ground, stepped into the driver's box, and pulled himself up to stare across the port side of the coach. Or was that starboard? Not being a sailor, but being a Missouri lad from the hills, he never could remember those little things.

Nothing caught his eye.

"What did you expect?" he asked himself. "A water keg?"

Then he leaped onto the ground and hurried to the back of the mud wagon. The boot. Yes. The boot might hold something. Canteen. Doctor's kit. Luggage. Water.

Nothing.

That perplexed Callahan. Why would a stagecoach be making this run without any passenger? Was this Abbott & Downing wreck delivering mail? And what was the deal with the Peaceful Valley Stagecoach Company? One of theirs must have been the wagon carrying the woman in its coach this afternoon.

He wet his lips and walked back to pick up his spoke-stick and the whiskey jug. "Job"—he turned to the gelding—"looks like we got us a—" He did not finish the statement.

Job was telling him what to do. And do it right quick.

CHAPTER 3

Snorting, the gelding started pawing the earth with its forelegs, his ears again flattened against its head. The horse focused on the hill. Job spun around and loped a good twenty yards away, stopped, whinnied a warning, and one more time stared at the hilltop.

"The second mud wagon," Callahan said aloud.

He didn't hear anything but Job's snorts and the wind, but he didn't have the ears of a horse. Callahan looked at what he did have. A broken spoke from a wagon wheel. And a jug of whiskey. Breaking into a run to the trail, he carried both with him.

Job was rearing, snorting, and dancing this way and that. As long as he had owned that horse, Callahan never had seen the animal act so wild. Dropping to a knee, he brought the jug to his mouth, sank his teeth into the cork, and pulled the jug down and his head up. A jigger of rotgut splashed out, the stench almost causing his pale eyes to melt. He didn't have to worry whether the contents weren't flammable.

The preacher set the clay jug on the ground, found the busted spoke, and laid it across a bent leg. Grabbing the jug with his other hand, he splashed liquor over the top edge of the wood. Three gulps worth, he figured.

He heard the traces, the wheels, those loud cracks of a whip, and more cussing from the driver.

Still kneeling, Callahan reached inside his Prince Albert and found the matches. The first one broke off in his hand. He cursed, but not a real bad one, and found another. It flared up but burned out before he could get it to the spoke.

The booming noise of the mud wagon sounded closer.

Callahan found a match, realized he had only one left. If this one didn't work . . . Shaking his head he moved it close to the spoke, used his thumbnail to set the match aflame, and lowered it to the wood slowly.

The *whoosh* almost singed the beard stubble on his face, and his eyes saw orange, red, and white dots for a moment. He stood and moved to the center of the trail as the mud wagon of, presumably, the Peaceful Valley Stagecoach Company crested the hill.

Callahan waved the burning torch over his head, east to west, right to left. He yelled, "Stop! We need help! Stop! There's been a terrible wreck!"

The lamps on each side of the vehicle glowed like the eyes of a giant beast. The driver held back the whip, and for one instant that lasted an eternity, Callahan thought the driver would send that black-snake a-popping, and just drive that coach over Callahan without a second thought. But a man of the cloth has to put his faith somewhere.

The whip dropped out of sight, and the man pulled brake and leather back, bellowing, "Whoa, mules! Whoa! Whoaaaaaaaaaa!"

Callahan kept waving the torch, which blew out just as the lead mules stopped maybe six or seven feet from him. The smoking spoke dropped to the ground, and he let out a long sigh of relief and a verbal prayer.

The driver wrapped the reins around the brake lever, pushed back his hat, spit out a plug of tobacco, and pointed a gloved finger at the circuit rider. "That's a good way to get yourself smashed to nothin' but raspberry jelly, mister!" the old man bellowed.

Callahan pointed to the injured man and the wrecked mud wagon.

"Yeah," the driver said as he climbed down to the ground. "That's the only reason I didn't ride right over you. Figured you to be some road agent. But then I spied the wrecked coach and . . . whoo-eeeeee!" He removed his hat and slapped it on his stubby thighs, startling the mules closest to him. "Looks like the Peaceful Valley Stagecoach Company is about to get itself a contract." The man did not look at Callahan as he walked to the lead mules, crossed in front of them, and made a beeline for the injured man.

Callahan followed.

He stood nearby as the happy driver knelt beside the hurt driver. A cloud passed over the moon, darkening the scene for a few seconds before it moved along, and when the light bathed the earth once more, the driver of the Peaceful Valley coach shrugged poor Absalom's shoulders.

The man's eyes slowly opened, and he whispered a soft curse.

"Yeah," said the Peaceful Valley man. "You had a real good idea there, Absalom. Gettin' me roostered in Peaceful Valley. Gettin' a good jump on me. You had this contract all wrapped up in fancy paper. But now, all I gots to do is get my mules and my mud wagon to Poudreville, and the contract belongs to us. Not you. Shucks, Absalom, you ain't even got a wagon no more." His knees popped as he rose, and he found a plug of tobacco in the back pocket of his denim britches.

Job became curious and started slowly walking to the gathering.

The driver looked around, smiled at Absalom, and turned to Callahan. "What happened to the team?"

Callahan nodded at the trail. "Kept running south."

The man studied on that for a while, even looked down the trail before shaking his head and grinning. "Nah. Don't count if the mules come in with no coach. Don't count at all."

Callahan didn't know what the old coot was talking about. "We need to get him to a doctor as fast as we can."

The man's jaw worked hard on the quid, and he nodded. "Yep. Absalom's got hisself a passel of injuries." He made a slight gesture toward the hill. "Peaceful Valley is, oh, ten-twelve miles. Just follow the trail. You can't miss it."

"What am I supposed to do?" Callahan felt temper rising. "Drag him there?"

"Leave him."

"So wolves can get to him while I'm gone?"

The man spit tobacco juice onto the grass. "Well, that is a possibility, I reckon. You can wait with him. Folks are bound to come by . . . tomorrow . . . next day. Ain't the most traveled route, though. Shucks, Benidoo"—he looked at Absalom again and shook his head—"he might croak in an hour or two."

Callahan said, "You need to turn that coach of yours around and help me load him in that contraption of yours and get him to Peaceful Valley."

The man was walking away before Callahan finished the sentence. When Callahan opened his mouth to shout something else, something the Major General in the Heavens might not consider polite, the man yelled, "Good luck to you, boys. I have to be in Poudreville in"—he pulled a watch from the small pocket in his britches—"three hours and fourteen minutes . . . which I believe I can do. That'll give the Peaceful Valley Stagecoach Company the contract."

Callahan bristled, then noticed Job grazing just a few feet from him. The Major General in the Heavens worked in unusual ways, but Callahan knew what he was supposed to do.

He walked directly to the white gelding, opened the saddle-bag, pulled out the long-barreled Colt .45, and followed the Peaceful Valley stagecoach driver.

The man had climbed into the driver's box and was gathering up the leather lines when he spit juice over the side and turned back to yell some insult or brag.

He didn't finish.

The lead slug clipped the top of the brake lever, caused the old-timer to swallow his tobacco, and the mules to take a few steps toward the east.

"What the—" the driver started.

The second bullet clipped leather and had the man dropping the reins, standing, and raising his hands high over his head. "Is this a robbery?"

"Get down." Callahan waved the smoking barrel.

Keeping his hands up once his feet rested on Wyoming grass, the man complied and walked around the back of the coach. The .45 remained aimed at the driver's torso, and Callahan's right arm did not waver.

"You," the minister said, "get over to Absalom. We're putting him in the back of that mud wagon. Then you're taking us back to Peaceful Valley."

"You'll answer to the Peaceful Valley Stagecoach Company for this," the man said, but his voice was too frightened to carry much threat.

"You'll answer to a higher power if you don't do exactly what I tell you to do." Callahan waved the Colt's barrel, and the man walked to the wounded Absalom.

"Take his shoulders," Callahan said. "Be careful with his head."

"How come I can't get his legs?"

"Because I'm carrying his legs. I can drop his legs, and draw my revolver and put a bullet between your eyes if you do something stupid like drop his upper torso." He holstered the revolver.

When they had laid the moaning Absalom on the floor of

the coach between the middle and rear benches, Callahan backed out. He removed his Prince Albert, and covered the man's legs and chest, then took off his hat and used his Boss of the Plains and the driver's weather-beaten monstrosity as a pillow. No one would call that comfortable, but it beat bouncing around in the coach with no covers and a head banging on hard wood.

"Turn the coach around," Callahan said. "I'll get my horse." He put his hand on the butt of the holstered revolver. "You've seen how good I am with a short gun. There are three more bullets in this hog leg. But I won't need more than one."

"You are a road agent," the man said.

"No. I'm a preacher. Ordained." The circuit rider hurried to Job.

Once in the saddle, he eased the gelding back to the coach which the driver was still struggling to turn around to head north. When that feat had been accomplished, the Peaceful Valley Stagecoach Company man turned and swallowed.

"Keep the coach slow and steady," Callahan said. "You're not out to win a contract for your stage line. I don't want Absalom bouncing around and doing more damage. *Slow. Steady.* An easy gait, but not a walk. I'll be right behind you. With my .45."

The man started to nod, but the nod stopped, and he wretched over the side of the coach.

Callahan cringed. "Now what?" he demanded.

The leather reins fell out of the driver's hands, gripping instead the side of the coach, and he hung his head over and vomited again.

Job snorted, shook his head, and tried to back away.

Vomit sprayed again.

Callahan made a quick look at the moon and wondered why the Major General in the Heavens always wanted to test a poor preacher so much.

Another waterfall of vomit, and the driver raised his head, and sobbed, "I swallered my 'baccy. I'm sicker than a dog." And he fell backward into the driver's box.

You wanted to see the ocean, Callahan thought as if talking to himself. *Remember? You got sidetracked in that little Texas town, but you could have kept drifting south. Seen the Gulf of Mexico. Or when you reached New Mexico Territory, you could have followed the old Butterfield line to California. You remember the Butterfield coaches. Don't you? 'Course, you do. They were something to see.*

How many did you take when that line was moving before the War Between the States? Tipton to Fort Smith that one time, wasn't it? In '59. When that pretty gal from St. Louis asked you to harmonize with her as she sang hymns to the fellow passengers. So sweet she sounded that two men riding on the top of the crowded coach got into a fight with a drummer and a Methodist to get to ride inside to hear her sing on the next line. You should have taken one of those coaches to California. Let your eyes gaze upon the majesty of the Pacific. But, no, Taylor Callahan. You just keep making poor choices when it comes to traveling.

Callahan swung off Job, led the gelding to the back of the coach, removed saddle and blanket and tossed both into the rear boot, then tethered the animal to the back of the Abbott & Downing.

The horse snorted.

Callahan shook his head. "It ain't exactly what I had in mind myself, boy." He rubbed the horse's neck, shook his head again, and walked to the side of the wagon. Putting a boot on the wheel cap, he grabbed hold, and made the climb into the driver's box.

The sick old dog of a driver had managed to crawl to the side where a guard usually sat, but the man wasn't sitting. He was on his knees, hanging his head over that side, and watering the train with . . . Callahan didn't want to know.

He found the leather, looked back, took the whip, and placed it in a holder. Never one to use a black-snake, he didn't think he would need to but kept it handy just in case.

The driver raised his head. The moonlight made that face look even whiter. "I'm sick."

Callahan nodded. "That's what happens, I hear, when a boy or a man swallows tobacco juice. Funny, though, ain't it?"

The man's eyes squinted.

"My ma. She dipped snuff probably from the time she was four years old. Filled air-tights and some of my daddies' jugs and bottles with juice." He shook his head. "Did that a-purpose, I figure. Just so when one of 'em drank, thinking he was filling his belly with corn liquor, they'd be a-running to the privy. Must be one of the differences between a man and a woman. Because my ma, well now, she swallowed juice her ownself. But I never once saw her lose her breakfast."

The driver turned even whiter, hung his head over the side, and retched again.

Callahan released the break, grubbed the leather, let out a Johnny Reb war cry that sent the mules heading up the hill, pulling the coach toward Peaceful Valley.

CHAPTER 4

When dawn broke, Taylor Callahan thanked the Major General in the Heavens for delivering another beautiful day. The driver, who had fallen asleep during the night, groaned, reached his right hand up to grab the side of the box, and slowly pulled himself up into a seated position. Callahan gave him a glance, then turned to make sure Job was okay trotting behind the mud wagon.

He clucked his tongue and flipped the heavy leather to keep the mules going. "Good morning," Callahan told the Peaceful Valley driver without looking at him.

The man spit phlegm between his legs, smacked his lips, and said in a ragged voice, "Ain't nothin' good about it."

Callahan smiled. "Canteen's on the seat."

The man glanced at the container and said, "Coffee'd be better. Whiskey'd be best."

"Can't help you on either of those requests."

The man's left hand reached up, grabbed the canvas strap, and pulled the canteen into his lap. After opening the top, he took a few swallows, then poured some in his hands and splashed his face.

"Bet you wouldn't do that with coffee or whiskey," Callahan said, still keeping his eyes on what passed for a road.

To his surprise, the man chuckled.

"You handle a team pretty good," the man said. "For a highwayman."

"Preacher," Callahan said. "Not a bandit."

The man turned his head and spit over the side.

"Never knowed a preacher who could handle mules and a mud wagon."

Callahan nodded at the compliment. "Something tells me you ain't knowed too many preachers."

The man laughed, and drank more water. "How's Absalom?"

One of the wheels on the left side struck a hole or a rock or something, and the coach bounced this way and that, but nothing too bad for the two men riding up top.

A yell came from inside the Abbott & Downing, followed by a curse. "You're tryin' to murder me, by grab!"

The Peaceful Valley man laughed, and took one more swallow of water, before holding it out toward the circuit rider.

Callahan shook his head. "Reckon Absalom'll live," he said, and set the canteen back on the floor.

Spotting another giant crater in the track, Callahan called out, "Gee," and leaned to his right just in case the mules didn't understand mule talk. But, of course, they did, and the team turned right to avoid tormenting Absalom farther.

"Like I said," the driver said, "you know a thing or two about driving a team."

Callahan smiled. "Wasn't always a preacher. And you make right pleasant conversation when you've a mind to."

The man laughed. "Well, it ain't like Absalom and the Poudreville bunch has a chance at gettin' this contract for the line with its wagon all busted to pieces. It'll be fun seein' the boys string you up for delayin' my victory once we get to

Peaceful Valley. You bein' a preacher, though, they might let you preach your own funeral before they string you up."

"That'd be most generous of them."

"I ain't kiddin' you, Preacher. It's a tough bunch of boys that have settled in Peaceful Valley."

"Figured that. Got to be tough to settle this country. Good, strong stock, I'd reckon."

"They'll hang you, man."

"Reckon so."

"I ain't foolin'."

Callahan grinned. "I figured you weren't much for jokes."

"You're crazy."

"Some say so, others say not. I, myself, haven't quite come to a decision one way or the other."

"I don't think you are a preacher. Not the way you handle yourself—and your short gun."

"Ordained I am. Got some writing in my saddlebags if you'd care to see it. Logan's Knob Seminary."

"Never heard of it."

Callahan shot the man another glance. "Can you name any seminary?"

The man chuckled. "Well, you called me on that one."

Callahan returned the laugh. "It's down south of Sparta. Sparta, Missouri. In the Ozarks."

"You're a long way from home."

The smile faded, and the eyes clouded. "Ain't home no more." Callahan made himself smile. "I'm riding the circuit. Preaching the gospel. Letting the Spirit guide my way. I thought I was being guided to Cheyenne. But maybe the Major General in the Heavens has decided I ought to help the kind souls in Peaceful Valley. For room and board. And whatever tithes they feel like contributing."

"Your room and board will be a six-foot hole covered with sod."

"Which is true, eventually, for all men."

"Mister, I ain't foolin'."

"You said that before. I didn't disagree with you then. Won't disagree with you now. You seem to be a man who speaks his mind."

"What'd you say your name was?" The man found the canteen and took another drink as Callahan told him.

"I'll try to remember that so we can carve your name into the rock we place on your grave."

"Appreciate it."

"I ain't—"

"Fooling," Callahan interrupted, cutting him off. "That'd be the third warning you've given me."

The man closed the canteen and shook his head again, muttering curses.

"Three's an important number in the Good Book."

"Yeah." The man turned to spit over the side again. "God created the Earth in three days."

Callahan laughed. "That'd be six, sir. But you knew that. You were just funning me. Rested on the seventh day. Seven's probably a more important number, but three's big. Take how we often say holy three times. Holy, holy, holy."

"Six is the big number in Peaceful Valley," the man said. "Six bullets in a Colt."

"Some people just put five beans in the wheel," Callahan said, "so they don't shoot their foot off."

"Not in Peaceful Valley."

Callahan nodded down the trail. "Fork in the road. Which way?"

"Peaceful Valley's to the west."

"What's to the east?"

"That'll take you to Cheyenne."

"Haw, mules!" Callahan shouted. "Haw. Haw. Haw!"

The coach turned left at the fork.

The man stared, blinked, stared again at Callahan, opened his mouth, then closed it. The coach kept on the path. Twenty yards. Fifty. One hundred.

"How much farther till we get to town?" Callahan asked.

"What the Sam Hill are you doin'?" the man asked.

"Taking Absalom, you, and me to Peaceful Valley, my good man."

"But—"

Callahan clucked his tongue, sang out at the team, and flicked the reins.

"Stop," the man said wearily.

Callahan gave him a curious look.

"Stop this coach!" the man barked.

"Whoa, mules. Whoa!" Callahan said, standing up, and pulling hard on the reins till the coach slowed and finally stopped.

"Are we there yet?" cried out Absalom from the coach.

"Not yet!" Callahan answered as he sat and twisted in the seat to look at the Peaceful Valley stagecoach driver. "You need to empty your bladder or something? Still sickly from that tobacco juice you swallowed last night?"

"No." The man sighed. "Slide over." He pushed himself to his feet. "I'll drive from here on out. If you're so dad-blasted set on getting yourself killed."

Callahan shrugged, set the brake, wrapped the leather around the long handle, and slid behind the driver. He found the canteen, and wet his own whistle as the man settled into the seat.

"Hang on, Absalom," the driver called down. "We're gonna bounce a mite before we bounce on down the trail."

"Gee!" he cried out, after releasing the brake, and pulled hard to his right. The mules turned, and the Abbott & Downing bounced roughly as the coach crossed the sloping country till it picked up the other trail, and began following the right fork.

Right, Callahan figured in the directional and correct senses of the word. "I misunderstand those directions?" he asked when the mud wagon began a less bouncing ride down the trail.

"No. You heard me right. I just lied to you, Preacher."

"I see."

The driver sighed. "I figured you'd be of mind to go to Cheyenne instead of Peaceful Valley."

Callahan nodded. "I see," he said again.

"That road don't go to Cheyenne." The driver flicked the lines, called out a few choice cuss words at the mules, and shook his head. The man looked and sounded like he was ashamed of himself. Maybe because Callahan had not taken the bait he had held out there, maybe because he realized Callahan was just what he had said he was, a circuit-riding preacher.

"You want to go to Cheyenne, you stay on this road past Peaceful Valley." The driver shook his head. "I figured you'd believe me to be lying so you wouldn't take the way I told you to take."

"I see."

They covered another fifty yards.

Callahan pointed to the west. "And where does that trail lead?"

"Thompson ranch." The driver waved his hand. "Thompsons claim all this land. They was here first."

"Second, most likely," Callahan said. "Indians first."

"Well, maybe so. But the Thompsons sure got it now. And the injuns won't be doin' no fightin' now that we gots a fort."

"Army post?"

The man nodded. "Fort Centennial. It ain't finished yet. Probably won't never get finished. They put it up to protect a railroad and Laramie."

"And the fort is . . . ?"

"Mile and a half from the town. Not a real fort or a real post. What they call a subpost, but some folks think it'll be a real fort with a full command. Especially if the injuns keep right on raiding and killing."

"Well, that's good news for a preacher." Callahan leaned back. "I can preach to the soldiers and the civilians. Though

I would certainly love to have Mr. Thompson and his cowboys hearing my words, and perhaps tithing some themselves."

"No, you wouldn't."

Callahan waited for the explanation.

"For one thing, there ain't no Mr. Thompson." The driver sighed heavily, and looked down the trail. "There are two sons, Knight and Walker, but don't go misterin' them. They ain't earned that respect. And the Widow Audrey Eleanor Thompson wears pants. Reckon the Bible has a few words to say that sure ain't right, good, or gospel." He snorted. "Reckon she wouldn't object to bein' called mister, neither."

"Well, you could have let me drive on to the ranch. Let me ask for a bed in the bunkhouse and some time to tend to Absalom."

"You don't get it, Preacher. If Audrey's two boys didn't kill the three of us, their ma sure would've."

"I see."

They rode another mile. The driver didn't seem to be taking the injured passenger into consideration until Callahan suggested that he slow down those mules.

When the man snarled, Callahan reminded him Absalom's stagecoach wasn't exactly competition any longer. "I'd like Absalom to get to town in one piece."

"Anything else?"

Callahan turned and waited till the man looked at him. "You remember how well I handle a six-shooter, I reckon."

The man sighed and pulled some on the reins. "Yeah. Reckon I do remember that."

They covered another mile or two before anyone spoke again.

"How big is Peaceful Valley?" Callahan asked.

"The town?" The man snorted. "Not big at all. Town proper, I mean. More than a dozen. No more than two dozen. My guess. Never took time to count 'em." He laughed. "Not that it would take long to count that high. And, yes, Preacher, I can count that high."

"Call me Taylor," Callahan said.

The man nodded, but he did not mention his name.

Callahan didn't press. He knew on the frontier asking a gent his name was downright rude, and had been known to lead to fisticuffs or gunplay. "So why would the United States Army build a fort, even just a subpost as you called it, to protect a town of fewer than twenty-four folks?"

The driver shrugged. "There's the Thompson spread."

"A woman, two sons. How many hired men? Ten? A dozen?"

"Doubt if it's even ten. Open range. Nary a barbed-wire fence in sight. Don't take many hands till spring or fall roundups. Then it's likely eighteen or so. My guess. I ain't counted them, neither. And I ain't never cowboyed."

They went down a hill.

"Indians?" Callahan asked when they started up the next low slope.

"None to speak of." The driver pointed toward the east. "The Arapaho come through now and then to trade mostly. The way the story goes is the big chief signed a treaty with Mr. Thompson before he got killed and Thompson gave the chief some land. But the deal was that Peace Treaty Peak would remain Arapaho land. Big medicine. It ain't rightly a mountain now." He nodded at the purple outlines farther north and west. "Not like them mountains. Least, that's how the story goes when I've heard it." He laughed. "I don't reckon the United States government will care that Old Man Thompson bought his ranch from the injuns, though. Do you?"

Callahan let a sad smile crease his face. "Knowing the government, I'd suspect you are right."

He held on as the driver seemed to deliberately hit a rock that rattled the coach and caused a whimper and a curse from Absalom. Callahan just shook his head as the driver chuckled.

"What's the nearest fort?" the circuit rider asked.

The driver nodded east. "Russell's just outside of Cheyenne." Then a bit west. "Sanders is by Laramie." He focused on the next climb. "Then Halleck is right at the base of Elk Mountain. And then there's Fort Steele where the Union Pacific crosses the North Platte."

"Seems like Peaceful Valley would be pretty well protected by those bluecoats."

"Seems like. But I ain't no soldier, and in case you ain't heard, them soldier boys have their minds set on killing Sitting Bull and Crazy Horse and as many Sioux and Cheyenne as they can this summer. And—" The driver stopped the stagecoach, stood, and stared hard.

Callahan followed his gaze.

"Hold on, Reverend!" the driver called out as he found the whip and cracked it five times, screaming profanity and sending the mules into a gallop.

Callahan did not mention the injured passenger. He just stared at the smoke. And remembered.

CHAPTER 5

Western Missouri, 1861–1862

It started out as just another beautiful August day in Clay County. Hot, muggy, the air filled with bugs, and the wind taking the day off. But still, a gorgeous afternoon.

Particularly when Taylor Callahan laid the last shingle onto the roof, looked down at his smiling wife, and said, while after wiping sweat off his brow, "Reckon that just about does it."

The petite auburn-haired love of his life smiled. "Why don't you come down and see for yourself?"

With a laugh, Callahan tossed the hammer over the side, watching it hit and somersault a few feet toward the well. He scooted down the slanted roof, hung his legs over, and dropped to the ground. His knees bent, and he almost fell over, but somehow righted himself and boosted back to a standing position. Then he turned and walked over to Karen, put his left arm over her shoulders, and they looked at the log cabin.

It wasn't much. A rectangular cabin of logs with a sharply pitched roof, two windows on the long sides, a large stone fireplace on the back wall, and two big double doors at the front, the side that faced the pike that ran from Liberty to the southeast and Harold's Crossroads to the northwest on the way to Excelsior Springs.

They had built it themselves with help from Karen's family and plenty of neighbors, not to mention some friends from the seminary at Logan's Knob. Harv Peacock had painted the shutters, and Harv's brother Lee had carved the crosses into them. Old Cooter Hamilton had donated the lightning rod, and Russell Brite, the carpenter from Harold's Crossroads, had worked on those heavy walnut doors, stained them to a rich brown, put the studs in so that when you got up close you could read the words *Holy, Holy, Holy.*

Yet both Callahans agreed the best feature of the cabin was the masonry on the chimney. Most churches had steeples, but this one had light-colored stones shaped into a cross against the dark granite. Cale Hendricks could have become an artist, one of those sculptors like Da Vinci and that one from France, who did that one of Mercury putting on his shoes before going for a run. Wearing the funny hat. What was that Frenchie's name? Jean something or other, but, well, yeah, weren't all those Frenchmen named Jean something or other?

Yes, sir, Callahan thought, nodding with much approval and pulling his wife closer, *this cabin is a mighty fine church.*

They had put in the pews the day before. Karen had sat in three of them and proclaimed them more comfortable than any church she had ever attended.

"Don't want them too comfortable," Callahan had teased her. "People might fall asleep."

"As loud as you talk?" She had grinned at him with that mischievous look that usually made him want to pull her into his arms and smother her slender neck with kisses.

"I don't talk that loud."

"Oh, it's pretty fiery and brimstoney when you get your dander up."

"I'll go gentle on them Sunday morning."

Her eyes told him she didn't believe him.

"No," he said, and looked again at the new church. "They'll need some gentleness, what with the war going on and all."

Her silence made him regret bringing the war into the conversation. Sometimes, he knew, he ought to think before he spit out words.

"Hey now," he said, and wrapped his arms around her. "That war's a long way from us, and we haven't seen much in the way of battles—I mean a real war—in Missouri so far. Some skirmishes. Small affairs at Booneville and Carthage, but nothing like we read about in the Old Testament. Right?"

Her eyes told him she had not been convinced. "Just seems wrong," she said after a long moment.

"It is wrong. War's wrong. The South is wrong. Pulling out of the Union isn't a smart thing to do. Lincoln's wrong. Fighting to keep in a bunch of crazy old coots who want to leave and form their own country. Let 'em go, I say, and see how long it takes before they come crawling back. Ask me, the only three states that's got any sense is Kentucky, Missouri, and whatever the third state is that says it's neutral. Not leaving the Union, but certainly not completely backing what the Northern states want. That's my thinking."

"We've had enough fighting already," she said.

"That's why we know fighting ain't the answer. But remember. John Brown is lying in his grave. That's all behind us."

John Brown was a Northerner who had brought his sons into Kansas Territory in the mid-1850s when the United States thought letting the territories decide if they wanted to be free states or allow slavery and passed the Kansas-Nebraska Act in 1854. Brown seemed to think freeing slaves and murdering—butchering—slave-owners was the way to bring Kansas into the Union as a free state. Missourians sacked Lawrence, burning a hotel and a newspaper office in May of '56, which led Brown and his boys to murder five men who'd defended the right of slavery in Pottawatomie. Massacred them. With broadswords.

The name "Bleeding Kansas" was soon born, and Brown made that state—and Missouri—bleed . . . till he went even crazier and thought raiding the federal arsenal at Harper's Ferry in Virginia was a good idea. That brought about the end of old John Brown. He was captured, tried, convicted, and executed.

But Karen was right, too. Missouri had seen its share of bloodshed during those violent years. Missourians had spilled a lot of Kansas blood. The boys who thought slavery was just, fair, and right accomplished nothing in the long run. In January, Kansas entered the United States as a free state. And in April, Southern rabble-rousers in Charleston, South Carolina, had fired upon Fort Sumter.

Missouri boys, most of them in the eastern part of the state, St. Louis and the likes, had joined up for the North. Western Missourians were more likely to back the Southern cause, and, indeed, Confederates or Missourians leaning toward the Confederacy raided the arsenal in Liberty a few days later. In May, Callahan read about a riot in St. Louis. In June, word came that the Yankees had taken the state capital, Jefferson City.

Missouri officially had declared itself neutral. It would not join the South, but it did not want to fight for the North.

Citizens, of course, were far from neutral.

The way Taylor Callahan saw things, it put his part of the country in a tough spot. Kansas was as blue as a territory— no, now a state—could be, filled with abolitionists and men who could not stand the sight of anybody from Missouri after Lawrence had been burned, and many Kansans killed.

Iowa above Missouri was strongly Union, too. So was much of eastern Missouri, especially around the St. Louis area. Arkansas to the south had pulled out of the Union, but Callahan had met a number of folks in the northern hills of that state who did not give one whit about the war, or the South, or slave owners.

Well, Taylor Callahan prayed every night that peace would come to Missouri, the United States, the new Confederate States, and the world.

He took Karen into his arms again, kissed her forehead, and led her to the open doors. "Holy, Holy, Holy," he said, tracing the studs on the doors after pulling them shut.

His wife broke into a lovely acapella soprano voice. "All the saints adore Thee," she sang. "Casting down their golden crowns around the glassy sea."

Karen's fears were for her family. She had four brothers, which meant Reggie, Don, Bacchus, and Jimbo, could be conscripted—if it came to that—or shanghaied into the service, for the Rebels or the Yankees. Or if things got ugly as it had been during the Bleeding Kansas years, they could be shot dead simply for saying the wrong thing to a Union man or a Southern man. Granted, Karen's folks and brothers were farther south, down Springfield way, but the last newspaper Callahan had seen and taken time to actually read said Confederate and Union forces were marching toward that town.

He thought *His Will be done.*

Then he wondered, whose will? Jefferson Davis's . . . or Abraham Lincoln's?

Nineteen folks showed up for the first Sunday services at the unnamed, nondenominational church. Roughly half of that belonged to the Widow Radzyminski's brood. Her two oldest spoke English with whatever accent a person named Radzyminski spoke.

The Reverend Taylor Callahan was not exactly prepared for a sermon—mainly because Karen soon put thoughts of war and family behind her and focused on the church they had built together. Gosh, her daddy had his doubts about the man who'd courted his daughter ever becoming anything close to respectable. Well, Mr. Breckenridge was not alone there. Most folks figured Taylor Callahan would wind up like one of his many daddies, strung up, shot down, cut to pieces with an Arkansas Toothpick in some alley behind a gambling house, saloon or some such, or run out of the state and maybe the entire continent. He had pretty much decided that was his fate, too.

But Taylor Callahan had turned over a new leaf, and that wasn't the half of it. He chopped down the old tree, dug up the roots, burned them till nothing was left but ash, and the ash got scattered by a dozen tornadoes. Then a new tree sprouted, and the new tree was sturdy and strong, a good tree. The new tree became the good man who found his way to the seminary at Logan's Knob. Or maybe Taylor Callahan found himself at the seminary. Then came the chopped down tree, and the fire, and the ashes and those twisters that left a new seed in the Missouri earth.

Either way, his teachers at Logan's Knob had taught him well. So when Karen got feeling sweet and massaged Callahan's shoulders as he looked through the big Bible and wrote down notes, and then started kissing his neck, well, the sermon and agenda for the first sermon at the first church he had ever built sort of didn't get finished.

But he remembered what he had learned at Logan's Knob.

The Good Lord loves to hear singing. So if you can't preach for forty minutes, let the Holy Spirit hear the songs that are meant to be sung—and that ain't "Yankee Doodle Dandy" and it sure ain't "Dixie."

"Nearer, My God, to Thee"

"Go, Labor On"

"Sweet Hour of Prayer" . . . just before the tithing plate was passed around.

"Just as I Am"

"Tarry with Me"

"Will We Meet"

They were singing one of the hymns Callahan's favorite daddy liked to sing—"From Every Stormy Wind"—and Callahan felt like he was singing practically in key—compared to the Radzyminski bunch, who could not carry a tune in a box car on the Weston and Atchison line.

> *From every stormy wind that blows,*
> *From every swelling tide of woes,*
> *There is a calm, a sure retreat;*
> *'Tis found beneath the mercy seat.*

They weren't singing with a whole lot of lungs when they'd started. Probably because they had sung themselves out—with no coffee, water, or whiskey to be had—about three or four songs earlier. But they got into it on the next to last verse.

> *There, there, on eagles' wings we soar,*
> *And time and sense seem all no more;*
> *And heav'n comes down, our souls to greet—*

The double doors swung open, and nobody got to sing the last line "And glory crowns the mercy seat" except Taylor and Karen Callahan, and they just mouthed the words.

He tried to remember why they had closed the doors to begin with, August being on the warm side of things in that part of Missouri . . . and every part of Missouri. The shutters were open on the windows, all four of them, and a breeze had been blowing. Besides, with less than two dozen people in a building that could hold seventy-one—if they squeezed in—it wasn't a sweat box, spread out as the folks were, except for the Radzyminski clan.

Every head turned, except Taylor Callahan's, who was facing the front—and only—door to the new cabin. He saw a lathered horse a few feet away, and after blinking and trying to look over Horace Harker's head—Horace had stood up to face the intruder, but just stood there, not moving, not speaking, and not saying anything to the visitor.

Callahan said, "Come in, friend. Come in. All are welcome in this church. Come in."

Horace Harker slowly moved to one side, and looked back at the pulpit and the preacher, which gave Callahan a clear look at the newcomer.

The preacher breathed a mite easier when he saw that it was Russell Brite. "Russell." Relief could not be hidden. The preacher practically beamed. "Folks, if you don't know Mr. Brite, well, you ought to. He's the master of wood and hammer and nails and studs, and stains. He's the man from Harold's Crossroads who built our fine doors."

"Is it all right if we clap our hands?" said the oldest of the Radzyminski girls.

At least, that's what Callahan thought the dark haired girl said, but that dialect was about as hard to crack as one of those walnuts at the McCutcheon grove.

"Absolutely," Callahan said. "We're clapping for the Lord and clapping for the Lord's helper!"

Everyone applauded.

"I might be able to preach and sing for another two hours," Callahan said, and enjoyed the laughter that followed.

But Russell Brite was not laughing.

When the noise died, he removed his hat—remembering at last that he was in a House of God—and shuffled his spurred boots. "I got some bad news, Reverend. Word come to the Crossroads from Excelsior Springs. There's been a big battle. Biggest one yet in Missouri. Don't know who won or what yet, just that it was ugly. Ugly on both sides."

"Where?" Horace Harker cried out.

"Wilson's Creek," came the answer.

Callahan's eyes immediately locked on Karen's. Wilson's Creek was near Springfield, his wife's hometown.

CHAPTER 6

Skirmishes followed. Brunswick and Kelpsford, Bird's Point and Lookout Station—places Callahan had never heard of. Yet late that month, word came of action at Lexington, less than forty miles due east, but on the other side of the Missouri River.

The letter from Karen's folks arrived in early September.

Callahan read it at the Sunday meeting at his church. "'Nathan Lyon, leader of the Union Army, was killed. The boys in blue suffered more than a thousand casualties. The South has its first real victory in the West, but it has been costly. Ben McCulloch's Rebs had some several hundred killed, wounded, missing. And war has come to our home. Your brothers have joined the fight, Don and Jimmy for the South, and Reggie, always the hothead, for the North. May God watch over our sons.'"

Callahan let the silence hold, then bowed his head, and prayed. "Father, watch over Clay County. Watch over our sons, our fathers, our mothers, our daughters, our homes."

The casualties at Wilson's Creek, he would soon realize,

were nothing compared to the slaughter that followed, mostly in the states on the eastern side of the Mississippi River.

In mid-September, the war reached Lexington again, this time between Colonel James A. Mulligan's boys in blue and General Sterling Price's seven thousand Confederates that soon expanded to at least ten thousand, maybe twelve thousand. Three days later, Price's boys were jubilant. The battle ended with the suffering Yankees surrendering after running out of water, but General John C. Frémont led a larger force and Price, knowing he could not win, retreated.

"Are you preaching for the bluecoats today?" Toby Hall asked one Sunday.

"I'm preaching for peace," Callahan said as he was passing his hat for the tithes that day. Sunday, September 22, 1861. "I'm always preaching for peace."

Hall sniggered. "You weren't always such a peaceable man. Remember that time in Kansas City, when you and me taken down them six boys who think themselves better'n us?"

"Left a piece of a good tooth on the floor that night," Callahan said, and waited for Hall to drop six pennies into the hat, better than he usually did. "And seem to recall that's why you can't bend them last two fingers on your right hand too good."

Hall grinned. Till the doors opened, and four men in blue uniforms entered, two of them holding Springfield rifles, and one a Walker Colt. The final man, wearing a black hat with the left side pinned up and a dyed-red ostrich plume waving in the breeze, held a saber.

"Hate to break up a meeting of seditionists," said the man with the fancy hat.

"We are Missourians," Callahan said. "Not seditionists."

The man studied the congregation, twenty-four, the best yet. "Meeting on the Sabbath?" the officer said with an ugly grin.

"It is the day most people gather to worship," Callahan said. "Not all, I agree. But it is the day we rest and give blessings. 'Then shall the land enjoy her sabbaths,' it says in Leviticus. We are enjoying ours. But you are welcome to join us, you and your men." He rattled the change in his hat. "No admission is demanded. But a donation is accepted."

"This is a church?" The man's saber point dropped to the floor.

"I tol' ya dem words said Holee, Holee, Holeee," one of the rifle-holding men pointed out.

To Callahan's surprise, the weapons were lowered, and the men gathered on the back pew, leaving their long arms leaning against the wall.

Callahan saw Karen, her eyes wide in surprise. She smiled at him, and he continued passing his hat. Two of the Union men dropped in two-bit pieces, and he returned to the front of the long room and led the congregation in song.

That night, Karen told him, "You could win over the biggest atheist in three states. You proved that today."

"No," he said, grinning, but he doubted that hat of his would fit on his head.

"Just about everyone in church today favors the South," she argued. "And they accepted those bluecoats."

"Those boys were armed," Callahan reminded her. "Other than the Widow Radzyminski's squirrel rifle, which she keeps underneath the seat of her wagon, there wasn't a weapon near our cabin. Except those brung in by the Yankees."

She stared at him blankly at first, then her face brightened with a smile. "You are blind to just about everything, Taylor. Toby Hall has a derringer in his left boot. Cale Hendricks has a big Bowie in his right one. And didn't you notice when Mr. Whitby put his right hand into the pocket of his Sunday-go-to-meeting coat? He wasn't reaching for an extra dollar to add to your collection for the day."

"I'll be . . ."

Well, one of those words he wasn't supposed to say slipped out.

Karen laughed. "I'll have to wash your mouth out with soap, young man."

A few days later, they learned about Osceola.

Tolliver, the mule trader from Benbow's Junction, brought word that the city about a hundred miles southeast had been sacked on the night of September 23. Redlegs from Kansas, under the command of Senator Jim Lane, had entered the town. Everyone knew Lane to be a jayhawker. Some said he came to the pretty city on the Osage River because he and other anti-slavers had been licked at Dry Wood Creek. Others said General Frémont had sent the Kansans to stop General Sterling Price's retreat. But Tolliver said what he heard was that the redlegs just came to take what they could.

They did.

Cows and chickens. Sheep, horses, mules. They busted into stores to take whatever they could load onto horses and wagons. Sacks of flour. Enough coffee to keep an army going for two years. Sugar, five hundred pounds of it, and just as much molasses. They freed two hundred slaves, and blew up the safe in the bank, making off with maybe a hundred thousand dollars.

"Nobody put up a fight?" Callahan asked.

"Oh, the State Guard was there. A hundred, two hundred, but Lane had two thousand with him. The boys put up a fight, I hear. Left one of their own dead, but had to skedaddle."

"Well"—Callahan sighed with relief—"one man dead. A loss but—"

"No, ten dead. Lane brung out some men and had them shot or hanged or both maybe. The redlegs said they was tried and executed. But we'll have to call that murder. And that ain't the worst of it. You ever been to Osceola?"

"Many a time," Callahan said. Though he hadn't passed through since his rowdy days.

"Ain't no reason to go back now," Tolliver said. "They burned the town to the ground. Not just the businesses, but the homes. Even some slave quarters. There had to be five hundred, no, more than that, homes in that town. Maybe not a thousand, but not far off that number. I been told that it's all ash and rubble now. Two, maybe three, homes is all that's left standing."

That's what really started the war on the Missouri-Kansas border.

But Taylor Callahan remained a man of peace. The double doors to his church remained open to all men and women, white or Negro, wearing blue or gray or butternut or a patchwork of all three.

He was hauling firewood from a wheelbarrow to the rack next to the fireplace one January morning when he heard horses. He looked up to see the tattered flag, neither Confederate nor Union, but black with a crooked bit of red silk sewed into it. It was not a flag he recognized; nor would anyone else that early in 1862, but before two years had passed, everyone would know that flag—and those who wore blue or supported the Federal cause would grow to fear it.

Most of the men, including the young boy holding the flag, remained back near the road. But three rode forward, and Callahan focused on the man in the middle, solid, dark-skinned, with eyes that appeared brooding and belligerent. He wore a cocked hat, had dark hair, a thick beard, and wore a green jacket, Union trousers, boots to his knees. At least four revolvers were tucked into holsters or his sash.

They reined up. The two men flanking the leader carried Colt revolvers in their right hands, and they, as well, had more six-shooters within easy reach. Callahan glanced at the rest of the riders, but as best as he could tell, maybe a third of them—if that many—had long guns.

Pistol fighters, he thought. He had heard of them, but never had seen such men. And he wondered if this were how he would die, carrying an armload of pine.

"Do I have the pleasure of addressin' the Rev'ren' Taylor?" asked the fierce-eyed man in the middle.

"Callahan," came the answer. "Taylor's my first name. After one of my daddies."

The man looked at the cabin. One of the doors was open, so all that could be read in the studs was . . . *ly, Holy.*

"Solid-lookin' cabin, suh," the man said. "Well made. I am tol' that you built this yourself."

"I had help." Callahan did not bother dropping the wood. He had considered it, but decided the pine though not the hardest of timber—might stop two or three .36-caliber lead balls if the shooting started.

"From God?" The man's eyes brightened.

"Well, He did not introduce himself as the Lord or Jehovah or Master or The Almighty, Most High or the Messiah or Yahweh-Rohi, and He—or She—did not snap her fingers. But brought instead citizens and neighbors, a mighty fine carpenter, a glorious stonemason and even a store owner who had a lightning rod he couldn't get rid of."

The man had not looked at Callahan, but kept his eyes trained on the cabin. "It is a fine building."

"I happily agree."

"Too bad I must burn it." The man turned his head and sensed something in the preacher's eyes. "But you did preach to the enemies of our cause two Sundays ago."

"Three federals and a tax-collector from Jackson County," Callahan said. "My doors are open to those who wish to hear."

"There is a war going on, Preacher."

Callahan nodded. "'And ye shall hear of wars and rumors of war'—"

"This war," the man interrupted, "is more than just rumors."

Callahan finished the verse. "'. . . see that ye be not troubled.'"

"We are all troubled," the man said.

Callahan nodded, paused, and then set out to complete the verse. "'. . . for all these things must come to pass—'"

"'. . . but the end is not yet, '" the man cut him off at the finish.

Callahan nodded. "I pray for the end."

"As do I."

Callahan glanced at the firewood he held, but still did not drop it. "I should remember you."

"I will be remembered," the man said. "That is written in stone."

"Kansas City," the preacher guessed.

"St. Joseph."

Callahan smiled. "Jim Stone's bucket of blood." He wet his lips, turned his head to the right just a bit, as that action might roll the memory back into its rightful place.

"Harvest moon," the man said.

"You had two blondes."

The man grinned. "And you had a straight flush."

"The Lord blessed me that night."

"And cursed me."

Callahan shook his head. "Those two girls, if I remember correctly, were not cursed to look at."

"They slipped me something that had me sleeping for three days. When I awakened, I indeed felt cursed. And broke."

The firewood toppled back into the wheelbarrow, with two good clean logs, falling over the edge and into the grass.

"Logan." Callahan's head bobbed.

"They call me Carbine Logan these days."

That caused the smile to fade and the preacher to straighten. "It is a name not spoken lightly."

"There is no light in Western Missouri."

"There is light. It just does not shine."

Carbine Logan, leader of a gang of Southern-sympathizing bushwhackers, leaned back in his saddle and gave Callahan a long stare. "You are not the same man I remember from that den of debauchery in St. Joseph."

"I am not that man."

"You saw the light?"

"I saw the darkness that would envelope me and condemn me if I did not change my ways."

The man on Carbine Logan's left spit out a waterfall of tobacco juice and let out a blasphemy. "Are we gonna burn this talkin' fool's cabin or sit here till bluebellies show up to shoot us down like dogs?"

That's when one of the men with the main group called out, "Capt'n. Somebody's comin' thisaway."

The leader of the bushwhackers twisted in his saddle, and the man who wanted Logan to hurry up and kill Callahan and burn the church, aimed his weapon at Callahan's chest.

"By all that is holy," a voice cried out, "it's a woman."

"My wife!" Callahan shouted.

Logan heard, and said, "Let the woman approach." The leader looked at the man who was drawing a bead on Callahan's chest. "And, you, suh, holster your sidearm. We may be border ruffians, but we have not forgotten to be gentlemen in the presence of ladies."

A long while later, Karen Callahan rounded the corner. She looked pale, and her hands were clenched, until she saw her husband. That caused her to breathe easier—just seeing that she was not a widow, yet—and she let out a long sigh before she walked straight to her husband, and put one shaking arm around his shoulders.

"Friends of yours, my husband?" she asked and stared at the three men closest to them.

"This is Carbine Logan, my dear." Callahan nodded.

Karen bowed. The man removed his hat. So did the two horsemen with him.

"Gentlemen," Callahan said, "may I present my lovely bride, Karen Callahan."

"A pleasure, Missus Callahan." Carbine Logan bowed in his saddle.

The two others muttered, doffing their hats, then settling them on their unkempt hair.

"I was telling your husband, the Reverend, that he has a fine place of worship," Logan said.

"We have been blessed," she said.

"May we all be blessed." Carbine Logan bowed again, turned his horse back toward the pike. The two men followed him.

"If you would remember us in your prayers, Reverend . . ."

"You are welcome in our church always," Callahan called back. "Capt'n Logan."

They watched them ride down the pike toward Liberty.

When the dust had settled, Taylor Callahan sank onto the ground and started shaking. Karen settled beside him, and put her arm around him, pulling him close.

"Logan?" she whispered. "Was that Carbine Logan . . . the butcher?"

Callahan wasn't sure if he nodded or spoke, but his wife started shaking, too.

CHAPTER 7

The Peacock brothers joined up with Quantrill's bunch. Harv was the first, but he always longed for some sort of excitement. Callahan did not care much for that bush whacker leader. William Quantrill acted more like a dandified bandit. Rumor was he had taught school in Kansas and Ohio, and to Callahan's thinking, Quantrill was no better than Jim Lane's Kansas redlegs. Instead of fighting Union troops, they murdered and robbed civilians, burned homes, whipped men for speaking to a man who favored the Union, or killed them for selling supplies.

Lee Peacock had a better reason to join the fight. He was beaten savagely at a dance at Harold's Crossroads by some Yankee volunteer soldiers from Peterson Towne. The reason was that Lee Peacock was Harv Peacock's brother, and Quantrill's men had ambushed a stagecoach, killed the federal paymaster, and stolen the payroll. One of the bluecoats pistol-whipped Cynthia Murdock, who had been dancing with young Lee. Those Murdock women riled quicker than the pants wearers in that clan, but it took fifteen stitches to sew up the gal's head—after the barber shaved off a bunch of that gorgeous red hair to stitch up the wound. Lee Peacock got his cracked ribs wrapped, and a wet rag to help his busted nose and lips. The boy didn't even go home. He just mounted his horse and rode off to find Quantrill.

Yankees couldn't find the bushwhacker leader in a month of Sundays. But volunteers had no problems.

The Peterson Towne boys did not make it back home, though.

Callahan read the account in the Liberty newspaper.

Their naked bodies were found near Saul Jenkins's hog farm. The uniforms would come in handy for bushwhackers, who often liked to disguise themselves as Yankees and then kill Yankees.

Jenkins told the federal captain and the county sheriff that it wasn't Quantrill's bunch who exacted revenge, it was Carbine Logan. "He wanted that to be known," the newspaper quoted the hog farmer. "He told me, 'This is not the work of Capt'n Quantrill. Tell the bluebellies and tell anyone this is what happens to vermin who mistreat Missouri ladies. And this is what happens to Yankees who won't let us live in peace."

Every time Callahan opened the shutters to the church, he thought about the two brothers. Harv who was such a fine carpenter and painter, and Lee who had carved the crosses into the wood.

Every day brought word of troubles, of battles, of raids, of death.

Old Cooter Hamilton was Callahan's first funeral. The first man buried in the cemetery behind the church.

"Men die in war," Callahan said at the graveside service. "They die in battle. They die of disease. They die fighting for the cause they believed in, and we are not here to say if the cause was just or was wrong. We are here to send a child of God home. Old Cooter Hamilton was a child of God. He came to Missouri from Ohio. That's all we know about him. I don't think his mama named him Old Cooter, but that's what he called himself, and that's what we shall carve on the cross we place on this hallowed ground. We don't ask a man his name in this part of the country. If he wants us to know, he'll tell us, and this fine merchant and neighbor wanted us to know him as Old Cooter Hamilton. He died in war. A dark war. All wars are dark, but this one is black as the Devil's heart. Men die in war, as I've said, but men should not die in war for selling salt and hemp to a man who was recognized as a man who remained loyal to the Union. That is not war, neighbors. That is not justice. That is murder. Let us pray."

Horace Harker was found dead in a ditch between the church and Liberty. Killed by redlegs, if you believed what you heard.

Someone said a Yankee brass button was found near the body, but bushwhackers often wore federal uniforms. Callahan was preaching that funeral when the doors opened and Carbine Logan walked in. The bushwhacker leader removed his hat, and let his spurs and saber jingle as he walked a few paces into the church.

Twelve women and two men had gathered for the funeral. Horace Harker had more friends than that, but it was getting to where men were leery about funerals. They stuck to their farms or businesses. If you went to see a Yankee buried, you might be visited by Carbine Logan or Quantrill or some other ruffian. Go to pay your last respects to a man who backed the South, and redlegs could hang you. Or a federal bunch might take you to the jail in Kansas City to beat whatever you knew out of you.

What would Washington, Adams, Jefferson, Franklin, and Hamilton be saying about this country, or these two countries, now?

Logan removed his hat. "Preacher, that freedman you're paying to dig Harker's grave . . ."

"Yes." Callahan stared.

"The boys told him to dig the grave on the other side of your cemetery. Just wanted you to know." He bowed slightly, turned, and headed for the door.

"Why on earth would you do that?"

Karen asked the question, and Callahan held his breath.

The bearded man turned, hat still in his hand, and bowed at Callahan's wife. "Ma'am, it just wouldn't be right to have a God-fearing and loyal Southern man like Horace to have to wait till Judgment Day lying next to a piece of Yankee trash like Old Cooter Hamilton." He bowed again, turned, and left the church.

Two of his men pulled the doors shut behind the bush-whacker leader.

The war news from the east was slow to come. McClellan was removed as commander of the Union armies. Ironclads *Monitor* of the Union and the *Virginia*, formerly a Yankee frigate called the *Merrimac*, pounded each other near Norfolk. New Orleans fell, and the Union had control of the Mississippi River. Then word came about a fight on the Tennessee River at a place near Shiloh Meeting House.

No one believed the casualty reports at first. That couldn't be. More than ten thousand Johnny Rebs killed? Thirteen thousand Union men dead? No battle could leave that many men dead. *Dead.* Not total casualties including wounded and missing. *Dead.* Gone to Glory. Twenty-three thousand men slain.

"Let's pray those are exaggerations," Callahan told the small congregation that Sunday. "But one man slain, one life lost—blue or gray—is still one too many."

The letter reached Karen the next week. It was from her

brother Phil. He was serving with the Twenty-fifth Missouri Infantry. They called the place Pittsburg Landing, but said it was near Shiloh Meeting House. Don was still alive, battered and bloodied, but not enough to keep him from marching with what was left of the command. But Jimmy had been killed. They had found him at a place they called the Bloody Pond, where Yankees and Rebels crawled to bathe their wounds.

They hoped the Yankees would give him a good burial. They didn't have time for such things as they limped south to Corinth, Mississippi. But they had given the bluebellies fits. The Yanks were too whipped to pursue the retreating Confederate Army.

She handed the letter to Callahan, too numb to speak, too drained and stunned to even shed a tear. "I wonder," Karen whispered.

"What do you wonder?" Callahan sat beside her, put his arm around her, and pulled her close.

"I wonder if Reggie was with the Yankees Don and Jimmy were fighting."

Taylor Callahan preached the funeral for Jimmy, even though the young man had only been to Clay County once. He had sent Karen a tintype from Corinth. Still in his teens, it showed him wearing brogans, Confederate Army pants, a collarless shirt, and an unbuttoned coat, of gray, maybe butternut, and a dark hat with a high crown and wide brim. He was holding a dog on his lap and a revolver in his hand.

Karen smiled. "It looks like he's about to shoot the dog." She sighed. "Jimmy wouldn't shoot a dog."

"I know that." Callahan set the photo on a stand atop a coffin he had built himself as people started filing in, more than had been inside the church since he'd started preaching.

"I wonder," Karen said, as he led her to the front pew.

"What do you wonder, sweetheart?"

"Why is Jimmy holding the revolver in his left hand? He's right-handed."

Callahan patted her shoulder. "The image is reversed. It's a tintype. The photos are always reversed. Just the way the technology works, I reckon." He stood.

She blinked.

He doubted she had heard his explanation, and did not think she would even remember the conversation.

That went both ways. He didn't remember what he had said in his eulogy, or even the hymns they sang before they walked outside to bury an empty coffin. They buried him beside Old Cooter Hamilton. Karen insisted on that. Hamilton might have been loyal to the North and Jimmy may have sided with the South, but they were dead now, and no matter what Carbine Logan said, they were at peace. Besides, Jimmy wasn't even in the grave. But his spirit was everywhere.

"Preacher?" It was the Widow Radzyminski. She had brought all her kids to the funeral.

Callahan was walking Karen back to the buckboard that would take them home. He turned, removed his hat, and bowed slightly. "Yes, ma'am."

"Shiloh," she said. "Shiloh Meeting House." The accent was hard, but Callahan understood the words.

"Yes, ma'am. That's where the fight was. In Tennessee."

"No." She pointed at the church. "Shiloh Meeting House."

He looked at the church he had built with help. Then stared at the woman unable to hide his confusion.

"You never name your church," the oldest daughter said. "She think you name it after her brother."

"For her brother," a brother corrected.

"Honor him," said the second-oldest girl.

The Widow Radzyminski's head went up and down, and she spoke whatever language she had grown up speaking, and Callahan figured that meant yes. "Shiloh Meeting House."

Callahan looked at the cabin he had built with help.

"'And the whole congregation of the children of Israel assembled together at Shiloh, and set up the tabernacle of the congregation there,'" said Mr. Prentiss, who drove out all the way from Liberty. He nodded. "Joshua, Chapter Eighteen, Verse One."

"Place needs a name," said someone from the crowd.

That took Callahan back to his wild days, back before he'd realized he was on a fast road to Hell while tarnishing a name blackened by foul and dastardly deeds done by quite a few of his daddies, and even his mama, but mostly by his own hand. And he remembered the names of the places he'd visited to gamble or consort with wicked women or drink gallons of beer and corn liquor and bad whiskey. Names like The Hole, The Hideaway, Jim's Place that became Jack's Place after Jim was killed, and then Kelley's Place, and then got burned down and became The Ruins, and finally just Ruin. *We're on the road to Ruin,* became a popular phrase in that part of Missouri. At least among the gamblers and gunmen and cheats and drunkards and knife fighters.

"Reckon it does." Callahan let his head bob, then looked at Karen, who smiled.

She smiled. "Jimmy would like that."

And so the cabin he had built became known as Shiloh Meeting Place.

The church was still open to anyone, no matter their faith, no matter their loyalty. Southern. Northern. Callahan had no stake in the war.

He just wanted to help people find the path that had eluded him for so many years.

He preached peace. He preached love.

He preached honesty and openness.

He preached from his heart.

He helped dig the graves when Carbine Logan executed

ten federals just south of the Crossroads. He let a Union patrol bury its dead—four men. But one of the wounded, Callahan knew, would not live to reach the doctor in Liberty.

Karen came up to him after the bluecoats left, and he looked at the mounds of graves.

His head shook. "When did we hold our first Sunday services?"

"Not a year ago," she whispered, and took his hand in hers.

"That sure looks like a lot of graves for a cemetery that didn't exist a few months ago," he said.

"Well, darling"—she squeezed his hand tightly—"we are in a civil war."

He squeezed back, shook his head, and exhaled. "There is absolutely nothing civil about this war."

"Darling," she said again. "There is nothing civil about any war."

They walked back to the fence. Callahan could not remember when the fence went up, but some of the neighbors had decided a cemetery ought to have structure, so they had erected a split-rail fence, though the Yankees had knocked down a section to make it easier to bury its dead—and not get caught in any ambush the bushwhackers might have been planning.

"I'm glad you're a preacher, honey," she told him, "and not a soldier."

"This isn't my fight," he said. "Besides, I'm done fighting."

"What are you doing?" he asked Karen one night in their log-cabin home.

"Embroidering." She did not look up.

He did not ask another question, but he stared at the shirt. It was the kind of shirt he saw often in those dark times. Worn by Missourians who rode with the bushwhackers. In fact, they were called Bushwhacker Shirts or Guerilla Shirts. They were loose fitting with pockets for cylinders for revolvers or revolvers themselves, and usually were embroidered with designs by their sweethearts, their mothers, sisters, even grandmothers or just women who wanted to support the cause somehow, some way.

CHAPTER 8

The Reverend Taylor Callahan sat in the gloaming, his hair singed, his hands burned, his arms and face and his clothes blackened from smoke and soot, and dust and ashes. He was not aware of anything except the ruins in front of him. The lower logs were left, though no longer good for anything, and the stone chimney remained standing, a monument, a tombstone. He could see some of the graves in the back of the cemetery behind what had been Shiloh Meeting House on the pike between Liberty and Excelsior Springs.

Men were digging. A horse snorted.

He heard the wind blow, then more horses. He breathed in, then out. He understood he was alive, though deep in his heart he wished he were dead.

A memory tried to push forward through his brain, but something blocked it out.

He heard the digging then more noise. He saw other men with shovels, but not in the graveyard. They were scooping up mounds of ash and dirt and tossing it onto the black ruins of the church. Four men carried buckets, dumping them on the smoking chunks that had once been pews.

More noise came behind him. Footfalls. Creaking leather. The popping of joints. He felt the presence at his side, but he did not look away from the church—or what had been a church—and the men in the graveyard. On any other day before that Thursday, he would not have been able to see the graveyard from where he sat. The church would have blocked his view.

A new scent reached him. Not one of burned wood. Not one of . . . well . . . he never wanted to remember that smell. But it was something he recognized, something from his past.

"Drink up, Preacher," a voice drawled.

His blue eyes looked down. He saw the greasy gauntlet holding a tin cup. Corn liquor. That's what he'd smelled. From his early teens and well into adulthood he had smelled enough of that brew.

His head shook. *I don't drink.*

He was unsure he said it but thought his lips moved. His throat ached from the effort. Or from all of the smoke he had drawn down his throat, or breathed into his lungs.

"It'll do you good," the voice said. The big hand tilted the cup back and forth, letting the liquor breathe, and the scents come up to him.

"You wouldn't like me when I'm drinking."

That caused him to remember a time a few years ago, when he had taken Karen Russell to the dance.

"I thought Baptists didn't dance," she chided him.

"Who says I'm a Baptist?" His eyes twinkled, and he had not had anything stronger than the tea the Appletons had brewed for the soiree.

"Isn't Logan's Knob—?"

He was shaking his head before she finished.

Rick Carter came over with a jug in his right hand. "How

about a snort, Taylor?" Carter held out the jug. "It's got a bit more bite than that tea you been drinkin'."

Taylor shook his head. "Give it up, Rick"—he looked at the farmer, but then his eyes fell back on Karen. And he sighed. "You wouldn't like me when I'm drinking."

Her grin reassured him even as she responded. "Who says I like you now?"

"You must like me a little bit. Else you wouldn't dance with me." He extended his hands toward her, and when her fingers touched him, they both smiled as he pulled her off the blanket.

She curtsied. "I guess I can give you one dance. But I promised Darby Keene I'd dance with him on the next quadrille."

"Of course." Taylor led her to the barn where the fiddlers, bassist, and banjo players rang out the last verses of "Sweet Betsy from Pike." "But I'll have you know I tipped the boys to play nothing but waltzes for the next ten songs."

He let her dance that quadrille with the Keene lad, twice, but when the band started up a varsouvienne, Taylor cut in.

Still sitting, Callahan wondered why his heart was not breaking. And he realized his heart was gone. Like it never existed.

The cup was pulled away from underneath his nose.

When Callahan turned his head, he saw the dark beard and merciless eyes of Carbine Logan. The commander of the bushwhackers drained the cup and set it on the scorched grass. "You know who done this?"

"Redlegs," Callahan whispered.

"Lane's bunch?"

Callahan shook his head. "Witt's." He remembered them busting into his cabin. Pounding his head with a revolver barrel, and sending him to the floor. He recalled their dog, that mongrel but loving girl, barking like he had never heard, and then the pistol shot that silenced her. "Least I heard someone address Major Witt."

"Figures. Witt and that bunch are worse than Lane, if that can be believed."

Callahan and the bushwhacker watched as a young slender man approached from the ruins, dragging a charred bit of chain in his left hand. His eyes were the same color as Callahan's . . . just not as dead as Callahan's cold blue eyes. The chain came forward, and dropped at the squatting Logan.

"They chained her to the pulpit." The boy could not have reached sixteen years.

"Lectern," Carbine Logan corrected.

Forty days must have passed.

"Anything else?" the bushwhacker commander asked.

The boy's head shook. "Ain't no way of knowin', suh." The boy's eyes considered Callahan for no more than a second, then focused on Carbine Logan. "Wrapped . . . her"— he swallowed, and then held down whatever wanted to rise out of his gut—"in a blanket." He swallowed again and held down the bile once more.

"I heard her scream," Callahan said, and the faces locked on him.

He had come to on the cabin floor. Why they hadn't burned his cabin he did not know. Why had they not murdered him, lynched him, had him drawn and quartered? But then he looked again at where the soldiers—he no longer considered Logan's bunch bushwhackers—were burying Karen Grace Russell Callahan, and understood. Living was his punishment.

He remembered words, or maybe he'd just dreamed them, but he thought he had heard Witt whisper to him before his world turned black. "Next church you get, boy, maybe you won't disgrace it by buryin' rebel trash next to our brave Kansas and Union men."

Callahan wondered why he did not cry. He wet his lips as best he could and shook his head.

Carbine Logan pressed a firm hand on his thigh and squeezed. "We'll avenge her, son. We'll avenge your wife, your dog, your church. Heads will roll, Preacher. And I mean that literally."

The world spun for a few moments, and then Callahan's head cleared some. He wet his lips again, but still could not summon much saliva. "What brought you here?" he asked, without looking at the teenager or Logan.

"We came to bury our dead, Preacher."

Callahan's head shot back to where men were coming out of the hole they had dug. He thought he could make out a blanket on the sod, but the darkness started creeping faster.

"That's your—" Logan thought, then finished. "That's your missus, Preacher. We buried our two boys with their fallen comrades. Had to wait to . . . retrieve . . . your wife's remains. It was too hot."

Callahan tried to nod as if he understood.

An older soldier came up behind them, kneeling on Callahan's right. He saw the big Bible in the man's leathery hands, and the Bible was placed by Callahan's thighs.

"Reckon they dropped this before they lit out," the man said. "Found it by the pike."

"I dropped it," Callahan said. "When I was running here." He reached for it, then the pain hit him, and he turned his hands over and saw the scorched flesh.

"You were still trying to get in there when we showed up, Preacher."

Callahan turned to Carbine Logan.

"My lieutenant had to pop you right where Witt or one of his mad-dog killers pistol-whipped you. Else we'd be burying you here, too."

I wish you were.

The bushwhacking captain turned to the kid who had brought the chain. "Fetch some of that salve Horace carried in his knapsack. He won't be needin' none no more. And rip up the cleanest shirt any of the boys got. We'll tend to the preacher's burns as best we can."

The boy nodded and took off out of Callahan's view.

Carbine Logan rose and looked up and down the road. "You'd figure folks would come to help. A fire brings out everybody. Used to, anyhows. And when folks see their church burnin' or smoke risin' from where any neighbor's home, any church, they know is there, they come to help."

"That was before," the older bushwhacker said. "Before Osceola. Before this blasted war started. Folks be scairt now, Capt'n."

"We're all scared," Carbine Logan whispered. He looked down at the preacher.

"You got a place you can stay?"

Callahan made no attempt at an answer.

"They didn't burn your home?"

Again, he did not answer. He had turned from them, and watched them shovel dirt back into the hole where they had laid whatever remained of his wife.

"We'da seed the smoke if they'd burnt his home, too, Capt'n," the old-timer said.

"Yeah. Reckon you're right." Logan drew in a long breath, shook his head, and exhaled. "All right, Clint, you take the preacher back to his place. Catch up with us when you can." He nodded down the road. "We won't be able to follow them. And if they's like they been doin', they'll split up into groups of twos and fours, take off in all directions, then skedaddle back to their farms around Lawrence." He looked down again at Taylor Callahan. "We will find them, Preacher. I promise you that. We will find them. And they will pay."

The kid was back with a muslin shirt and a jar of something.

Carbine Logan bent and picked up Callahan's Bible. "I'll use this, Preacher, if you don't mind. Say some words."

"She was partial to Psalms." Callahan heard his voice, though it sounded like it came all the way down from Logan's Knob.

"Psalms." Carbine Logan's head bobbed. Then he looked at the kid, gave him an order without speaking, and started walking to the opening in the split-rail fence that led to the cemetery.

The boy squatted beside Callahan, tossed the shirt to the old-timer, and began straining to open the jar. The old man started to rip apart the shirt.

Callahan called out to Carbine Logan's back. "Reckon I'll be coming with you, Captain."

Logan stopped, still holding the heavy Bible, and turned back toward the preacher. "If you're up to it, Preacher. After all, she was your wife."

He tried to stand, but it took the boy and the old man to pull him to his feet. Callahan stared in the darkening day at the notorious bushwhacker. "I'll be riding with you, too," he said, "after we finish what we got to do here."

"We ain't ridin' to no church social, Preacher," Carbine Logan said.

"I know where we're riding to, Captain," Callahan heard himself say. "We're all bound for Hell. But I'll be riding with you just the same. The men that did this will soon learn that Hell rides with us, and we shall send every last one of them to the hottest pits of Hell."

For two years or thereabouts, Taylor Callahan lived in Hell . . . the Hell that was Missouri and Kansas, with some trips into Arkansas and Texas, once into Kentucky to hide from federal pursuit. Though some Yankee papers said Carbine Logan rode with Quantrill's guerillas in the 1863 raid of Lawrence, Kansas, Callahan knew that to be hogwash. They were dug in, deep in the thickets of the Sni-a-Bar when Missourians torched that city.

Taylor Callahan fired revolvers during the war, but he never set any home, any permanent structure, afire. Federal wagons that were captured, well, they could burn. But no home. No barn. Certainly not a church. Not even a shed. Not even an outhouse.

He wore the embroidered shirt of a bushwhacker, a gift from Rebecca Kelley, whose husband rode with Carbine Logan until that scrape near Lone Elm, probably the bloodiest fight the boys got into, and while they were hurt, and Jim Kelley and fifteen other bushwhackers killed, they had broken the spirit of Witt's Marauders. Major Sylvester Witt himself was left on the field, his body punctured by at least fifteen—if the account in the *Liberty Weekly Gazette* was accurate—leaden balls.

Before the war was over, Witt and Jim Kelley and more bushwhackers and redlegs and legitimate Confederate and Union soldiers than Callahan could count were dead.

Callahan probably would have been dead, too, except the Major General in the Heavens had brought fate into play. Callahan and another bushwhacker had been left behind in the Sni-a-Bar to look after a kid whose leg had been amputated—surgery performed by Callahan and reluctant comrades. When they rode out to find Logan's Irregulars, a federal patrol intercepted them. Callahan's smooth talking and preaching had miraculously—he knew the Major General in the Heavens did not perform miracles every day—gotten his comrades free to travel on in the night. But Callahan was taken with the bluecoats to a town called New Jerusalem.

Which no longer was a town. Rebels had burned it.

Ironically, the bushwhackers had not burned the church—just every other structure, practically, and most of the population in New Jerusalem backed the Southern cause. He remembered a fireman saying "the whole state's turned plumb loco. Don't nothin' matter no more."

He remembered the dead, including children. He remembered the smoke, but that had not triggered thoughts of that terrible evening when Witt's Marauders had knocked him out and dragged his wife to the Shiloh Meeting House where . . .

He would not recall all of that.

What he remembered was a Union man, a soldier who had found the bound copies of a newspaper, and had read about what had happened at the Shiloh Meeting House on the road out of Liberty. The officer would have been in his right to shoot Taylor Callahan dead, but he did not. Instead, he had offered Taylor Callahan a revolver.

"You'll need this, Preacher," the bluebelly had said.

And before he rode out, Callahan had answered, "No, I won't."

CHAPTER 9

Wyoming Territory, 1876

Gripping the bottom of the hard bench to keep from bouncing off the Abbott & Downing as the stagecoach cleared the rise, Callahan forced away the memories of a long-ago war, when he felt as though he would never see a blue sky again, and when full moons raised fear. He just remembered the smoke and a long-dead spouse.

From the top of the hill, he saw the burning building and what must have been the town of Peaceful Valley. He took in the surrounding area, the mountains far to the north, south, and west, the endless expanse of wind-blown grass and small hills that rose and fell like ocean waves—not that Taylor Callahan had seen any ocean, at least, personally, with his clear eyes. But he sure had seen pictures of those giant blue, foamy waters.

A thought struck him as the coach rolled down into the town and the driver cursed and spit. *Where, pray tell, is the valley?*

It looked like a combination of prairie towns he had seen in Kansas and the mountain towns of Colorado, though he could see one prominent hill a bit off to the northeast.

Most of the buildings were log cabins, including the one burning, though some frame structures, including a two-story structure he figured had to be a hotel. Since the Union Pacific went through Cheyenne and off to the Pacific, building framed wooden buildings wasn't that uncommon. More expensive than chopping down your own trees, but either way, you had to travel a far piece to get that lumber. To the mountains for the logs, to the railroad towns for the two-by-fours and fine planks. No one had gotten around to painting any of the frame houses, except for, again, what Callahan guessed to be the hotel, and another one, a brilliant white, he knew was the saloon. The south-facing side spelled out *SA-LOOON* in giant orange letters.

Three O's?

Well, the middle one seemed to have been used as a bull's eye for target practice. A lot of target practice. Or someone was slopping with black paint or thought polka dots were artistic. Callahan couldn't tell from the distance, but he'd be sure to check it out.

The mud wagon headed straight for the burning structure as the driver kept cursing. Men, and a few women, had given up trying to save the building, and stood around watching the flames finish devouring what was left. Most of them turned to look at the approaching wagon.

A handful of horses were tethered at the hitch rail in front of the saloon, and some cowboys lounged, drinking and watching the show. One man pulled off a bowler hat, slapped it against his thigh, and walked toward the coach as the driver began pulling hard on the reins, and calling out to his team.

"Whoa! Whoa, mules, whoa!"

When the coach stopped, the driver set the brake and yelled to the man with the bowler hat, "What the Sam Hill happened to my stagecoach station?"

From inside the coach, Absalom giggled.

The man returned the bowler to his bald head and stopped

when he reached the front wheel of the Abbott & Downing. He snapped, "What the Sam Hill are you doin' back so soon? There ain't no contract if you didn't get to Poudreville."

"There ain't no contract if we ain't got no station in Peaceful Valley," the driver barked.

Inside the coach, Absalom howled like a coyote.

"There ain't no contract for us, if—" The man in the bowler hat must have recognized Absalom's laugh. He walked to the door and peered inside the window. "What the Sam Hill is Absalom doing in your coach, Buster?"

Well, at least Callahan now knew the name of the mud wagon driver.

"Ask him." Buster hooked a thumb toward Callahan.

The man in the bowler hat stepped back. He studied Callahan, and ran a hand across the stubble on his cheeks and chin. "Who the Sam Hill are you, mister?"

"Well," Callahan said with a smile, "I'm not Sam Hill." He climbed down from the coach, walked around the back, untied Job, took the reins in his hand, and led the horse to a watering trough near a log cabin with a sign painted above the door that read SUPPLYS.

Spelling seemed not to be a strong suit for the population of Peaceful Valley.

"My name's Taylor Callahan," he called out, turning and checking to make sure the wind was still blowing away from the supply store.

"Gunfighter?" asked the man in the bowler hat.

"Circuit-riding preacher," Callahan said as he walked toward the coach.

"Who ain't no sloth or slouch when it comes to working a Colt .45 Peacemaker," Buster said.

"Preacher." The man in the bowler hat laughed. "With a *Peacemaker*." He must have thought Buster was joking.

"Ordained after studying at the seminary at Logan's Knob over Missouri way." Callahan waved toward the east, grabbed the handle, and opened the door. "We got a man here who's in need of a doctor." He looked at the people standing at the building as the fire began to die.

The man in the bowler hat looked up at Buster. "Where's the Poudre River coach?" he asked.

Buster waved back to the south. "Smashed to pieces."

"Huh," the man in the bowler hat muttered, not like he was asking a question, just a statement that said nothing. "Well." He scratched his cheek, and said again, "Huh."

"No stagecoach for Poudre River," Buster said. "No station for us."

"Question is," the man in the bowler hat said, "which can get done first? New station? Or a new coach?"

"Don't have to be nothin' fancy," Buster said. "Meanin' a coach. Them Poudre River boys could throw some chairs in a covered wagon and haul passengers."

"That's a fact," said the man in the bowler hat. "But we could let a room in the hotel." He pointed at the two-story frame building. "Call it our office. Lots of stagecoach companies have offices in a town's hotel. I think."

Callahan opened the door to the Abbott & Downing. "Mister, there's a hurt man inside, despite his giggling. The noble thing to do would be get him to a doctor. Is there a doctor in this town?"

Bowler Hat turned around, and his right hand moved closer to the Remington pistol in his waistband. He looked back up at Buster. "Where does this rascal come into the picture?"

"He stopped me last night," Buster said. "I come across the wreck, figured we had this contract all signed, sealed, and delivered. The preacher here . . . he had other notions and made me haul Absalom back."

"A preacher." The man turned back to Callahan. "You mean you wasn't trying to be funny?" He looked at Buster. "A preacher stopped you? Armed? When does a preacher pack a Colt?"

"Ordinarily, I don't," Callahan said with a smile. "Fact is,

I'd like to put it back in my saddlebags. After Job is finished drinking. And then I'd like to see about finding a place to bring the Word to this lovely town. For tithes, whatever the heart tells you and all these fine citizens to offer when I pass my hat."

The man in the bowler hat stared at Callahan for a long while as some of the firefighters began leaving the smoking hull of the stagecoach station to see what was going on at the Peaceful Valley mud wagon.

"This yahoo cost us a contract for the rights to haul folks to and from Poudreville?" the bowler hat wearer asked Buster.

Buster did not answer.

"You let a slick-talking confidence man buffalo you?" said the man in the bowler hat.

"He ain't no greenhorn, Frank."

Well, Callahan thought with a smile, he was learning all sorts of things without having to ask prying questions. The driver's name was Buster. The man in the bowler hat was called Frank. You didn't have to be rude in this country to learn how a man wanted to be called. You just had to be patient and polite.

"Mister," Frank said, moving his hand closer to the Remington, "I'm going to shoot you dead. Then I'm going to put Absalom out of his misery. It ain't like we'll put a name on the cross we put over your grave, but in case somebody comes asking about the body, what is your name?"

"Already told you that. Callahan. Taylor Callahan. The Reverend Taylor Callahan. And I thought it was considered rude to ask a man his name in this country."

"Well," said the man in the bowler hat, "I reckon that's why folks call me Rude Frank." He grinned.

Buster whispered, "I wouldn't try nothin', Frank."

Frank chuckled. "He don't look much like a preacher. Except for the black. Reminds me of a priest I gunned down in New Mexico Territory five, six years back."

"Why did you gun down a priest?" Buster asked.

"He kept ringing that dad-blasted bell. Had to be six o'clock on a Sunday morn. And I was trying to sleep off a mighty good drunk."

Most of the firefighters had started moving, probably to get out of the line of an errant bullet, but possibly to get closer to the forthcoming showdown between Frank and the circuit rider.

Callahan just stood easily, listening to the crackling wood and the sound of Job slaking his thirst. The white gelding had hardly stopped to swallow. The horse might drink the trough dry and possibly could turn Wyoming into something resembling that drought-stricken country down in South Texas that Callahan and Job had spent some time in last summer.

"I never told you about me killing that priest, Buster?" Frank asked.

"Nope."

The man in the bowler hat was stalling, but not because of fear, and not because he liked to talk. Callahan had already figured out that part. He was a man who liked an audience, and if the Poudreville Stagecoach Company's Abbott & Downing coach had not already been wrecked and ruined, the man likely would have kept on running his mouth till the coach arrived, even if it only carried Absalom.

The door on the side of the Peaceful Valley coach opened, and Absalom's legs hung out. Somehow the battered old driver managed to sit up.

"You must be feeling better, Absalom," Frank said, finding something else he could talk about till people arrived from the hotel and the saloon and whatever other businesses had decided to give Peaceful Valley a go.

"Maybe," the driver said in a pained voice, "I just want to see you cut down to size."

Frank's face tightened. "After I've sent this preacher to

meet his Maker, I'll be putting a couple of holes in your belly."

"I don't reckon you will."

"We'll see."

More people gathered. Even a man in black sleeve garters and red whiskers came out of the store that sold *supplys*.

Out of the corner of his eye, Callahan noticed a few of the newcomers looking over toward the tall hill, but Callahan had not forgotten his wild and woolly days, or those ugly years riding with Carbine Logan's Irregulars. He kept looking at Frank.

The mules snorted, and Buster coughed and spit.

"If you're gonna shoot this cardsharper," said a young man with a big mustache and batwing chaps who had joined a few others from the saloon with the extra shot-up *O*. The young waddie casually raised his hand and pointed off toward the northeast. "You best do it before Grant Lee gets here, Frank."

"Grant?" Callahan asked. "Lee?"

The cowboy stared at Callahan. "Yeah. You know him?"

That almost made Callahan take his eyes off Frank. "You don't see the irony of that name, son?" the minister asked.

"Irony?" the cowboy said.

Callahan had to stifle a laugh. That would have been something St. Peter never would have let Taylor Callahan live down. He could see the angel standing at the Pearly Gates, laughing his head off. "You got killed because you were cackling like a wet hen, laughing so hard, snot run out of your mouth. As good a preacher as you could be on Earth sometimes, Callahan, I just don't know that the gates are open for a man who laughed his way to death in a gunfight." He paused at that thought. Would St. Peter use the word *snot*?

"Grant," Absalom managed to say, "was a Yankee general. Lee would be Robert E. Lee. He was the general of the Army of Northern Virginia."

"Northern Virginia has its own army?" asked the cowboy.

"You never heard of the War Between the States?" someone asked the youngster.

"The Civil War," a woman corrected.

"Ohhhh." The youngster finally understood the irony, though Callahan decided that the boy still didn't know what *irony* meant.

"Where's Marshal Lee?" Frank asked.

An older, leaner cowboy who was savvy enough to have brought a bottle of whiskey from the saloon with the extra *O* took a swig and swallowed. "He's coming down from Peace Treaty Peak."

"Walking or loping?" Frank asked.

"Walking."

Frank's grin widened. "Then I got a few minutes."

A man and a woman rounded the corner of the smoldering cabin. The man wore a two-gun rig, and the two guns were silver plated and had ivory handles. The woman was playing with a deck of cards.

"You interrupted my game, Frank," the man said. "Kill this stranger so I can win some more money from these waddies."

The man with the red whiskers who sold supplys said, "You'd think Marshal Grant would spur his horse into a trot."

"Marshal Lee, Harry," said the woman with the cards. "Not Grant."

"He ain't blind," Harry finished. "He has to see the smoke"—he looked at the woman—"and I know his name's Grant Lee, Kit. But me and Grant's on first-name basis."

"Ask me," someone said from behind Callahan, "Grant Lee has always favored Poudre River over Peaceful Valley."

"Amen," said another voice behind Callahan.

"How far away is our lawdog?" Frank asked.

"If you're gonna kill this stranger," someone else said, "you ought to do it right now. Appears our lawdog has finally seen there ain't no Peaceful Valley Stagecoach Company headquarters no more."

"Nah," said a woman Callahan could not see. "He just sees all of us gathered around to watch a shootin'."

"You ready, cardsharp?" Frank stepped back a couple of paces, and his face hardened. The smile flattened into a grim line, and his eyes focused on Callahan while his fingers on his right hand began to twitch.

"Callahan," the circuit rider said with a smile. "Taylor Callahan. Preacher. Not a cardsharp."

"We'll get that right on your tombstone," Frank said.

Callahan laughed. "From what I've read so far on your buildings, I have my doubts that you will get anything right."

That silenced everybody in the crowd, except the woman with the cards.

The pretty blonde woman laughed. "I like this guy. He has wit."

"That can be his epilogue," Frank said.

"Epitaph," Callahan corrected. He could see in the face of the gunman, Frank did not like to be corrected.

"I wouldn't do it, Frank," Buster said again.

But Rude Frank was already making a play for his Remington.

CHAPTER 10

Sometimes, Grant Lee wished Old Man Thompson had shot him dead that day in what became Peaceful Valley, instead of the other way around. It sure would have made life a lot simpler. Lee clucked his tongue and pulled on the reins to stop his horse.

It sure would have made life a lot simpler? "Not, I reckon," he said aloud, "if I was deader than Old Man Thompson is now."

The horse swished its tail, snorted, and decided, since they had stopped the easy walk, to defecate.

Lee took advantage of the unexpected delay to drape the reins over the neck of the animal and lean back, stretching out his back and shoulder muscles. He let a giant yawn stretch his jaw, mouth, and cheek muscles, hoping to dull the ache in the top molar on the left side of his mouth that had been chipped two nights ago. He'd buffaloed young Walker Thompson with the barrel of his Smith & Wesson. The fool had gulped down too much of Kit Van Dorn's doctored-up rye whiskey and started acting like the dang fools acted when they were young and drunk.

Grant Lee had plenty of experience, firsthand as a dang fool many years ago, and secondhand since they had pinned the star on his vest. Of course, it wasn't Walker Thompson who chipped that big tooth of Lee's. Nope. The Widow Audrey Eleanor Thompson had done that herself, with the hard leather-knobbed end of the quirt she fancied. All Lee had done was take the boy home, rather than lock him up in the jail and let him sleep off a drunk. The moon had been full, and Lee always liked to ride across the rolling country of that part of Wyoming at night, listening to the night birds and the bull bats and the coyote and the wind.

The Wyoming wind didn't sound so full of thunder and bluster in the evenings. Most evenings, anyhow. Not like the daytime winds. *Maybe,* Lee thought, *it's on account you can't see the wind at nighttime.*

He clucked his tongue, ran that thought through his brain again, then tested it by speaking it aloud. "On account you can't see the wind at nighttime." He scratched his nose, shook his head, then spit. "You can't see the wind at daytime, either, you dad-blasted knucklehead."

The horse, done with its bodily function, snorted. Or maybe the gelding was just laughing at Grant Lee's lack of sophistication and intelligence.

The lawman gathered the reins, and felt the wind—that which he could not see blow dust off his thick mustache and cool his ears. He replayed the scene that had given him the toothache.

"That tin star don't give you the right to go about addling the brains of my youngest!" Standing on the porch of the two-story ranch home Old Man Thompson had built, legend said, with his own hands, the Widow Audrey Eleanor Thompson glared at Grant Lee. "No man addles the brains of my children. Only I am allowed to do that."

"Well, Missus Thompson," Marshal Grant Lee said in his

slow drawl, "it was either knock the boy out or let him shoot Kit Van Dorn deader than the rat Rude Frank shot a few minutes earlier."

"Kit Van Dorn ain't no better than the rat Rude Frank shot. Nobody in Wyoming Territory would have missed her."

"Several would disagree with you on that count, ma'am— the waddies you hire for roundups, the soldier boys who come through on payday, those dang fools who keep ruinin' my sleep with their stagecoaches, Tin Horne and Rude Frank, the hide hunters who come by every three or four months, those surveyors that showed up last week, the sheriff and his deputies over Laramie way, and the United States marshal up in Cheyenne."

The Widow Audrey Eleanor Thompson frowned. To Grant Lee's surprise, she didn't say anything.

However, her other son, Knight, did. "You wouldn't have done that iffen my pappy was still alive." Twenty minutes older than Walker, Knight took after his pappy; Walker had his mother's soft features.

Marshal Lee nodded. "Wouldn't have had to, son. Your pa would have hided the boy a whole lot worse than I done him."

Knight's right hand flashed for the Colt on his right hip, but Grant Lee knew he did not have to defend himself.

The Widow Audrey Eleanor Thompson—nobody in Peaceful Valley called her anything other than the Widow Audrey Eleanor Thompson when speaking of her, excepting at Sunday services, whenever folks remembered it was the Sabbath. Not Mrs. Thompson. Not the Widow Thompson. And when they spoke *to* her, they generally just said, "ma'am". Although Tin Horne had once suggested they ought to change that *ma'am* to *sir*.

"You pull that hogleg, boy," the Widow Audrey Eleanor Thompson told her oldest, "and I'll bust every finger you got at every knuckle on your left hand. And chop off your right hand."

Knight's .45, halfway clear of leather, slid back into the holster.

"Go fetch your stupid brother," the lad's mother ordered.

The kid frowned, muttered a respectful, "Yes, ma'am," stepped down to the ground, and began moving to the horse Lee had pulled from town.

Still in the saddle, for the Widow Audrey Eleanor Thompson had not invited him to step down, Lee looked over at the bunkhouse, but saw just a few waddies standing underneath the picket and thatch awning over the door. No porch for the bunkhouse, just rocks and sage.

"I didn't hit Walker too hard," Grant Lee told the boy's ma. "Suspect the whiskey he drunk—if you call what they serve in that bucket of blood *whiskey*—is what he's mostly sleeping off."

"You a doctor now?" the Widow Audrey Eleanor Thompson growled.

"Jack of all trades." Grant Lee smiled.

The Widow Audrey Eleanor Thompson found nothing amusing.

The older boy grabbed his twin's britches by the waist between the suspenders and jerked him down. Using the side of the horse to brace the groaning kid up, Knight Thompson steadied his brother, then let the boy jackknife over Knight's right shoulder while Lee kept a tight grip on the reins to the Thompson gelding until the meaner of the two kids was carrying his younger brother toward the big house.

"Boutelle!" the Widow Audrey Eleanor Thompson shouted toward the bunkhouse. "Come fetch Red Wing and put him in the barn."

Boutelle, who had been foreman of the place since the dead Thompson first established the spread, pitched his cigar onto the ground in front of the bunkhouse, and stepped down, crushing out the smoke with the toe of his right boot before his bowed legs took him to Lee and the horse. Lee handed the reins to the foreman, who nodded without comment, and began leading the animal to the big barn.

Boutelle was a pretty decent man. Good cowboy. Probably would have made a mighty fine foreman at any other spread. But on the Thompson range, a foreman was nothing but a dollar-a-day hired hand. He didn't boss anything. The bossing had always been done by a Thompson—first the old man, now dead, and now the old hardcase's widow.

Grant Lee turned, planning to tip his hat, apologize to the Widow Audrey Eleanor Thompson for riding in at such a late hour of the night and uninvited, but saw the woman coming straight for him. She stopped and looked up when a cloud drifted over the moon. He could not get a real good look at the widow's face.

"Light down," she ordered.

In his stupidity, his ignorance, his dumb Texas upbringing, Marshal Grant Lee stepped off his horse. He could not recollect exactly what he'd expected, but maybe, just maybe, the Widow Audrey Eleanor Thompson was going to invite him inside for some coffee. Or he halfway imagined her voice turning sweet as honeydew.

"Marshal, we might be a long way from the Sioux and Cheyenne that are on the prod north of here, but it is dark, and there's no sense in you riding back to Peaceful Valley at this time of night. We'll put you up, feed you breakfast, and then . . . I don't know . . . hang you or drag you to the Colorado line."

Instead, she slammed the heavy end of a quirt against his cheek. He fell back against the horse, but gathered the horn on the saddle with his left hand, and kept a firm grip on the reins with the right. The horse shied away, and he almost went down to his knees but kept himself on his feet, muttered something that was meant to calm the horse, and shook some sense back into his head.

Some of the cowboys standing in front of the bunkhouse chuckled, but the Widow Audrey Eleanor Thompson said nothing. She just strode back to the porch, stepped up, and then turned around. "Hurt one of my boys again, Marshal," she called out, "and next time you get the other end of my quirt." She turned back, opened the door, turned around and yelled at her hired men at the bunkhouse. "Get to bed. Work starts before dawn on this ranch. You boys might remember."

Boutelle had vanished into the barn.

The bunkhouse door opened, spreading light a few yards across the ground, then figured blocked out the yellowish glow till the door closed.

The door to the ranch house slammed shut.

Marshal Grant Lee's horse snorted.

Grant Lee spit out some blood, and, he figured out later, a piece of that molar. He pulled himself into the saddle, shook his head, spit again, and rode back to town.

For a Texan, Grant Lee had never been a fan of horses. Oh, he rode well enough, but he did not care that much for all the bouncing around. No matter what he wore—chaps, long-handle undergarments, britches with thighs and seat reinforced with wool, leather or both, he always felt chaffed after just three or four miles. Pathetic. That's what his pa would have called it.

As he returned to Peaceful Valley, his thighs ached, his butt hurt, and that dad-blasted tooth hurt like blazes. Bouncing around at a trot had not helped so he was keeping the horse's gait to a slow walk. When he had decided to take the job as Peaceful Valley lawman, he did not think he would have to ride much. It wasn't much of a town. Legally, it wasn't even a town. Legally, if things came to court in Cheyenne, he wasn't even a lawman. But all that might change . . . and why he had ridden up to Fort Centennial yesterday afternoon.

The bluebelly major of those soldier boys had wanted to

talk to him. As he had talked, they had ridden across the prairie together with some other soldier boys to keep them all safe. He had spent the night at the post, learning more from soldiers and surveyors and a bigwig who had come all the way from Washington, District of Columbia, by way of Omaha, which is where the big wig lived ten months out of each year. After hearing about what all was going on, and why the United States Army had decided a subpost was needed, Grant Lee realized he might have bitten off more than he could chew. Being Peaceful Valley lawman, that is.

He sighed again. *Bitten off more than I can chew.* That busted molar hurt even more just from thinking that phrase.

On the other hand, if he was smart, if he could play his cards right, and live long enough, he could become richer and more powerful than the Widow Audrey Eleanor Thompson.

He caught a whiff of an unnatural scent and looked up. He wouldn't live long at all if he kept daydreaming and thinking too much while he rode in this country, instead of paying attention to what was going around. It might not be Montana, but it sure wasn't the tamest and safest country in the United States and her territories.

Pulling on the reins, he stopped his horse again.

The stagecoach station was rubble. Place had burned down to the ground. That's likely where the scent came from. Smelled like burned wood, but not firewood or smoke from a cookfire. Scents had different smells, Grant Lee had learned, and a man knowed when something smelled wrong. Even smoke.

But smoke wasn't what held Grant Lee's attention. Fires were common in frontier towns, big ones like Cheyenne, littler ones like Poudreville, and tiny ones like Peaceful Valley. Just about every town Grant Lee had spent time in had seen an outbreak of fires.

Gunfights were another story, though Peaceful Valley had seen its share for a town with not a whole lot of gunfighters. It wasn't Dodge City or Abilene. It wasn't San Antonio or Fort Worth. Wasn't old San Francisco during the Gold Rush or Denver during the Pikes Peak run, either.

He could tell Rude Frank was about to make his play.

What he couldn't figure out was who Rude Frank aimed to kill. Marshal Grant Lee's eyes were pretty sharp. Sharper than his wits. Sharper than the two blades of that Barlow knife he kept tucked in the right pocket of his britches, yet. He couldn't make out the man in black.

Black? Didn't only gunfighters wear black outfits like that Prince Albert fluttering in the wind? And a black Boss of the Plains hat made by John B. Stetson's company? Black boots, too. If Lee's eyes were not playing tricks on him, the fellow had a black ribbon tie. Only thing white on him was his shirt, which was partially hidden by a black vest.

Grant Lee put spurs to his horse, but that just pained his tooth and his backside and his thighs. Maybe if Rude Frank killed the stranger, the residents of Peaceful Valley would back the marshal and run that gun slinging, card-cheating mean scoundrel back to the Indian Territory where he had hailed from.

But that wasn't the actions a good man, a God-fearing man, nor what a man sworn to keep the peace ought to do. He spurred on the horse and shouted out a warning. Leaning into the wind, he let the horse gallop.

He gritted his teeth, then pulled his revolver from his holster, hoping to fire a warning shot.

But he couldn't get that old thumb-busting pistol to cock.

He was too late. He saw that clear as day.

Rude Frank had made his play. His gun was coming up to kill the stranger.

CHAPTER 11

The Reverend Taylor Callahan smiled.

Rude Frank's face turned about ten times paler than the white collar of a St. Louis priest on Easter Sunday. The blowhard drew in a deep breath. Off to his right, the woman laughed.

"Kill him," said a black-hatted hombre with his thumbs hooked in the front of his trousers.

Callahan waved the barrel of his Colt revolver, which was aimed in the direction of Rude Frank's chest.

"We'll all testify Frank drew first," said a man in the crowd. "Self-defense. Go ahead. Shoot him down like the lowdown dirty dog he is."

The woman laughed again.

Rude Frank did not dare look at the man, or the woman, or even at Callahan's eyes. He could not take his eyes off the .45 that gleamed in the sun.

"You gonna try to finish that draw, son?" Callahan's eyes twinkled. "I mean, if I was you, I wouldn't try it." He waved the Colt slightly. "Seein' how all I got to do is touch this trigger, and that would be the end of poor Rude Frank. But you seem too young and too ignorant to be cut down and buried. We all learn from our mistakes, and that's something that never changes, no matter how old you get. The way you have been acting, ain't likely to be too many more years."

Rude Frank looked at his revolver, which wasn't quite halfway out of the holster. His Adam's apple bobbed, and he started to lower the weapon, but Callahan cleared his throat, shook his head, and waved the barrel just a tad more, never taking his finger off the trigger.

"No." Callahan waited till the wannabe gunfighter looked back in his direction, and their eyes met. "No, I don't reckon it would be a good idea for me to let you keep on—" He laughed. "Sonny, you thought I was gonna say *livin'*, but that would not be the kind and generous and forgivin' thing for a circuit rider to do. Especially on his first day. First few minutes in a new town. Makes a bad impression. Cuts down on the generosity of tithe-givin' patrons at my meetin's. No, sonny, I was gonna say keep on packin' that hogleg. You might partake of too much liquor, or what passes for liquor here, and liquor can make a man, especially a hotheaded youngster like yourself, not think too clearly. Make him quick to rile. Seek revenge. Especially if he thinks he's been shamed. You feelin' shamed, Frankie?"

The punk's head shook slightly.

"Glad to hear it. I think the best thing for you to do is—" He paused, hearing the clopping of a horse's hooves sounding behind him.

That would be the lawman he had heard was making his way down the hills and into town. Lee Grant. No, *Grant Lee*. What a handle to be labeled with! The town marshal who seemed to like the Poudre River Stagecoach Company over the one from Peaceful Valley, which sounded strange, since the Poudre River was in Colorado.

"Maybe unbuckle that gun rig you got. That's right. Nice and gentle, no sudden moves." Callahan watched Rude Frank unbuckle the belt then ordered, "Wrap the belt around the holster. And remember, we're being real careful, real gentle, real easy, because you don't want nobody—especially me—to think you might be trying to slicker a man. Folks used to say, before I seen the error of my youthful and ignorant ways, I wasn't the type of fellow who got slickered often and made those who tried to slicker me regret their poor choice immensely."

"You talk a whole lot, Preacher." The woman wasn't the woman in the green dress he had caught a glimpse of in the stagecoach last night. Well, she wasn't wearing that green dress anyway.

Callahan smiled. "Wait till you hear my sermons." But he did not take his eyes off Rude Frank.

The gunman did not take his eyes off Taylor Callahan, either. Beads of sweat were popping up on his forehead underneath his hat, and his sideburns were getting slick from perspiration.

"You're doing fine work, Frank," Callahan said. "Mighty fine."

The horse stopped. Leather creaked. Callahan could feel the presence of the lawman but kept his gun pointed at Rude Frank. Callahan did not look at anyone except the big-mouthed gunfighter.

"Just leave the rig and the hogleg atop that spittoon. Careful. You don't want a nice-looking gun and fancy leather rig with all them pretty conchos and them shining brass cartridges falling into all that nasty stuff folks expectorate into them brass cuspidors." He watched the gunman carefully. "Good. Yes, sir, Frank, you follow directions right good. Now, if you'd be ever so kind to stand up and back away, keeping your hands up just a bit. That's fine. Real fine. That's far enough."

The Colt clicked as Callahan touched the trigger with his finger while his thumb braked the hammer and slowly settled it as the revolver moved forward. With a bow, he carefully let the Colt drop to the side of his trousers.

"Frank, you look as if you need a bracer," Callahan said. "I'd admire to stand you to a whiskey, if my credit's good. I don't partake of ardent spirits myself—not anymore—but I suppose a young man like you can handle a libation or two, though I'm just buying you one. You reckon that's okay, ma'am?" For the first time, he let his eyes fall on the handsome woman.

"Your credit's good with me," she said before adding with a wink, "for a drink. Just one."

Rude Frank muttered what probably was a profanity before he made a beeline for the Three O'd Saloon. The mean-spirited man followed, whispering something to the woman that from the gal's reaction was not anything she cared to hear.

The residents of Peaceful Valley decided the fun was over and began to go their separate ways. The woman still stood there, though, and appeared to be sizing up Callahan as he turned to look at the man on the horse.

The man wore a dented and tarnished tin star.

"Marshal," Callahan said, nodding a polite greeting, "my name is Taylor Callahan, and I'd like to preach the Word to sinners and non-sinners alike—though I've yet to meet a body who was completely without sin—if that meets with your approval."

"I was hoping," the lawman said, "that your first act would be the preaching at Rude Frank's funeral."

Callahan chuckled. "He's just a youngster, Marshal. Sometimes once a punk kid looks into the face of death, his wicked ways come to an end."

"Sometimes." The lawman nodded. "But I don't think it'll take to Rude Frank." He lifted his gaze at the woman. "Kit, the stagecoach station ain't exactly in the same condition it was in when I rode out of town."

"You got good eyesight, Grant," she said. "And the preacher here can tell you that Absalom's stagecoach ain't in the same condition it was in when it left Peaceful Valley on what appears to be its last run. And Buster can tell you that, thanks to our itinerant minister, neither company, Poudre City nor Peaceful Valley, has won any contract. For now."

"Where have you been, Marshal?" The voice came from a man who'd reemerged and hooked his thumbs near two holsters that hung low on his hips.

"Fort Centennial," Lee answered, "if it's any of your business, Tin Horne."

Tin Horne. Callahan turned to study the man. The nom de plume fit. Tin Horne undoubtedly was a better gunfighter than Rude Frank.

"Well, you better run this sharper out of town," the gambler said, pointing a finger on his right hand at Callahan, while not moving his hand from the nearest revolver.

"He says he's a preacher," Marshal Grant Lee said. "Not a cardsharper."

"I say he is one." Stepping down and walking toward Callahan, Tin Horne let his fingers fall over the butts of his holstered revolvers. He stopped a few yards in front of Callahan. "I say you ought to run him out of town. Pronto."

"There's no law that says a town can't have two sharpers," Grant Lee said coldly.

The gunman turned and delivered a vehement stare at the lawman. "You calling me a cheat?"

"I don't think the word *cheat* left my mouth, Horne," Lee said. "Why don't you go inside and make sure Rude Frank don't drink more than the one whiskey this stranger bought him."

"On credit," Kit Van Dorn clarified.

Marshal Grant Lee nodded. "On credit."

"You best run him out of town," the sharper said. "Or the funeral he preaches, will be his own." He walked to Kit, grabbed the pretty woman's upper left arm firmly, turning her around, and practically shoving her into the gambling house.

Callahan walked over and collected Rude Frank's rig. When he looked up, he realized the streets were suddenly deserted. The marshal dismounted and, pulling his horse by the reins, covered the distance. "You look like a man who has ridden hard," Lee said. "No offense."

Callahan smiled. "Well, I did have a rather not-dull ride on a mud wagon into town. After a fairly eventful night. After a pretty long journey from Colorado."

"Poudreville?" Lee asked.

"With a respite at Virginia Dale."

"That your horse?" The lawman pointed at Job.

"If your definition of horse includes things that don't giddyap and are pigheaded."

"He don't look all that bad to me."

"Looks ain't always accurate."

"I know what you mean. I'm handsome enough to be a thespian, but here I am, lawin'."

They stared at each other, then the marshal began leading his horse to his office. "I got a corral behind the courthouse, or what we call the courthouse. You can put your gelding in there with mine. For the time being."

"So I'm allowed to preach here?" Callahan sought confirmation.

"No permits required. As long as you don't go off half-cocked."

"What's your split?"

The marshal stopped and turned back to look over the circuit rider. "Split?"

"Last towns I've visited, the folks in charge wanted a split of the profits—or the split of my take. Ten percent in Denver, but twenty-three and one-third in Trinidad."

They started their journey to the courthouse.

"I don't reckon we have the same way of thinking here, Preacher. You hungry?"

"Marshal, I like the way you talk."

* * *

Marshal Grant Lee fried eggs and salt pork on the top of the stove in his office, serving supper at his desk with stale bread and not the worst coffee Taylor Callahan had ever tasted, but not that far from tying for last place. The lawman sat in his chair and motioned to a barrel in the corner. "Pull that up for your seat, Reverend," he drawled. "It's better than anything else I got, and you probably would like to take a load off your feet and legs."

"Oh, that looks like a fine settee," Callahan said. Leaving his supper on the edge of the cluttered desk, he walked for the makeshift furniture.

"You don't smoke, do you, Callahan?" Grant Lee called out.

"No, sir."

"That's good."

Which seemed like an odd question and statement, until Callahan squatted and saw the stamped black letters on the top of the keg. DANGER. As he spun the heavy barrel around, his throat turned on the dry side. GUNPOWDER. He turned his head and stared at the lawman.

"Don't worry." Lee sipped coffee. "I don't smoke, either. And it's too warm to start a fire."

Callahan made himself smile and half carried, half dragged the heavy keg to the desk.

"You load your own bullets?" Callahan asked, then settled his hindquarters over the DANGER warning.

"Habit I picked up during the War of the Rebellion," the lawman answered.

The choice of what to call the Civil War labeled Grant Lee a Yankee. A Southerner, or a former bushwhacker from western Missouri, would have called it the War for Southern Independence or the War Between the States, or something a whole lot harsher. Or maybe the marshal was trying to figure out Callahan's past.

Callahan just smiled and nodded. "All my daddies loaded

their own. 'Course, we had to back then. Couldn't buy pre-loaded ca'tridges."

"Where was that?" Grant Lee asked.

Callahan knew that was not a polite question. In the Western country, a man did not ask a stranger his name, nor did a man ask where the stranger hailed from. To do so was plumb rude. To do so could bring about an old-fashioned row.

But Callahan was going to be a peaceable preacher. "Missouri."

"That's what I figured." Lee nodded and lifted his coffee cup. "The accent for one thing. The way you handled that six-shooter when you were showing up Rude Frank was another. I seen many a night rider and many a bushwhacker. I'm a Kansas man."

"Red Leg?" Callahan studied the lawman's face.

The man just smiled. "What do you think?"

Callahan sipped the awful coffee. "I think with a name like Grant Lee, you got the best, and worst, of both worlds. Kinda straddling the fence."

"Straddling a fence can hurt many a man," the lawman said. "And I didn't have a say in what my mammie and my old pappy named me. Besides, I'm forty-seven years old. That means I was born before most folks knowed who Grant was or who Lee was."

"Some people would change their name," Callahan said. "Stop the jokes. Save the torment."

"Some folks would indeed." The man picked up a piece of meat and chewed on it.

Callahan forked a chunk of egg into his mouth. Good, hot, greasy, and just the right amount of salt and pepper. "I like you, Grant Lee," he said after swallowing.

Grant Lee sipped some coffee. "I like you, Reverend Callahan. How long you expect to be here?"

The preacher shrugged. "Oh, I was aiming to make Cheyenne."

"That city sure could use some good preachers."

Callahan smiled. "You might have noticed, Marshal—"

"Call me Grant," the lawman said.

Callahan's smile widened. "That's a right hard name for a western Missouri man to say."

The lawman laughed. "Then call me Lee."

Callahan chuckled. "Grant," he said, testing the word. "I think I might like you."

The lawman gestured his coffee cup. "You were saying?"

After backtracking to where he had been interrupted, Callahan relocated his train of thought. "I was saying, Grant, you might have noticed Peaceful Valley seems to have its share of sinners and some hardcases who might need some fire and brimstone shoved down their throats. And quite a few folks seem in need of comforting."

"I don't know about the comforting, Preacher, but—"

"Call me Taylor."

"Taylor." Their coffee mugs clinked.

"As I was saying, Taylor, I don't know about the comforting, but there's better than an even money chance we sure will need some preaching done here. This town was always about to bust wide open. Those two dang fool stagecoach companies is just a little boil on one's buttocks. Not even a boil. Just a nuisance. But things are changing, and they are about to change a whole lot. Makes me wish I was still back home in Prairie Dog Creek."

Prairie Dog Creek. That was good to hear. Taylor Callahan had never heard of Prairie Dog Creek, Kansas. It wasn't one of those towns Missouri bushwhackers had targeted like Lawrence or Fort Baxter.

But the lawman's next sentence was not comforting in the least. "Yes, sir, Taylor, we'll have need of a real good preacher. 'Cause I sure do expect we'll be busy burying a lot of citizens."

CHAPTER 12

Callahan set his coffee cup on the edge of the cluttered desk. He could not hide the twinkle in his blue eyes as he said softly, "From what I've seen of Peaceful Valley, even if smallpox swept through here, there wouldn't be *that* many folks to bury."

The lawman smiled slightly. "And the territory of Wyoming and the rest of these here United States of America and the entire rest of the world would not miss those that were planted. Including me."

"And me as well," Callahan said.

"I don't know about that, Preacher. There's something about you that—I don't know just how to put it—but . . . well . . . let's see—" Lee paused. He drained his cup, set it atop his cleaned, but greasy plate, and shook his head. "Yeah, there's just something about you."

"Well, I thank you for that. And there's something about you, too."

Grant Lee wiped his mouth and chin with his bandanna. "There's not many people here now, Preacher, but there's about to be."

Callahan tried to take in all he had seen, remembering what he could about the town. It did not appear to be gold country, nor silver. There was a ranch—the Thompson spread—but Wyoming Territory had plenty of ranches and enough cattle to keep the railroad crews full of beef for the Union Pacific. Nothing was impressive about what Callahan had seen—of the town or that part of the territory. In fact, he could not think of a whole lot to say about the people who populated the town. The marshal was nice. And that woman Kit Van Dorn was quite pleasant to look at. But you probably would not want to look at her too much. Her associates, Rude Frank and Tin Horne were not pleasant at all. Their temperaments tended to run on the easy-to-rile side. Callahan figured they also were the jealous types.

And then there were those two stagecoach lines with crazy drivers.

Callahan smiled. "Two stagecoach companies vying for the rights to a contract from Poudreville to Peaceful Valley. Having spent a few days in Poudreville, preaching in a livcry—the mules and horses liked my sermons, Psalms, and hymn selections far more than the asses and jackasses of the two-legged variety—I can't see much profit in that for either company."

Grant Lee nodded slightly, and his left hand moved to open a desk drawer. He pulled out a bottle close to three-quarters full of dark liquid, withdrew the cork, and extended the bottle toward the circuit rider.

Shaking his head slightly, Callahan grinned. "Unless that's tea, I reckon I ought to pass."

"Reckon I could call it communion wine, Reverend," Lee said, "though when you taste it you might think the wine has turned."

"I'd still have to thank you for the offer, but decline with my sincerest regrets."

"You sure?"

"You'd be sure if you'd ever seen me when I was liquored up."

"Fair enough. I like a man who's honest about what he can handle and what he can't. I don't drink too much. Bad habit. Especially when you're packing a star. In a flea trap of a town in the middle of nowhere. I just drink a bit after I've rid a hoss more than I'd care to." He splashed no more than a finger or two of the whiskey into his cup, found the cork and pushed it back into the neck, and let the bottle disappear inside the drawer, which he pushed shut.

Callahan wondered if the drawer would be opened and the lawman would drink another slug or two. Then dismissed the thought. He could tell Grant Lee was not lying to him about his lack of fondness for John Barleycorn.

The lawman even made a face as he sipped the dark liquor.

"Back to the current situation at your humble little town. And a stagecoach war. I mean, if they were running a stage to Cheyenne," Callahan said. "Or even Laramie. From what I've heard, that would make sense. I guess those two stagecoach companies could continue on to those towns." He studied the lawman's reaction. After wetting his lips with his tongue, Callahan continued. "But that's not what's going on. Is it?"

"Won't be no need for a stagecoach to run to Laramie. Cheyenne?" He shrugged. "I reckon that's a possibility. We'll have to see."

"A spur," Callahan said.

Grant Lee nodded, and he took a healthier swallow of his whiskey, but coughed a bit, and wiped his nose—more proof he wasn't much of a drinker of Western whiskey.

"I still don't see the reason to build a railroad here," Callahan said. "From what I gather, the Thompson ranch doesn't produce enough flank steaks and beef ribs to warrant a shipping yard. This isn't Dodge City or Wichita."

"Do you know what a Hell-on-Wheels is?" Lee asked.

Callahan nodded. "Temporary camp of sorts. When they're building a railroad." He shook his head and let a mirthless grin cross his face. "From my brief stay, so far, in Peaceful Valley, I'd say it is well on its way to becoming a Hell-on-Wheels."

The lawman finished his liquor and set the cup down. He did not open the drawer for a second round.

"That's what the commander at Fort Centennial told me," Lee said. "Some rich railroad investors have concocted this idea to lay tracks for a spur from Laramie to Denver."

"Why not Cheyenne?"

Lee shrugged. "Cheyenne's got a railroad to Denver. Denver Pacific and the Kansas Pacific sort of partnered. To compete with the U.P. That line was completed, oh, five, six years ago. You could have saved the soles on your boots by taking the train from Denver to Cheyenne."

Callahan smiled. "Except that railroads give passes to lawmen, politicians, land agents, friends of the railroad. They don't part with passes for preachers."

"I suppose you're right. The way I think, Laramie wants its own direct line to Denver. The money's in Denver. Did you see the U.S. Mint there?"

"Can't say that I did."

Grant Lee pointed at the map hanging on the wall to his left. "I'm told laying track should be easy. Well, maybe not a straight line south like it is from Denver to Cheyenne. That line runs through Greeley. But an engineer and a surveyor said it's easier to go from Laramie to Denver. Maybe because you don't have to stop in Greeley."

He chuckled. "Hard to meet many people with something pleasant to say about Greeley."

"Woman I met in Poudreville hailed from Greeley. She said it's a nice, young, thriving town. But I'd never heard of Greeley before."

"You mean to tell me you'd heard of Peaceful Valley or Poudreville before you got up this way?"

"Well, no. Anyway, I was directed from Fort Collins to Poudreville and Virginia Dale, and at Virginia Dale, I was sent to Peaceful Valley, and told from there I could make it to Cheyenne. Had I spent more time in Denver, I guess I could have gone through Greeley. But then I never would have made your acquaintance."

"And I never would have gotten to see you shame Rude Frank." Lee rose, gathered the dishes, and dumped them in the skillet on the cast-iron stove. "Well, I have my own theories. For a spur from Laramie to Denver. It could be that the territorial prison is in Laramie. Cheyenne might control the government, but prisons are where a state or territory makes money."

Callahan gave that some consideration.

"Besides, the Cheyenne crowd is full of cattlemen. And cattlemen don't cotton to cattle women. When Old Man Thompson was alive, he was riding up to Cheyenne often, drinking with the governor, making friends with bankers and Union Pacific men, and the"—he stopped to clear his throat—"well, the lovely hostesses at the hifalutin . . . ummmm . . ." His voice trailed off then he continued. "They keep talking about building a Cheyenne Social Club. Till they do, well, it's sort of like Kit Van Dorn."

"I see the picture you're trying to draw with words," Callahan said with a smile.

"And you call yourself a preacher?" the lawman said, grinning wider than Callahan.

"A preacher is just a man," Callahan said, but hoped the marshal would move on to more genteel conversation.

Grant Lee glanced at the drawer that held the whiskey bottle. Callahan gave the man credit for his resolve as he did not reach to grab the knob and open the drawer.

"Well, once the old man died and the Widow Audrey

Eleanor Thompson became the bull of the woods, so to speak, Cheyenne's civic leaders, state bigwigs, and most of the railroad folks stopped treating the ranch here like it was anything of importance. They ain't the kind that would call a lady a rustler. Mark my words, Preacher, she ain't. She's a good woman. Good woman in a hard business. But this country might be about to go up in flames."

Callahan remembered the smoke from the burning stagecoach station. He remembered the memories it resurrected. He remembered his dead wife. And he remembered all he had done, all the sins he had committed, all the blood he had shed, and the deaths he had seen. The deaths he had caused, and the hell he had helped create during those terrible years.

In a daze, he sat in the small cabin in a village—that was stretching the definition a mite—nestled in a remote part of Wyoming Territory but knew he had never heard of the town until someone had mentioned it while putting a nickel into his hat down in Colorado.

He stared ahead, hearing the reports of revolvers, the thundering of hooves, and the loud screams of men of violence. The gunpowder keg he sat on felt like the saddle of a galloping horse. Instead of coffee and the pleasing scent of fried bacon, hot bacon grease, and fried eggs, he smelled burnt powder. White smoke filled his eyes. He saw the blackness of night, and muzzle blasts that looked like fireflies in western Missouri.

He heard the commands of his leader, Carbine Logan—commands no real soldier in a legitimate army would have ordered. "Kill them all! Shoot them down like the mongrel dogs they are. They are murderers. We are in the right. We take no prisoners! Nor shall they. So if you die, boys, die game!"

"I say something wrong, Reverend?"

Callahan made himself look up. Was he sweating? He felt like it, but suddenly he realized where he was. In Peaceful

Valley, Wyoming. Six hundred? Seven hundred miles west of Clay County?

He shook off the chill, blocked those images again, and wondered how long he would be haunted?

Then he remembered the peace he had known. The peace he had been living—or trying to live—for better than ten years. No longer was he the bushwhacker, the killer. He was a minister. *Ordained.* What he had been before the War Between the States. He had vowed in 1864 he would never take another life, that he would live up to what he was supposed to be.

A man of peace. A man of God.

He smiled.

Though at that moment, had Grant Lee opened the drawer and pulled out the bottle, Taylor Callahan was not convinced he would have summoned up the willpower to say no.

"Well"—he swallowed—"I guess I'm not . . ." He faltered. "I wonder if I can forgive all Kansans."

"You forgive me?"

"I don't think I have to forgive you. If you're looking to make a confession, that's not the religion of my tribe. I'm not saying anything against it. I'm just saying that's not the way I preach. You want forgiveness, just ask the Major General in the Heavens."

A silence filled the room.

"Where were we?" Grant Lee asked after the long uneasiness.

"The Widow Thompson," Callahan answered, though he wasn't exactly sure that was the correct answer.

"Yep. She's a handful. You'll find out for yourself. Here's what you come into, Preacher. You might wish someone had directed you to Greeley. Or kept holding your camp meetings in Virginia Dale. It's a right nice place these days. Kit Van Dorn could be richer than the Widow Audrey Eleanor

Thompson when the tracks reach Peaceful Valley. Even before that, folks who want to make a buck will be hightailing it from parts unknown to either Laramie or here. Not much else between."

"Will they be laying tracks from Denver?" Callahan asked.

"I don't think so. The commander at Fort Centennial seems to think this is a Laramie enterprise. The way I hear it, the tracks have to be to the Colorado line by—" He frowned. "I disremember the exact date, but it's sort of like the deal between the Poudreville Stagecoach Company and the Peaceful Valley Stagecoach Company. You got to prove your worth and meet your deadline before you get to see a contract and then you can anticipate all the money you might make."

The marshal opened another drawer and pulled out two cigars. He handed one to Callahan, bit off the end of the other one, and stuck it in his mouth.

"You partial to the weed?" he asked, the cigar in his teeth dancing as he made the words.

"Not particularly," Callahan answered, but he bit off the end of his cigar, too.

"A smart man, Preacher, would keep right on walking to Cheyenne."

"I suspect you're right. But I have a feeling I was called here. That I'm needed here. Right here. In Peaceful Valley."

"That calling, Preacher," the lawman said, after removing the cigar. "It could be Death calling."

Callahan nodded.

"You got guts, Taylor. I admire a man with guts."

"I admire a man with a match." He held out his cigar.

Marshal Grant Lee laughed and shook his head. "I was hoping you had one."

CHAPTER 13

"Where can I hold my revival meetings?" Callahan asked over breakfast the next morning. More fried bacon and eggs and bad coffee, courtesy of Marshal Grant Lee.

The Kansan pushed back his chair. "You serious?"

Callahan took a sip of the hot brew. "It's what I do," he said, and speared a chunk of scrambled egg with his fork.

"If the ashes have cooled down, I reckon what's left of the stagecoach station would work."

It took a moment for Callahan to swallow his egg. He washed it down with the bad coffee, and studied the marshal's face. "You're serious."

"It's sort of the center of town. Near the road. Good place. Not that I think you'll be preaching to the thousands like there were at the Sermon on the Mount. Good thing. I don't have any more loaves of bread and the fish haven't been biting lately."

Callahan smiled and did not correct the lawman on his Scripture. The Sermon on the Mount and the Feeding of the

Multitude were different events. "The Supplys store?" he asked.

Grant's head shook soberly. "He can hardly fit four customers in at a time. 'Course, four of anybody is a crowd in Peaceful Valley. And I reckon the Three O'd Saloon is out."

"Oh, I don't know. I've had some of my best tithes given in saloons, some of them worse than what you have here."

"Yeah, but you didn't have Rude Frank and Tin Horne in those places. They'd gun you down. Kit Van Dorn might even shoot you if you interfered with profits."

Maybe, Callahan thought, *Marshal Lee is trying to urge me to leave town.*

That would not be a bad thing—leaving Peaceful Valley. Just saddle up Job and meander his way to Cheyenne. That had been his plan anyway. There was a railroad in Cheyenne. The Union Pacific. Two railroads. The Denver Pacific, which linked with the Kansas Pacific in Denver. There was the Bozeman Trail, or whatever folks called the path to Montana Territory these days. Callahan wasn't sure he wanted to be in Montana Territory. Not this year. Not with the Sioux and Cheyennes mad—with good reason—at the United States government, and the War Department threatening to wipe out the whole lot of Indians on the Northern Plains if they did not return to the poorly maintained reservations.

But he could go somewhere.

Yet something told him he needed to be here. The Major General in the Heavens had His reasons, but He rarely shared those reasons.

"The old stagecoach station, eh?" Callahan heard himself whispering.

"The stones at the bottom and on the floor were solid," said Grant Lee, who had nothing wrong with his hearing. "Not calling that fine masonry, but by Wyoming Territory standards, it wasn't half bad. Chimney didn't collapse none from the fire, so you could get a fire going if it got cold. And it ain't being used right now."

"Shucks," Callahan said, "I've preached in worse places." He was already thinking about how to use the ruins not as a meeting place, but as a theatrical prop.

"Ain't no roof, but it don't look much like rain. You could move out those burned remnants. If I had any prisoners, I would make them work for you. But the jail I got . . ."

That would be the stone structure, which likely had no cells, and would not hold more than six men, if they were skinny like most cowboys—and traveling preachers.

Grant Lee shrugged. "I'd help you with the cleaning, but I need to saddle up and ride south."

"On business?" Callahan asked, though he knew it was none of his affair.

"A bit of an investigation, you might say. See if something I also heard at Fort Centennial pans out." He laughed. "If it happens to be true, maybe I'll ride south to Denver. Maybe catch the Kansas Pacific and go back home."

Callahan did not push things any further. It was not his affair. Wasn't his town, either. Besides, he liked cleaning up places. Some of the places he had preached had been livery stables or saloons, and he might have had to muck the stalls or swamp the rough drinking holes before he could do any preaching. He also liked manual labor. He could think things through while he worked.

Though cleaning a burned-out rubble would be a true test.

Maybe that was the Major General in the Heavens' plan. A test. To see what kind of man, what kind of circuit rider, Taylor Callahan was after a dozen years.

The two left the humble office, shaking hands at the corral, and Lee telling the preacher he could stay as long as he wanted. Callahan thanked him again and left the lawman saddling his horse while the circuit rider walked to the burned-out shell that had been a stagecoach station. Buster, the driver of the Peaceful Valley Stagecoach Company's mud wagon, was standing in front of the wreck. He eyed

Callahan but said nothing until the preacher stepped through what once was a doorway and kicked a mound of ash and charred log with his boot.

"Your company own this?" Callahan asked, breathing in the still strong odor of fire and ruin before turning around to look at the driver.

Buster's face was scrunched up. "Huh?" he finally said.

"Did the Peaceful Valley Stagecoach Company own this cabin? Or was your employer just renting it?"

"I dunno."

Callahan's eyebrows arched. "You reckon you still got a job?"

"Dunno."

"You want to earn some money?"

Buster studied Callahan, scratched his cheek, shifted a wad of tobacco from his left cheek to his right, spit, and then scratched the other cheek. "What I got to do?"

"Find a shovel. Help me move this ash and this rubble to—" Callahan had to stop and look around. The wind seemed to come in from north or west mostly, so moving the mess to the south side might be the best. That way, folks standing in the ruins to hear some of the Word wouldn't get ashes in their nostrils or choke while singing some fine songs of Gospel and Glory. "Help me move it there." He pointed. "Won't even need a wheelbarrow to move it. Just scoop and toss, scoop and toss." He kicked at a fallen rafter. "Or pick up and toss."

"How much?"

Callahan thought a moment, then said, "Four bits."

"That ain't much."

"I ain't got much." Callahan grinned. "But I'm guessing . . . you ain't got nothing."

Buster frowned and nodded toward the Three O'd Saloon. "Got cheated last night."

Another thought came to Callahan. "Did you send word

to Poudreville about what happened here last night? That the company's stagecoach station burned down?"

"Ain't got no way to get word to Poudreville. Lessen I walk."

"You got a team of mules. And a coach. That's more than Absalom and the Poudreville Stagecoach Company has."

"Mules got stole last night. Took my stagecoach, too."

Callahan pushed back the brim of his Boss of the Plains Stetson. "Why didn't you tell Marshal Grant?"

"Didn't think about it. Reckon I should have?"

Hooves clopped, and Callahan turned to see the lawman riding south.

"Well, you'll have to wait," he told the stagecoach driver and turned back to look at that sad, big man. "Till the marshal gets back. Till then, I got two bits."

"Thought you said six bits!" Buster fired back.

Callahan grinned. "I believe I said *four* bits. Yours to earn. If you're hungry. Or should I say, *thirsty*, enough."

"Where you gonna get a shovel?"

Callahan pointed at the SUPPLYS store.

"It ain't open."

"It will be."

"Think you might advance me my pay?" Buster looked over at the SALOOON with one of the o's filled with bullet holes.

"It's not even eight in the morning, Buster, and you want something to drink?"

"Uh-huh."

"Is the saloon open?"

"It don't never close."

Callahan saw the door was open, but there was not much activity to be seen or heard. "Well, it's closed for you, Buster, till you earn your pay."

The man shrugged, but then he surprised Callahan by saying, "Reckon we can get started moving some of them logs and charred timbers out of the way. Till you can buy some shovels."

Buy shovels? Callahan certainly hoped that would not be required.

They worked steadily, the preacher and the stagecoach driver becoming filthy from the ashes, soot, and charred timbers they moved. As they worked, the small town slowly came to life. First, smoke started coming from the fireplaces banked during the night. It wasn't cold, but Callahan would not have called the morning warm. After all, it was Wyoming Territory.

At first, he attempted conversation, but soon determined that a hopeless cause. So they buried themselves—sometimes it felt literally as the ash and charred flakes fell upon them—moving what they could to the southern side of what remained of the cabin.

"Whose cabin was this before your company took it over?"

It had to be pushing ten in the morning, by then, and the owner of the store had yet to show up. But some man in a bowler hat and mismatched brogans came from the other side of the street and entered the saloon. Buster was right. The saloon must have been open twenty-four hours a day.

"Kit Van Dorn's," came the matter-of-fact answer.

Conversation was harder, what with the wind picking up—from the northeast. Both men pulled their bandannas over their noses and mouth to keep from filling their insides with the nasty remnants of the log structure.

Callahan looked up for confirmation.

"That's what I got told," the driver said, and tugged on a stuck bit of black wood.

"She didn't seem too upset over the loss of a fine rental property."

"Kit's got other investments."

Callahan could not hide his grin. "I have seen the truth in

that statement, Buster. I surely have." He moved over to help the big man with the black wood.

When they had managed to unwedge the piece and drag it through the dust, Callahan figured it was time to rest a bit. They walked to the well, and Callahan lowered the bucket, then cranked the turn. They dipped their bandannas in the bucket, scrubbed their faces and hands as best they could, emptied the bucket, and sent it down again. When the bucket was raised again, they drank.

By then, a man walked from a cabin behind the hotel, and Buster nodded. "Guess the store's 'bout to open. Here comes Peterman."

He would have to walk right past the well, so Callahan tried to make himself as presentable as possible. Buster scratched himself, farted, and then sat down on a stump.

"Morning," Callahan greeted the storekeeper.

The man stopped. "You still here?"

"Appears to be the case, sir."

The storekeeper grunted, then frowned when he saw Buster. He also saw just how dirty, despite their scrubbing, the two men were. Especially since they'd had no soap.

Well, there never was a good time to ask the owner of a store to turn over a new leaf and become generous, so Callahan removed his hat and slapped it on his dirty pants. It didn't matter. Charcoal and soot were black. So were his hat and pants. "Mr. Peterman, this good man here and I have been cleaning up what remains of the old stagecoach station. I aim to do my preaching there for a few days."

"In that wreck?"

"We are all wrecks when the Major General in the Heavens looks down on us."

"Why not just preach outside in the open?"

"Sir." Callahan tried to look as though he were shocked by such an outrageous proposal. "This is not a dog-and-pony show. I am not a swindler nor a seller of snake oil. I am a preacher, ordained from Logan's Knob Seminary."

"Never heard of it."

"Well, it has produced finer theologians and ministers than me, I assure you. I am here to preach."

"I ain't stopping you."

"But you could be of great assistance. If you could loan us two shovels. That's all we ask. Shovels to remove the ash. So I can stand—"

"I don't understand why you want to preach in what's left. Place ought to be torn down. We can put another business there." He pointed at the stagecoach driver. "That's what you ought to be doing, Buster. So you can win that contract you and Absalom been trying to get."

Callahan figured this to be another lost cause, but he had to try. "You're right on many counts, Mr. Peterman. You have a business mind and a mind that thinks. This burned-out wreck will be torn down. But first, it will be used as my pulpit. The donation—temporarily, of course—of two shovels will be the first step. You would be helping clean things up . . . as a man with civic pride would do anywhere."

He wasn't going to get those shovels.

"I don't rent. I don't give. And I don't—"

"Give them the shovels, Harry," a musical voice sang out. "I'll pay for them and take the cost out of your bill at my saloon."

CHAPTER 14

Whatever Harry Peterman told Kit Van Dorn those shovels were worth was a lie. But Taylor Callahan was not about to issue any complaints. Buster complained enough for six or seven Jackson County men, and anyone from Clay County knew nobody grumbled about anything as much as those who hailed from Jackson County, Missouri.

Of course, the cantankerous old Peaceful Valley Stagecoach Company employee's directed most of his grievances at Taylor Callahan. "Iffen you told me I'd be doing farmer work, I'da brung some gloves with me."

"Iffen you is so dad-blasted determined to do some preachin', you ought to just build yourself a church. It'd be cleaner than this pigsty."

* * *

"This is the most ridiculous job I ever signed on fer."

"Fifty cents. All the ashes I've swallered, it'll take me fifty dollars' worth of beer to clear out my mouth, throat, esophagus, stomach, and intestines."

"You is the confoundest boss man I ever worked for."

"There ain't no roof. Ain't no walls. Ain't no place to sit. What kind of preacher did you say you was? Some hard-shell outfit, gotta be. Make folks stand all the time. Stand in ash and soot and burned mess. That's cruel."

"Cruel. That ain't the half of it. They don't treat prisoners this bad at the territorial prison up in Laramie."

"Not only ain't you got no good sense, you is a miser. Four bits for this work. I bet you owned slaves before the Rebellion."

"You bet wrong." After two hours and twenty minutes of working to Buster's incessant griping, Callahan finally spoke. "Reckon I won't have to pay you that fifty cents you just lost."

Buster flustered, clutching the shovel's handle and staring wildly. "Now wait just a confounded minute, Preacher. When I said *bet*, I wasn't meaning in the literary sense. It was one of them fun bets, you see. Not moneymaking sense."

"Oh." Callahan scooped up more ash and tossed it into the ever-growing mound of rubble and waste. "I see. Maybe you should work on the keeping-your-mouth-shut sense."

"Maybe I should." Buster nodded, wiped his brow, and went back to work.

But he did not keep his mouth shut, though the complaints became fewer and the stories on the whimsical side increased—those about mules, getting drunk, stagecoach races, getting drunk, women he had danced with, getting drunk, and a gold nugget he found up around Breckenridge that was larger than his big toe on his left foot . . . which was a bit wider than the big toe on his right foot, but only on account of the Percheron that flattened it with its big right forefoot when Buster was freighting for that skinflint operator in Fairplay.

He looked up from shoveling. "Misnamed as any town in the territory of Colorado because not one dad-blasted citizen—male, female, or dog—that lived in that mining town knowed one dad-blasted thing about fair play."

"You boys must be hungry." That voice sounded nothing like Buster's nasal whines.

Buster reached up and removed his hat even before Callahan could see Kit Van Dorn.

The preacher found the brim of the Boss of the Plains and bowed slightly as he took off his hat. "Ma'am."

"I'm practically starved," Buster told the saloon girl.

"Well, there's more food in my place than I can eat. You're both welcome to some."

The stagecoach driver dropped the shovel and took off.

Callahan watched, thinking Buster ran faster than the team of mules he drove for the Peaceful Valley Stagecoach Company. He did not stop to wash his face or hands.

After placing the hat back on his head, Callahan leaned his shovel against the fireplace, and knelt to turn over the shovel Buster had dropped so that if someone stepped on the end, the shovel would not pop up and smack that someone in the face.

"Your generosity is much appreciated, ma'am." Callahan

touched the brim of his hat, but he wasn't sure Kit Van Dorn had heard him or seen him.

She stared at the ruins of the old cabin.

"Ma'am?" Callahan waited.

She looked at him, her face showing something he could not read. Those blue eyes seemed haunted, though, which one might expect considering her line of work. Those eyes showed a lot of rough years, but she remained attractive.

By Jehovah, he might even call her beautiful—though not as lovely as—

Her question stopped his own haunted memories.

He wasn't sure he understood what she had asked. "I'm sorry," he said. "I didn't quite catch—"

"What are you?" she repeated.

He made himself smile. That was a question he had been asked for years and years. "I'm a circuit-riding preacher. Just without any planned trail. Drifter, I guess you'd call it. But I'm ordained. From—"

Her head shook, interrupting him again.

Buster was already in the saloon, the batwing doors banging in the late-morning air.

Kit Van Dorn pointed at the ruins. "You plan on preaching in that? Nobody would step inside that. Not until you tear it down and put something up in its place. It's what you'd do to a place that has been torched. It's not safe. The timbers still standing could fall."

He pushed back his hat and smiled. Most of the preachers he had known would have said, "Oh, ye of little faith." But Callahan was not one to use any cliché when he could help it. "It would just fall on me."

She misunderstood. "Oh, no, I think people will come to hear you preach, Reverend. Some for the show. Some because they are bored. Some because, deep down, they want religion."

His smile never faded. Now it widened. "They'll be smart

enough to stand away from that mess. No matter how much cleaner Buster and I can make it." He turned and looked at the wreck of the old log cabin. "There's all sorts of lessons I can pass on, sermons I can preach, from standing inside that mess. Ashes to ashes. Rising from the ruins. Job sat down among the ashes. Isaiah planted an ash. 'Beauty for ashes,' from Isaiah. The turning of Sodom and Gomorrah into ashes. The Bible's full of scripture about ashes."

"That's not why you're doing this," she said.

He tried to widen his smile.

"Oh, I'm sure you can preach some fine words about ashes. Resurrection. Or, yeah, Peaceful Valley might not quite be as wicked as Sodom or Gomorrah, but it ain't far from becoming ashes. And maybe it deserves to be burned to the ground. But you don't need props to do that. Folks here are simple-minded, maybe, but they aren't all that ignorant."

He looked back at the burned shell, and he knew he did it so she could not read the truth of her statement in his eyes, or even deeper into his soul. The woman had intuition. No, this might be more than that. She seemed to know him about as well as—

Sighing, he looked back at her. "Well, ma'am," he said, and grinned. "I reckon you done figured me out. But you are at a slight disadvantage. You've seen me outdraw your pal Frank."

"He's not my pal," she corrected.

He shrugged. "Your employee. Whatever. And you got me pegged, but you ain't never heard me preach. You see, the fact is, I ain't that good of a preacher, so I need props. And what's left of that cabin, it'll serve me well."

Kit Van Dorn didn't believe him. Callahan knew that. But she chewed on her bottom lip for a moment, and started to say something. But of all the unlikely residents of Peaceful Valley, Wyoming Territory, Buster came to the circuit rider's rescue.

He popped through the batwing doors and bellowed, "I thought there was grub waitin' for us to eat."

The woman turned away from Callahan and barked, "It's on the stove, you durned fool."

"But I can't find nothin' to put it on. Or find a spoon or somethin' to shove it into my mouth. And I'm durned about starved, woman."

She sighed, stifled a curse, and looked back at Callahan. "I don't know how he survives on his own."

Callahan smiled. "He's a stagecoach driver. Gets his meals at every station along his route."

"He's a child."

"A big one."

"And ugly." She looked back at the saloon. "Hold your horses—mean, *mules*. I'm coming." But first she turned back and stared into Callahan's clear eyes. "We'll continue this debate another time, *Reverend*." She stressed, or maybe mocked, the last word.

Callahan just touched the brim of his hat again and gave her a pleasing grin. "I look forward to it, Miss Van Dorn."

"The name," she said as she turned and started walking to her saloon, "is Kit."

Inside the Three O'd Saloon, Buster sat at a table. Callahan did not see a bartender, so guessed the ash-covered stagecoach driver had helped himself to the glass of beer in front of him. About half of the beer had been drained, but the man was ready to eat. Buster had untied his bandanna and stuck the stained and frayed piece of cotton over the top button of his shirt, sort of like a napkin. He wasn't alone in the saloon.

At a far table, where poker and faro players usually would be, Tin Horne sat alone, dealing solitaire. A cup of steaming coffee sat next to the various decks he had shuffled.

Practice makes perfect, Callahan reminded himself, *even for a professional gambler.*

On the other end of the saloon, Rude Frank sat, whiskey

bottle in front of him, no food, no bowl, no plate, no cards, not even a shot glass. But there was a cork. Seeing Callahan come through the swinging doors made the scoundrel grab the bottle and take a pull.

No other saloon girls were inside. But then, it was pushing noon, and Callahan figured the chippies likely were still sleeping in. Those women worked long hours, even in a small dot on a map like Peaceful Valley.

Tin Horne did not look up. Rude Frank could not take his eyes off Callahan.

Maybe, he thought, *this is not a good idea.* But his growling stomach quashed such a debate.

The inside of the saloon smelled not of sawdust and vomit and spilled beer and smoke from cigars and cigarettes. It smelled of wonderful stew. He saw the pot atop the stove.

"Have a seat," Kit told him. "What'll you have to drink?"

"Coffee would sure hit the spot, ma'am," he said.

"I have a fine bottle of Scotch," she tempted him.

"But I'm Irish."

"I bet we could find some Irish whiskey, too."

"Coffee will be just fine."

She grinned. "Milk?"

That surprised him. "If you have some, just a splash."

"Sugar?"

He shook his head.

"All right." She turned and headed toward the bar.

"Miss Kit!" Buster called out and held out his glass. "You reckon you might spare me another beer?"

Callahan tried to work his way around that sentence.

"It's a powerful load of ash I swallowed." Buster coughed. And his eyes looked like those of one of the coon hounds Callahan's pappies had favored all those years ago in Missouri.

"Maybe one more," the woman called out, and she disappeared underneath the bar.

Callahan caught the sound of dishes and utensils rattling. Then he heard the icy voice of her partner.

"You're mighty generous with my beer," Tin Horne called out.

Held by the woman's hands, two bowls appeared and dropped onto the bar. The hands disappeared.

Rude Frank slowly lowered the bottle he had been drinking from, and stared at the cardsharper, who kept his eyes, not on the bar and the woman finding what she needed to serve her guests, but on Callahan.

Callahan ignored the cheat and walked to Buster, grabbed a chair from a nearby table, pulled it up alongside the stagecoach man, and found a spot where he could keep his eyes on both Tin Horne and Rude Frank. By looking into the mirror behind the bar, he saw Kit Van Dorn, too, when she stood.

Putting the silverware in the bowl, she stared at her partner. "Your half comes from the gambling. Mine comes from the booze. And the back rooms."

"I never liked those terms," Tin Horne said.

"Then the next time you're in Cheyenne, approach my lawyer." She carried the bowls and utensils to the stove, laid them atop, and ladled in the brown stew, then took the bowls over to Callahan and Buster. "But I don't think you can afford his rates."

"Not from what I'm making in this fleabag of a town," Tin Horne said. "For now." He found his coffee, took a sip, and smiled. "But soon."

"Smells good," Callahan said with a smile, trying to distract Kit.

Buster was already shoveling spoonfuls into his mouth.

"I'll fetch you your coffee. And your beer." She shook her head and sighed.

Buster probably didn't even hear her. In fact, it was hard for Callahan to hear what the saloon owner said over the stagecoach driver's snorting and slurping. Pigs ate quieter than Buster.

The coffee, for a change, was good. The stew tasted delicious, maybe on account of the fact that Taylor Callahan was hungry, or perhaps because Kit Van Dorn, having returned with a fresh beer for Buster and the coffeepot, found a chair and sat beside him. She had managed to bring an empty cup herself, and after topping off Callahan's coffee, she poured some into her own.

Callahan licked his lips, smiled, and asked, "Elk?"

"Antelope." It was Buster who answered. "Ain't never got sick of it." His eyes lifted from staring at the bowl and he smiled slightly at Kit. "You cook it just fine, ma'am. Better'n any I ever et."

"Thank you." She sipped from her cup.

Callahan kept his eyes on the mirror. The gambler seemed to debate himself over what he should do next. Drink his coffee. Play his game of solitaire. Or go over and start a row with either Kit Van Dorn or Taylor Callahan. The middle option finally won out.

Rude Frank kept sucking from the bottle, and found enough nerve to stand, although remaining steady on his feet proved something of a challenge. Callahan saw Tin Horne glance up, and a smile stretched across his pale face before he began gathering the cards and shuffling the deck—probably what the cardsharper was betting on anyway . . . that Rude Frank would find enough courage in his whiskey bottle to start a row with Taylor Callahan.

"I'm sick and—" Rude Frank seemed to forget his place. He was that drunk.

"Tired," Buster filled in the missing word. Then he looked up, and realized who'd been talking. He swallowed his mouthful of stew, drained his beer in record time, and scraped the legs of his chair on the floor. He stood, picked up the bowl, and looked at Kit. "All right if I help myself to some more antelope stew, ma'am?"

Kit kept her eyes on Rude Frank. "Of course, Buster. Eat your fill."

When the stagecoach man had found his way to the stove, Rude Frank rested his right hand on a revolver. It wasn't the one he had drawn too slowly on Callahan the day before. It looked like a Navy Colt, but likely converted to take brass cartridges rather than paper cartridges and percussion caps. "I'm gonna kill you, Preacher." His words were slurred.

But Callahan figured even a drunkard might not miss at that range.

Callahan looked up and tried to appear pleasant. "I'm not wearing a gun, Frank," he said calmly.

The evil grin spread across the drunkard's face. "I know. That's how come I'm gonna kill you." His right hand darted for the deadly .36.

CHAPTER 15

The Navy Colt was halfway out of Rude Frank's holster when three gunshots boomed just outside the saloon, followed by a wild, high-pitched cry. The Three O'd Saloon's batwing doors banged open, and a slim, young waddie with a short crowned hat pushed his way inside, spurs jingling, and shouting, "Where's that danged lawdog?"

Rude Frank started turning on his heels at the first report of a pistol, his bowler hat falling off, while the long-barreled weapon cleared the holster, his thumb working on the hammer. Too late, he understood his mistake and cursed.

The cowboy's face whitened, but his smoking revolver was pointed at the floor. He wasn't looking for any trouble. Spinning around, dropping to a knee, Rude Frank tried to bring his own gun level. His eyes widened, and he brought up his left arm in a defensive move. But the time he had spent, no more than two seconds, had cost him.

Taylor Callahan's first instinct was to toss the coffee from his cup—maybe the whole cup—at Rude Frank. That thought was dismissed instantly. The cup was only half full and the coffee was lukewarm at best.

But the coffeepot Kit had brought to the table was the answer. Unless Tin Horne decided to put a bullet in Rude Frank's back—fat chance of that—or she had a hideaway gun, the coffeepot was Callahan's only chance. Seeing her standing and reaching for the pot herself, he moved fast. He was also closer and probably more desperate. He had the coffeepot in his hand and slung it as hard as he could.

The table overturned. Kit lost her balance. Buster fell backward in his chair, taking his bowl of antelope stew with him.

Rude Frank cursed again, tried to duck and bring his left hand up to block the flying blue-speckled pot with a bottom blackened from years of use. His reflexes were quick enough to keep the pot from smashing his face, but not lightning fast. He deflected the pot, hurting his left hand like blazes, tearing flesh and likely breaking a couple of fingers. However, the movement knocked the lid ajar and tilted the pot down. Worse, with the lid open, some of the coffee—not scalding but hot enough—found his right shoulder.

He triggered the Navy, but the .36 ball splintered the table that had been overturned by the actions of Callahan, Buster, and Kit.

The pot caught the top of Rude Frank's collarbone, flipped over, showering the rough wood with the rest of the coffee before bouncing off another table, then clattering across the floor. Rude Frank went down, the Colt still in his hand.

Callahan lifted his foot to kick a chair away from him, then thought better of it. He grabbed the back in a quick motion, raising it over his head, all the while covering the short distance separating him from the vicious gunfighter. Rude Frank was coming up to a sitting position on the floor, and trying to raise his right hand with the .36. He saw the chair, though, and lifted his left hand to block the blow.

The gun fired again, splintering the planked floor as the chair crushed Rude Frank's left arm, breaking at least one of the bones in the forearm, then smashing against the man's head. The bowler hat might have cushioned the blow somewhat, so that Rude Frank escaped a fractured skull, but that was all for him. At least for the time being.

Callahan's momentum carried him past the sprawled figure. His boots slipped on the coffee, and he fell against a table, overturning it and landing on his knees.

He spun quickly, coming up to see Kit holding another chair over her head, but she stopped herself from smashing it against Rude Frank. The man would not have felt it anyway. At least, not until he woke up.

Callahan rose, sucked in a deep breath, and moved fast. He found the Navy Colt, picked it up, and aimed it at the unconscious man.

Twelve, thirteen years ago, Taylor Callahan would have shot the man. But that was during the war and a different Taylor Callahan. He looked at the Colt, shook his head at the pathetic figure on the floor, and turned to Buster, whose shirtfront was covered with the remnants of his antelope stew. Callahan extended his left hand and helped the big stagecoach driver to his feet. Then he spun the Navy and extended it, butt forward, to Kit.

"Thanks," he said.

"For what?" Her smile and eyes were charming.

He had to catch his breath. "Helping out."

"I don't think you needed any help."

"Oh." He made himself smile. The saloon smelled of coffee and gunpowder. "I reckon the Major General in the Heavens provided some help." He turned to the batwing doors.

"What the Sam Hill was that all about?" the cowboy said. A grin stretched across his young face. "Ma and ever'body is gonna be sorry they missed seeing this." He was looking at Rude Frank, and then he spit tobacco juice onto Rude Frank's torn shirt. "We've been wantin' to do this for years."

The waddie could not have been older than twenty years

old. He chewed his tobacco some more before turning to Tin Horne. "I need that marshal, Tin."

The gambler did not look up. He stayed focused on his cards. "I am not Grant Lee's keeper, boy."

The kid frowned, then spotted Buster, and recognition came quickly. "Well, Buster, you're the guy who ought to know. Walker and me seen your stagecoach."

"What?"

"Your stagecoach. And mules."

"Where? Somebody stole my coach and team last night." Buster brushed the stew remnants off his shirt, then licked his fingers.

The cowhand looked again at Rude Frank. Then his eyes met Callahan's. "Looked like I busted in on something. But I like what I seen of this here show."

"What about my mules?" Buster demanded. "My stage-coach."

Satisfied Rude Frank was no longer a threat for the time being, Callahan shoved the .36-caliber pistol into his waist-band. He caught only part of the conversation between the young cowboy and the agitated stagecoach driver but figured he had lost Buster as his fifty-cents-a-day helper. He had gotten his money's worth.

And Taylor Callahan had not had any violent memories of the church that had burned in Missouri and set him travel-ing another path, one that could have—*should have,* some might argue—sent him to the hottest pits in Hades.

But then the cowboy said three words that got Callahan's attention, even Kit Van Dorn's and Tin Horne's. "Injuns took it."

"What?" Buster screamed.

"You're drunk, Thompson," Tin Horne said from his table.

"No, sir. I ain't had a drop. Ma don't tolerate nobody drinkin' when we is workin'." The boy talked fast.

And Callahan now had a name for the kid. He was one of

the Widow Audrey Eleanor Thompson's boys. From the ranch. The one whose father was dead.

The gambler rose from his chair, gathered his cards and stuck them in one of his top vest pockets, finished his coffee, and walked over. "How many?" he asked.

"Six?" The boy shrugged. "Eight?" He shrugged again. "We just got a glance of 'em."

The gambler's derisive laugh caused the boy's face to fluster. "They had braided hair, mister, riding paint hosses. Yipping like coyotes, with quivers on their backs, and two of 'em held lances. Another had a Winchester Yellow Boy." He glanced at Callahan, then stared harder at the gambler. "I ain't as old as you, Horne, but I know an injun when I see one. And they had them mules taking that stagecoach southwest."

"How?" Buster asked.

"One of 'em was sittin' atop just like you. Didn't use no whip, though. Least till he got over the hill."

Kit cleared her throat. "If that's true, those Indians had to have come through town last night. Taken the mud wagon and the mules."

"They would have had to harness the team, too," Tin Horne added.

Callahan cleared his throat. "Indians aren't stupid, folks. I had to learn to hitch a team when I was eight years old."

"Pa made me do it when I was eight," the boy said with a grin. "Well, I just thought the marshal would want to get a posse up."

"He ain't in town," Buster grumbled.

"What the heck happened to that cabin?" the cowhand asked. Then he looked at Callahan, and stuck out his right hand. "Name's Knight. Knight Thompson." With a grin, he pointed at Rude Frank flat on his back and not moving except for the rising and falling of his chest as he breathed. "That was quite a show, mister."

Callahan liked the lad's grip. "I would not have cared for the ending had you not popped in the way you did, Knight. Name's Callahan. The Reverend Taylor Callahan."

The boy whistled. "You is a preacher? Honest?"

Callahan laughed. "I'm a preacher. Ordained. Honest? To God, yes. To everyone else, well, I try to be."

"What are we gonna do to get my mules back?" Buster demanded.

"No telling when Marshal Grant Lee will be back," Kit said.

"We don't need no marshal," Tin Horne said. "Not to go after a bunch of Indians."

"Riley Staples was with us when we spotted them redskins makin' their way south with the coach. I sent him back to the ranch. But town was closer so I come here. Walker went to trail after the stagecoach-stealing hostiles."

"That's dangerous," Kit said.

"Oh, you know Walker, Miss Kit. He ain't stupid." He smiled again at the sprawled body of Rude Frank. "Like some folks."

"We'll ride after them bucks and teach them to steal from a white man. Indians"—Tin Horne spit—"stealing a stagecoach. Think they're playing a joke on us. Preacher, you tell your pal the lawman what we're doing . . . if that yellow dog ever comes back. Just like him, to be out of town when Indians raid our settlement. They could have burned the whole place down and scalped us all."

"But they didn't," Callahan said. "From what I gather, based on this bright young man's story, is they—"

"Horse theft is a hanging offense in this country," Tin Horne said. "We string thieves up who make off with our mules, too. Especially when the thieves are no-good, lyin' injuns. Buster, get some good ropes from that miser."

"Reckon I'll be riding with you," Callahan said. His eyes locked on the gambler's.

"Those thievin' injuns don't likely follow the teachin's from your Good Book, preacher man."

"They's six, maybe eight, who knows how many injuns made off with my mud wagon. And my babies. My mules. I sure hope they ain't eatin' my babies." Buster cleared his throat. "But, Tin, we could use the preacher. You seen for yourself he's right handy with a gun. Ain't like most preachers, you know."

The gambler frowned, but his eyes moved from Callahan to Rude Frank, who moaned, but did not open his eyes.

"All right, Preacher," Tin Horne relented. "Saddle that tired old nag of yours. Maybe write a note and leave it for our fine, courageous lawman Perhaps he'll see fit to join us and do his job."

Callahan was already walking out the door before the gambler finished. He walked directly to the marshal's office, grabbing his saddle, blanket and bridle, and then moving outside to the corral to saddle Job. He did not take time to write a note for Marshal Grant Lee. People in town would spread the news, and Callahan did not think Tin Horne, who had appointed himself in charge of the alleged posse, would wait for him. Callahan would have a hard enough time keeping up with the vengeance-minded fools on Job.

He checked the saddlebags, saw the long-barreled Colt 45, and thought about pulling out the revolver. He could carry it and the Navy .36 he had picked up after his brief tussle with Rude Frank. Instead, he left the modern weapon where it was. Swinging into the saddle, he tugged the reins to turn around the white gelding, then trotted over to the saloon.

There had been no need to rush. The only person in the saddle, other than the circuit rider, was the Thompson boy.

"Preacher," he said, "I knew it was a bad idea to come to Peaceful Valley. Them injuns will be halfway through Colorado by the time we get out of town."

We can only hope, Callahan thought, looking toward the sky, wishing the Major General in the Heavens understood and might actually do something for once.

But, as usual when it came to the Major General in the Heavens' dealings with the Reverend Taylor Callahan, that old codger was deaf. For here came Buster on a big brown gelding. The gambler, carrying a Sharps rifle affixed with a long, brass telescopic sight, rode a sleek black steed.

"Let's go take us some scalps," Tin Horne said, and kicked his horse to move in a lope. But he stopped quickly and stood in his stirrups, looking past Callahan off to the northeast.

Callahan studied the gambler's face. No, it didn't look like a trick—a way for Tin Horne to put a bullet in Callahan's back. Horne looked confused, maybe concerned. Hearing the clopping of hooves, Callahan turned around, trusting the Major General in the Heavens to keep the faithful minister of the Word from getting killed like some fool sucker.

Well, if Tin Horne planned on murdering the circuit rider, he'd have to take care of six, no seven, eyewitnesses.

CHAPTER 16

The riders descended the same hill that had brought Marshal Grant Lee into the settlement yesterday.

A big man with a wide-brimmed Stetson—the same style as Callahan's but the color of a dun horse—led the party. Two riders pulled pack mules behind them. Two big wagons, both with two big gray draft horses in the harnesses, carried a pair of men each. Another rider, dressed in black, brought up the rear, and that man had a big Henry rifle braced against his right hip, the barrel reflecting sunlight and pointing straight at the heavens.

"Are we goin'?" Knight Thompson said. "Those red devils are getting away with Thompson property."

"And my mules and my mud wagon," Buster added.

"Your brother's trailing them," Tin Horne said. "Those thieving injuns aren't getting away."

Kit Van Dorn took a few steps forward, bit her lower lip, and shook her head. "Strangers. Look like city folk."

"Not the one with the rifle," Buster amended.

"You recognize 'em, Buster?" Tin Horne asked.

"Can't say I do."

The young Thompson lad sighed, but said, "Well, the one with the rifle might be helpful to us."

"Maybe." Tin Horne remained noncommittal.

The party kept approaching, the mules and horses snorting, metal rattling in the backs of the two wagons that approached with no urgency. The man bringing up the rear brought his rifle down, laying it across his thighs.

"Howdy!" Kit Van Dorn called out, raising her right hand in the universal greeting.

The leader reined up a few yards in front of them, and the drivers pulled their mules to a stop. The man with the pack mule halted between the two wagons, but the rider with the Henry rifle rode over to the southeast a few feet.

"Ma'am." The leader tipped the brim of his hat.

Rude Frank pushed his way out of the saloon, moaned, and staggered back against the wall as the swinging doors banged. Sliding down, he tilted over and put his left arm over his eyes.

The man with the wide-brimmed Stetson smiled. "Looks like we missed the prizefight." He nodded at the others. "Marquis of Queensbury rules, I assume."

Only Taylor Callahan laughed at the joke, and that brought the stranger's attention to the circuit rider.

"Folks call me Iron Tom," he said. "This is my crew." He introduced the names of the men in the wagon, and the one with the pack mule, but Callahan would not remember any name except Iron Tom and the name of the man with the .44-caliber Henry.

"And Missoula Milford."

"You mean," young Knight Thompson inquired, "the very same Missoula Milford who killed all them eighteen men, red and white, who tried to stand up to the railroad?"

"Eighteen white men," the man with the Henry corrected. He let the reins drape over his horse's neck, while he pushed back the brim of his black pork-pie hat. "Never counted the Indians." His head bobbed slightly as he raised his rifle.

"But I can up that number of white corpses to nineteen." The cold eyes moved to Callahan. "Maybe even twenty."

No, Taylor Callahan thought. Missoula Milford had reached twenty killings a long, long time before he started hiring out for railroads.

His memories took him back to—

He thought hard. *When was that? December, January, February? We'd lost track of months that cold winter of 1863 and '64.*

They found the men lying in a hollow, but only because Tyson Barnes insisted those circling buzzards weren't waiting for some wild hog to die.

Discovering dead Missourians had become common at that point in the war. The bodies might be hanging from the solid limb of a fine oak tree, but usually were just left to rot after an engagement with Kansas redlegs or regular Union patrols.

Yet those eight men lay bunched together. The man known as Shakespeare swung out of his saddle, holding a revolver in his right hand, and walked to the corpses.

"Shot in the back," he said, holstering the Colt, and pulling the body off the next dead man.

"Why," Billy Joe McTavish cried out, "that's Rudolph Parmenter of Centerville." Young Billy Joe before he wound up getting half an infected leg cut off—by Callahan.

"One of Sedalia Slim's boys," Todd Hamer said, removing his corncob pipe and tapping it on the horn of his saddle. "Slim and his boys parted ways with George Todd."

"Bet he wish he hadn't now," said someone well back in the ranks. Not that it would have mattered. Todd himself would be dead before the end of the year.

"Bullet came through and—" Shakespeare spit disgust and hatred from his mouth, and rolled the next body over. And the next.

The men riding at the front of the column, who included Carbine Logan and the Reverend Taylor Callahan, saw with their own eyes. They knew by the time the fifth body had been pulled out of the pile.

They knew as some of the boys dismounted and started digging graves with their Arkansas Toothpicks, to give these brave lads maybe not a proper burial, but at least keep the buzzards from picking their bodies clean. They knew the preacher who rode with them would read from his Bible, deliver a eulogy, and maybe have this rough men, the boys and old raiders who had seen so much, and done so much killing themselves, sing a hymn or two before they rode on, and maybe avenged these deaths. Or maybe they'd be killed themselves, and no one would find them till after the buzzards had done nature's work.

"They lined them up," Shakespeare said, looking up from the next body he'd rolled over. A body with a hole in the back of his embroidered bushwhacker's shirt, and a bigger hole in the chest.

And they could see the small hole with dried blood in the back of the next man.

Knives dug into the wet ground. Knives and the hands of disgusted men, soldiers who had become gravediggers . . . though many people refused to call them irregulars soldiers. Murderers. Assassins. Mad-dog killers. Rebel trash.

Often, Taylor Callahan thought of himself as a mad-dog, murderer, Rebel trash of an assassin. But on this day, he just felt . . . like a poor, lost human soul.

The last body moaned as Shakespeare rolled him over. And there was no ghastly exit wound in the front of his once-pretty, now grimy, bushwhacker shirt.

Callahan went to the body and put his left arm on the boy's left shoulder as Shakespeare leaned closer.

"Sonny," Shakespeare whispered.

The boy sighed. He couldn't be older than fifteen. Calla-

han looked past Carbine Logan and down the line of the closest Confederates. "Anyone know this boy?"

No answer came. Callahan looked back at the pale, filthy face.

"So young."

" 'He wears the rose of youth upon him,' " Shakespeare said.

Callahan pushed wet blond bangs from the boy's eyes. "Antony and Cleopatra," *he whispered.*

Shakespeare grinned with solemnity. "You always surprise me, Preacher. Even when you preach New Testament rather than the Old."

"I was taught both," Callahan said.

"But we live in the Old Testament today. An eye for an eye. Vengeance and fire and—"

"Mommy."

They both turned to the kid, whose eyes fluttered, then held open, darting this way and that. Maybe he saw the two bushwhackers kneeling over him. Maybe he even saw Carbine Logan. But Callahan thought he saw something none of the men could see. At least, they could not see what the boy was seeing. But the way the war was turning, they likely would all see whatever one saw right before death . . . and soon.

"Mommy." The boy smiled.

Rarely—maybe never—had Callahan seen what looked like a peaceful death in the past several months. But the boy whose name he would never know smiled, sighed, and closed his eyes as death came and stilled him.

Shakespeare whispered a curse, and Callahan removed his hat and began to pray.

When he stood, Carbine Logan said, "More work of that Yankee blackheart."

And one bushwhacker whispered the name Missoula Milford.

* * *

But now Missoula Milford killed for money, not in war. He had been doing that since the last of the Confederate generals surrendered their armies. First in Texas, if the stories were true. A bit of unpleasantness over land and water just above the Rio Grande. A feud in New Mexico Territory. A range war in Arizona. And then he had discovered the railroads. That's when his legend blossomed.

And now he was in Wyoming Territory. Peaceful Valley.

Was this part of the Major General in the Heavens' master plan?

"Milford," Iron Tom said, "we are peaceable surveyors. And these are the residents of Peaceful Valley, a befitting name. I am sure they do not want to get into a row with us."

"I think they got word that we were comin'," Missoula Milford said. "That's why they're armed and mounted and ready to ride."

"We're ridin' against some injuns that stole a stagecoach and mules," Knight Thompson said.

Missoula Milford nudged his horse forward until he came alongside Iron Tom. The two men eyed each other, then Iron Tom looked over, picked Callahan to be the leader—for all men make mistakes, Callahan knew—and asked, "What tribe?"

"I dunno!" It was Knight Thompson who answered. "They wore buckskins and feathers and rode injun ponies."

"You be one of the Thompson hands?" Iron Tom asked.

"No." The boy straightened in his saddle. "I be one of the Thompsons. Period. Knight Thompson, if it's any of your business, stranger."

Milford's eyes narrowed and the Henry started to move, but Iron Tom whispered a warning or rebuke, possibly just an order, and the stock of the rifle settled back on the man-killer's thigh.

"We're surveyors," Iron Tom said again. "For the newly formed Denver City and Laramie Railway Corporation. To see about a possible track to link Laramie to the rest of the eastern United States without having to deal with Cheyenne."

Kit Van Dorn whistled. "So the rumors are true."

The surveyor boss nodded. "*If* we can plat a road. *If* the corrupt sons of guns in Washington don't sink our plan. And *if* we can meet a deadline imposed by our financial backers."

"And," the mankiller with the Henry added with a wicked grin, "the injuns don't—"

"That's enough." Iron Tom was maybe one man who Missoula Milford did not intimidate. Perhaps because the hired gunman knew who paid his fee.

Missoula Milford smiled at Callahan. "I take it you are the law in this two-bit town. Grant Lee." He started to lower the rifle again, and Iron Tom made no orders to stop.

"You take it wrong, friend." Callahan smiled. "The law of Peaceful Valley lit out this morning on business. What business I cannot say. My name is Taylor Callahan. The Reverend Taylor Callahan. Circuit-riding preacher setting up for a few nights and afternoons of bringing the Word to anyone who cares to listen. In my humble abode." He gestured toward the burned-out shell.

The rifle stopped. The gunman appeared to be weighing Callahan's statement.

"There's a Bible in my saddlebags, sir. And a diploma from the seminary at Logan's Knob. Way over east in Missouri. If you'd like to hear me pray, I can pray right now. For your coming to Peaceful Valley and bringing these citizens news that they—"

"Save it for Sunday," Iron Tom said.

"You're just talkin' so them injuns get away with all their plunder they stole," the young Thompson kid said.

Callahan grinned. The boy had more sense than practically the entire population of Peaceful Valley, including the surveyors and hired killer from a new railroad company up in Laramie.

"How far away were those Indians, boy?" Iron Tom turned his attention to Knight Thompson.

The kid pointed. "Couple miles. But they're ridin' south. My brother's trailin' 'em."

"Horse thieves?" the surveyor asked.

"Mules!" Buster bellowed. "And my mud wagon. I done tol' you folks that. So did the kid."

"All right." The big man turned in his saddle. "Frank," he called to the one pulling the pack mule. "Set up camp." He pointed at a flat spot next to the Three O'd Saloon, but immediately corrected himself, and found another likely location between a couple of cabins about as far away from the saloon as possible. Not that it would keep any of them from getting liquored up or having a dance or two if Callahan knew what was in the hearts of surveying crews . . . and anyone else who happened to find a place like Peaceful Valley after weeks or months on the Wyoming plains.

"Earl"—Iron Tom pointed to one of the men in the nearest wagon—"chop down a tree over there. Turn it into a trough. We'll have to get water from the well. That'll keep our stock." He looked over at Kit. "The town won't have any problem with us using water from your well, will they, ma'am? To keep our stock healthy. And keep our men filled with coffee."

She smiled. "I'm not the mayor, sir. But I think I can say if you're bringing a railroad to Peaceful Valley, we'll give you just about anything you want. Without charge."

The man grinned, showing he was human. "Anything, ma'am?"

"Just about, Iron Tom," she said, matching his grin. "But not . . . *everything*."

He laughed. "All right. Whit and Bob, you'll ride with us. The rest of you boys, set up camp. Earl, you're in charge. Pitch your tents. Cook your grub. Missoula and I will assist these citizens and get this man's mules and"—he looked over at Buster—"mud wagon."

"Mud wagon back from those thieving Indians," Buster added after a short sigh. "Though don't reckon we'll have no need of no stagecoach line if there's a railroad coming through town." He spit and then looked up at the solidly built man. "That track you planning on building? It'll go through Poudreville?"

"I have been told that's the straightest line to Denver, sir," Iron Tom answered, "but we'll have to see for ourselves."

"Well." Buster sighed again. "I always wanted to be a conductor or somethin' like that."

"I'll put in a word for ye," said one of the men in the wagon, speaking in an Irish brogue.

"Preacher," Iron Tom said, turning back to Callahan, "you'll stay here." He pointed at the burned out cabin. "I think your church might need some more improvements before you can perform blessings and baptisms, sir. We'll take care of your Indian problem. Compliments of the Denver City and Laramie Railway Corporation."

Callahan had already turned Job and was riding south. "Thanks for the offer, sir, but I answer to a higher calling."

CHAPTER 17

The Major General in the Heavens worked in inexplicable ways.

On most days, Job would feign arthritis or ligament desmitis or colic or cracked heels or mud fever or just I-ain't-in-no-hurry-and-deep-down-neither-are-you, so the gelding's pace would resemble that old tortoise's rather than some hare's. But that day was turning into nothing like most days for Taylor Callahan.

Young Knight Thompson had galloped his horse a couple of miles to Peaceful Valley—and Callahan figured the kid never enjoyed putting a horse at a walk or a trot—so while the animal had rested some since arriving in town, he was far from being ready to run in some match race. Iron Tom and the man-killing Missoula Milford had not been riding their mounts hard, traveling a good many miles. Not from Laramie, either. Cheyenne most likely. The railroad company they were hired by might have been working for the greater good of Laramie, but most of the money in the territory came out of Cheyenne. Taylor Callahan had figured out that much already. Tin Horne rode a good animal, but as eager to collect some Indian scalps as his mouth made him out to be, he did not ride boldly at the head of the column, or volunteer to ride ahead and see if he could find the Indians that had stolen an Abbott & Downing coach and some poor mules.

And poor Buster? Well, the way he sat on a mule showed everyone he was a stagecoach driver, not a fine *caballero*.

It was a strange posse.

That quickly grew stranger.

Callahan turned in the saddle to the sound of thundering hooves. Tin Horne cursed slightly and reined up after he, too, looked over his shoulder.

"What the devil do you think you're doing?" he barked as she slowed her gray mare after she caught up with the riders.

"Figured some of you might need some help," she said.

"I don't need no help," the gambler growled.

She smiled, then kicked her mare up until stopping it alongside Callahan. "But he might."

Callahan could not help but grin.

Disgust masked Tin Horne's face. His mouth opened, and he likely wanted to spew Kit Van Dorn and Taylor Callahan with vile epithets, but Knight Thompson spoke first.

"We ain't gonna catch them thieving redskins sitting around here palavering." The kid spurred his horse and headed for the next rise.

"You get back to town, woman," the gambler ordered.

"Let her come." The words had a chilling tone, spoken by Missoula Milford. He tipped his hat and grinned a wicked, lecherous stare.

"The cowboy is right," Iron Tom said, kicking his horse into a trot and riding after Knight Thompson.

"You get killed," Tin Horne said, "it's your fault." He rode after the Thompson lad.

"He's right," Callahan said, pulling his hat down and gathering the reins tighter.

"And what's your excuse?" Not waiting for an answer, Kit nudged her horse into a lope.

Buster was already urging his mule after the cardsharper, and Kit nudged her horse into a lope.

Callahan looked at the sky. "Sure hope you know what you're doing, General," he whispered, and followed the party.

He guessed they had been riding better than two hours when they saw a cowboy atop another hill. The rider rode down a bit, reined in, then waved his hat over his head. Once the hat was planted firmly on his head, he spurred his sorrel and thundered to them.

Riding at the head of the Peaceful Valley column—well, *column* was a bit of a stretch—Tin Horne raised his right hand and reined his horse to a stop. Job, Callahan knew, enjoyed stopping.

The young Thompson boy rode out a few yards ahead. Before the rider reached him, Knight slid his horse to a dusty stop.

"What the blazes kept you, Brother!" the man said angrily.

Callahan thought to recall the other Thompson brother's name.

"I come as fast as I could, Walker," Knight Thompson said.

Yes, of course. Walker. Callahan declared to himself he would have thought of the name, eventually. They taught that in the seminary at Logan's Knob.

"This is all you come back with?" Walker looked at the war party from Peaceful Valley with disgust.

"It's Wednesday," Buster said.

"What the Sam Hill does that have to do with anything?" Walker Thompson roared.

Wednesday. Callahan tried to decipher where all the days had gone. *Wednesday. Yes, that must be right.*

"It's also Peaceful Valley," the stagecoach driver said.

"And there's an army post a few miles from Peaceful

Valley," Walker reminded his brother . . . and the town's residents. "When I sent you to fetch some help, I figured you'd bring back the law. Where is Marshal Lee?"

"He rode off somewhere," Knight answered. "And you know what Pa always said about bluebellies. They ain't got the sand of us Texans. Ma says the same."

"Well, there's a lot more injuns than they is of us. Even with these—" He waved his hand in disgust at the posse assembled in town. "You bring a hussy to ride with us."

"This hussy," Kit said pleasantly, "can shoot better than you or your brother or any of those thirty-a-month waddies riding for your brand."

Callahan could see the brotherly resemblance. He could also see something else. Walker was the leader. Walker was the reckless one. Knight thought things through. The circuit rider wondered who was more like the dead father, and the widowed, hard rock of a mother.

"Where are the injuns?" Missoula Milford demanded.

"Who are you?" Walker demanded.

The killer just grinned, but his right hand moved toward a holstered revolver.

"Walker," Knight cautioned, "that's Missoula Milford."

"In the flesh," Iron Tom added with a grin.

The hothead gave Iron Tom a glance, then stared hard at the cold-blooded killer. His eyes shifted to Callahan. "You ride with them, stranger?"

Callahan smiled easily and shook his head. "I'm here to keep the peace, son. Usually, I ride by myself. Well, that's not altogether true." He lifted his head skyward, and let his smile spread before locking eyes on the younger Thompson boy. "Name's Callahan. Taylor Callahan. The Reverend Taylor Callahan. Was riding to Cheyenne. Got delayed a bit in Peaceful Valley."

"Don't let him fool you, Walker," Buster said. "He's outdrawed Rude Frank and whupped him something spectacular."

"All right. If this is what we got, this is what we got." He turned his horse around, and his brother rode up beside him.

"The injuns stopped at Windy Creek a couple hills over. Let's ride."

They rode. But they rode hard and fast.

They found the rest of the cowboys at the bottom of the hill, smoking cigarettes, holding the reins to their horses, the cinches of the saddles loosened. Callahan spotted two other cowboys at the top of the hill. He could just make out the sun reflecting off the spurs of one Thompson rider. He would be looking at the war party—or mud-wagon-stealing party, rather—while his pard kept studying the rolling hills around them.

"Guess they ain't moved." Walker Thompson looked back. "Keep your horses quiet." The cowboy dismounted and began walking his horse down the hill. "Don't run 'em. Those injuns don't know we're here."

Callahan grinned. How naïve were today's youth. But he dismounted. While most of the posse led their animals by the bridle, Callahan just tugged Job's reins. That horse would not whinny or snort. He'd barely even break wind no matter what scent he caught of an Indian horse on the other side of a sloping hill.

"What's happening?" Walker asked when they reached the bottom.

"Nothin'," said a cowboy with a battered hat and thick gray mustache. "Same as when you left." He gestured up the hill. "Sittin', smokin' pipes or whatever. Waitin'."

"Maybe for a renegade white man," guessed a cowhand who had to be younger than even Walker Thompson. "I've read many a bad man—even women—will buy stolen horses from injuns."

"You read too much," Knight said.

"This is all that come with you?" the gray-mustached man asked.

"It's enough," Tin Horne said. "I'm here." He gestured to his left. "And this, boys, is Missoula Milford."

Someone whistled.

"Not so loud, you dumb oaf," Walker snapped.

Callahan started walking toward the hill.

"Where you think you're going?" Tin Horne demanded.

"To see what kind of pickle I got myself into." At least, he thought, *the slope up the hill isn't very steep.*

He hoped no one would follow him, but did not waste a prayer to the Major General in the Heavens because he understood what the answer would be.

One of the Thompson boys said, "The rest of you stay put," but Callahan could not tell which one had spoken for their voices were quite similar.

Callahan did not look behind him, but he could tell he was not climbing the hill alone.

"Where you goin'?" asked one of the Thompson hired men.

"Them's my mules," Callahan heard Buster say. "And my stagecoach."

Crawling on his belly, Callahan reached the whiplike kid on the side of the hill and said, "Name's Callahan. The Reverend Taylor Callahan." He held out his right hand.

The Thompson hand shook it, then he turned around to look up and whisper, "Harv, Knight brung us a preacher."

Harv started backing up, revealing gray-striped britches, chaps, a gun belt, faded blue shirt, brown vest, red bandanna, blond hair, and a black hat he held with a gloved left hand. The waddie rolled over, revealing something a young cowboy might call a mustache, and pale blue eyes.

"Callahan." The preacher smiled.

"You a real preacher?" the waddie asked.

"Afraid so."

The cowboy grinned. "Don't reckon them's followin' you is your choir."

"I don't know, son." Callahan set his hat on the ground. "I've never heard any one of them sing." He tilted his head up the ridge. "Mind if I have myself a looksee?"

The boy shrugged. "Just don't let 'em see you."

As Callahan slithered his way up the hill, he heard the first cowhand ask, "Buster, you come for your mud wagon?"

"That's right," the driver whispered, "and I brung Missoula Milford with me."

That stopped the conversation.

By then, Callahan was on the top. He swallowed, breathed in and out, and took in everything he could see below.

The creek sparkled with sunlight, and the Indians sat around the mud wagon. The team of mules had been unhitched, and they grazed at the side of the creek. Even the horses of the wagon thieves grazed loosely, though two Indians with feathers hanging from their braids, stayed close.

"They's jus' sittin' there." Buster had joined him.

"Most of them are standing," Callahan whispered.

The driver grumbled, then breathed out with relief. "Well, they ain't et my mules. Dadgum stagecoach company would prob'ly take the price of a good mule out of my pay."

"You know what tribe?" Callahan asked.

"Yep." He picked a stem of grass and put it between his lips. "Arapaho."

"Perfect." Callahan turned around to see Missoula Milford coming up on the circuit rider's left. He was not the man the preacher wished to see, especially with him carrying that rifle. Next came Iron Tom, and he brought his rifle, too.

On the other side of Buster, the two Thompson brothers bellied their way through the already flattened grass.

"Dumb injuns," Missoula Milford whispered. "They's all sittin' ducks. Don't know we're even here."

"I count ten," Iron Tom said.

"Like I say"—Missoula Milford thumbed back the hammer of his rifle—"sittin' ducks. Easy pickin's."

"Hold on," Knight Thompson said.

"Hold on nothin'," his younger brother said. "We got those thievin' devils in our gunsights."

"They could have been miles away by now," Knight argued. "They've stopped here for a reason."

"Yep." Callahan didn't know much about Indians. Most of his dealings had been with the Five Civilized Tribes in the Indian Nations, and those dealings had been few and far between. But he knew the people camped below were not resting their animals, or waiting in hopes of being cut down in an avalanche. They were simply waiting.

"What would you know about Arapaho devils?" Missoula Milford said. "You . . . a preacher. Those redskins are probably headin' up to Montana Territory to join up with those murdering curs ridin' with Sittin' Bull and Crazy Horse."

"They're going the wrong way then," Callahan said. "They're headed south."

The mankiller snorted and spit, then looked across the hilltop at his boss. "I say we open up on them. We can cut them all down. I can kill eight myself."

Callahan had heard enough. "Not unless you lined them up back to back to see how many bodies one of your bullets could go through—after they had surrendered." He let out a breath. *That temper*, he could hear the Major General in the Heavens telling him, *is going to get you in a heap of trouble one of these days*.

Missoula Milford stared at him, remembering, and trying to figure out who this Taylor Callahan really was.

"I think the preacher's right," Knight said.

"What would you know?" his brother barked.

"I know we've never had no troubles with the Arapaho before. I know Pa trusted them, and they trusted Pa. He and Stands Firm were blood brothers. And Pa always said that made us blood brothers with Stands Firm and his sons, too."

"And I say," Missoula Milford whispered while still trying to read Callahan's unreadable face, "the only good injun is one who has had his scalp lifted."

Callahan decided to put his trust in the Major General in the Heavens. He stood up, picking up his hat as he rose, and began walking down the hill.

The voices behind him were part gasps, mostly curses. But Callahan kept walking, keeping his hands spread apart.

Someone was coming behind him, and to his surprise, Buster joined him.

"Buster!" That was Kit's voice. She'd made her way up, too. "Reverend!"

The Indians below looked up. Those sitting now stood. And they stood holding bows, spears, or worn-looking rifles.

"You can go back now, Buster." Callahan was surprised he could say anything aloud.

"Nope. Them's my mules. My wagon. Well, technically ain't neither mine. But I'm like them young jaspers of cowboys behind us. I ride for the brand."

Callahan smiled. "So do I . . . in a way."

"I'm hopin' your boss is a whole lot better than mine."

"He is." Callahan took a peek at the sky, hoping the Major General in the Heavens heard him.

CHAPTER 18

Johnnie Harris started to put his right hand atop the swinging door to the Aces Up Saloon in Crawford's Junction, Colorado, a dingy little town that had nothing going for it, except it was a water stop on the Kansas Pacific Railroad. He stopped quickly.

That was a habit he thought he had broken. Broken like the hand that had been ruined by a gunfighting preacher named Taylor Callahan in some miserable town on the Texas side of the Red River more than a year ago.

He shoved the useless hand into the pocket of his linen duster. Someone was coming. He could have gone inside before the man in the black bowler reached the door, but the flash of tin on the man's vest startled him. So he stepped aside and looked across the street.

Everett Harris, one of Johnnie's outlaw brothers, frowned, but the youngest of the four boys shook his head, tapping his chest with his left hand.

Everett wasn't a fool. The oldest of the Harris no-accounts had taught those signals to his three brothers. Tap on the chest. That means only one thing.

Lawdog.

Everett backed up against the wall of the general store, pulled down the brim of his black hat as far as he could, and fished out the makings for a cigarette, which he began to roll, ever so slowly.

The lawman pushed through the doors, and let them sling and clatter their way shut. He glanced at Johnnie, then his eyes settled on the hand in the duster.

Right hand. Right pocket.

This was no greenhorn for a lawman.

A man could be holding a knife or a gun in that pocket, though Johnnie knew his right hand would not hold much of anything anymore. He had learned to hold a Colt with his left hand at an early age. Boss Harris had taught all his brothers to do that, too.

But in Crawford's Junction, Colorado, signs had been posted everywhere.

> **THE CARRYING OF FIREARMS**
> **IN THE OPEN OR CONCEALED**
> **IS STRICTLY PROHIBITED**
> **WITHIN THE CITY LIMITS**
> **OF CRAWFORD'S JUNCTION**
> **FINES OF UP TO $25**
> **MAY BE IMPOSED**

"Howdy," the man said. The badge did not read *DEPUTY*. It read *MARSHAL*.

Johnnie spilled more flakes onto the boardwalk than in the paper. He wasn't much of a smoker anyway. And though he had seen many a man able to roll a cigarette with just one hand, that was not one of his talents. He didn't even like to smoke.

Some outlaw he had become.

He sighed, and made himself look at the lawman. Johnnie doubted any WANTED posters for a gang of no-good brothers in Texas would have reached way up north into Colorado. Well, maybe his big brother's had. But Johnnie took after his ma, not his pa, or his three brothers.

"Marshal." Johnnie managed to say, and he brought out the crippled hand from his pocket.

The lawman's face changed, softened, and he stepped closer. His voice softened. "Need help with that, son?"

He knew what he should do. What Boss Harris, even Everett and Digger, would want him to do. Expect him to do.

Let the lawman roll that cigarette for the crippled little boy. Say something about the wind. That wouldn't even be a lie on these plains east of the Front Range of Colorado's Rocky Mountains. Despite the hodgepodge of buildings— including the bank the brothers were supposed to rob—the wind swept down Railroad Avenue. Get the lawman back into the saloon. Maybe offer to buy him a drink. When the cry of "Robbery!" sounded, act shocked and scared like everyone else. The lawman would run out of the saloon, not knowing that Everett was stationed outside the bank to cut down anyone who might try to stop Digger and Boss from getting out of town with enough money that could help them continue their quest—the quest to catch up with the gun slinging devil of a preacher, Taylor Callahan.

"I don't really like smokin'," Johnnie heard himself saying.

And then the lawman did something different. Unexpected. He pulled off the black glove covering his left hand.

Johnnie sucked in a deep breath. He had only the pinky and ring finger. The thumb was nothing but a nub. And the two other fingers were gone. The hand looked as though it had been crushed.

"Coupler," the lawman said, and nodded toward the iron rails. He grinned without much humor. "The conductor said if you get into a fight with a coupler, you're gonna lose." He took the papers. "He was right."

"Yeah," Johnnie said, trying to be brave and strong and mean. "But it's your left hand."

"Uh-huh." The man began to roll the smoke with one hand as though he had been doing it forever. Finished, he licked the paper, handed it to Johnnie, and then tightened the string to the pouch of tobacco. Johnnie took the cigarette, put it in his mouth, and then took the tobacco, and dropped it into the pocket of the duster that also held a hideaway pistol.

The marshal found a match, struck it against the batwing doors of the saloon and, cupping his hands to keep the flame from being blown out, lifted it toward the dangling cigarette.

Johnnie sucked till the cigarette smoke flavored his mouth.

"But the thing is, son," the lawman said as he took away the match, shook it out, and flicked it into the dusty street. "I was left-handed at the time."

Johnnie looked up. He felt ashamed.

"How long?" The lawman jutted his chin down at the ruined hand.

"Year," Johnnie heard himself saying. "Little bit longer."

"Mine was in June of eighteen and sixty-nine." The marshal smiled. "So you see, I've had a bit more schooling in the finer arts of rolling smokes, or becoming right-handed."

Johnnie took the cigarette out and pointed at the badge. Then at the holstered revolver. "Reckon you've had plenty of practice," he said, and brought the smoke back to his mouth, though he still did not care for the taste at all.

"You were going into the saloon," the lawman said. "How about let me buy you a beer?"

Well, that's what the brothers would want him to do. Of course, if things got ticklish—and they likely would. Boss had said the town would be deserted, but that afternoon it had looked about as popular as a main street in Denver on a Saturday night. Johnnie knew he would also be expected to do something else if push came to shove. When the lawman was heading to stop the robbery, Johnnie could pull his .36 and put one or two bullets in the one-handed lawdog's back.

Instead, Johnnie decided to keep the lawman on the street. There was a risk involved. A lot of risk. Everett could signal Digger to let Boss know they could go ahead and rob the bank. Maybe that's what Everett thought Johnnie wanted him to do. Maybe Everett figured he could kill the lawman with an easy shot. He could do that quite well; Johnnie knew how fine a shot all of his brothers were.

But maybe not.

Johnnie pulled on the smoke.

"I told you how I lost my hand," the lawman said. "Think you could share with me how you hurt yours?"

Johnnie smiled. "I did something stupid."

The lawman grinned. "I know that feeling." He raised his mangled hand, then began to pull the leather glove back on. "I like your courage, though, kid." He grimaced as his right hand pulled the glove tight over the disfigured piece of skin and bone. "See, I don't have the courage to leave my hand out for public view. You do. That takes guts."

"Guts?"

"Especially out here in the West. I heard people calling me half a man. Half a man?" He turned and spit into the street. "A hand. I don't think one miserable hand is even one-twentieth of a man. Doesn't weigh much. One twentieth. Maybe one-fiftieth. I have two legs. Two arms. Two eyes. Two lungs." He raised his gloved hand and looked at it. "I wonder. I wonder . . ." His voice trailed off then he smiled again. "How about that beer? Or might you be a whiskey drinker?"

Johnnie tried to look cheerful. "I drank too much whiskey before."

"I see. I know. I rode down that trail, too." He extended the hand. "For about two years after this." The arm dropped to his side. "But then . . . well . . . my mama always said that you never stop learning."

"I hope that's true." Johnnie didn't mean to say it out loud. He looked across the street.

Everett stared at him. Stared? No, he glared.

Two cowboys rode up toward the saloon, but the hitch rails were full, so they turned their mounts and headed to the general store. Again, Everett jerked down the brim of his hat and busied himself by pretending to be scraping mud off the sole of his right boot on a rock in the alley between the general store and a barbershop.

The bank was five doors up Railroad Avenue.

The cowboys started walking, their spurs jingling, and the taller of the two began speaking. Johnnie didn't listen but did catch a few phrases.

"I'm just tellin' you that's what I heard."

"Rude Frank got out-drawed? And not by Tin Horne? I don't believe that for one second. Somebody's hurrawin' ya."

The lawman said, "It took me months to learn how to draw, cock, fire, and hit what I was aiming at. Mind you, I was a railroad bum. Not a lawman. Not a gunman."

As the cowboys continued on their way to the saloon, one said, "I tell you, the word done come down to Poudreville that's exactly what happened."

Johnnie looked at the lawman. "How long have you been marshaling?"

"Four years. Started as a deputy. Took over when Marshal Jim Phillips was gunned down in a bank robbery."

A man pushed his way out of the saloon, and said to the lawman, "You avenged Jimmy, Wade. You avenged him good." The man was drunk. Johnnie could see that in the man's eyes, but the words came out strong, solid, and probably truthful. "Shot those three bank robbers dead."

"Nothin' I'm proud of, Matt," the lawman said.

The cowboys had reached the boardwalk, and Johnnie heard two words that stunned him.

"*Taylor . . . Callahan.*"

The drunk stepped out of the cowboys way and put his

hand on the lawman's shoulder. "You done good. And you done good ever since."

Johnnie Harris watched the two waddies enter the saloon.

"Never heard no gunfighter by that handle," one of the men said.

They were through the entrance, and the pounding as the doors swung back and forth drowned out some of the words, but not one.

"Preacher."

The drunk staggered on down the boardwalk. The marshal shook his head and chuckled. "He's a good man. Owns the bank. Heading back to work, I suspect. I hope Amos he's the teller—knows better than to let Matt handle any withdrawals. And leaves everything else to Eric, the assistant cashier."

Hours later, when the brothers were riding toward Poudreville Johnnie Harris would wonder about that lawman—whose name he never knew—and the stories he had overheard. Did the marshal know what Johnnie was part of? That he was a lookout for a gang of bank robbers and killers? If Johnnie had brought that up to any of his brothers, they would have called him crazy to even think of such a far-fetched story. And if Johnnie told Everett, Digger or especially Boss that maybe it was the hand of a Higher Power that had caused the marshal to stop, the conversation that followed between the two men who had lost the use of their stronger hands. Not to mention hearing the story of a preacher named Taylor Callahan who had outdrawn a fast draw named Rude Frank in some town. Some town that was up from Poudreville.

"How about that drink?" The marshal's voice brought Johnnie Harris back to the streets of Crawford's Junction. "Or the café down the street. Across from the bank. Betty Sue serves good coffee and real fine slices of pie. Think today's pies are apple."

Johnnie tried to smile. "I'm sorry, Marshal." He pointed

across the street. Everett stepped back and moved toward his saddled horse at the hitch rail. Johnnie prayed his stupid brother would not pull out the Winchester and open up. "But that's my brother over there. And I guess he's ready to ride over Denver City way."

The lawman glanced at Everett, nodded with politeness, and looked back at Johnnie.

"Well, son." His head bobbed. "Safe travels. It was fine talking to you. Stay out of trouble." He held out his right hand.

Johnnie lifted his left. It was an odd handshake. But it felt good.

"Stay out of trouble," the marshal said again. And he went down the boardwalk toward the bank and the café, whistling.

Johnnie quickly crossed the street.

His brother looked over the saddle and cursed, then started to pull the Winchester from the scabbard.

"No!" Johnnie snapped.

"He's headin' right for Digger and Boss. To the bank. You ignorant oaf."

"He's going to the café," Johnnie said.

"Which is right by the bank."

The rifle came halfway out.

"We're not robbing the bank," Johnnie said. "I know where Taylor Callahan is."

The rifle stopped moving. Everett stared hard.

"Two men were talkin'. I overheard them. They said a preacher outdrew some fast-dealing, quick-gunning card-sharper."

The rifle slid back into the scabbard.

"Where?"

"Near Poudreville."

Everett spit. "I ain't never heard of no Poudreville."

"We'd never heard of Crawford's Junction till three days ago," Johnnie reminded him.

"We can still rob the bank," his brother argued.

"Yeah. And be on the run from the law. While the preacher that done this"—he raised his crippled hand for effect—"is this close to us."

Everett knew he was right. He grabbed the reins, untied his horse, and walked the horse toward the center of the street.

Johnnie unloosened his horse and swung into the saddle. He remembered how awkward it was, after his right hand had first been ruined, climbing into a saddle and dismounting. Now he was getting good at it. Maybe the Crawford's Junction lawman was right.

He turned the horse around and saw Everett pulling his flat right hand across the front of his throat, three times, four, then sighing, and lowering his hand to the horn of the saddle. Johnnie spotted Digger and Boss moving toward their hitched horses in front of the bank. Then he looked over on the other side of the street.

But he did not see the marshal. He wondered what the lawman's name was.

"You best be right," Everett Harris growled as he turned his horse around. "Or Boss'll tan your hide till you can't sit a saddle for months." He spurred his horse out of town. Johnnie rode after him. The two other brothers would catch up to them soon. And Johnnie hoped he had done the right thing.

Saving the marshal's life. The town's money.

While possibly condemning a preacher to his death.

CHAPTER 19

One of the Arapaho braves began singing.
Two walked slowly to the pony herd.

The rest gathered in a semicircle, fitting arrows from their quivers into their bows, but—at least for the time being—keeping the arrows aimed at the flattened grass of the plains.

"I've walked into friendlier places, Preacher," Buster said in a dry, quiet voice.

The Reverend Taylor Callahan wanted to swallow, but he could not make his mouth produce enough moisture to spit. He might have blamed it on the dry wind blowing all the time, but the Major General in the Heavens would have laughed off that excuse. Still, he managed to find his voice. "You want to turn back?"

They kept walking. And sweating the cold sweat Callahan had not felt since the late War Between the States.

A horse whinnied. Another answered. The lone brave still sang.

Callahan did not know the words. "You speak Arapaho?" he asked as they neared the Indians. The tune and rhythm

were unlike any he had heard at all those churches and re-
vivals and camp meetings he had attended in his life, but the
song had a spiritual quality. Sweet and powerful.

The warriors in the semicircle *looked* powerful, but they
sure did not have any sweetness etched on their faces.

"I don't see any war paint on them." Callahan hoped that
was a reassuring sign.

"Don't mean they won't kill us, scalp us, then chop us
into mincemeat."

"You're not exactly instilling confidence."

"That's your job, ain't it?"

Reaching the semicircle, they stopped, then Callahan
covered a few more paces. He tried to pick out a leader, but
they all had a sameness to them. No more than two or three
feathers. All in buckskin. All copper skinned, black-eyed,
hair in braids. All holding those bows and arrows.

"You speak Arapaho?" Callahan asked again, realizing
Buster had never answered the question he posed just moments ago.

Moments? It felt like years.

"Nope." Buster's voice was an octave or two higher.
"Absalom does. Well, he says he does. But you can't believe
nothin' he says."

"Well"—Callahan's voice went into a whisper—"maybe
now you regret putting Absalom at death's door."

"I ain't regretting nothin' I done to that old coot." Buster
coughed, cleared his throat, spit, and said, "Any . . . here . . .
savvy . . . Eng-lish?" The words were spaced apart, and the
old stagecoach driver enunciated like that schoolteacher did
back in Clay County—before some scandal sent him out of
town on a rail.

No answer came. Not even a grunt. No Indian shook his
head. The lone brave stopped singing.

"Now what?" Callahan asked.

Buster grunted and took a step forward. "What you want
to tell 'em?"

Callahan blinked, confused. The fool had just said he did not speak Arapaho. Then Buster's hands raised out toward the men in the middle of the semicircle, and his fingers and hands began moving rapidly. The eyes of the men in the center watched closely. The others, Callahan noticed, kept their sharp eyes trained on either Callahan, or up on the hilltop.

To the circuit rider's amazement, the Arapaho warrior in the center, knelt, placing his bow and arrow on the ground. Still kneeling—so his weapons were not out of reach, in case these peace talks petered out—the brave's own hands and fingers moved.

Shaking his head at his own stupidity, Callahan somehow managed to smile. Sign language. *Of course.* He had seen a few men talk with their hands down in the Indian Nations and suddenly realized just how scared he had been coming down that hill and into the encampment.

Once the Arapaho lowered his hands, Buster sucked in a lungful of air, held it, then let it out. He did not look over at Callahan, but spoke to the minister while keeping his eyes on the spokesman for the Arapaho.

"Them's was just the formalities—howdics, good afternoons, nice weather, hope your travels have been productive and all's well, and such," the stagecoach driver said. "Now to get to the introductions."

His hands flashed again, the Indian's eyes moving with each flash of fingers, and waves of both of the man's knotty, big hands. The brave's head nodded, and then his own hands went into action—too fast for Callahan to remember, not that it would matter. He had struggled with Latin, and many said his English was not particularly strong.

"He calls hisself Killer of Ten Crows," Buster said, giving Callahan a sideways glance as he explained. "And that don't mean birds he's done in. Them ain't crow feathers tied to that ol' hoss's elk-skin shirt. I told him who I was. Told him you was our holy man." He chuckled. "Killer of Ten Crows said you don't look like no holy man."

"I've been told that before," Callahan said.

"Well, I think he means you are a mite young to be a holy man."

"I'm older than the both of you think."

Buster wiped his mouth. "The next few minutes we won't talk about nothin' much. Weather. Family. Huntin' and such. Not much sense in it. No point to it. But that's the way these here meetin's go."

"No different from the way we beat around the bush when we visit one another," Callahan said, and started thinking about a sermon. "Nice weather. Good-lookin' corn you got in the fields. River looks high. Catfish been bitin'? I saw a fat deer on my way down the pike. Hope she wasn't fat on your butterbeans."

With a grunt, Buster went back to talking with his hands.

Callahan wet his lips and waited.

The hands went this way and that. The Indian spoke. Buster spoke. But no words were heard.

A pause followed, a lengthy one, and then Killer of Ten Crows worked his arms and hands, grunted, and waited.

Buster sucked in a deep breath. His shoulders straightened. "That's bad. Real bad."

"What is it?" Callahan whispered.

But the stagecoach driver's hands were already flashing silent words to Killer of Ten Crows.

The conversation continued as the wind blew. The only sound came from the milling horses, and the omnipresent wind.

"He wants to see Iron Hand," Buster said.

The voice startled Callahan. It took him a moment to recover. "Iron Hand?" he finally asked.

"Yeah. What the injuns called Old Man Thompson. The dead daddy of young Knight and Walker. Guess the Arapaho didn't hear that ol' Iron Hand got hisself kilt a few years back down in Texas."

"He died in Texas?" Callahan asked.

"Range war. Sheepherders agin' cattlemen. Pretty common out west, Preacher. Thompson had ranches in Texas, somewhere south of San Antonio, and then liked the looks of the area here when he was pushing some beef to feed the U.P. boys in Laramie. He bought this land from Stands Firm."

"Bought it?"

Buster nodded. "Don't know what he paid for it. Then he claimed most of it. How much the government—territorial and them cheatin' swine in Washington City—will agree to that, especially now the old man's deader than dirt. But that's what he done. Bought the land, signed a treaty so to speak, not between soldiers and Arapaho, and no bill of sale, I reckon. The old man treated the injuns fair, and they done the same to him."

"And the town?" Callahan said, though he still did not think from what he had seen of Peaceful Valley that *town* was an accurate description.

"The old man had the town platted. I think that's the right word."

"You'll have to tell him Mr. Thompson is dead, Buster," Callahan said.

"Yeah."

"How will Stands Firm react to this news?"

"He won't." Now Buster turned to look Callahan in the eye. "The old chief's dead, too. That's why they come. That's why they stole my mules and my coach. Wanted to steal Absalom's." He spat and shook his head. "Stupid redskins thought his coach and mules was better'n mine. Dumb heathen red devils." He spat again. "They want to bury the ol' man. Their chief. Stands Firm. On Peace Treaty Peak." He laughed dryly. "That's why they taken my rig. Guess they figure a mud wagon in these parts is better than a hearse."

"Where's Peace Treaty Peak?"

"That's the rub, Preacher. It's on the hill overlookin' Peaceful Valley. I just don't know how our fine citizens will take kindly to seein' a dead injun on his burial stand atop that hill ever' morn."

The spokesman for the tribe spoke in a deep voice again, and Buster and Callahan turned toward him. The man stood, leaving his bow and arrow on the ground, and he nodded at his own men. Without a word, those Indians took their arrows from their bow, and shoved them back into the quivers on their backs. They held their bows. The young warrior with the wonderful voice began to sing once more.

Callahan felt relief wash over him.

Buster nodded, signed something to the leader, and then looked at the circuit rider. "Killer of Ten Crows asks if you are really our holy man."

Callahan smiled, and nodded at the Arapaho leader. "Tell him I . . ."

Maybe it was habit, but the preacher started to talk with his hands. Not sign language, not anything an Indian or a frontiersman like Buster would recognize, but the old Missouri way of talking with one's hands. "Tell him I travel from south to north, from east to west. Tell him I preach my faith to all who will listen. That includes my red brothers. And my white brothers. All men are my brothers. All women are my sisters. I speak to men of peace. Of love. Of charity. Of forgiveness."

Buster made some gestures. Killer of Ten Crows responded quickly.

"He says you are a warrior, too. He sees that in your face. He hears that in your voice. He knows that peace is in your heart, but that was not always so."

The wind seemed cooler, and Callahan realized he was biting his bottom lip. He nodded at Killer of Ten Crows. "He sees better than many white men. Tell him, yes, there is much truth in what he says. But tell him I want nothing more than to bring peace and comfort to all."

There was a long silence. Then the Arapaho's hands flashed.

"He asks if you will bring Iron Hand to him."

Callahan wet his lips. *How did I get elected spokesman for a town I had never heard of, never seen since . . . Let's see. If today is Wednesday . . .* His eyes met the deep black ones of Killer of Ten Crows.

"Buster," said Callahan, not taking his eyes off the Arapaho leader. "Tell him the truth. That Iron Hand will be greeting his chief, Stands Firm, in the Happy Hunting Ground."

The stagecoach driver spit between his teeth. He tried to stop his curse, but couldn't, and shook his head, rolled his eyes. "Happy Huntin' Ground. Don't be preposterous, Preacher."

"Just tell him the truth."

The hands moved, and Callahan realized all those stories he had read—in Western newspapers—were wrong. This was not the stoic Indian. The eyes of Killer of Ten Crows welled with tears, and he bowed his head, clasped his hands, and slowly turned to his fellow warriors. He spoke in the deep baritone. One of the warriors turned, screamed in anguish, and dropped to his knees. Two others began singing, and the boy with the rich voice, joined them.

It was beautiful. Sad. Emotional. True. The mourning touched Callahan's heart. A white man, he knew, could learn much from these Arapaho.

Killer of Ten Crows spoke, and two of his warriors rushed over, lifted him to his feet. The leader did not wipe the tears streaming down his copper cheeks, but he continued to speak to the men. The songs stopped, except for the young boy's, and he sang softer, more of a hum than song.

The Indian asked Buster a question with his hands.

Buster bit his lip. "He asks where is Iron Hand buried?"

"Texas?" Callahan asked.

The driver's head shook. "Nope. His wife brung him back.

You figure that one out, Preacher. Thousand. Twelve hundred miles. Hauled them boys' dead pappy all that distance to bury him . . . atop Peace Treaty Peak."

Callahan turned and looked up the hill. He could see the figures of men, and Kit Van Dorn, standing, watching, but could not make out the two brothers.

Callahan looked back at Killer of Ten Crows. "Tell them the truth."

"I-I d-d-d-don't know if I-I-I oughta, Preacher," the man stuttered. "That's s-su-posed to be s-s-sacred—"

"Tell them the truth."

The stuttering stopped. And Buster talked with his hands again.

The Arapaho leader bowed his head, nodded, and spoke again in the universal sign language.

"He says the two great chiefs will rest together, one above the ground, as is the way of the Arapaho. One below the ground, which is the way of the white men. And they will hunt together for all time."

Callahan smiled. He liked that way of thinking.

"Tell him it is the way it should be," Callahan said. "The way it will be. Forever."

After the translation, Killer of Ten Crows nodded. He might have smiled. Then he started walking toward Callahan, extending his arms.

For a second, Taylor Callahan envisioned himself as the great white peacemaker, a simple ordained circuit rider a long way from Missouri, but a man who—with a little help from the Major General in the Heavens—could maybe ride up to Montana Territory and stop a war between the Sioux and the Yankee army.

The Major General in the Heavens, though, quickly showed the error of Callahan's thinking.

The roar of what sounded like a Howitzer boomed from the top of the hill. And Killer of Ten Crows dropped to the ground.

CHAPTER 20

It all happened, the way Taylor Callahan later recalled, as though each second stretched into half a minute. The hair at the top of the Arapaho leader's hair parted. Blood sprayed. The feathers dangling from his left braids flew back as though a strong gust of wind had blown. Those dark eyes revealed a tremendous shock while his mouth and the rest of his face exhibited excruciating pain. The moccasins lifted off the ground. His arms flailed. And he catapulted backward, landed, bounced up, landed again, then he did not move.

But the other Indians did.

Callahan saw them charging, picking up their bows and arrows, or drawing knives from sheathes. The ponies began racing around, but not galloping off.

As the report of the gunshot echoed, Callahan spun. He saw the figure of a man on the hilltop, a man holding a rifle, and working the lever again. Shouts and curses sounded from the hill. Callahan could not make out the man. He didn't have to. The man who had shot Killer of Ten Crows was Missoula Milford.

"Hold your fire!" Callahan cried out. *Idiots.* He tried to comprehend what had made the hired killer shoot. "Hold—"

Something hit him in the back. Something hard. But it wasn't a bullet. Nor a knife. He felt the arms wrapping around him, smelled the sweat, the scent of old rawhide, well cured, and knew one of the Arapaho warriors was about to kill him.

His hat flew off and he landed hard, his arms stretched out before him. His teeth slammed together, but he didn't lose any, though the cracking sure did not sound pleasant. Blood leaked from his nose. His mouth tasted nothing but grass and dirt. His chin bled as a hand gripped his hair and jerked it forward. Then he caught the flash of sunlight on metal and saw the knife, a ragged, ugly thing, held by the red hand of an Indian.

But Callahan had a good view of the hilltop. His right hand lifted and he pointed, and somehow he managed to say, "Wait! Look! *Look!*"

The Indian, he knew, would not understand a word of English.

The blade bit into his throat.

Another voice growled, guttural and strong, a voice Callahan recognized, but a word he had never heard—if it was a word, and not a grunt or moan or the cry a man uttered just before Death came to visit him.

Yet the knife stopped.

Oh, the hand still gripped his hair, strong and hard, and Callahan feared a good chunk might be ripped from the top of his skull. He blinked away tears from pain and stress. Waited till the hilltop and the figures atop it came back into focus.

The voice near him yelled again, stronger, and whatever had been uttered was followed by a curse in English and then, "Dern idiots."

That was Buster.

The next words were in a tongue Callahan did not know. Arapaho.

Footfalls sounded, and the buckskin britches and beaded moccasins rustled through the tall grass as an Indian stepped a few paces in front of Callahan, on the right.

The man holding Callahan's head at an uncomfortable angle and an even more uncomfortable knife blade at his bleeding throat, said something short, brusque, apparently a question. The Indian standing before him answered, waving his left hand in what the circuit rider assumed was a *Don't Bother Me* signal.

Then came another voice from one of the Arapaho Taylor Callahan was mighty glad to see.

"Thank your guidin' spirit, Preacher," Buster said. "Killer of Ten Crows ain't been kilt."

"He's . . . your spir . . . it . . . too . . . Buster," Callahan said, though the words came hard and soft, his head being pulled up and a knife pressed tight underneath his Adam's apple.

A moccasin stopped near Callahan's left eye. Then the legs continued forward. Killer of Ten Crows stopped about two yards in front of Callahan, his left hand planted atop his head, his right hand hanging by his side. He stared up, then turned, and looked down at Callahan. Blood leaked down his forehead, over the bridge of his nose, and streaked down past his lips, dripped off his chin.

"This," he said, flinching from the pain each syllable caused, "is why . . . we . . . never trusted . . . any . . . pale-face . . . but . . . Iron Hand."

Callahan blinked.

But Buster swore "You secretive red devil. You savvy and speak English."

"Better than"—the Arapaho removed his blooded left hand and let it fall to his side—"you do, Talks Too Much For His Own Good."

"Is that my Arapaho name, Chief?"

The Indian did not answer, but looked down at Callahan.

Killer of Ten Crows did not speak but the knife against the minister's throat jerked away, and the hand released his hair. Callahan's head planted against the grass, but the pressure on his back was removed, and he could breathe a bit easier. His arms worked. His legs worked. He pushed himself up to his knees, spit out grass, and said, "Killer of Ten Crows can trust me."

The Indian smiled and held out his blood-stained left hand. "Trust you."

Callahan pushed himself to his feet, drew in a deep breath, and nodded at the hill. "There hasn't been another shot fired." He knew why. Someone was holding a gun on the man who had fired the shot. Someone else was aiming a revolver at the other man. He couldn't tell who, but if he had to guess, he'd reckon one of the Thompson brothers had gotten the drop on Missoula Milford before he could shoot again, and the other kid had drawn on Iron Tom.

Iron Tom. Iron Hand. Two men with similar names, but Iron Tom could not have carried the dead rancher's hat.

"Why did they shoot me?" the Arapaho asked.

"Likely," Buster begun, "they thought you was gonna cut off the preacher's head. Scalp him. Likely—"

"Buster," Callahan said softly. "Shut up."

The stagecoach driver stopped, frowned, and looked up the hill.

Killer of Ten Crows smiled slightly, but flinched at the pain just moving his lips caused. Yet when one of the warriors moved close to him, to help him, the Arapaho barked something in his own language, a sharp rebuke. A statement made from pride.

"I do not know I can trust you," Killer of Ten Crows said.

"Give me a few minutes, and I'll earn that trust," Callahan said.

The Indian stared hard, waiting.

"Let me walk up that hill," Callahan said. "I'll earn your trust."

"How?"

"You just leave that to me."

"You go up there. You might take that poor shot's rifle." The Indian smiled. "And I think you shoot better than the fool who parted my scalp."

Callahan answered honestly. "I never was much of a hand . . . with a long gun."

"You are a strong leader," the Arapaho said. "You might be a worthy adversary." He smiled. "Yes, I know. Adversary. Big word for dumb injun."

"You're no dumb Indian, Killer of Ten Crows. I'm going to walk up that hill. I'm going to show you that not all white men are liars, cheats, and cold-blooded assassins. And I'm going to bring down the sons of Iron Hand."

"And if you lie?"

Callahan shrugged. "Well, you can kill and scalp, old Buster here, I reckon."

Buster started to protest, but a knife went up against his throat, and he paled.

Killer of Ten Crows grinned. "Go. You amuse me. But before you think you can kill a small party of Stands Firm's band of Arapaho, know this. The entire village is coming to say farewell to our chief, Stands Firm. We outnumber you fifteen to one. And our friends from other tribes will be coming, too. It will be a gathering of red nations. Much like what is going on in the north with our Cheyenne and Sioux brothers."

"I'll be back," Callahan said, and he started for the hill.

Leaning forward, he moved up the hill. Sweating, partially from anger—likely a great deal from the realization of just how close he came to meeting the Major General in the Heavens in person—and mostly because no matter how much he preached, he still had the temper of his mother and plenty of his daddies. And he'd had the fortune, good or bad, to have been born in western Missouri and lived there when the whole country turned mad during the late unpleasantness.

The hill, he came to understand, was a mite steeper and hard to climb, than it had been to descend.

"He's just about here!" It was Kit Van Dorn's voice.

Callahan's throat was dry, his chest heaving, the sides of his shirt wet from sweat. He reached the top, pushed damp bangs from his eyes, and only then did he realize he had left his Boss of the Plains in the valley below. He blinked, refocused, made sure he was seeing things the way they actually were.

He had guessed wrong.

Missoula Milford had not fired the shot that almost tore off the top of Killer of Ten Crows' head. It was Iron Tom. Oh, the rifle that lay near the surveyor chief's boots was the one that belonged to the hired killer and butcher of surrendered Confederate irregulars, but Missoula Milford stood with his thumbs hooked in his gun belt. Grinning without humor, his eyes focused on the circuit rider and not Knight Thompson, who had him covered with his Winchester Yellow Boy.

The rest of the crew stood at the edge of the hill. Apparently they had come up at the sound of the rifle shot, though by Callahan's quick count, a few of the cowboys must still be on the other side of the hill, holding the horses. The surveyors had their arms spread far from their waists, and, most likely, their weapons. Walker Knight kept his revolver on them. Two of the cowboys made sure none of the strangers tried something.

Tin Horne sat Indian-style, grinning and chewing on a blade of Wyoming grass. "You missed a good show."

Nobody aimed a gun at him, so Callahan figured that, as a gambler, the cardsharper had decided the odds were against him had he decided to join the fracas on Iron Tom's play.

"I think you just had poor seats." Callahan sucked in plenty of oxygen, breathed out, and gestured down the slope to the south. "It was quite a melodrama down there for a bit." He looked at Iron Tom, who shrugged.

"One less Arapaho for the army to kill," Iron Tom said. "And I guess this proved those injuns are yellow dogs. And it proves once you kill an injun chief, the rest of the band won't fight till they get themselves a new chief. So long, Stands Firm."

"What this proves," Callahan said, "is that you're a lousy shot."

The surveyor's eyes narrowed. Then the cocksure attitude vanished. "You mean—"

"You gave him a haircut and a bit of a headache, but he's not dead." Callahan looked at Knight. "Only that's not Stands Firm down there. It's an Arapaho named Killer of Ten Crows."

"Where's Stands Firm?" Knight Thompson asked.

"He's dead. Died a while back." Callahan wet his lips. "The Arapahos want to bury him atop Peace Treaty Peak. Alongside your daddy."

"Even better," Iron Tom said. "That'll make getting this railroad built a lot quicker. It—"

"Shut up." Both of the Thompson brothers studied one another.

Walker spoke first. "That's what Pa would have wanted."

"It's what Stands Firm wanted," Callahan said.

"You can't bury no Indian on the top of that hill." Tin Horne stood. "Think what that'll do for business. For settlers. No white man's gonna want to look up at a dead Indian. That—"

"Shut up." It was Kit who spoke.

"I reckon," Missoula Milford said, "it's time for me to take that Henry of mine and rid the world of them injuns. I know injuns. They won't let us out of here alive."

"Shut up," Walker Thompson said.

Callahan walked to the sitting Iron Tom.

"I think they will," Callahan said. "They came in peace. They'll go in peace. And we'll leave in peace. Providing one thing happens."

Trying to sound nonchalant, Iron Tom asked, "Which is?"

"This." Callahan jerked him to his feet, then sent a left haymaker to the fool's jaw, knocking him toward the south facing slope.

As the surveyor pushed himself up with his hands, the circuit rider's right boot caught the railroader's chin, sending him flailing and somersaulting down the incline. Callahan followed. He kept his feet, sliding a ways when the slope got real ticklish, usually just walking fast. He only stopped to kick, shove, or push the fool who had almost gotten every white person nearby killed. The man groaned, cursed, cried. Callahan just sent him tumbling.

Slipping on his last kick, he lost his balance. *Stupid. I should have bent down and pushed the man down those last few yards.* He slid on his buttocks but felt no embarrassment.

"No"—Iron Tom wheezed— "more."

Callahan did not have the breath to respond, but he was far from total exhaustion. He came to his knees, and when Iron Tom pushed himself up with his hands, Callahan kicked him in the chest, sending the man rolling. It almost planted the circuit rider on his backside, but he somehow regained his balance.

He heard laughter then, chants, maybe another song. Callahan reached down, grabbed Iron Tom's ripped coat, pulled the man to his knees, and hurled him forward.

He fell facedown, but was still conscious. He managed to rise once more, and Callahan planted a boot in the buttocks.

Iron Tom fell flat on his face. He pushed himself up, then collapsed, unconscious.

Callahan had to take a full minute to catch his breath. He didn't know how he could find enough strength to keep going. But the Major General in the Heavens must get the credit.

He put his right foot in front. Brought the left one to its side. He was still standing. He kept at it, reached the unconscious would-be assassin, and somehow managed to drop to his knees, let his right hand grip the collar. He got back up under his own power, and dragged Iron Tom the remaining fifteen yards.

Dropping the idiot in front of Killer of Ten Crows, Callahan straightened. Wondering how he could still be on his feet, he realized everything was now in the hands of the Major General in the Heavens.

CHAPTER 21

"**H**ere's the man . . .". Callahan had to fill his lungs with oxygen again. He exhaled, breathed in deeply once more, and pointed at the prostate form of Iron Tom. "He shot you." His lungs still worked hard, but maybe not as hard as his legs had to work to keep him from dropping on top of the surveyor boss. "Don't know . . . why."

He had to clear his head, which he did by shaking it. "No, I do know why." He thought a drink of spring water would be mighty helpful. Or like back in his younger, wilder years, a swallow or two of Bubba Sam McTavish's corn liquor. "He thought you were Stands Firm."

Killer of Ten Crows nodded as if he already knew, cringing at the pain the mere movement of his head caused. "We have ways of dealing with his kind."

Callahan's eyes found the warrior closest to the Arapaho leader. A younger man than Killer of Ten Crows, his body not as scarred, the eyes not as wise. Shirtless, and wearing only a loin cloth made of some wild, furry animal, and moccasins, his dark eyes looked at the form of Iron Tom with pure hatred. His left hand gripped a knife that remained in its fringed and beaded deerskin sheath.

Killer of Ten Crows said something in the language of the Arapaho, and the younger warrior bristled, but said nothing. Looking at Callahan, Killer of Ten Crows asked, "You give him to us?"

"He shot you. It's your call, but you should know this about him." Callahan wet his lips and swallowed. "This man." His right arm swept up toward the hilltop where the rest of the party looked down, ready to fight, or ready to hightail it back to Peaceful Valley or, more than likely, Fort Centennial. "He and the men he brought with him have been hired by the . . . Iron Horse."

Killer of Ten Crows smiled. "You mean . . . railroad."

Callahan's lips curved upward. He liked this Arapaho. "Yes. The railroad is powerful among my people. And the railroad has the soldiers to protect it. You kill him"—he jutted his jaw toward Iron Tom—"there could be trouble between your people and mine. Our army is powerful." He turned to look up the hill. What he saw made him take a step back.

Kit Van Dorn stood, not ten feet from him. Flanking her were the two Thompson boys, and beside them, looking mean but nervous, was Missoula Milford.

Callahan frowned, and stared up the ridge.

"Don't worry, Preacher," Knight Thompson said. "Our boys are keeping an eye on his boys." His right finger pointed at the groaning surveyor.

"And," Knight's brother added, "we thought Mr. Milford would be better off with us."

Callahan felt stronger and turned back to face the Arapahos. "Killer of Ten Crows, these are the sons of Iron Hand. They are your friends, as Iron Hand was your friend. This man is called Knight. And this is his brother, Walker."

They were twins, but far from identical.

Killer of Ten Crows walked to each brother and clasped

his hands. He stepped back and smiled. "Yes, these are the sons of Iron Hand. I see their father in their eyes. Your father was a friend to my people. My people shall be a friend to you."

He looked at Kit Van Dorn. "And this woman?" He turned back to face Callahan. "Is she your woman?"

Missoula Milford snorted. "His woman. Any man's woman. For a nickel."

The Arapaho showed no emotion. Kit, however, paled.

"She is one of the settlers in the town Iron Hand built," Callahan explained. "She, too, shall be a friend of the Arapaho."

Killer of Ten Crows nodded. He turned and looked at Missoula Milford. "I do not need to know the name of this paleface. I do not want to know his name. I can see the death in his eyes, hatred in his heart. He does not just hate the Arapaho, or all men and women and children of my color. He hates everyone. This woman. These brothers. Even you, a holy man among your people." He turned back and nodded at Callahan. "Mostly, this man hates himself."

The Indian walked to Iron Tom. His eyes had opened, but he was too afraid to move, especially as he lay staring up at the bloodied face of the Arapaho he had tried to murder. Killer of Ten Crows knelt beside him. Iron Tom's face turned whiter than the cloud drifting across the blue sky.

"In the old times," Killer of Ten Crows whispered, "you would not be so lucky. In the old times, you would live a long time, but you would not enjoy life. You would pray for death. But you would not die—until I got tired of torturing you. We would torture you to gain your strength. But I see that would be no use. For you are not strong. You are weak. You are a coward. You are not worth my time. You are nothing." He spit in the man's face, and rose.

The younger brave, the fierce warrior, spoke sharply in Arapaho. But a few guttural words from Killer of Ten Crows shamed him, and he looked down at his moccasins.

The Indian leader turned to Callahan.

"His scalp would not be worth taking," the Arapaho said. "Take him with you. We will be at the place you call Peace Treaty Peak in three days. We will come with our fallen leader. On the fourth day, we will bury him above the place where his friend—the father of these two strong men—rests. It will be good. You are all invited. We will mourn the leaders we have lost. And then we will celebrate their lives, and all they have taught us."

With that, Killer of Ten Crows turned around and walked back to his people.

Taylor Callahan wished he could remember everything the Arapaho had said. He could sure work it into a funeral service or a good sermon at a crowded camp meeting.

Buster walked over and cleared his throat. The Indians were busy catching up their ponies, and Killer of Ten Crows was talking to the fierce warrior.

"Buster," Callahan said. "You reckon we could load Iron Tom here in your mud wagon. I don't think he'll be riding much for a while."

"Thing is, Preacher," the burly man said, "I ain't ridin' back with y'all." He gestured toward the Abbott & Downing. "That's how come them bucks stole my mules and my stagecoach. Yep. They figured it for a hearse. So I'm to go with them. We'll bring ol' Stands Firm in it. Give him a good sendoff." He shrugged, spit out tobacco juice and smiled. "Besides, if there's a railroad comin' to Peaceful Valley that'll be runnin' through Poudreville comin' and a-goin', there ain't gonna be no use for no stagecoach company. Lessen we can run 'er to Cheyenne, I reckon."

He shifted his chaw, and scratched his beard. "Reckon you can break the news to Absalom."

"Sure thing." Callahan extended his hand.

Buster's grip was strong, but his eyes were bright. "See ya Saturday night, Preacher."

"Good luck to you, Buster. And thanks. You're a man to ride the river with."

The stagecoach driver grinned. "As long as it ain't the River Stinks."

Styx, Callahan thought, but he did not correct the old coot.

The Arapaho warriors made a travois out of two polls. Where they came from, Callahan had no clue, They also came up with a couple of trade blankets. The horses of the Peaceful Valley contingent were brought down by the rest of the party. Callahan mounted Job, and one of the hired hands pulled Iron Tom behind him. At the top of the hill, Callahan turned Job around and watched the stagecoach, surrounded by Arapahos, head south.

"How'd you ever become a preacher?"

As the stagecoach and the Indians disappeared, he turned to look at Kit. "I got tired of sinning."

She grinned. "That's a shame, pardner." She turned her horse, and kicked it into a trot to catch up with the others.

Before they reached the fork in the trail, Knight Thompson spurred his horse and caught Taylor Callahan. Both reined up, and the youngster asked, "We best get back home, tell Ma what all happened and what all's gonna happen."

Callahan nodded and held out his hand, which the youngster just stared at.

Knight worked his Adam's apple, looked over at Kit, who, likewise, had stopped, and drew in a deep breath. After exhaling, he thumbed to the party behind him. "I can send some of my boys to ride with you," he said, uneasy. "I mean—" He started to look back at the survey crew and Missoula Milford, but stopped.

Callahan smiled. "I'll be all right, son."

"You sure?"

He nodded, and jerked a thumb at the saloon girl. "That crew with Iron Tom may be tough, and Missoula Milford's a cold-blooded killer who don't know the meanin' of the word *remorse*, but I don't reckon those surveyors would let him murder a woman. Any woman."

"I ain't so rightly sure."

Callahan grinned again. "Tin Horne wouldn't stand for it. Killin' me? Sure. But not Kit."

Twisting in his saddle, Callahan pointed at one of the survey men, snapped his finger until he recalled the name. "Bob. Spell that young waddie and take the lead rope to your boss. Be gentle on the ride down to Peaceful Valley."

When the exchanges were made, and the brothers and riders for the Thompson ranch took their trail home, Kit Van Dorn made a request. "Tin, do us a favor and bring up the rear. If Missoula Milford or Bob or Whit raise a gun in our general direction, shoot them all out of the saddle."

The gambler tipped his hat.

Callahan shrugged and kicked Job into a walk as Kit rode alongside him. "Is Tin Horne that fast?" he asked softly.

"He's not slow. But if he was to shoot anyone, it'd likely be you." Kit let their horses cover a few more yards before adding, "But they don't know that."

Spotting Marshal Grant Lee's horse in the corral lifted Callahan's spirits. Harry with the red whiskers stepped out of the SUPPLYS store, and Rude Frank pushed through the batwing doors at the Three O'd Saloon. Smoke rose from a cookfire in the camp other surveyors had set up, and Peaceful Valley almost resembled an actual community.

Callahan turned to Kit, and tipped his hat. "Guess I ought to report to Marshal Lee what all he has missed."

"Don't scare him off," Kit said with a grin then whispered, "No one would blame you, Preacher, if you weren't in these parts first thing tomorrow morn."

He looked into her eyes. She really was concerned for his well-being.

"Just a thought," she added.

"But then you'd never get to hear my preaching, ma'am."

"My soul's not worth saving, Reverend."

"Neither was mine. But the Major General in the Heavens proved me wrong."

"I'm no soldier."

"Neither was I." He nodded and smiled, turned Job out of the procession and kicked the horse into a trot.

Marshal Grant Lee was stepping out of the cabin he had for an office before Callahan reined up.

With Job unsaddled and turned loose in the corral, with oats and the core of an apple the marshal had finished for supper, Callahan sat on his gunpowder keg and let the lawman pour him a cup of coffee.

"I met the railroad surveyors," Lee said as he pulled up his chair and filled his tin cup from a bottle of whiskey. "Railroad workers can be a hard lot, but I never thought much about those men with those telescopes and funny boxes and charts and such. As bein' tough, you understand."

"That's what folks call a stereotype," Callahan said.

"Reckon it is. But them boys in camp ain't no stereo-nothin'. They wear two guns each. And they's four of them. Plus the two that rode in with you. And that ain't countin' Missoula Milford. Or . . ." He snapped his fingers. "What's the boss man's name?"

"Iron Tom is what they call him." Callahan blew on his coffee cup. "But he's not feeling solid as iron right now."

"I'm guessin' you beat the spirit of the Lord in him?"

"Let's just say I whupped him good."

By the time he'd related the story of everything that had happened, Callahan's coffee was cool enough to gulp down.

Marshal Grant Lee remained silent and unblinking for a long while, then wordlessly reached over for the bottle he had not corked and filled his cup about a third full. He drank about half of that, swallowed, wet his lips, and killed the rest of the liquor. After putting the cup on the table, he wiped his lips with his shirtsleeve. "Your day," he said as he looked Callahan in the eye, "was bigger than mine."

"Where were you?" Callahan drank some more coffee. "If you don't mind saying."

"I don't mind saying." Lee stared at the bottle, and his right hand started for it but pulled back quickly, and he let his arm drop off the table. "I don't have much in the way of secrets. I went to see the boss soldier at Fort Centennial."

Callahan nodded, then waited. He waited a full three minutes.

"There ain't no soldiers at Fort Centennial." Lee burped a rank whiskey burp then waved his hand. "Oh, there's a handful in what passes for the post hospital. Sick with the grippe or some other malady. And an orderly there to nursemaid them. And a few boys to take care of the horses and all. And an officer to do what officers do, which is, you might know, not one blasted thing."

Callahan nodded.

"That might be a good thing," Callahan said at last. "With all that's been going on with the Indians up Montana way, some bluebellies seeing a bunch of Arapaho Indians on a hilltop might lead to some trouble."

"I reckon so." Grant Lee looked again at that bottle. "Except having some bluecoats on Peace Treaty Peak might've kept a war from breaking out among the Arapaho and us white folks."

Callahan felt the coffee roiling in his belly. He managed

to swallow down something that wanted to crawl out of his throat and formed a question. "How's that?"

Grant Lee waved. "Earl. He's one of those surveyors that come in with that boss you clobbered and almost turned over to be butchered by Indians. Not a bad sort, Earl. Tougher, like I said, than expected, but he knows a lot about surveying. That trail . . . that railroad . . . they want to run from Laramie to Denver? The way it's looking, right now, it's gonna go right over Peace Treaty Peak."

Callahan had to sit on his own right hand to keep from reaching for that bottle of whiskey.

"How you reckon the warriors in the late Stands Firm's band will react to that, Reverend?"

CHAPTER 22

Most Indian tribes on the Western frontier did not love the Iron Horse. Callahan knew that. Railroads scared away game Arapahos, Cheyennes, Sioux, Comanches, Kiowas—you name it—depended on. If that Iron Horse cut through the land those people claimed, then you could count on some trouble. Of course, most of the Comanches and Kiowas were pinned up on reservations. The army, the Texans, the settlers—and, yes, the railroad—had eventually defeated them. So had disease.

But the Sioux and Cheyennes, especially the northern band of the latter, could still fight. Some of the Arapahos, too. Not to mention the Apaches in the southwestern territories and parts of Texas.

"I've heard," Callahan told the marshal, "buffalo won't cross a railroad track."

"Don't blame 'em," Grant Lee, feeling his tongue loosened by the whiskey, agreed. "I don't like crossing them myself. Ever seen a man or woman or horse or dog that got run over by a train?" He did not wait for an answer. "It ain't a pretty sight." He shook his head, and refilled the cups of coffee.

They were eating supper, ham instead of bacon and eggs, with a few potatoes, thinly sliced, and fried up in the grease.

Something had been troubling Callahan since the lawman had explained the railroad's route. He did not add to the conversation about horrible deaths from train accidents. Trains crisscrossed all of Missouri, so he had heard a few ghastly descriptions, and had preached one funeral—no, it was two—or an old man and a young boy who had been struck and killed.

"I'm no engineer," Callahan began as a way of qualifying his ignorance, "but why would you lay a railroad track up and down a hill? When a creek bed runs around the side of the hill and the country flattens out a bit before the next hills, which aren't that high for a ways."

The lawman grinned. "You ain't seen a flood, I reckon, exceptin' what you read in the Good Book about Moses."

"Noah," Callahan corrected. "I've seen floods, Marshal. The Missouri River can raise Cain when she gets angry. And you should have seen the flash flood that came close to carrying me and an entire town in southern Texas right up to those glorious Pearly Gates." He wet his throat with coffee. "Puttin' the tracks on a trestle over the creek, beats making a train huff and puff and pull and groan up and down a hill."

Grant Lee grinned. "Thought you said you ain't no engineer."

Callahan just smiled.

"Listen, Preacher," the lawman said, serious now. "Somebody's gonna find fault with any plan. Like you said, you ain't an engineer . . . or a surveyor. Run that track around the creek bed, folks will complain the smoke from those locomotives ruin the view atop Peace Treaty Peak. Climb the hill, and they'll say it ruins the views from up there and down here. The old man is buried up there, but he's the only person. We got a regular boneyard just forty yards from where we're eating and drinking right this very minute. Maybe we can talk the Widow Audrey Eleanor Thompson into planting her husband alongside the other people who have died in these parts." He frowned. "Well, I don't know that the residents of this village and this county would want to have an Arapaho on his burial platform when they come to put flowers on their loved one's grave, or seeing his bones sticking out from his rawhide, or a raven pecking at him, or—"

"I get the picture, Marshal," Callahan said.

Lee grinned again. "Well, truth be told, it ain't likely most of the folks who have been planted here got any loved ones bringing them flowers or nothin'. Most of 'em ain't even got names carved into the crosses, them's that gots crosses anyway."

They stopped talking to drink coffee.

"But if that railroad comes through here," Lee said, "it'll do wonders for this town. We won't just be a place for cowboys from the Widow Audrey Eleanor Thompson's ranch to come get roostered or lose their wages to a slick like Tin Horne. It'll be a thrivin' little town . . . which means I'll be moving on."

"You don't like progress?" Callahan asked.

"I don't like gettin' shot," Grant Lee answered.

The horses in the corral began snorting. Hooves sounded. Job and the lawman's horse had to be running in circles around the edge of the corral, and the noises they made were not curious or friendly whinnies.

Grant Lee knocked over his coffee cup, but did not stop to pick it up. He grabbed a Winchester rifle from the gun rack and headed for the door. "Must be a dad-blasted wolf," he snapped. "That's another thing I don't like about Wyoming Territory."

Right behind the lawman went the circuit rider. He did not grab a weapon, figuring the marshal had enough firepower for a wolf. The door opened, and sunlight almost blinded him. The marshal was out the door, and Callahan was thinking again. *Sunlight. The sun might have been ready to sink in a few minutes, but there was plenty of light for the time being. Why would a wolf or even a coyote come into a town in daylight when it can be seen? Unless the wolf's rabid.*

He wondered if he had made a mistake not grabbing a revolver or even a stick he could shake or rattle then remembered what his daddy—the one who got fifteen years at the state prison in Jefferson City—often told him. "Don't never step into nothin' you don't know nothin' about."

An instant later he heard the gunshot.

Above the roar of a rifle, Callahan recognized another sound immediately. One he had heard far too often in his life, especially during his years riding with Carbine Logan's Irregulars.

The easiest noise for Callahan to recognize, he figured, was a bullet or ball striking flesh.

Grant Lee grunted, slammed against the side of the building next to the door as his rifle clattered on the ground. The town marshal slapped his left hand across his right shoulder and his head banged against the wall. His feet flew out from under him and he hit the ground hard. His legs sprayed out, his head rattling against the frame of his office and home as he slid down into a seated position.

He said a few choice words, but the Major General in the Heavens would not let Saint Peter hold those sentiments against him when Grant Lee stood at the Pearly Gates. Much can be forgiven when you've been shot from ambush.

Of course, the marshal might have stretched the limits of the Major General in the Heavens' generosity. He was still letting those curses flail.

Callahan dropped to his belly, and crawled forward. His right hand gripped the barrel of the unfired Winchester Lee had dropped. He pulled the trigger.

A bullet struck inches in front of Callahan's face, kicking dirt up into his hair.

He jerked the barrel again, but the rifle scarcely budged.

"Lift your leg!" Callahan ordered, only he added a few choice descriptions of the marshal's leg, and punctuated that with certain unflattering comments about the lawman's parentage. But the Major General in the Heavens might forgive those sins, too, given the circumstances.

The next bullet hit a post, and sent splinters into Callahan's forehead and cheek. One brushed his eyebrow. A little lower, Callahan figured, and he might be wearing a patch over that eye for the rest of his life.

Which would not be long from now if he did not get any cooperation from Grant Lee.

"Lift your confounded leg, Lee, or we're all dead."

Confounded was the word Callahan used when he told the story later. It was not the adjective he picked during the ambush.

Lee managed to work his left leg up enough the Winchester came into Callahan's possession.

He jacked the lever, pressed the stock to his shoulder and fired three shots at the powder of smoke he saw behind some sagebrush.

The next shot, however, clipped a few hairs atop the preacher's head. "To your left," Grant Lee said through grinding teeth.

Callahan did not need any instructions. He rolled over, working the lever of the Winchester, finding the likely spot behind the chimney of the ruins of the old stagecoach station he was turning into his pulpit . . . if he lived long enough to preach there.

The figure came around the chimney, and Callahan squeezed the trigger. He heard the whine of a bullet ricocheting off the stone, and the high-pitched scream as the second assassin dropped out of sight.

Callahan came to his knees, cocked the rifle, and aimed

at the sagebrush. A head appeared, and he squeezed the trigger. The head disappeared. The preacher smelled the pungent odor of gun smoke. He tasted gall. He felt the heat from the barrel of the Winchester.

He turned, shot at the chimney again when he saw what had to be a rifle barrel moving into the open.

The barrel disappeared.

And now came other gunshots. Callahan turned to his right, bringing the rifle lever up, but stopping.

"Son of a . . . gun . . ." Marshal Grant Lee managed to say. "Is that—"

"Absalom!" Callahan yelled. He wanted to laugh. But he wanted to stay alive even more.

Absalom was walking. Limping, actually. Somehow that crazy, ornery old cuss of a stagecoach driver was moving gingerly and firing a Winchester rifle. Right behind him came the red-whiskered gent who ran the SUPPLYS store. He held one of those old revolving rifles Samuel Colt had manufactured years back.

The Lord works in mysterious ways, Callahan thought briefly. A man survived a gunfight, especially one started from ambush, only from luck, or the hand of the Major General in the Heavens.

"You derned fool assassins!" Absalom yelled. "Ruint my beauty sleep. Tryin' to murder the bestest lawman this ter'tory ever knowed. Tryin' to cut down a preacher—a preacher who saved my worthless life. I'll send you all to—"

His rifle roared.

Working his own rifle, Harry from the SUPPLYS store glanced at the marshal's office. "Get Lee inside, Preacher!" he yelled, and let his gun roar. "We got this covered." He growled, aimed the old relic of a long gun. "Attack our town! Shoot our marshal! Try to kill a gol-blasted preacher man!" The rifle barked again. "Take that, ye miserable swine!"

They were sitting ducks. Especially Grant Lee.

Callahan set the marshal's rifle aside, climbed to his feet, and grabbed the marshal's shoulders, which caused even more unflattering curses from the lawman, then dragged him into the small cabin and dropped him on the floor. He did not apologize, but raced back outside, shutting the door.

He found the rifle, heard a shot to his left, and spun around. Kit Van Dorn and Tin Horne, of all people, were shooting at the burned-out building.

"Are you all right, Reverend?" Kit called out.

Callahan's ears were ringing. He could hardly make her words. Maybe that's not what she said. Maybe he just wanted to think the woman cared about him. Maybe she had asked about Marshal Grant Lee.

Another idea struck him just moments after the echoes of the gunshots faded. An idea he could formulate into a good sermon, or Sunday school lesson, or just a story to tell to some wayward soul . . .

At first glance, Peaceful Valley looked like absolutely nothing. A scattering of ramshackle structures—one of those now practically burned to the ground—in the middle of nowhere. Not much going on. Nothing special about the residents at first glance. It was a town nobody would really care about. But the people who lived there saw something different. When attacked, they came to the defense. Sort of like those musketeers in that book written by that Frenchman, Alexandre Dumb-something-another. "All for one, one for all." When the chips were down, they'd come to the defense of a citizen and a passer-by.

Callahan thought he'd close with a kicker to the story. *How many men might we say the same thing about? A man who isn't worth saving? I've never met such a man.*

A figure darted away from the ruins of the stagecoach station, bringing Callahan's attention back to the moment as bullets clipped dust at the man's feet. The Winchester's stock came up against the preacher's shoulder. He drew a bead on the man's back. He could tell the sun was going down, but he would be able to see clearly for a good while yet. Right then a bullet sang past his forehead, the heat and wind blinding him for a moment. He dropped to his knees, turned, snapped a shot in the direction of the first assassin. He worked the lever, and saw that man running, too.

Callahan aimed. *All men are worth saving? Well, maybe not all of them.* "Forgive me, Lord," he whispered, "for the life of a man I am about to take," then amended his prayer. "Not that he is much of a man."

It would be several hours later, after his nerves had settled, and the smell of cordite, blood, dust, and near-death had diminished that he would think about Absalom riding—no, walking—to the rescue. Backed by the storeowner.

The gunfighting preacher touched the trigger.

CHAPTER 23

The hammer struck with a loud snap.

And nothing more.

Callahan stopped the curse before it left his throat as the running man disappeared over the ridgeline. He would have to find where Marshal Grant Lee kept the bullets. By the time he reloaded the rifle, and struck out after the would-be assassins, it would be dark. Taylor Callahan had his share of skills—but tracking wasn't one of them.

He entered the cabin and leaned the Winchester against the cabin wall. Kneeling beside Lee, he asked, "How bad is it?" He heard soft footfalls and knew it was Kit.

The marshal groaned. "Well, it hurts like a son of a—"

Outside, Absalom drowned out the marshal's sentiment, cursing at the cowardly assassins who had fled being the cowards that they were. Tin Horne walking cautiously toward the old stagecoach station where the second gunman had hidden.

Kit looked down at the marshal, then at Callahan. "You get a good look at them?"

Callahan shook his head. "Too far away." He turned back to the lawman. "How 'bout you, Grant? See anything?"

"Nothing," he said through gritted teeth. "Stepped outside. Then went down. Don't think I even heard the shot."

Still outside, Absalom cursed some more.

"Shut up, you old fool!" the storekeeper barked.

The horses had stopped running, but were milling around. Tin Horne was walking back. Other citizens had gathered, some carrying weapons—shotguns, rifles, one old Walker Colt. Even some surveyors for the railroad drifted over.

Harry of the SUPPLYS store entered the cabin and knelt beside the marshal, and began pulling away the shirt. "Went through," he said. Then his eyes moved to Callahan. "You hit?"

Callahan shook his head.

"Harry's a pretty good hand at doctoring gunshots," Kit explained. "Pulls teeth, too."

Callahan said, "I thought barbers were the doctors in towns like this."

"Not our barber," Tin Horne said, as he entered the cabin. "He can barely cut hair."

While the others attended the marshal, Callahan grabbed a lantern, which he lighted, and walked to the corral. Full dark would not come for a while, but the light was fading. He found his Peacemaker in the saddlebags, put the Colt .45 in his waistband, and worked his way around the corral. Footsteps sounded, and he glanced up, his right hand moving toward the butt of the revolver, but stopping when he saw the limping Absalom.

The contrary old stagecoach driver wasn't alone. One of the surveyors had come with him, and so had the barber.

Job and the marshal's horse moved away from the men. The animals were nervous, but Callahan understood that feeling. After all those rifle shots, the minister was a long way from feeling relaxed. He held the lantern closer to the ground, studying and remembering.

"You lose somethin'?" Absalom asked.

"Looking for a sign."

"Ain't you lookin' in the wrong direction? Shouldn't you be lookin' up toward Heaven?" The old coot chuckled at his joke.

Callahan set the lantern on the ground and knelt. His hand moved over the dirt.

"What is it?" Absalom started to squat beside the preacher, but groaned and decided against that plan. He might not be able to get back to his feet.

"You ought to be in bed," Callahan said.

"You find something, Preacher?" the barber asked.

Callahan did not answer. The horses had been spooked. But it was no wolf, no coyote, nothing like that which had frightened them. He found the footprint of the two-legged variety. He looked over at the camp of teamsters. Anyone paying attention would have had a clear view of the corral. And an easy path to get from there.

Picking up the lantern, he moved away from the footprint and walked to the edge of the corral. There was another print, this one clearer.

Absalom hovered over Callahan's shoulder. The railroad man kept a few yards back.

"What you make of that, Absalom?" Callahan asked, holding the lantern over the print.

"Boot print," the curmudgeon said, smiling as though he had just answered a question and wanted his prize.

"Man came over here, startled the horses," Callahan said. "To get us out of the cabin. So they could open up on me."

"You?" the barber said. "It was Marshal Grant who got shot."

"Their mistake," Callahan said, but then he thought *Or was it?*

"That print could have come from your boot. Or the lawman's. Or that saloon gal." The surveyor had decided to talk.

Callahan rose and put his right foot on the bottom rail of the corral. "Not my boot." He pointed to his boot. "This is a cowboy boot. Not that I'm a cowboy, but I ride a lot." He pointed to his boot again. "This is a boot more for riding than walking. The print is different."

Absalom put his boot next to the print. "Well, it sure ain't Miss Kit's," the old-timer said. "Her feet ain't that big. Besides, she wears sandals." He sighed. "From Paris."

Callahan nodded at the barber's feet. "Not yours, either. Your toes are more pointed."

"Cordovan's," the barber said, smiling, then pulling up the legs of his britches to show them off. "Bought 'em at Denver. Three dollars and fifteen cents."

Callahan moved the lantern back over the print. "These came from work boots. Heavy soles. That aren't smooth. Like mine. Or Absalom's. Or yours." He brought the lamp up high, and let the light bathe the ground near the surveyor. "But yours."

The man's mouth dropped open. His eyes widened, and he brought up his right hand. "Now, just you wait a minute, mister. I ain't had nothing to do with nothing. I was over yonder"—he waved at the camp—"fixing our supper. When this ruckus started."

Callahan smiled, nodded, and turned away. He walked along the edge of the corral, following the prints. "Yeah. I know. Your feet are too small anyhow. This was a bigger man." He stopped and looked at the shell of the cabin that was to be his pulpit.

"The man here spooked the horses," he explained, testing the words and his theory for himself—and the others. Let them know what he was thinking. Maybe they'd agree with him. Maybe they'd have other thoughts. But he was pretty sure he had figured it out.

"Once the horses started running, the spook took off." Callahan tilted his head forward, toward the dark ruins of the cabin. "Hid behind the chimney. Figured to get us in a crossfire if his pard wasn't aiming straight."

"Why . . . why . . . why . . ." Absalom sounded like a teakettle right before it started to whistle on a hot stove. Rattling. Shaking. And steam practically coming out of his spout. "This ain't right. This is a darned consecration."

Callahan looked at the old man. "Do you mean *conspiracy*?"

Absalom blinked, and followed that with a slight shrug.

The lantern lowered, and Callahan glanced down, smiled, and dropped to a knee. His free hand reached over, scooped up something, and dropped it in the pocket of his Prince Albert. "Well, well, well, well. Now we might be getting somewhere."

"What did you find?" Absalom asked.

Callahan stood, kicking up dust with his right boot in a sweeping motion that sent debris and grass into the corral.

"I guess one of the horses kicked some apples out of the corral." He nodded, but did not bring the lantern closer. "And whoever spooked the horses stepped into a pile of . . . well—" He turned around, looked at the member of Iron Tom's surveying group, and smiled.

The man was staring at his work boots.

"Like I said, sonny, your feet aren't this big. But I bet, if all your crew wears boots like those you've got on, one of them might be smellin' a mite. Not that horse apples stink. Always found the aroma of horse apples fairly pleasant, in the turd sense, of course. But with the spikes and ridges and all them fancy work-boot things, I bet whoever stepped in this pile of droppings will have the dickens of a time cleanin' off the bottoms of his boots."

The man swallowed. Then he glanced at the surveyors' camp.

Absalom limped past just as far as the glow of the lantern

reached. "Whoever it was"—he pointed at the remains of the cabin—"looks like he taken off for what's left of the old Peaceful Valley station." He turned back and stared hard at Callahan. "Just like you done said."

"We think alike," Callahan said with a grin.

The old-timer shrugged. "We could follow." He pointed at Callahan's lantern. "Just to be sure we's right."

"We're right," Callahan said. "No point in wasting time. I want to check something else." He rounded the corral and headed on the side of the marshal's office, but stopped when he reached the corner of the building.

Absalom was behind him. So was the barber. The surveyor stopped at the edge of the corral, staring down where Callahan had kicked the dirt, though he likely couldn't see anything clearly.

"You comin' with us, bub?" Absalom asked.

The man pointed at his camp. "Reckon not. Reckon I better . . . well, see you gents. Tomorrow. Or . . . somewhere."

"Thanks for your help," Callahan said, and led the two other men past the cabin.

"What help?" Absalom grumbled.

When they reached the ridge where the first not-quite sharpshooter had set up, Callahan lifted the lantern well over his head.

"You ain't gonna find no tracks here, Preacher," Absalom said. "Maybe some bent grass, but that won't do you no good. Ain't like finding turd on a fellow's boots."

"Why didn't you go to that camp?" the barber asked. "You could have found the fouled boots and had your man."

"Yeah," Absalom agreed. "Match the flattened turd with them boots and—" The stagecoach driver looked insulted. "What the blazes is so funny? What you laughin' 'bout?"

Callahan's right hand reached into his pocket. It came out as a fist. Moving the lantern in his left hand closer, he let his fingers unclench and spread out.

"Where's the turd?" the bartender asked.

"Wasn't any." Callahan shook his hand and let the wind carry away the dirt, pebbles, and bits of dead grass.

"I don't get it," the barber said.

"I do." Absalom chuckled. "You wanted to put a little fear in 'em boys." He laughed harder. "They'll all be looking ever so closely at their boots, cleanin' 'em, scrapin' the bottoms."

"Well, shucks," the barber said. "I thought you knew which one of them dirty curs tried to bushwhack you."

Turning, Callahan held the lantern lower. "I do know," he said. "You saw the size of those footprints. Belong to a big man. You can tell by the prints he left that he wasn't walking too steady."

Absalom cackled. "Not after the whuppin' you put on him. I done heard tell 'bout all that has been happenin' here from Josiah here"—he nodded at the barber—"And Miss Kit. And Harry. A few others who come to visit me and bring me"—he coughed—"my medicine."

"Iron Tom?" the barber asked.

"Of course," Callahan said. "I think the rest of that crew are actual surveyors. They hired on to do a job. A job with instruments meant to plat out maps and such. Not murder. Not some kind of land swindle."

"Swindle?" The barber tugged on his mustache.

Callahan dropped to a knee.

"So," Absalom said, "if it were Iron Tom who done this, then the feller who shot—" He paused.

Callahan set the lantern in the blowing tall grass, and reached down with his left hand. It brought up a tiny cylinder he held with the tips of his thumb and forefinger. "Ever seen one of these?"

"Brass ca'tridge," Absalom answered.

"Rimfire." Callahan held the casing closer for inspection. A little less than an inch long. He let his finger and thumb turn over the bit of brass. "Forty-four caliber." His nose picked up the scent of gunpowder. "Henry rifle."

"Don't see too many Henry rifles in this part of the country," Josiah the barber said. "Don't see them much of anywhere anymore. Winchesters mostly."

"That assassin could have blowed the head off the both of you, Preacher," Absalom said.

"We saw some during the late war," Callahan said, and slid the brass into his pocket. "You can fire a lot of lead with one of those long guns, but the bullets travel slow. Range wouldn't top two hundred yards on the best day. And in this wind"—he motioned to the west—"and shooting into the sinking sun. He was lucky to have hit Marshal Lee."

"We ought to tar and feather and then string up that no-good assassin," Absalom said. "Missoula Milford ain't fit to live."

"If he finds out you know he's the one " the barber began.

"He knows I know," Callahan said, and rose.

"He'll try to shoot you dead. Now that he missed and accidentally hit the marshal." Absalom stiffened. "Been six or seven months since we had to lynch somebody in these here parts."

"We won't take the law in our own hands." Callahan sighed. "And I don't think shooting Marshal Lee was an accident. I think they wanted the law out of the picture here." He shrugged. "But I imagine Iron Tom hoped I would catch a bullet or two."

"What would they have agin the marshal?" Josiah asked.

"I don't know," Callahan said. "I don't know why they want to put a railroad through here. I don't know why they want to put it right over Peace Treaty Peak. And I didn't know for certain why the Major General in the Heavens brought me to Peaceful Valley when I could very well be sleeping in a nice hotel, or some kind-hearted soul's house—free of charge, of course—in Cheyenne. But I'm starting to figure out I was brought here."

"Yeah," Absalom said. "I had a hand in that. But I still think we ought to lynch Missoula Milford and Iron Tom."

"You know, I almost killed him when he was running away." Callahan just let the words fall off his tongue. He wasn't speaking to the barber, or the old stagecoach driver. Nor was he talking to himself. He looked at the stars that were beginning to show. "But the Major General in the Heavens decided it was not the right thing to do. And I'm glad of that. Mighty glad. He's a smart guy, that general. The smartest there ever was."

"Awww," Absalom said. "You don't know what you're talkin' 'bout. Best general there ever was Ulysses S. Grant."

"George Washington," the barber countered.

CHAPTER 24

Marshal Grant Lee rolled the spent brass casing of the .44-caliber Henry between his thumb and forefinger, then laid it on the table by his cot.

The Reverend Taylor Callahan had dragged his keg of gunpowder closer. He found the bottle of whiskey and topped off the lawman's coffee mug. After laying the rimfire slug aside, Lee picked up the tin cup with his good arm and took a few swallows, then set the cup on the small bench serving as a table.

"Gunnin' for you, I reckon." He picked up the piece of brass and handed it back to Callahan.

The preacher's head shook. "We don't look that much alike, Marshal." He flipped the casing up, caught it, then slipped it back into the pocket of his Prince Albert. "Way I figure things, Missoula Milford was to kill you. Iron Tom thought he might do me in."

"They need better shots to do the job." Grant Lee had a few more sips of whiskey.

Callahan shrugged. "Better rifle anyway."

"Didn't allow for that Wyoming wind." Lee managed to

smile, but it did not last long. "Why in Sam Hill would they want me dead?"

The circuit rider gave another shrug. "Maybe not dead. Just incapacitated. Like you said, the cavalry at Fort Centennial up and vamoosed. You're the only law between Laramie and Cheyenne."

"They should have killed me," Lee said. "Because I'll kill them."

"If they killed you, likely a deputy federal marshal would have been sent in from Cheyenne." Callahan reached back into his pocket and pulled out the rimfire shell. After studying it for a moment, he shook his head. "I don't know, Grant. Maybe Missoula Milford didn't miss his aim. Maybe he just wanted to wing you."

"And you?"

Callahan grinned. "Oh, I'm pretty sure Iron Tom would rather have me six feet under."

"Then you need to be careful."

"I usually am."

The marshal finished his whiskey, coughed, and sighed. "Well, I ain't gonna be doing much for a spell. Maybe that's why they wanted me shot. Figured I'd hire Milford as a deputy."

Callahan laughed. "I don't think they would think you're that daft."

"I don't know. Things have been stirred up here. Not many folks in town would agree to pinning on a tin star."

Callahan did not like the way the lawman's eyes were focusing on him. "Josiah?" he tried. "The barber. He seems like a good man."

"Better man than he is a barber. But he's got a wife and four children. With a fifth due in about three months, Lord willing."

"Absalom?"

The lawman snorted. "Don't be ridiculous." He raised his good arm and pointed a long finger. "And if you recommend

Rude Frank or even Tin Horne, I'll whup you till you're crying for your mama. Even with a hole in my shoulder."

"One of the Thompson brothers?"

"It's gonna be you, Callahan." The man's face tightened from the pain. "It's got to be you."

Callahan made himself laugh. "I am no lawman, Marshal. I'm a preacher. An itinerant preacher."

The lawman used his good arm to point to a wooden box on a shelf next to the hat and coat racks.

"There's a couple of tin stars in there. The blacksmith made them for the marshal who was here before I got this job. Take one and pin it on your Prince Albert."

"Grant—" The start of a plea never got past that one syllable. Slowly, he got up, walked to the shelf, opened the box, pulled out a five-point star, and looked at the stamped letters.

DEPITY MARRSHAL
P.V., W.T.

What was it about Peaceful Valley's spelling?

Callahan muttered a bit of a cuss word. Not a real bad one, though. In fact, a body could find those four letters right together in the Good Book. First time, if he recollected right, in the thirty-second chapter of Deuteronomy. *For a fire is kindled in mine anger, and shall burn unto the lowest hell, and shall consume the earth with her increase, and set on fire the foundations of the mountains.*

It seemed to be an apt description of what had been happening ever since he set foot in Wyoming Territory. And was likely about to repeat itself again.

By the time Callahan made it back to the bunk, Grant Lee had pushed himself up partway, looked around, then sighed. "Why am I looking for a Bible? You've got one."

"You gonna swear me in?" Callahan asked.

"Yeah."

The two men studied each other, then Lee drew in a deep breath, thought for a good long while, and exhaled. "Reckon I ought to ask you first, though." He stopped to clear his throat. "After General Lee and the others surrendered, did you take the oath of allegiance?"

Callahan gave a faint grin. "Marshal, I took an oath to a higher party long before that war started."

Their eyes held for a while, then the lawman shrugged. "Just say I do. Or I will." He snorted. "Or I'll try."

Callahan said all three.

That's when the door opened.

Callahan didn't recognize two of the men. Two others he knew were townsfolks, though he had not learned their names or what exactly they did. He didn't pay much attention to any of the four, but he could not take his eyes off Kit Van Dorn.

She marched straight to the bunk, put her hands on her hips, and shook her head as she looked around the office. "This is no place for a sick man to recover," she barked. Then stared at Callahan as though he were to blame.

Before either Lee or Callahan could speak, she spun around to the men with her. "Well, get to it."

Two disappeared behind the doorway, coming back with one of those stretchers Callahan had seen orderlies scurrying about with during the War Between the States.

"We're taking you so you can be cared for, Marshal," the woman said.

"I got work to do," the lawman protested.

"Well, this town will just have to take care of itself for a change," Kit snapped. A nod sent the men forward.

Marshal Grant Lee started to complain, but she paid no attention to him. Her eyes left the incapacitated lawman and landed on the Reverend Taylor Callahan as he pinned the tin star onto the front of his black coat.

"Or," she said softly, "let your deputy earn his keep for a spell."

"He's already earned more than this county or town could ever pay him," Grant Lee said, then cursed and snorted and ground his teeth to block out the pain as two of the men lifted him and set him on the narrow blanket between two narrow poles the two other men held.

"Take him to my room," she ordered the men. "I'll be along directly."

The marshal started to protest, but pain in his shoulder caused an interruption, and he ground his teeth and clenched his fists while the stretcher bearers hauled him through the doorway, one man opening the door ahead of them, the other man closing the door behind them, leaving Kit Van Dorn alone with the circuit rider.

"This is a different kind of peacekeeping," she said when the sounds of grunting men and a groaning marshal had been replaced by the winds of Wyoming Territory. "You know that, I hope."

He tried to find something witty to say. When that failed, he tried to find something logical to say. When that failed, he simply shrugged.

Kit pointed at his right hip. "You're naked for a marshal."

He immediately thought of a witty response but also immediately understood if he cracked that joke, his face would be stinging from a slap, and she might never speak to him, or even look at him with those pretty eyes again.

So, he figured if a shrug was an all right response the first time, it would work again.

"You're gonna get yourself killed, Preacher," she said.

He smiled. "People have been telling me that for years, ma'am." He watched her eyes lose their anger. "And I'm still here."

Her mouth opened, closed, and she shrugged. Turning, she walked to the door and opened it, letting the wind in, letting it send her blond curls flying. She looked back at him as she stepped outside. "Try to stick around, Preacher. This town needs you."

The door closed, and Taylor Callahan sat on the empty bunk. His eyes looked at the ceiling, and he whispered, "I sure hope you know what you're doin'. 'Cause I ain't got a clue." He turned toward the bottle of whiskey that lay within an easy reach.

But he did not get a chance to test his willpower.

The door opened and in limped Absalom. When the old reprobate saw the badge, he chuckled. "You just is a jack o' all trades, ain't ye." He looked around, found the whiskey bottle and said, "That'll cut the dust out of my mouth. Where's Marshal Grant?"

"You need the law?" Callahan asked.

"No. I need a drink." He pulled out the cork with his teeth, removed it with his left hand, and drank a healthy swallow. Then he sighed with satisfaction. "But just to satisfy my curiosity, he ain't dead, is he?"

Callahan shook his head. "Miss Kit decided to look after him."

The man's eyes brightened. "I bet she can do just that." He took another slug, burped, and held the bottle out to Callahan. "Want a snort?"

"No," Callahan lied.

The door flew open. It was so windy, he hadn't heard the pounding hooves of a horse. He'd been trying to figure out where he had left his Peacemaker, or where any of Marshal Grant Lee's weapons were, and briefly wondered if Absalom had set him up to be assassinated. Quickly, though, he recognized the face, and knew his life was not in jeopardy.

"Where's the mar—" Knight Thompson's face changed. His eyes almost popped out of their sockets as they focused on the deputy's badge pinned to the black frock coat. "You taken up lawin'?"

Absalom almost dropped the bottle of whiskey he was laughing so hard.

Callahan sighed. "It's longer than Psalms," he told the young cowboy.

"Where's Marshal Lee?"

"He took a bullet earlier this evening," Callahan answered, and quickly added, "but he should recover."

"And he made you his deputy?"

Callahan sighed again. "Wasn't my idea."

The stagecoach driver cackled like a crazy hen.

The boy chewed his lip but for a moment. "Well, come on. Cletus has gone to fetch Harry. We gots to get back home. And quick."

Callahan was moving. He could hear the urgency in the cowboy's voice. He found his hat. He found the saddlebags, and while he was opening one to withdraw the .45-caliber Colt revolver, Knight Thompson said something else.

"It's Walker. He's been shot."

Absalom wasn't laughing when Callahan found the box and tossed the second misspelled deputy marshal's badge at him, and said, "You're deputized," though he was pretty sure a deputy had no legal authority to deputize anyone. That had to be the marshal's job. But when push came to shove, Callahan wasn't exactly sure Grant Lee was a real marshal since he hadn't been convinced Peaceful Valley was a real town.

"Somebody's got to keep the peace, Absalom. And that's gotta be you. I'll be back as soon as I can."

"Come on, Preacher . . . umm . . . Deputy! We got to move. And fast. Walker's been hit bad."

Absalom set the bottle down. His face lost its ruddiness and his voice sounded cold sober for the first time Callahan could remember. "Go on. I'll look after this pigsty of a community."

The moon had risen, and the clouds had been blown to Texas by the force of the winds, so once Callahan had saddled Job, they rode hard—or as hard as Job was willing to go—to the Thompson ranch.

It seemed closer than Callahan had figured. Or maybe, after all he had been through in just that day, he had lost all sense of time.

He stood in the parlor, turning his black Stetson around and around with the fingers on the brim. A fire was going. The wind howled outside. Harry was in the parlor across the short hallway, operating on Walker Thompson. Callahan had just gotten a glimpse at the boy and managed to say a short prayer before he was ordered out. The room was small, and the barber had said he didn't want any relatives in the room while he was performing surgery. And that the preacher would be of better service to mother and brother than as a nurse.

Knight had dragged a chair over, and sat in the doorway, staring across the hall to the closed parlor door.

The Widow Audrey Eleanor Thompson stood by the fireplace in the family parlor. She did not take her eyes off Callahan. "Just who in the devil are you, mister?" the woman finally said.

Callahan turned to look at her. She seemed younger than she ought to be, with her dark hair held up in a bun. As she toyed with a well-braided quirt she held in her right hand, her eyes were dark and cold. Leathered by the sun and wind, her face was not handsome. But not ugly. Strong though, with not an iota of weakness to be found anywhere.

She was the woman in the green dress, though she had looked younger and more attractive, with that lovely smile when the mud wagon had gone sailing past him a few nights back.

"Name's Callahan, ma'am." He reached for the Stetson that was no longer in his hands, but laying on the desk that had belonged to the woman's late husband. "Taylor Callahan. I'm a circuit rider. Preacher. Just got to Peaceful Valley—"

"Preacher." She coughed out the word. Her eyes locked on the .45 at Callahan's waist and opened a small tin box, and stuffed snuff into her mouth. To Knight, she said, "I send you to Peaceful Valley for a lawman and a doctor. I get Harry and a . . . nobody."

"You're right there, ma'am," Callahan said, suddenly remembering the Colt in his waistband. "I'm a nobody. Sure enough."

"He's a better man than anyone in town," Knight said.

"Now, son," Callahan said, "that ain't rightly so." He nodded at the closed door across the hall. "Josiah the barber. He's a real good man. And Harry's a mighty fine doctor. Got that slug out of Marshal Lee's shoulder fine."

"The bullet in my son," the Widow Audrey Eleanor Thompson said, "isn't in his shoulder."

Callahan breathed in and out. The mother was dead right on that account. The wound was in the boy's chest. With luck, it might have missed the lung, but Callahan wasn't sure. The bullet had not exited, either. Callahan looked down at the badge on his Prince Albert.

Lawman, he reminded himself. *Grant Lee's depending on you.*

He caught a whiff of perfume he knew he was just imagining. The Widow Audrey Eleanor Thompson was not the kind of woman to spray something sweet-smelling onto her neck or wrists.

Kit Van Dorn's depending on you, too. "Son," Callahan said, waiting for Knight Thompson to look him in the eye. "It's about time you told me just what happened to your kid brother."

"Why?" The mother's tone was biting, condescending.

But Taylor Callahan had heard that kind of mockery often enough, and it was something he could handle. "So you might have a story to tell at your next camp meetin'."

She pointed to the door. "If my boy dies, Reverend, you won't be preaching at his funeral. You—"

"I'm talking to your son, ma'am," Callahan said without looking at the hard rock of a woman. "And you're not talking to a preacher right now." He grabbed his Prince Albert and pulled it open, first toward her, then toward the kid. He let them see the badge again, misspellings and all.

"You're talking to the law."

CHAPTER 25

It was after suppertime, Knight Thompson told Callahan. The brothers ate with their mother. "Ma always insisted on that."

The preacher understood the boys' mother got her way, always and forever. Well, he could relate to that. His own mother was known as Old Ironclad in Clay County, Missouri.

"After supper, Ma dismissed us, and we moseyed over to the bunkhouse. Just to pass the time. And plan for work that had to be done."

The Widow Audrey Eleanor Thompson always let her sons and her hired men know work on a ranch was never finished.

Callahan, of course, could read between the sentences Knight Thompson did not say.

While he was no cowboy, Callahan had preached at a few bunkhouses—for chuck and a place to sleep, though sometimes a sermon and a Psalm and one or two hymns was not enough for a supper and a place to sleep *and* breakfast the next morning. Often he had to chop wood, gather eggs, mend fence, saddle-stitch some tack, muck a stall, or try to break a green colt.

He figured since Old Man Thompson was dead, cards might be dealt in the bunkhouse. And wagers might be placed on the cards. Table stakes. Dealer's choice. Nickel ante. No limit.

After a couple of hours and a pot of coffee—translated to after several hands and a bottle of John Barleycorn—the brothers had said work would start early come morning, so they stepped outside. The first bullet sent Walker flying back into the bunkhouse. The second and third grazed Knight, who showed the gash on his left forearm, and untucked his shirt and showed a burn on his left side.

"It was too dark to see anything," said one of the cowboys who the foreman had sent to the house to make sure no one else tried to kill a Thompson.

Knight nodded in agreement. "We shut the door. Carter here"—he nodded at the man with the Winchester peering out the break in the curtain hanging over the floor-to-ceiling window—"kept an eye out."

Carter did not look away from the window. "Nothin' to see."

"Harley was visitin' the privy when the shootin' started," the cowboy said. "He heard hooves about five or ten minutes after the first shots. That's when I opened the door. No more shootin'."

Callahan considered this, then shook his head. "You ever been ambushed like this before?"

"No, sir," Knight said.

"Nobody would have dared done this while their father was alive," the mother said. "Nobody." She sighed, shook her head, and added, "My sons have done nothing to have anyone want to gun them down in cold blood. That's as gospel as anything you'll ever preach, sir."

"Ma . . ." Knight sighed.

"Full dark?" Callahan asked, just to make sure. "You mean around . . ."

One of the cowboys gave an exact time, then held up a Waltham repeater as to attest to the veracity of his statement.

That meant a man like Missoula Milford could have ridden to the Thompson ranch after his botched attempt of murdering Taylor Callahan and Iron Tom's successful job of putting Marshal Grant Lee out of action for a few weeks.

"One horse?" Callahan asked. "Or more."

"One horse," Carter said. "One rifle. A repeater. Naturally."

"Naturally," Callahan said.

"Did you say . . . Marshal Lee was shot today, too?" asked the cowboy with the watch.

Callahan nodded. "Caught a .44 slug in the shoulder. Harry patched him up. He's hurting, but he'll be fine." He looked up at the Major General in the Heavens, silently pleading with the old soldier not to go making a liar out of this circuit rider. "Just before sundown."

The men eyed one another. They did the same math and the same theorizing as Taylor Callahan. But no one voiced that theory aloud.

Because the door across the hallway opened.

Harry had had one long, hard day and night. He looked pale, gaunt, his eyes red, and roughly a dozen new wrinkles in his forehead. His white shirtsleeves had been rolled up, and his hands and arms were stained with blood that had been wiped down with a rag or towel or maybe even a tablecloth. From the appearance he gave, how the man was still on his feet had to be a mystery.

The Widow Audrey Eleanor Thompson bulled her way to the open doorway.

"How is my son?" she demanded.

"Sleeping, ma'am," the merchant said. "And if somebody don't bring me a brandy right quick, I'll have you know I cannot be held responsible for my actions."

Knight Thompson did not bother hunting for a snifter or shot glass. He took over the decanter, and the merchant practically ripped it from the youngster's grasp.

"You can see him," Harry said softly. "Don't wake him up, though."

The mother was already across the hallway, and her oldest son did not let her get too far ahead of him.

Harry held the lid to the decanter in one hand, and brought the brandy to his mouth and drank about a third of it. Lowering the glassware, he started to wipe his mouth with his sleeves, then noticed the condition of his sleeves. He looked over his shoulder and said, "Don't hug him. Don't kiss him. You can hold his hand if you must, but don't get near his chest. That wound opens up, and I ain't sure he'll be long for the world. But let him sleep, and I figure he's got a decent chance."

He held the decanter toward Callahan. "Join me?"

"It's all yours, Doc," Callahan said.

The not-quite-a-doctor's eyes showed a bit of life.

Carter, the watching cowboy, left his position by the window, cradling the rifle underneath a shoulder. He reached out for the decanter. "Don't want you to drink alone, Doc."

The merchant passed over the decanter and walked across the hallway. His blood-stained right hand disappeared into the deep pockets of his equally stained trousers. Looking Callahan in the eyes, he pulled out a chunk of lead, and held it closer to the preacher for inspection. "Reckon I've seen enough of these today," he said, and looked out the window. "It's still today, ain't it?"

Callahan tried to find a clock, but saw nothing. He sighed. "I'm not sure." Then he took the piece of flattened metal from the merchant-doctor's finger and thumb. "Forty-four caliber from the weight."

"Henry," Harry said. "Maybe."

Callahan nodded in confirmation. "Maybe. Not sure it could be proved in a court of law."

The merchant-doctor grinned without humor. "You might not have noticed, and you ain't been in Wyoming Territory for very long, but court of law don't have the same meaning up here as it do anywhere else in these United States and her territories."

Callahan gave him a knowing smile. "But I am bound to a higher court, sir."

"Indeed." Harry turned back to Carter, the cowhand. "I'm the guest on this property, boy, and I'm a bit older than you. So I get a larger share of that brandy than you do."

The decanter was returned to the doctor.

His sip was a short one, and he handed the brandy back to the cowhand. "Boy's lucky to be alive," Harry said, and stifled a cough.

Callahan turned to Carter. "You got any good trackers on this spread?"

The cowboy swallowed the brandy and set the decanter on a table in the hallway. "Mister"—he wiped his mouth with the back of his left hand—"the way the wind's a-blowin' tonight, there ain't gonna be nothin' we could follow come daybreak."

"Anybody you know who would want one or both of those young men dead?" Callahan asked.

Harry laughed and reached over and pretended to polish the tin star on the preacher's coat with his blood-stained fingers. "Get yerself a badge, and you move from preacher to detective right quick. Don't you?"

The brandy had gone to the man's head, but Callahan did not hold that against him. He waited for an answer.

"Only enemies the Thompsons ever had," Carter said, "was down Texas way. And the boys had nothin' to do with that." He had turned and was staring through the doorway into the other parlor, where everyone could hear the Widow Audrey Eleanor Thompson talking to her unconscious son.

*   *   *

"Preacher . . . I   mean . . . Marshal . . . I   mean . . . I . . . ummm . . . *sir*?"

Callahan's eyes slowly opened. His neck hurt. His side hurt. He just plain hurt. And what he really wanted was to sleep. A long, long time.

It took a moment to remember where he was. He saw the curtains. The flickering flames from the candles. He smelled the brandy but knew he had not broken his vow, that he was sober. For he tasted nothing but coffee on his tongue. Old coffee. Marshal Grant Lee's coffee.

"Mr. Callahan."

Knight Thompson's blue eyes with the green dots in them came slowly into focus.

Callahan was sitting in the parlor. No, he had to be lying down. On the sofa. He groaned, closed his eyes, then tried to blink the sleep out of them. Slowly, he lifted his head off the arm of the sofa. It had not been a comfortable arm.

"Yeah." Callahan thought he had said that, but he wasn't altogether sure.

The next thing he knew, he was sitting up. Well, at least, it felt like he was sitting up. No longer was he staring up into the face of young Knight Walker. No, no, that wasn't the right name. Knight and Walker were brothers. It was Knight Thompson. And Walker Thompson. And . . . yeah . . . the Widow Audrey Eleanor Thompson. Thank the Major General in the Heavens she wasn't staring down at him.

"Yeah." Callahan heard his own voice. "Yeah. Yeah, son. I'm awake." The thought about adding he would be certainly a great deal more awake if someone handed him a cup of good, strong, black coffee neither he nor Marshal Grant Lee had brewed.

"It's Walker—"

The young man's two words brought the circuit rider up straight from a sleepy, hurting deputy marshal and itinerant circuit riding and ordained minister from the Logan's Knob

Seminary in western Missouri to a wide awake lawman and preacher. "Yes?"

"He's awake."

Two words Taylor Callahan was mighty glad to hear.

For some reason, the Reverend Taylor Callahan—at first, anyway—tried to make himself look like a real preacher. Ramrod backbone. Stand tall. Straight. Look stern. Look like a . . . a . . . a . . . a . . . Methodist! Full of vinegar and fire and brimstone and Old Testament lessons. Then he thought *this boy has been at Death's Door. With Satan and the Good Guy pulling him one way and the other. Let's give the kid a bit of a break. What would you say to that, you ornery old Major General in the Heavens?*

"How do you feel, Walker?" Callahan heard himself ask.

"Like I just got caught in a stampede." The boy's voice was strong, clear. His eyes—identical to his slightly older brother's—were well focused on the badge still pinned on the Prince Albert of the Reverend Taylor Callahan's.

A good sign.

Noticing, the preacher presented himself more like a deputy marshal. He tried to make himself look as though he had not slept the past two and three-quarters of an hour on the most expensive—and equally uncomfortable—sofa to sleep on in the miserable little town he had never heard of until a day or a week or an eternity ago.

He looked down on Walker Thompson, knowing the boy had survived surgery to extract a flattened leaden bullet—the misshapen chunk of lead Callahan held in his fisted left hand.

"How you feelin', sonny?" Callahan asked again, immediately regretting he had issued the stupid query twice. "Don't feel obligated to answer that one honest, Walker," he amended. "How about . . . do you need anything?"

The boy tried to smile, and shook his head.

"Good."

Well, that was one word Callahan used again from his limited vocabulary. He stared into the boy's eyes and a calmness overcame him. He felt younger than his years. He even smiled. "I don't reckon there's anything you can really tell me, is there, Knight?"

The eyes in the pale face changed, seemed to sink deeper into death that had been hanging just an inch or so from Death's Door.

Callahan sucked in his breath, and held it. He did not know what the boy might say, but anything would help. So Callahan waited hopefully for a revealing confession.

"My name"—the boy paused—"is . . . Walker. Knight's . . . my . . . brother."

CHAPTER 26

The boy's eyes closed, then opened. Callahan slowly exhaled.

"You remember anything, Walker?" the preacher asked.

The boy's eyes closed. Opened. He slowly focused on the circuit rider standing over him.

"I must remember . . ." The kid had to think. "Well . . ."

This, Callahan thought, *could take as long as Esther. Chapter Eight. Verse Nine. Hear that, you wily ol' teachers at Logan's Knob Seminary. Taylor Callahan has answered one of your so-called queries correctly.*

Well, he wasn't stupid. Certainly not a genius, but for a farming boy in Clay County he had something other than corncobs in his noggin.

"I just need to know, sonny," he said in a soothing voice. "If there's anything you recall . . . you saw . . . you heard . . . you thought . . . you sensed . . . you realized . . . before that .44-caliber chunk of lead darned near sent you to meet Saint Peter in the flesh . . . or whatever angels call flesh."

* * *

"My sons," the Widow Audrey Eleanor Thompson said the next morning at breakfast, "have no enemies."

She made good coffee. Well, Taylor Callahan assumed she had brewed it as he did not see the bunkhouse cook anywhere.

He had spent the night in the bunkhouse, sleeping despite loud snores coming from every bunk but his. Nobody snored when you were a bushwhacker during the late war. Snoring could give away your hiding place, and Carbine Logan's Irregulars were hunted by plenty of redlegs and Yankee soldiers.

He thought he would be eating chuck with the crew, but Knight Thompson had come inside before Callahan had his boots on.

"Ma wants to see you."

"How's your brother?" one of the hired hands had asked.

The boy had nodded. Every eye was on him. "Sleeping. Doc says he's doing fine. Long as infection doesn't set in."

Callahan found his hat and coat. "See you boys," he had said to the group of hard-working, underpaid waddies.

They were nice kids. Good at what they did. Bowlegged and full of bluster, but fun to be around.

"Just to remind you, I should be preaching in town. So if you'd care to hear the Word and sing some mighty fine songs of praise and hope and glory, feel free to come to town."

None of the eyes he'd seen had showed much enthusiasm, so Callahan had tugged on his Boss of the Plains and followed young Knight Thompson to the main house. The coffee greeted him. So did snores from Harry the merchant-doctor. The snores came from the parlor across from where Walker Thompson still slept.

"Ma wanted Harry to take him to his own bed," Knight explained, "but the doc . . . he said, no, best not move him till he's got some more strength, replenished the blood he lost and all." The kid shrugged. "Reckon he's right."

"Sounds like good advice." Callahan had looked in on the boy, then hung his hat on a rack and followed Knight to the dining room, where the Widow Audrey Eleanor Thompson sat at the end of the table, drinking coffee.

Callahan took a drink of his coffee. "Any strangers in town?" he asked, and regretted the question because he knew the answer before the widow set her cup on the saucer.

"Just you."

He nodded. "But I don't have a .44-caliber rifle. Or any rifle. And I have no quarrel with your sons or you."

She stared at him, and he drank more coffee. No food, though. The widow just had coffee out. Callahan bet the boys in the bunkhouse were filling up on bacon and beans and sourdough biscuits, laughing, and telling jokes, and bragging about their exploits, and debating who all might have tried to gun down both of the sons of the owner of the brand they rode for. And he was drinking coffee—granted, mighty fine coffee—with a hard rock of a woman. He heard the front door open and close, and knew Knight Thompson had left. Probably for the bunkhouse. To eat.

Callahan tried to remember when was the last time he had any vittles of substance. "There are some strangers in town," he told her. "A railroad surveyor and his crew."

She did not blink. No surprise showed in her eyes.

"Knight and Walker probably mentioned that to you. And the Arapahos. The stolen mud wagon."

"They spoke of it." She was one cold lady. Not much for conversation.

He wondered why she had wanted him to come over and drink coffee with her. "Did you know about the plan for this railroad they hope to connect Laramie with Denver?"

"No."

"It might be good for you," he said. "Shipping cattle to Denver via rail instead of driving them to . . . wherever you can sell them."

"You are a preacher after all." She stood, found the pot and walked over to refresh his cup, then returned and poured some steaming black liquid into her own. The pot was put on a wooden holder on the table. "You don't have any inkling how much a railroad charges to ship livestock."

He nodded and smiled. "Yes, ma'am, I reckon you are right. But maybe buyers will come here. Like they do at the Kansas cattle towns. Dodge City. Wichita."

"The railroad will not come through," she said. "It is a ludicrous dream by a bunch of schemers."

"They are surveying it," he said. "I guess they figure—"

"They are wasting their time."

He started to open his mouth, but she held up her right hand. "We shall not waste time talking about a foolish railroad. I want to know what you plan to do about the scoundrels that dared try to murder one of my sons."

Callahan said, "Missus Thompson. They tried to murder both of your sons."

Her face finally showed emotion. Then Callahan heard a noise behind him, and saw her eyes lift. He turned to find the yawning Harry slipping his suspenders over his shoulders and walking in his stocking feet to the coffeepot.

"You got an extra cup, ma'am?" he asked.

She pointed to a cabinet and the worn-out merchant-doctor opened the door, rattling expensive china before coming out with a small bowl. He filled that with coffee, and drank it black and hot, like one might do with soup.

"No fever," he said as he refilled the bowl. "For Walker. That's a good sign." He drank half of the bowl, then turned and coughed. "I don't want to wake him up, so I'll hold off on changing his bandages. Reckon I must've plugged him up pretty good, on account that the torn sheets I wrapped around that bullet hole and scalpel cuts ain't festered or turned ugly looking."

He finished the bowl, set it on the table, and looked at Callahan. "You goin' back to town, Preacher?"

Callahan looked at the Widow Audrey Eleanor Thompson. "Am I going back to Peaceful Valley, ma'am?"

She frowned. "Don't act foolish. I am not keeping you here against your will."

"You coming?" Callahan asked Harry while standing and finding his hat.

"No." The man dragged a chair from the table and planted himself in it. "Marshal Lee shouldn't have any problems. If the wound starts festering, cut it open, drain it, pour some whiskey down it—not good whiskey, but not the forty-rod they sell at Miss Kit's place, neither. Make sure it's real whiskey. I prefer rye. Gots more healing properties than Irish."

"What makes you think the gunman wanted both of my boys dead?" the woman said.

"Bullets scratched him," Callahan said.

"That could have been meant for Walker."

He nodded. "That's a possibility. But I don't think that's what happened. I think somebody wants both of your kids dead, ma'am. Any reason you can think of might help me."

"No one wants my boys dead," she said.

"The railroad?"

Her head shook. "I own this ranch."

"Does the name Missoula Milford mean anything to you?"

"No." She found her cup but just held it. "I had never heard his name until Walker and Knight used it after they returned home."

"You're about the onliest person in town who ain't never heard of that gun slick and coward," Harry said, and yawned.

"How about Iron Tom?" Callahan looked at the woman but still could not read her face. "I don't know his last name. He's a surveyor."

"The only Iron I knew of was Iron Hand. That is what the Arapaho Indians named my late husband."

Callahan turned toward Harry. "You need me to send anything here from town? For you? For Walker?"

The man yawned again before shaking his head. "There ain't nothing I need from Peaceful Valley. But if you get to Cheyenne or Laramie, you could ask for a real sawbones. The only reason I got to doctorin' is because my scissors and razors are sharper than Josiah's. He thinks himself a barber. And some of my tonic is pert' much pure alcohol so it's good for what ails anybody."

Callahan thanked the widow for the coffee, then headed for the door.

"You will find the man who tried to kill my youngest son," she called out when his right hand gripped the door. It was an order. Not a suggestion. Not a plea.

"Both sons, ma'am." Callahan pulled the door open and donned his hat. He looked back down the hallway that emptied into the dining room where he had a clear view of the widow. "And, ma'am, that killer might be after you, too." He shut the door, and found Knight Thompson coming from the bunkhouse.

"What you mean by that?" the young man asked.

"I think the man who shot your brother, as I've told you already, wanted to gun you down, too. Your mother doesn't think so. Well, if she owns the ranch—" He waited.

The boy understood. "She owns the ranch."

"If whoever shot Walker, almost put him under, and grazed you is after the ranch, they'd have to get rid of your mother, too." He let that sink in. "Unless there's something you haven't been telling me."

The boy shook his head, and Callahan figured he wasn't lying. He didn't have the look of a liar, and Callahan usually could pick a liar fairly quickly. *It takes a liar to recognize a liar.*

"Only enemies my pa had was down in Texas," said the young cowboy—or was he actually a young *rancher*? "Everybody in Wyoming Territory respected him and admired him and practically worshipped him. Me and Walker don't get to Cheyenne much. Hardly ever get to Laramie, neither. We don't know nobody. Don't see why anyone would want us dead. It just don't make no sense at all."

Callahan put his right hand on the lad's shoulder. "Don't fret. Just stay close. Keep your eyes sharp. And if you hear a loud metallic click, or catch a glimpse of sunlight reflecting off metal, hit the dirt. Take cover. Then shoot to kill."

What would the Major General in the Heavens have to say about that piece of advice? Telling a young kid, probably still in his teens, to shoot someone dead before that someone killed him. What about preaching love and charity and forgiveness? Well, Wyoming Territory seemed to be more of an Old Testament kind of place. The Major General in the Heavens would understand.

"All of your riders need to stick close. Ride together. Nobody goes alone."

"That's asking a lot, Preacher. We got plenty of cattle here and a lot of range to cover."

"I know." He saw Job looking out from a round pen, eyeing him, as if saying he was a town horse and did not get along with these rank, half-broke mustangs kicking up dust and preventing him from getting enough to eat. "But with the blessing of my boss, we'll get this mystery solved and have the man who tried to end your twin brother's life spending some time in the territorial prison in Laramie."

"I sure hope you can find out who did it."

Callahan fished the bullet that had been taken out of Walker's body. *I know who did it,* he told himself. *I just have to figure out how I can prove he did it. And why.* He returned the bullet to the pocket. "Don't leave your mother alone, either."

You sound like you know what you're talking about, he told himself. *Just like you sound when you're preaching. Maybe one day you'll actually know what you're talking about.*

He held out his hand. The boy's grip was good and strong.

"You gonna do some scouting?" Knight asked. "Try to see if you can find any clues? Any tracks?"

Callahan shook his head. "You don't know where the shots came from. Just a general direction. It was dark. You didn't see anything. That would just waste my time. Waste all of our time. The way I figure it, in a legal sense, this is a job for the county sheriff. I'm supposed to be the acting marshal of Peaceful Valley. But I'll have to get Grant Lee to verify that for me."

He nodded again. His stomach growled. Good coffee could only do so much for an old bushwhacking guerilla from Missouri.

"Stay close. Watch after your mother. Look after your brother. And if you need anything, send a couple of riders to town to fetch me. Remember, nobody works alone. Not till we get this mystery solved."

The cook at the bunkhouse gave him some cold biscuits and two burned pieces of bacon to eat on the ride back to town. Callahan had finished those before he was fifty yards away from the ranch compound.

He kept his eyes sharp on the ride back to Peaceful Valley, trying to piece together a puzzle without any pieces. He had a chunk of lead that might have come from a Henry rifle. But he could not even say for certain that it was a .44-caliber slug. No witnesses. No motive. Not a clue.

Callahan sighed as he put Job into a canter for a while.

The thing to do, he understood, would be just keep riding. Past Peaceful Valley. Go to Cheyenne. That was his original plan. Even if he preached in that burned out building, he couldn't see making enough money to pay for one night's lodging in Cheyenne if he ever got there.

That was no good.

"You need to think positive," he told himself.

Then Job crested the rise and he looked down upon the village of Peaceful Valley. He also looked up at Peace Treaty Peak.

And he could not stop the curse before it sang out in the wind, a sharp bark of profanity that caused Job to buck a little.

CHAPTER 27

Sheep. Sheep. Those furry little animals covered almost every yard of the peak, from the top, down to the edge of the settlement. Taylor Callahan had never seen so many sheep in his life.

How many? He couldn't tell. Some of the animals remained so close together, there was no way to count—especially from that distance. They looked like cotton balls rolling this way and that, and the noise they made caused Job to buck a little more.

Callahan stuck with the horse, then kicked him into a lope down the hill, then made him lope back up. When he reached the top, he reined hard, and growled at the white gelding to stop acting up.

He looked down at the town. He could make out Kit Van Dorn and two other women. Kit shielded her eyes and stared at the sheep. The railroad men had gathered, too. Callahan did not see Missoula Milford, but that meant absolutely nothing. He glanced at the marshal's office. Grant Lee's horse remained in the corral. A couple of figures stood in front of the batwing doors at the Three O'd Saloon.

He glanced behind him, thinking about the Thompson ranch. He remembered the old man, the father of the two boys, had been killed in some range war in Texas. A war that pitted cattlemen, like the late Iron Hand Thompson, against a sheepherder or bunch of sheepherders. Callahan could not recall any rancher or any cowboy ever saying anything complimentary or close to nice about sheep. Or shepherds.

He had learned sheep and shepherds might get plenty of mentions in the Good Book, but it was best not to speak of sheep in any positive sense at any place in the Great State of Texas or any state or territory west or due north of there.

"Sheep," Callahan said, or maybe it was a word that sounded somewhat like that noun. "I don't think this is a good omen of peaceful days in Peaceful Valley."

He kicked Job into a walk down the hill.

The covered wagon at the base of Peace Treaty Peak was new. Smoke drifted from the front of the wagon.

Callahan turned toward it. The mules that had pulled the vehicle grazed among some of the sheep that liked the grass in the valley rather than what grew at the top of the hill. Drawing closer, he spotted Tin Horne, Rude Frank, and a few other townsmen heading toward the wagon. He kicked Job into a lope.

It was not a covered wagon. Well, it had a yellowed canvas over the top, but it wasn't a Conestoga or freight wagon or anything he had seen in all his days. The frame had been painted green, but the sun, wind, and rain had faded it over the miles and years. The wheels were solid and sturdy. A tool box or chuck box or something along those lines was built into the wagon's side between the rear and front wheels.

Stopping near the front of the wagon, he dismounted and saw a tall, thin, closed door instead of a driver's bench. More than just a wagon, it was like a house on wheels—

though he could not yet figure out how a man drove the mules, unless the owner removed the door. Or walked alongside the wagon like he had seen drawings in magazines and books of folks doing along the California, Mormon, or Oregon trails.

The door opened, and out stepped a tall, robust man with a thick brown mustache and beard and black patch over his left eye. The man leaped down, holding nothing more than a crooked shepherd's cane, though he was dressed nothing like the sheep tenders Callahan had seen drawn on church walls and in a few illustrated Bibles and such. No, sir, the man wasn't like anything Callahan had seen or read about in the Bible—Old Testament or New.

Not with that Walker Colt stuck in his waistband.

"Aye," the man said in a thick Scottish brogue. "The law has come to welcome me and my flock."

Callahan had forgotten about the badge pinned to his Prince Albert.

"Me name is Angus MacLerie." He smiled at Callahan, then turned toward the settlement. "Aye. Yes. Mighty fine, mighty fine. A citizens' welcoming committee. Right on time."

Looking at the approaching settlers, Callahan found nothing welcoming in their faces.

The unwelcoming party stopped about twenty yards from the wagon. Most of the settlers stared at the strange wagon as Callahan measured Mr. MacLerie standing a good six feet, four inches, and weighing maybe two hundred and twenty pounds . . . even without the heavy Walker Colt.

"Who are you and what are you doing here?" Tin Horne asked.

"The name is MacLerie, as I was telling ye constable." He waved at the preacher. "I bring sheep to this fine country."

"This is cattle country, mister," Rude Frank said.

The man smiled. "Is that a fact, sir?" He looked up at

Peace Treaty Peak, then across the valley, taking his time, savoring the spectacle of his performance. East. West. North. South. He studied the settlement, the misspellings, the burned-out stagecoach station, the corrals, the marshal's office, the stone jail, the saloon, and general store. He looked at the road that ran south to Poudreville and north to Cheyenne. He even gazed upon those majestic Rocky Mountains, the purple rises with peaks still capped with snow far off in the distance.

Then he looked right back into Rude Frank's eyes. "Laddie, I see nary a bovine anywhere. Just sheep. And"— he nodded at Job—"what, I guess, is what ye Wyoming frontiersmen might call a horse."

"You think we're gonna let your furballs eat our grass till there ain't nothing but dirt here," said a black-mustached man whose name Callahan had not learned, "you got an-other think comin'."

Angus MacLerie laughed, and waved his cane toward the summit of Peace Treaty Peak. "I believe they are eating as we speak. But I dinnae think they will eat it all the way to the roots, me good man."

Other residents began making their way toward the sheep-herder's wagon. So did a few men who did not live there. Those were the men who worried Taylor Callahan—two of the surveyors. And Iron Tom. And Missoula Milford.

He also saw Kit look back at the surveyors and mankiller. She turned quickly, lifting the hems of her dress, and mov-ing straight to the marshal's office.

Absalom stepped out from a lean-to—probably just now waking up after a bender—and saw Missoula Milford and the men with him. Then he saw the residents. Finally he saw the wagon and the party of men around it. Then he saw the sheep. He rubbed his eyes, looked again, and made a beeline for the marshal's office.

Good, Callahan thought. *This might call for an experi-enced lawman, which I am not.* But he walked over to Job and unfastened a saddlebag. Keeping the white gelding between him and the approaching townsmen and the Milford-Iron Tom gang, he withdrew the .45 Colt, checked the loads in the cylinder, then pushed away the tails of the black coat and shoved the weapon inside the back of his britches.

He walked back to the strange wagon. Angus MacLerie had seen him take the revolver, but he did not seem to care.

"What the blazes are those sheep doin' here?" Iron Tom said, planting his feet firm on the sod, spread out, and pointing a rough finger at the Scotsman. Missoula Milford cradled the Henry rifle in his arms. The two surveyors, Callahan realized, had pistols shoved inside their waistbands.

He looked down at the marshal's cabin, but saw no movement, no door opening, not even a window being cracked.

"They are having their noon meal," the Scotsman answered.

"It'll be their last meal," Missoula Milford said. "Mutton for supper, folks. Mutton for supper." He laughed.

So did Angus MacLerie.

"Listen, we are building a railroad from Laramie to Denver," Iron Tom said, "and that railroad is going to go up that ridge, then down, and therefore you must take this . . . this . . . flock . . . somewhere else."

"They like it right there."

"There's also a good man buried on the top of that hill," said one of the bartenders from the Three O'd Saloon. "And he got kilt by some low-down sheepman in Texas."

"A shame," Angus MacLerie said. "But this is open range, I have been told. And my sheep are there. Let us call it . . . eminent domain."

"Huh?" a few townsmen and Missoula Milford said.

Another man spit out tobacco juice, wiped his mouth, and gazed up Peace Treaty Peak. "Must be five hundred head," he whispered.

Angus MacLerie laughed. "Nay, me good man. You are

not even half there. Twelve hundred head." The Scot sighed. "We lost a few hundred more on the drive up from Texas. Twelve hundred head of the finest Mexican Churros you will ever see."

"What the Sam Hill are you gonna do with twelve hundred sheep, mister?" the man with the black mustache asked.

"Provide you with woolen shirts and britches for the winter," Angus MacLerie answered. "And"—he tilted his head toward Missoula Milford—"as this charming young man said, mutton for a good meal. Maybe lamb chops for supper. Tasty food."

The door opened at the marshal's cabin. Kit came out. So did Grant Lee, but he just pulled out a chair, set it beside the door, and sat down. Absalom exited the cabin and handed the lawman a rifle. As Lee made himself comfortable, he cradled the rifle over his legs and watched as the old stagecoach driver and the beautiful saloon girl started for the gathering around the strange wagon.

"Problem is, mister," a Peaceful Valley man said, "you're just one person. With a lot of woolies. And the blood from you and your confounded sheep will soon be flowing all the way to the crick down yonder."

Angus MacLerie laughed.

"But, gentlemen, gentlemen, I did not travel all the way from South Texas to Wyoming Territory alone."

One man appeared near where Callahan thought the late rancher Thompson was buried. Sunlight reflected off the rifle he aimed down the slope. Another rose out of the flock, and when he worked the lever on his repeater, the noise reached over the noisy sheep.

The door to the sheepherders wagon cracked open and the barrel of a double barrel shotgun pointed at Missoula Milford's back.

Callahan saw another man step out of the grove of trees along the creek bed. And yet another rose out from about a half dozen *baaaahhing* Mexican Churros at the edge of town.

"Allow me to present to you my sons, Arran, Bram, and Dalziel," Angus MacLerie said. "And two of the finest sheepmen you'll find on this side of the globe. Hipolito Sanchez and Severino de la Baca. They've been working with me for ten years. Cousins. Don't call them Mexicans. They are *Tejanos*. Their fathers both served with Sam Houston when he was winning independence for the Lone Star State from that devil Santa Anna."

The hammer on Missoula Milford's Henry clicked, but Callahan saw that the killer was lowering the hammer. Then he set the stock of the rifle on the ground near his boot, and held the barrel with his right hand. He smiled good-naturedly.

"What about me, Papa?" A redheaded woman with fiery green eyes stepped out from the back of the wagon. She held a long-barreled Colt in her right hand, pointed in the general direction of Iron Tom.

"Ah, indeed," Angus MacLerie said. "Gentlemen, good people of Wyoming, this is my charming and beautiful daughter, Freya."

No one spoke. The only sound for the next two minutes came from the twelve hundred Mexican Churros and the Wyoming wind. Till Job decided to empty his bladder.

Callahan looked off to the north. Cheyenne. He could be in Cheyenne. He could be anywhere. But where was he? Right in the middle of a bunch of ugliness. When he finally got to stand at those Pearly Gates, he would demand to know what the Major General in the Heavens was thinking by putting him, a peace-loving, good-natured sort, in the middle of all these ugly confrontations. He just prayed that that meeting would not be in the next few minutes. Too many good people, along with some folks rotten to the core, could be called to answer alongside Taylor Callahan.

And, yeah, those Mexican Churros sure were pretty looking animals. A lot more handsomer than that silly white gelding called Job.

"Ah, and here comes one of the most beautiful creatures I have ever seen." Angus MacLerie bowed as Kit walked up. Absalom reached toward a lamb, but the frightened animal scurried away from his thick, gnarly hand and did not stop until it was beside its mother.

"Golly," Absalom said. "Them's sure are pretty little things. I ain't never seen nothin' like them afore. Except in storybooks. They look like fluffy pillows with legs."

"More profitable than cattle, too," Angus MacLerie said. "And in country like this, they can make a man a fortune."

"You're on railroad property," Iron Tom said. "This territory is big enough. Find yourself another pasture to turn to ruined earth."

"We like it here."

"You might find yourself buried here."

Angus MacLerie laughed. "Indeed. But for the moment, I think if a fracas were to begin, the first dead man would be you. And when it was all over, all of the dead men would be you good, silly, ignorant people."

"I bet I could snuggle up with one of them critters and sleep a month of Sundays," Absalom said. "They sure is perty."

"What about it, Marshal?" someone said.

Callahan looked at the badge he wore, then down at the cabin where the real lawman kept an eye out from the safety of his cabin. With a rifle across his lap. Shooting uphill. At this range. With this wind. Nope, Angus MacLerie was right.

"Why don't we all just go about our business for this day?" Callahan said. "Let our new sheepherders and their flocks go about their business, and maybe we can have a peaceful, friendly meeting at the marshal's office tomorrow morning." He patted the badge pinned to his coat. "I'm just filling in, Mr. MacLerie, while Peaceful Valley's town marshal recovers from a slight wound."

Angus MacLerie grinned. "I would love to talk to your constable. Why don't we say over breakfast? Freya makes the finest haggis there is. Haggis for breakfast. Haggis for dinner. Haggis for supper. Haggis forever."

"I'm sure we can come to an understanding." Callahan tipped his hat at Freya. "And perhaps you and your children and your employees would like to come hear what I really do for a living—preaching—on Sunday in a few days. Any tithes would be welcome, but not demanded, of course."

"Of course." Angus MacLerie bowed.

"What did you call him?" Kit demanded.

Callahan glanced at the beautiful woman. It took a moment for the question to work through the myriad thoughts bouncing through his brain. "MacLerie," the circuit rider finally answered, and decided to introduce the two. "Angus MacLerie, may I present to you the loveliest blossom in Peaceful Valley, Kit Van Dorn."

The Scotsman bowed.

The saloon girl gasped. "Angus MacLerie! You mean the same sheepherding Angus MacLerie who shot Old Man Thompson dead in Texas all those years ago?"

CHAPTER 28

The sheepman rose from his bow, donned the cap he had flamboyantly removed, and said, "My reputation precedes me." He was calm.

Calmer than most men would act, Callahan thought. *Calmer than he had any right to be.*

Absalom pointed up the hill. "Don't you know who is planted atop that hill, mister?"

"Why, of course I do, my good man," MacLerie said. "John Jacob Thompson. Old Iron Hand himself. After all, I buried him there."

Missoula Milford laughed. "Well, Scotsman, I guess I won't have to bother with killing you and your Mexicans and your sons that smell like sheep dip." He glanced over at Freya and let a lecherous grin cross his face. "And make the acquaintance of your fine lookin' daughter." He turned and started to walk back to camp. "That Thompson kid will kill you, I'm sure. And he's got six or eight cowboys to back his play."

Iron Tom chuckled, and then gingerly began to make his way back to the surveyors camp in the middle of the settlement, the hired men following him. Callahan watched the hired killer, replaying the words Missoula Milford had said a few times, just to make sure he had heard clearly. Then he cleared his throat and called out the assassin's name.

The killer stopped, and slowly turned around.

Callahan let him stare for a moment, then the preacher smiled. "Don't you mean Thompson's *two* sons?"

The man's laugh sounded cold. "Yeah, I reckon so." He turned and took another four steps before Callahan called out his name again.

Missoula Milford just turned his head.

"In case you haven't heard, Walker Thompson is still alive."

The killer's eyes hardened.

Callahan grinned. "You're not the shot you used to be, I reckon."

"I don't know what you're talking about, Preacher."

"Don't you?"

The man let out something between a cough and a grunt. "You'll find out just how good I am with a Henry, Preacher, if you don't watch your mouth. This here is Wyomin' Territory. And the tin stars, the judges, and the juries figure if you insult a man and get killed, why that ain't nothin' more than self-defense."

Callahan nodded. "The thing is," he said, spacing the words the way he had been taught at the seminary at Logan's Knob. "I never insult . . . a *man*."

"Preacher," Absalom said as he limped alongside Callahan and Kit Van Dorn as they walked back to the marshal's office, "you gonna get yourself kilt if you don't watch what you say to a mad-dog hombre." He gestured toward the surveyors camp.

They reached the marshal's office, and Grant Lee leaned the rifle against the wall.

The Mexican Churros *baa'ed* and *baa'ed*—a noise,

Callahan figured, would take some getting used to in that part of the West.

"Nice choir," Lee said, nodding toward Peace Treaty Peak. "How many woolies are there?"

"Angus MacLerie says twelve hundred."

The lawman stiffened. "MacLerie? *Angus MacLerie?*"

Kit nodded. "That's what he says."

"From Texas?" the marshal asked.

"With three sons, a daughter, and two Mexican shepherds," Callahan said.

Staring up at Peace Treaty Peak, Grant Lee whistled and shook his head, before turning to face Callahan. "You got your work cut out for you, *Marshal.*"

Callahan sipped coffee. Grant Lee nursed a coffee cup filled with whiskey. Absalom smoked his pipe. Kit just stared at the hill covered with furry animals on four legs.

"Tell me the story again," the preacher said.

Absalom tapped his pipe on the keg he was sitting on. "In the beginning, God created the heaven and the earth."

"Not that story." Callahan sighed. "I know that story."

"You ought to," Grant Lee said.

"And stop tapping your pipe on that keg. You want to blow us all up to Kingdom Come. Here." Callahan rose, extended his hand. "Get up. You sit on that stump. I'll sit on the gunpowder."

Kit turned around. Grant Lee stared at his coffee cup, tossed out the remaining whiskey and muttered something.

Callahan practically jerked Absalom off the keg and sat down. "I want to hear about Iron Hand Thompson."

The three Peaceful Valley residents stared at one another.

"He was dead before I got here," Kit said.

"Me, too," Grant Lee whispered.

Absalom shrugged. "Harry was the first person to build here." He pointed at the SUPPLYS store.

"Buster told me the late Mr. Thompson platted the town," Callahan said.

"I don't know," Absalom said, "about no plattin', but I do know I wouldn't believe nothin' Buster told nobody. He's a liar."

"I always thought this was open range," the marshal said.

Kit shrugged. Slowly, she started with what she had heard. Absalom filled in a few things he thought he remembered. Lee added what he knew as a lawman.

Iron Hand Thompson drove a herd of cattle from Texas to feed the Union Pacific Construction crews in Cheyenne and Laramie shortly after the War Between the States. He liked what he saw near the peak, so he hired an old mountain man to take him to visit with Stands Firm in an Arapaho camp. They agreed on price—though nobody knew exactly what the price was—and Thompson brought a herd of cattle up the following summer. Or maybe it was two or three summers later. But certainly at least six years ago there was a ranch house and a bunkhouse—or at least a bunkhouse and a dugout—where the main compound of the Thompson spread was. He hired several cowboys to work the cattle, and the Arapaho were allowed a few beeves, more if they were hungry.

"He must have had twenty men working for him," Grant Lee said.

Before Absalom could say something else, Callahan stated, "That's more than they have working for them now."

"Different times," Grant Lee offered. "This country was a whole lot wilder back then."

"And it ain't tame right now," Absalom interjected.

"When did Harry set up his store?" Callahan asked.

"I'd say three, four years ago," Kit answered.

"Four or five," Absalom corrected. "Iron Hand got kilt in Texas in"—he held up his fingers and subtracted digits— "'seventy-two. Yep. That's when he got kilt, so four years ago. Harry was here the year before. But Harry could confirm that. Though his memory is about as shot as Buster's."

"But this town was platted?" Callahan asked.

Grant Lee snorted, and waved his arm around. "Platted like the spread of birdshot in a tornado. Look around, Reverend. Does this town look like it was platted?"

Callahan did not answer. He had seen some towns in Missouri that were supposed to have been platted that looked as scattershot as this village. "If he had title—"

"I don't know about any title. I just took a job here because Mrs. Thompson said we needed a peace officer here." Lee shrugged. "We didn't. Not until Buster and Absalom and the stagecoach wars began three or four months ago." He looked at his empty coffee cup. From what his face revealed, he regretted tossing out that whiskey.

"I'm guessing any records of deeds and such would be at the county seat?"

"County?" Absalom asked. "They's counties in this ter'tory?"

Grant Lee grunted, and rubbed the top of his shoulder, above the bullet wound. "There appears to be some discrepancy as to whether we are in Albany or Laramie County," asked Callahan.

"Railroad'll change that," Kit said.

Lee sighed. "I reckon." He flexed his arm, grimacing from the pain, then looked up at Callahan. "Nobody wants anything to do with Peaceful Valley. They just want the cattle that the Thompsons will sell them."

The old stagecoach driver snorted. "Wonder how they'll take to eatin' mutton?"

Callahan smiled at the joke—if it were a joke—but kept his eyes on the marshal. "If I were looking for land records . . . ?"

Lee waved his good arm. "Cheyenne. Most likely."

"How long would it take me to ride there?"

"On a good horse"—the lawman pondered the question—"six or seven hours. With a smart rider."

Callahan heard the horses snorting in the corral. One of them sounded like it was yawning. "A good horse?" He filled his lungs, shook his head, and exhaled loudly.

The sheep ate and made noises. The wind blew. There seemed to be a bit of excitement in the Three O'd Saloon, but Kit showed no interest in leaving the front of the marshal's office.

"Here's another discrepancy in the stories I've heard," Callahan said, returning back to the story of the life, times, and tragic death of Iron Hand Thompson. "The legend I hear in Peaceful Valley is that the widow Thompson brought the body of their old man from southern Texas to be buried right up there atop Peace Treaty Peak. But the Scotsman said he brought the body here and buried the old man himself."

They turned and looked up at the sheep-covered hill.

"They sure is funny lookin' critters," Absalom said. "Prettier than cattle."

"You think so?" Lee asked.

When no one responded, the lawman said, "What do you think the Arapahos will say when they see twelve hundred head of . . . what did you say they were, Preacher?"

"Mexican Churros," Callahan answered.

"Right. Twelve hundred head of bawling sheep are dropping sheep dip all over the grave of one of the few white men Indians admired and respected and treated justly because he was just with them. And where they want to bury their great chief. How you think the Arapahos will take that?"

"Maybe I ought to head up to Laramie," Kit said. "Buy a ticket to . . . I don't know . . . Rawlings? Sacramento? China?"

Grant Lee shook his head. "This was a peaceful little town for a while." He pushed himself to his feet. "Sure am glad I'm incapacitated and have a couple of deputies filling in for me."

Callahan eyed the lawman, who stared down the road. Then he heard the sound of running horses. Some of the sheep did, too, and started scurrying up the slope. Callahan looked up, then rose.

"Didn't take long for word to spread, did it?" Grant Lee said. "You want me to help you, Preacher?"

Taylor Callahan looked at the lawman. From the corner of his eye, he saw Kit, her face pleading, hopeful.

Callahan shook his head. "You need to nurse that shoulder. We'll take care of this."

"We?" Absalom's face paled.

"Come on, Deputy." Callahan grinned.

Knight Thompson had brought just one cowboy with him. Callahan reckoned he could thank the Major General in the Heavens for that. Holding his hand up straight, he breathed a bit easier when the young riders reined up, stopping their horses in front of him and a nervous Absalom, who kept rubbing his thighs and groaning about all the aches and injuries he had suffered of late.

"Where's the man who gunned down my pa?" Knight asked.

"How's your brother?" Callahan inquired easily.

"About the same. Where's MacLerie?"

Callahan took a few steps, and held out his left hand, palm down, under the flaring nostrils of the roan gelding Knight sat atop. The horse eyed him with suspicion, snorted, and shook its head. Callahan then looked at the bay the thirty-a-month cowhand rode. "You got pretty good horses, son. Both of you."

"Quit stalling, Preacher," Knight said. "We're here to kill Angus MacLerie."

Callahan nodded. "I need good horses." He gestured toward the corral. "I have a horse. But Job is not what I would call . . . a good horse. I'd like to rent these two horses from you. Give you half of the tithes I collect when I preach on Sunday."

The cowboy chuckled. "You gonna ride like the Romans? A foot on the back of each hoss? You don't look like you could do that too good, Sky Pilot."

Callahan smiled good-naturedly. "No, sonny. I pull one horse behind me. So I don't wear either of them out. I'm off to Cheyenne. And you two"—the smile faded—"are under arrest."

He let out the Rebel cry like he was riding with Carbine Logan—high-pitched, squealing, the sound of a hundred wild demons from the deepest and most savage pits of Hades. He raised his arms over his head and waved them back and forth. Yelling, his eyes were wild as he moved between the horses.

The cowboy reached for the horn, but Callahan grabbed the cinch and jerked it. The bay was starting to buck, and the cowboy felt the saddle slide. He dived off.

"Grab the reins, Absalom!" Callahan roared, slamming into the neck of the frightened roan that carried Knight Thompson. The bay disappeared from Callahan's view. He heard Absalom shout something, but the snorting horses, and pounding hooves cut off most of it. So did Knight's curses and grunts as the roan arched its back. Callahan stumbled into the boy's left leg, which sent his spurs raking against the horse's flesh.

That ended the ride for Knight Thompson. He pitched over the left and hit the ground. The roan took off toward Peace Treaty Peak. The sheep bawled loudly. Hooves pounded.

Callahan stepped where the roan had been standing, spotted young Thompson coming to his knees and reaching for the holstered revolver. Callahan reached him in an instant, and let his right boot do the rest of the work. It caught the kid under the jaw. Teeth snapped. The boy grunted and fell on his back while his revolver spiraled a few feet to his right.

Callahan looked over his shoulder for just a second. He estimated how much time he had. The cowboy was coming up. Absalom was running after the horse. The sheep were running from the roan. MacLerie's shepherds, sons and daughter were trying to stop the sheep from taking off to, oh, Montana Territory perhaps.

Spotting Knight Thompson's revolver, Callahan bent, snatched it up, and then saw the kid coming to his knees. Callahan swung the Colt, heard the barrel pound into the boy's skull. Those gentle eyes glazed over as the boy fell, while in the same motion, Callahan spun around, dropped to a knee, and thumbed back the hammer of Thompson's revolver.

The cowhand who rode for the Thompson brand was just getting his gun leveled when Callahan bellowed, "Don't rush your own demise, sonny!"

CHAPTER 29

"What is it . . ." Angus MacLerie said again, ". . . that ye want me to do?"

Callahan sighed. He thought his explanation was satisfactory and clear. Pointing to the small stone building just past the corral behind the marshal's cabin, the circuit rider said, "You see that jail?"

MacLerie stared. "Ye call that a jail? But I dunno see a door?"

"It fell down." Callahan tried to sum everything up in a hurry. "Listen, as the deputy marshal of Peaceful Valley—till Marshal Lee has recovered enough to resume his duties—I'm putting these two knuckleheaded hotheads in the jail."

"That jail?" The Scotsman laughed.

"Well, sir, I don't reckon I can take them to the territorial prison in Laramie till after a trial." Of course, Callahan did not think any trial would be necessary. But he had to keep the young Thompson lad from starting a range war or killing somebody—which might result in a hanging instead of a prison sentence in Laramie—or a more likely scenario, getting himself killed.

Callahan looked at the crumbling building. It would hold Knight Thompson and the cowhand. Well, it would keep them dry from the rain—if it ever rained—and maybe keep most of the dust the wind kept blowing from dirtying them up a mite. The roof hadn't caved in yet. There could be some snakes nesting inside, but he had seen cowboys pop the heads of rattlesnakes with their lariats, so a diamondback or two wouldn't scare a good waddie. The grass growing around that shack was good and high. In fact, one could mistake that part of town as an overgrown English garden.

"I want you to surround the jail with your sheep," Callahan told MacLerie again.

"All my Churros?"

Callahan's head shook. "Not all of them. Of course not." He had heard that sheep could mow through a prairie closer than one of old Cyrus McCormick's mechanical reapers. He bit his lip, looked at the four-legged furry critters grazing up and down Peace Treaty Peak. "Fifty ought to be enough."

The Scotsman cackled. "You know, laddie . . . padre, bishop, reverend, rector, deacon, monk, sky pilot, friar, whatever you want to be called . . . my sheep are sturdy and strong, but they are not as intimidating as a mountain lion or a grizzly bear or a burly man with a sawed-off twelve gauge and murder in his black eyes and blacker heart."

"You can call me Callahan. Those sheep will bawl or run around, if either that kid or his hired cowboy, step out of that shed," Callahan said. "And that will alert my guard." He turned and pointed at Absalom.

The old codger's eyes widened, and his mouth moved up and down but no words came out for a couple of seconds. "But . . . but . . . but . . ." was all that came out.

Standing next to the stagecoach driver, Marshal Grant Lee scratched his head. He looked at the shed, then at the sheep, then at the two Thompson riders, still unconscious. "It might work. We can spell each other on guard duty. Might need a third man."

"Ye'll have one," MacLerie said. "I'll have one of me laddies down here to mind my fifty sheep." He scratched his chin, studying the town. "Nay. I'll make it seventy-five. There's enough fresh grass for seventy-five, me thinks." He looked back at Callahan. "How long will ye be gone, Marshal Preacher?"

"With luck, I'm back tomorrow."

MacLerie laughed. "Preacher, I admire ye faith. But you dinnae look like the type of man who can ride to Cheyenne and back in a day." He laughed.

"If I were riding my own horse"—Callahan was walking away—"I'd say you were right. But I think these two Thompson mounts can do the job just fine."

He caught up the roan and held the reins in his left hand, then mounted the bay. The stirrups were a bit on the short side, but he was not going to take the time to loosen them. They were laced-up stirrups, and he did not have the hours it would take him to lower them.

"Killer of Ten Crows says he'll be back by Saturday," Absalom reminded him.

"I know."

"Tomorrow's Friday," Marshal Lee said.

"I know that, too."

"You haven't told us what you expect to find in Cheyenne."

"Likely," Absalom said, "a ticket to Omaha."

Callahan smiled, pulled his hat down tight, and kicked the bay into a walk.

The horses had been ridden hard from the Thompson ranch, so Callahan figured the best way to get to Cheyenne and back was to walk the horses for a couple of miles.

After that, he reined up in a dip, out of the wind, and let the animals relieve themselves. He dismounted, tightened the cinches, checked both horses, and examined all four hooves on each animal, then walked both horses up the hill before he swung into the saddle on the bay again.

Unlike Job, the bay horse ran. It was a smooth gait, too, and Callahan gave the gelding its head as he wrapped the roan's reins around his hand. Wind pushed the brim of his Boss of the Plains up, but the Stetson remained firm on his head. He found the rhythm of a running horse exciting.

He had not been much of a rider—not growing up on a farm—and while he had ridden horses as a young teen and growing man, no one would have ever called him a *caballero muy grande*.

The war had changed that. The war had changed everything.

It had been a long time since he had ridden a horse like that—galloped without the reins in his teeth and two revolvers in his hand, shooting at Yankee soldiers. Rode without expecting death at any moment, his death or the death of the soldiers he would kill. He felt . . . invigorated. And he remembered a time before the blood and flames and ruination of a land, a time when he and Karen had ridden together.

"I bet I can beat you to the creek," she said.

"On that nag?" He laughed.

"What would you care to bet?"

"Gambling is a sin?"

She smiled. "Chapter and verse, Reverend?"

He laughed. "Gambling is the child of avarice, the brother of iniquity, and the father of mischief."

She reined in her sorrel and stopped the dun.

"Proverbs?" she asked.

He laughed. "George Washington. Or so I was told. In a

tavern. On my journey to ruin. He was a professor—the man who used the quote—and it sure did sound like something George Washington would have said. Certainly not many of my daddies."

"You're silly. I'll beat you."

She did. He let her, of course, but he lost nothing in the wager. In fact, he was rewarded with her laughter, and the life in her eyes after she splashed across the creek and reined up underneath the maple tree.

The hills were not too steep. The path—nobody, not even a farm kid from Clay County, Missouri, would call it a pike, road, or even a marked trail—remained fairly easy to follow. He moved from trot to canter, which always felt like poetry (unless he was riding Job).

Callahan stopped again between two hills where he spied a small creek running from the mountains. He was sweating, but the animals appeared to be fine. Cowponies, he had heard, were tough little critters, wiry, more mustang than anything else. They weren't thoroughbreds for sure, but they could cover some ground when they had to.

Taylor Callahan figured they had to.

He let the animals cool before he led them to the creek, and while they drank, he moved upstream, dropped to his belly, and leaned into the cold, mountain water. He drank, then came to his knees, scooping water in his hands and bathing his face, his forehead, his throat, and neck. He drank again, but did not want to drink too much—or let the horses get fat and full.

After pulling on his hat, he grabbed the reins to the bay, then the roan, and led them away from the water.

He let the animals rest a minute—and he rested, too, rubbing his backside and his thighs, and stretching his shoulders. A hawk—or maybe it was a falcon—soared overhead. The sky remained azure, cloudless. He figured he could

reach Cheyenne in the night, find a kindhearted man who
ran a livery stable who would let him bed the horses down
and give him a stall to sleep in, then get to work when businesses opened in the morning. It would be up to the Major
General in the Heavens—not to mention the clerks in the
land office—but he should be able to return to Peaceful
Valley by late tomorrow evening.

What happened the day after that depended on what he
learned in Cheyenne.

Both horses looked up the hill to the northeast. Their ears
perked, and the roan whinnied.

Callahan listened, but heard just the wind. He looked at
the saddlebags. And he could hear the Major General in the
Heavens laughing.

*Preacher, you rode with Carbine Logan long enough to
know that you ride your own saddle. How long would it have
taken you to take the saddle off ol' Job and put it on that
bay? The stirrups would suit you to a T. Oh, no, Reverend,
don't look at that saddlebag. Don't even look at the saddlebags on the roan. Your .45-caliber Peacemaker, is back yonder in Peaceful Valley. Where you left it.*

*Sure, sure, go ahead and look. There's a chance a cow
puncher who works for thirty dollars a month and found it
might have a pistol in one of them pouches. But my money
would be on some coffee, maybe a biscuit no more than a
week old, folded up slicker or something, maybe some doctoring medicine for cows and calves and bulls.*

He saw the scabbards, though, and the stock of a Winchester. That was on Knight Thompson's horse. The hired
hand's saddle had no scabbard, but there were lariats hanging from both horns.

Yeah, that's a great idea, Reverend. The Major General in
the Heavens started to laugh. *I bet you can rope whoever it is
that's riding up that slope right now. This is gonna be fun to
watch, Callahan. Mighty fun.*

Callahan went between the two animals, and grabbed the

reins instead of the Winchester. He could hear the hooves of horses and the clanking of metal. The metal meant the horses were not wild mustangs. He knew that sound. Sabers in scabbards. Maybe carbines.

He was not surprised to see black hats, yellow scarves, blue blouses and sun- and wind-burned faces of cavalrymen appear at the top of the ridge.

They saw him, too.

The commander held up a right hand covered by a pale yellow gauntlet. The horsemen stopped atop the ridge. One man reached for the carbine, but the commander—a lean, wisp of a man with sandy hair and a thick mustache and goatee—barked an order. Other riders appeared now, forming a line on either side of the men who had first appeared.

"Yankees." Callahan breathed in and out, sweating even more. There was a time, a dozen years ago, when Callahan would have filled his hands with revolvers and blasted his way out of such a ticklish situation or wound up facing a smiling Satan. He tried to tell himself that not all Yankees were bad men. He recalled the bedraggled commander of the Union forces at New Jerusalem, Missouri, a burned-out wreck of a town, back in '64. The officer from Indiana had let Taylor Callahan ride out on his own, unharmed. It was then Callahan had made his vow that he would live by the Word—the True Word—and not the word Confederates and Unionists proclaimed. He would live the way he thought men and women should live. *In peace.*

Well, he had to concede, he had stumbled a time or two.

Four men rode down the hill, including the officer in command. About a dozen or more stayed atop, all pulling up their carbines and bracing the stocks against their thighs in a show of force.

Callahan ran his right finger around the collar of his shirt, stained with sweat and grime, and thought about how much easier things would be had he become Catholic, or some other religion that turned a holy man's collar around. Dead giveaway. See that white collar and you know what that man was.

See a circuit rider from Logan's Knob Seminary and you didn't know exactly what you were getting.

"Who are you and what is your business here?" shouted the officer, a lieutenant if Callahan read the number of bars correctly.

"Callahan," came an easy answer, somehow not sounding like the frog that was stuck in his throat. "Taylor Callahan. I'm a circuit rider. Preaching the Word. The Good Word. Just came from Peaceful Valley by way of Virginia Dale and Poudre City. Heading to my next Sunday-go-to-meeting . . . in Cheyenne." He removed his hat and bowed. "But I can sure take time to preach and sing some to you soldiers, dedicated to peace and justice, and loyal to all citizens of our United States and her territories. Maybe sing a hymn or two. Tithes are purely at your own discretion, of course."

Two rifles came to shoulders, and Callahan heard the distinct *clickings* of hammers being pulled to full cock. The troopers stopped their horses.

The man in charge pushed back his slouch hat. "Where did you say you came from?" the lieutenant asked.

"Peaceful Valley," Callahan managed to say.

"On two horses?" the lieutenant asked.

"I was told there's a real fine blacksmith in Cheyenne," Callahan said, thinking that one little white lie could be forgiven.

The faces and the rifle barrels informed Callahan otherwise.

"Preacher," the lieutenant said. "You're coming with us."

CHAPTER 30

Taylor Callahan rode between two troopers up and down a few hills until they reached a tent city. Well, a tent town. *City* was on the generous side. Sibley tents had been erected, and a makeshift corral had been established to hold the horses and mules. A guidon fluttered in the wind behind one tent, and for a moment, Callahan wondered if it might be the fort, Centennial, that had been established. But something told him otherwise.

No campfires. No cookfires. And when one of the soldiers ahead of him started to light his pipe, the lieutenant rebuked him. "You heard the major's orders."

Grumbling, the soldier stuck his pipe back in a pocket on his dark blue blouse.

The lieutenant ordered Callahan and the patrol to stop when they reached the corrals. "Dismount."

On the ground, Callahan was shoved aside as soldiers grabbed the reins to the two Thompson mounts and led them into the corral with the cavalry mounts.

"Give them both a good rubdown, my friends," Callahan

called out cheerily. "Perhaps a double helping of oats. We have a long ride to Cheyenne." He smiled at the lieutenant.

The young officer did not smile back. Nor did he lower the barrel of his Remington revolver. "To the Sibley," he said, nodding behind Callahan. "You'll speak to Major Dance."

Callahan turned and found the Sibley tent. He didn't see many soldiers, but had not Marshal Grant told him that Fort Centennial was just a subpost? The fort was only a mile and a half out of town, and if the commanding major had left on some sort of mission, he had not gone very far from his starting point.

He saw the artillery—two mountain howitzers and two Gatling guns. Soldiers honed their bayonets and sabers with whetstones. No cigarettes. No lanterns. No campfires. Those he saw drinking used canteens. Callahan looked around the hills. They would be well shielded . . . but why were they there?

The major was stepping through the canvas opening when Callahan and the lieutenant reached the tent.

The lieutenant saluted, almost pounding the barrel of the .44 against his temple. "Sir," he said when he recovered. "We found this man riding from Peaceful Valley to Cheyenne. Leading one horse."

The major was a short fellow, stout for a cavalry man, but with the cannons and Gatling guns, maybe he was artillery. Callahan couldn't tell for sure. The man wore buckskin britches and a red silk shirt. His blouse with his insignia must have been in the tent. He was balding, with a crooked nose, wrinkled forehead, and well-groomed mustache and pointed goatee, both showing more gray hairs than black ones.

"I don't believe I know you, mister," the major said in an accent Callahan could not place.

Callahan tested his warmest smile. "The Reverend Taylor

Callahan, Major. Circuit-riding preacher—no denomination—spreading the Word and the News to all who are willing to listen. I've been in Peaceful Valley, and now I'm riding to Cheyenne."

"On two horses," the lieutenant reminded the major.

Callahan nodded. "The good souls of Peaceful Valley were generous with their tithes."

"Both horses wore Thompson brands," the lieutenant said.

The major looked over Callahan's shoulder at the lieutenant, then stroked his pointed beard. "You in any particular hurry to get to Cheyenne, Reverend?" the major asked.

"There are souls that need saving," Callahan answered, "and who knows how much time those poor creatures have left on this world?"

"How'd you find this camp?"

Callahan paused. That wasn't a question he expected. "I didn't find this camp, Major. I was riding to Cheyenne and ran into your lieutenant here and his patrol. They brought me here."

The eyes went past Callahan's shoulder again. "Mr. Mason?"

"He looked suspicious, sir," came a feeble answer.

"So you brought him *here*?"

Lieutenant Mason stammered.

"See to your men, Mason. Remind them of my orders. Then report back here in thirty minutes. That is all, Lieutenant." The chastised young sapling snapped a salute the major did not return, then turned sharply and hurried back to the corral. The major took a step back, pulled open the flap, and smiled.

"Officers from West Point aren't what they used to be, Reverend. Please step inside my humble abode. You, I hope, can be of service to the United States Army and the people of Wyoming Territory."

* * *

Callahan declined the rye whiskey the major poured, but accepted a cup of coffee. Cold coffee. It probably had been brewed two or three days ago from the taste, and he sat on a folding wood-and-canvas chair while the major sat on the edge of a wooden table that could also be folded.

"What is the situation at Peaceful Valley, Reverend?" the major asked as he opened a box and pulled out two cigars, putting one in his mouth, and handing the other to Callahan.

Again, Callahan shook his head.

"The situation?" the major repeated.

It was odd, Callahan thought, that the officer had not introduced himself.

"Situation?" Callahan did not have to act confused. He did not know what the Yankee meant.

"We heard that the stagecoach station was burned down by Indians," the major said.

"Indians?"

"Arapaho," came the answer, "to be precise. Led by that butchering Stands Firm." The major stopped to light his cigar, flicking away the match when the tip glowed orange, then chasing the taste of smoke with some strong rye whiskey. "Stands Firm aims to join up with Sitting Bull."

Callahan managed to blink. "Nobody mentioned Indians or Arapahos or Stands Firm when I got to town, Major."

"When did you get to Peaceful Valley?"

"The night the station burned," Callahan answered. "But—"

"These are perilous times," the major interrupted. "I take it you have met the railroad surveyors under Thomas Aldridge."

Somehow *Thomas Aldridge* did not quite fit Iron Tom. But, well, nobody had a say in what handle their parents put on them.

"I've met his acquaintance." Callahan rubbed the knuckles on his right hand.

"The territory of Wyoming needs this railroad. The Arapa-hos are out to stop it."

Callahan breathed in and out. He said nothing.

Just then the flap opened, and a red-bearded man in buck-skins stepped inside, saw Callahan and straightened in sur-prise, then spotted the major. "Beggin' yer pardon—"

"Don't you know how to knock, Culbertson?" the major bellowed.

The man spit on the grass carpet. "Didn't think ye would hear it on yer cloth door."

Callahan thought the major would die from apoplexy and the scout appeared to enjoy his joke, but quickly got down to business. "I did figger you might want to know there's about a million sheep atop Peace Treaty Peak right now."

"What?"

Callahan thought the major would keel over dead.

"Sheep. Tons of 'em. Got one of them sheep wagons. You know. On wheels with a chimney stickin' out top. Grazin' up and down that no-count hill. Five, six men. I think."

"Sheep?" The major gulped down his whiskey.

"That's what I been tellin' you, ain't it. *Baa-baa-baaaaaaa.* Sheep!"

The major looked at Callahan. "Is this true?"

He decided to be honest. "Twelve hundred Mexican Churros. On Peace Treaty Peak."

"What are the Thompsons doing about this outrage?"

Callahan decided not to be honest. "They don't mind." He cleared his throat. "That's a myth, you know. That sheep and cattle don't get along. That sheepmen and ranchers can't get along. Remember in Genesis, when Jacob's working for Laban, we read about brown cattle, speckled cattle, spotted cattle and they're milling right among the sheep—'and of such shall be my hire.'" He smiled. "Did you see any goats on that hill, mister?"

The major picked up the whiskey bottle but did not

bother with the cup. He drank several swallows, then wiped his mouth, and stared at the canvas behind Callahan. "Has Aldridge and his men started setting markers for the tracks?"

"No. Don't look like it. If he had, I'd reckon the sheep might have knocked down any stakes."

"Sheep!" The bottle slammed on the table. "Confound it." But just like that the major's eyes showed a spark. "Maybe not. Maybe everything will work. Barbarity. Sheep. Sheep massacred. That could play to our advantage."

Callahan decided the major was out of his mind, and if he asked the scout for his educated opinion, the verdict would likely be the same. He stood. "Well, gentlemen, this has been a right social gatherin', but my flock awaits me in Cheyenne. I bid you both a mighty fine evening."

He had reached the flap when he heard the cock of the major's revolver.

No gunshot followed. So that was a good sign. Silently thanking the Major General in the Heavens, Callahan turned around.

"I'm afraid, Pastor, that we will need your company." The gun waved. Callahan gave a feeble shrug and stepped back inside the tent.

"Culbertson," the major said, "step outside. Holler for Lieutenant Mason."

When the officer entered the tent, the major aimed his revolver at Callahan. "This preacher—if he is actually one—has decided to put roots in this valley, Lieutenant, if you get my meaning."

The young kid did, because his face blanched.

"You and Culbertson will take care of him. But do not let any of the men see this. They might lose their faith."

"How do you want it done?" the scout asked.

The head shook. "That is your world, Culbertson. I am a soldier for the United States of America. I have my duty. You have yours."

Ever the good host, the major slipped behind the scout and held the tent flap open for the two men and the condemned preacher to walk into the gloaming.

Two troopers rode up to the corral, then dismounted, and Lieutenant Mason called out, "Karl, Spacey! Leave your mounts saddled. Culbertson and I have a mission for the major."

"Won't get no argument from us," Karl, or Spacey, called back, punched his companion on the shoulder good-naturedly, and then they walked to a cold camp where a handful of troopers were rolling dice before the sun's last glows faded and left the men and the camp in darkness.

Darkness. No smoke. No lanterns. They wanted to be hidden.

"How we gonna do this?" Culbertson asked.

"That's your job. I'm an officer. I don't—" He could not finish the sentence.

Callahan wasn't one to beg, but he figured it would not be cowardly to make a suggestion. "You could just let me go. I am riding to Cheyenne. That's where I was going when I ran into you boys."

The lieutenant snorted. "Your bad luck. The major's got a grand plan here. If you think Custer is going to be in all the newspapers after he wipes out the Sioux, wait till you see how big my name is."

They had reached the two horses, cavalry mounts, McClellan saddles.

"I could cut his throat," Culbertson said, "but horses will balk at the blood."

"Just knock him out." The lieutenant grinned at Callahan and said as though that would make death come easier. "It'll be better that way. You'll be asleep. Won't even feel a thing."

Callahan drew in a deep breath, exhaled, and made his head move up and down. His Adam's apple moved, and he said, "Boys, I am a preacher. And I know this is none of your doing. That you are good soldiers to our country, and must obey your commanding officers. I will be glad to stand before my Master and walk the Streets of God. But—" His voice caught. "Will you . . . ?" He sniffed. "Would you just grant a condemned soul's last request? Join me . . . in a . . . real . . . quick . . . prayer." He extended his arms, brought them around each man's shoulders.

And slammed their skulls together.

It sounded like a gunshot. The men dropped. The horses balked. One of the dice rollers yelled out, "What the—"

Callahan grabbed the far side of the tiny saddle and ran alongside the frightened animal. He heard a gunshot. Felt the hot air as the slug flew past his neck and over the horse's back. Once in Missouri, in St. Joe, before the war broke out, he had watched a rider—one of those orphan boys working for Russell, Majors, and Waddell's Pony Express—do a running mount. The crowd had cheered him on, and even Taylor Callahan had muttered, "Amen, and Godspeed, son!"

Watching it one time, sixteen years ago, was one thing. The horse was at a canter, and Callahan was running alongside him.

Another shot whined off a stone.

Someone behind him screamed out profanity that would make a sailor blush, then commanded, "Hold your fire!"

Callahan was running at the same pace. He pictured that Pony Express kid, who was a whole lot thinner, faster, younger, and experienced. He knew he would have one chance. Miss—and he was dead.

He landed on both feet, then pushed himself up. The legs went over his head, he felt himself moving. His head came up, and he knew he was in the saddle.

If any self-respecting man called a McClellan a saddle.

His boots found the stirrups, he gathered the reins, and he let the horse break into a hard gallop. Up the hill.

More shots rang out. He thought he heard the major's curses and orders.

There was no horn to hang on to. Another thing Callahan disliked about Yankee saddles. He leaned low, the wind whipping his face, watching the grass sweep past him. Then he knew he was riding downhill. He came up, got a better handle on the reins but did not slow down the horse.

He figured the Major General in the Heavens was looking after him. The other horse had taken off, too. He was running about fifty yards ahead of Callahan.

Callahan leaned forward, finding the right rhythm. He had a little bit of daylight left. "Come on," he urged his purloined horse. "Let's catch up to your friend yonder."

He was riding a good horse, but he still would need two mounts to get to Cheyenne. And he would have to ride doubly hard. That crazy army commander was certain to send some bluebellies after him.

CHAPTER 31

The first man appeared at the top of the hill, moving slowly, taking a few steps before stopping and kneeling, his left hand touching the ground, feeling the blades of grass, then the head rose and he scanned the land that stretched down and then up, undulating like ocean waves.

He came to his feet and began the descent.

By now, the moon was up, and though not full, the stars of the Milky Way and other galaxies, stars, and planets lighted the Wyoming landscape enough to see. It wasn't as bright as day, as some dime novelist might write, but it was a long way from pitch black.

Riders came over the ridge next, but just two of them, though the trailing man pulled a pinto pony behind him. The pinto belonged to the tracker, and as the tracker moved slowly down the hill, Taylor Callahan reckoned him to be an Indian.

Pawnee, the circuit rider guessed. One of the residents in Virginia Dale had mentioned the army often used Pawnees as scouts when they could. Farther north, in Montana, the soldier boys employed Crows, but in Wyoming Territory,

Pawnees were more likely to be hired. Pawnees did not care a whit for Arapahos, and Arapahos did not care a whit for Pawnees. They mixed like Kansans and Missourians. Or Texans and anybody else.

Callahan hid in the thicket that grew in the flats along the creek bed. He lay on his belly, keeping the Spencer carbine aimed in the general direction of the two soldiers and the scout. The Major General in the Heavens had looked after the preacher. Callahan had figured the carbine in the scabbard on the horse he had purloined—he did not want to use the word *stolen*, for the time being, at least—would be a single-shot Springfield. But to his liking, he found a repeater. A repeating carbine that packed a wallop.

He had left his horse on the far side of the thicket. Having thrown a shoe, the mount wasn't going anywhere. With his horse a bit west and the wind blowing south, Callahan hoped neither that horse nor the three coming down the hill would catch any scent.

They might not . . . as long as the wind did not change directions.

The Pawnee scout was a cautious type. Taking his own sweet time.

Callahan looked up the hill. Three men. He might be able to handle that, but if a patrol appeared . . . if this was just a scouting party for a whole lot of bluebellies, then the game was up. And Callahan would be standing before Saint Peter in a jiffy.

The Pawnee stopped. The two soldiers nudged their horses and did not rein up until they were a few feet behind him. The bearded one stuck a cigar in his mouth and struck a match against the carbine in the scabbard and brought it up to the cigar.

"Good," the Pawnee grunted. "White man see your ugly face better to blow it off."

The match shook out quickly, and the soldier said, "You think he's around here?"

"Maybe so."

The clean-shaven soldier stood in his stirrups and looked around, even looked right over where Callahan lay flat. "In those woods?" the trooper's voice squeaked out.

The flowing creek bubbled. Somewhere off in the distance, a wolf greeted the moon.

Callahan shifted his eyes and studied the hill. Nothing to see, except a heavy cloud heading toward the moon.

"Man wouldn't stop," the bearded soldier said. "He'd be riding to save his hide." He found another match and struck it.

Callahan knew he couldn't hold out there forever. "Hands up, boys." He didn't shout, fearing the echo and not knowing how close any other soldiers—or Pawnee scouts might be—but he certainly made sure his voice was heard. "I've got a Spencer on you."

Only the Pawnee did not move.

The match again was shook out as the bearded man spit out his cigar and reached for the stock of the carbine.

The clean-shaven lieutenant barked, "Don't be a fool, Banks!" His left hand dropped the hackamore to the Pawnee's pony, and slapped down on the bearded man's hand. "He ain't bluffing."

The pinto horse turned and trotted off a few yards.

The Pawnee still did not move.

"Hands up," Callahan ordered again, and was relieved when all six arms stretched toward the moon. Slowly, he rose, keeping the Spencer pointed in the general direction of the three men. He took one more look up the hill, and then walked slowly toward his pursuers.

A Navy Colt .36 was stuck inside the Indian's buckskin britches.

"Lose the hardware," Callahan said. "But be real careful."

The revolver was pulled out.

"Throw it toward the creek," Callahan said.

The Indian obeyed.

"Same with the knife."

Again, the Pawnee did as he was told.

Callahan kept the Spencer steady.

"Your turn," he told the bearded man. "Pull out the long gun." It was a Springfield, standard army issue. "Eject the cartridge." The man complied. "Give it a big heave."

It landed a few feet away, but the noise caused the pinto horse to trot off a bit farther toward the bottom of the hill the riders had descended.

"Side arm?" Callahan did not see one.

The man's head shook.

"You?" Callahan turned the barrel slightly toward the clean-shaven one.

He withdrew his carbine from the scabbard, ejected the cartridge, and pitched the Springfield to land a few feet near the bearded man's weapon.

"How many others are after me?" Callahan asked.

"Just us," the clean-shaven soldier said. "The major figured Squaw Killer would be enough." He gestured at the Pawnee.

Callahan considered that. He wasn't sure he believed the shavetail, but didn't have any time left for argument or debate. "All right. You first." He waved the barrel of the Spencer at the clean-shaven trooper. "Dismount."

He glanced at the cloud and let out a silent thank-you to the Major General in the Heavens. It would slip right underneath the moon, giving him enough light to maybe get out of this ticklish situation alive. "Walk toward those long guns."

The young soldier did as he was told.

"Pick up the first Springfield. Then jam it into the dirt as hard as you can, barrel-first."

That was done just as Callahan asked.

"Now the second."

The kid was good at obeying orders with a .56-50 rimfire aimed in his general direction.

"Your turn," Callahan told the bearded man, who sighed and dismounted.

"Any one of you three want to tell me what the devil this crazy major of yours is doing?"

They did not answer.

"He was going to have me murdered." Callahan brought the rifle up to his shoulder and aimed it directly at the clean-shaven young man. "I am a *minister*. I was doing absolutely nothing wrong. The army is not supposed to go around ordering the execution of any civilian without a trial. Not a military tribunal. But a trial by the territorial court." He wasn't exactly sure about the veracity of his statement, but it wasn't likely two troopers or a Pawnee scout would put up any argument.

"We don't know." To Callahan's surprise, it was the bearded man who answered. "Old Iron Butt ordered us from Fort Centennial. Said we were gonna show the world we could whip any redskins as good as Custer's boys."

Callahan looked at the Pawnee. "How about you?"

The Indian looked like a bronze statue.

"All right. The three of you walk through the creek and through the woods," Callahan said. "You'll find a horse there. Don't ride him. He lost a shoe, and I don't want him to go lame."

When they were past him but not yet to the creek, he ordered the three men to stop and turn around.

He let them watch as he gathered the reins to the black-bearded man's horse before mounting the clean-shaven trooper's bay. Sticking the reins to the bay in his mouth, he wrapped the reins to the other mount tightly around his left hand and raised the Spencer carbine in his right.

"You're gonna shoot us down," the bearded man said, his voice rising a few octaves. "Murder us in cold blood. You don't have to do that. We ain't gonna do you no harm."

Keeping the Spencer aimed in the vicinity of the three men, Callahan asked, "What's that fort's name? The one in

Cheyenne?" He hoped the men could understand since he was speaking with his mouth full of leather.

"Russell," the clean-shaven one answered. "D.A. Russell."

The dark-bearded man stopped bawling like a newborn calf.

Nodding, Callahan spit out the reins. He wanted to make sure the soldiers understood him clearly. "If you boys want to be heroes, living heroes, you ought to walk to Fort Russell, D.A. Russell, instead of heading back to that camp where your major is planning something that is likely gonna land him before a general court-martial and firing squad. Tell the commander what's going on. I have a notion nobody knows about the campaign you have been ordered to take part in . . . except your martinet of a major. And maybe some railroad surveyors." He figured the three men weren't going to attack him now.

He needed three or four hands as the Spencer went into the scabbard, the reins he had spit out went back into his mouth, the carbine came back out of the scabbard and the stock braced against Callahan's thigh, the barrel pointing at the stars above.

He touched the trigger.

The .56-50 rimfire kicked hard. Callahan knew he'd have a right big bruise on that thigh, and he saw the Indian's pinto bolting up the ridge. He hoped the bluebelly wasn't lying, that no other scouting patrols were in the vicinity, but he did not want the Pawnee to catch up to that pinto. He might enjoy taking part in some premeditated massacre.

Besides, Callahan had his hands full. His horse was galloping toward the next hill, the trailing gelding trying to pull his left shoulder out of the socket. Somehow, he managed to not drop the Spencer and get it back into the scabbard. That freed up his right hand and allowed him to get those nasty-tasting reins out of his mouth.

Taylor Callahan felt the night wind in his face as he

crested the hill. He did not look back at the Pawnee scout and the two soldiers.

And he did not hear the Indian say, "He no ride like paleface preacher."

Callahan realized the brilliance of the Major General in the Heavens, or as nonbelievers might put it, his own dumb luck. He was mounted on a horse that belonged to the United States Cavalry, and was pulling another gelding belonging to the same outfit—animals that had to cover great distances, that were used to hard rides. The horse he rode ran like he was born to gallop. It had some Arabian blood, probably mixed with a thoroughbred—certainly not a cowpony like the Thompsons owned, good for a short burst of speed, and could run fast over a quarter mile or so. A rider had to remember not to run a cowpony too hard and too fast for too long.

On the other hand, Callahan was not stupid. Only an idiot would ride a horse at a gallop for too long. He reined in, gave the horse a breather, and let it walk for a while, then dismounted and tried the other horse, starting it off at a walk as well, then letting it pick up the pace into a trot.

He kept that up, alternating horses, and when the path he followed showed more use, became wider, the ruts deeper from wagon wheels and the hooves of horses, mules, oxen, he turned off the road. He could be wrong about everything. More importantly, the major from Fort Centennial might have sent a galloper ahead. The local boys had to know of short cuts and other ways to reach Cheyenne.

Seeing the smoke from the city, he circled around as dawn began breaking in soft but mesmerizing colors off to the east. He crossed the railroad tracks west of town, kept a wide loop until he found an arroyo—though in that part of the country it was called a coulee. He placed his Boss of the

Plains on the ground, and emptied one of the canteens inside the crown.

The horses had not been ridden hard for a while, so he let the first one drink, then let the second one finish.

He jerked the second one's head away when it nuzzled the brim of the black hat. "You eat grass," Callahan said. "Not my Stetson."

The hat returned to his head, and though it smelled like horses, the coolness from the wet fur revived him. Next, he removed the saddles and bridles, then checked the saddlebags to see if he might have any luck.

Hardtack. A box of shells for the Spencer. A map of the territory that might come in handy, so he folded that up and stuck it in the Prince Albert's inside pocket. A pencil and a note pad, the pages new and clean. He kept that, as well.

No orders of any kind, but that would have been a surprise.

Carbine Logan had not believed in written orders. "Written orders," he once said, "can get men killed if they wind up in the wrong hands. And written orders could get me hung."

Callahan drank from the second canteen, finding nothing in the other saddlebags except a five-dollar gold piece, a tintype of a pretty girl, and a bowl. He accepted the money as a tithe, and prayed the pretty girl would change the wrongful ways of either the clean-shaven or bearded soldier.

The bowl he placed on the ground and emptied the second canteen in it. He pitched the canteen and walked away, leaving the water for the two horses. Pulling his Stetson down tight, he climbed up to the trail that led north, and began walking south. To Cheyenne.

It was much bigger than he expected. Noisy, too. He marveled at the locomotive, its smokestack belching blackness into the air, as it chugged in from the east. A church bell chimed eight times. The town would be awake, although he had his doubts Cheyenne, Wyoming Territory, ever slept.

Reaching the first livery, he saw a young Negro lad fork-
ing hay into a corral, where several horses revealed their ap-
preciation. "Top of the morning to you, my fine, young
man," Callahan said when the boy turned around.

"Mornin'," the stable hand said.

"Could you direct me to the land office?"

The kid leaned the pitchfork against the corral and
walked to the edge of the street. He pointed. "The frame
buildin' yonder. The one that ain't been painted. Jus' the
color of wood."

"Yes, my good man, I should have known. The United
States government would see no need to spend money on
paint."

"Nobody should, I reckon. The wind just peels it all off
anyhow."

Callahan thanked the young man again and walked toward the single-story building. He waited for a freight
wagon to pass, then a buggy carrying a well-dressed man
and a handsome woman. A trapper followed, his mule laden
with fur pelts. Only then Callahan figured he might be able
to cross the street without getting killed.

He looked through the lettering on the big window, and
thanked his good fortune again. The land office was empty.
He opened the door, heard the bell ringing above him, and
saw a man at a roll-top desk slide his chair back, turn
around, and push up his wire spectacles.

"How may I help you, sir?" the man said.

"I wish I knew." Callahan smiled.

CHAPTER 32

The Royal Flush dominated Cheyenne's main street. Johnnie Harris had seen many fancy gambling halls in the big towns of Texas—San Antonio, Waco, Four Notch Flats—but this one beat everything the Lone Star State could have even dreamed up. It was something that would fit in at that Coney Island park in New York City that Johnnie had read about.

Well, he had not actually read the article in that illustrated magazine, but he had seen the drawing of that carousel with those carved horses and zebras and camels and things.

There was no carousel inside the Royal Flush. There was a real horse, a white stallion, and on it was a red-headed woman with hair down to her buttocks, and she wore nothing more than a silk sheet. She wasn't riding sidesaddle, either. There wasn't a saddle on the horse. She just sat on it, laughing, and grinning or winking at the card players and the house dealers and the drummers and merchants who were tossing her flowers they'd bought from the school-age vendors for two bits a piece, and the railroad men who said vile words that would have made any woman except the redhead blush, and cattlemen and cattle buyers who looked annoyed because the place got so loud a body could hardly hear themselves talk.

"I don't think!" Boss Harris had to yell to be heard, and Boss stood only a couple of feet to Johnnie's left. "I don't think!" he shouted again.

Johnnie turned, saw his older brother, then leaned closer and cupped his left ear with his hand.

"I don't think that white horse is the one the circuit rider who crippled you rode! Do you?"

Of course, it wasn't the same horse. The horse the redhead sat atop was a stallion. Any fool could see that. That fast-shooting preacher named Taylor Callahan—the one who had ruined Johnnie's gun hand in Nathan, Texas—rode a white gelding. Or had been riding a gelding the last time the preacher had been seen.

"That store tender in Virginia Dale said he was comin' to Cheyenne, didn't he?" Johnnie said. "So did that sawbones in Poudreville."

"And," Johnnie's oldest brother pointed out, "we've been here three days and ain't seen that preacher nowhere."

A saloon girl walked by with a tray over her head that held about a dozen glasses of whiskey and beer. Boss deftly picked up a shot glass with the woman never the wiser. He killed the whiskey in one swallow, then tossed the empty glass onto a table behind him filled with poker players.

"Watch it, buster!" bellowed a man in a tweed suit.

Boss spun around, putting his hands on his revolvers and glaring at the city slicker. The man quickly muttered something that might have been an apology, and set the glass upright near his dwindling stack of chips, cash, and coins, and picked up the cards the dealer had slid in front of him.

Boss Harris was just grouchy and drunk, itching for a fight. They had left the railroad town east of Denver and ridden hard and fast to Poudreville, where, indeed, the circuit rider named Taylor Callahan had been a while back. On to

Virginia Dale, where again they had missed the man they were trailing for revenge. So they had ridden into Wyoming Territory, passing a family of sheepherders pushing north, then pressing hard for the territorial capital, seeing nothing except antelope and coyotes and a collection of pathetic buildings that would not have been considered a town down in Texas. Everett had suggested maybe they could rob the saloon, and Boss might have been considering it, but Digger said, no. He remembered one of them hayseeds in Poudreville saying the settlement of Peaceful Valley might not amount to much but they had one hard-rock of a lawman keeping peace there. Cheyenne was a much wilder place—bigger, richer, more fun, and a whole lot easier for an outlaw to go unnoticed.

The only preachers they had seen were the regulars, the old Catholic priest, the red-bearded Presbyterian Scotsman, and a few others—even one they had seen in the saloon, not preaching about the evils of intoxicating spirits, but having a snort of French Brandy before the church bells started pealing.

Just before the four brothers had decided to cut the dust at the Royal Flush, Digger had suggested they might take the next U.P. train west to Laramie. The preacher could have gone there.

"If we go to Laramie, we'll ride our horses," Boss had told them. "Only train the Harris brothers will take is the one we feel like robbin'. And I ain't heard of no big gold shipments or payrolls. Have you?"

Another saloon girl began working her way through the throngs, giggling when someone pinched her rear end although her face and eyes revealed just how unamused she truly felt. But she held a tray of beer and liquor high over her head, and she was even shorter than the last one who came right by Boss Harris. Once again, he swiped a whiskey. But the girl caught his movement out of the corner of her eye.

She stopped suddenly, turning, and the tray went flying

onto the poker table. The gamblers cursed. One fell backward and smashed his head against a spittoon, spilling the
contents over the well-polished shoes of a man in a fancy
striped suit. His mustache must have been groomed with
four dollars' worth of wax.

A hide hunter, greasy and stinking of blood and guts,
came out of his chair and roared at the saloon girl's clumsi-
ness.

The saloon girl spit at him, told him where he could go
with his insults, then pointed a wrinkled finger at Boss
Harris.

"You ain't jus' payin' for that drink you stole. You're
payin' fer ever' glass you busted, ever' beer you spilt, and
ever' drop of whiskey that he soakin' the floor. And you're
payin' me the tips I done lost, too, you four-flushin' miser."

The hide hunter turned his anger from the saloon girl to
Boss Harris.

Digger knew how to get the brothers out of a jam like
this. He tossed his empty mug of beer onto another table,
reached over, and grabbed Boss's shoulder, spun him around,
and sent his right fist into his brother's jaw. Boss fell backward onto another table, overturning it, sending cards, liquor,
cash, chips, and players onto the floor.

"Fight!" a drunken cowhand said from somewhere.

Men started standing while others dived for cover. The
horse carrying the redhead whinnied, and Everett pulled his
hideaway gun from a pocket and snapped a shot.

"Gun!" someone yelled, but few in the Royal Flush heard
the shout because the bullet Everett fired burned the rear end
of the white stallion, the hindquarters lifted high, one of the
rear hooves took a fat merchant in his thigh and sent him
over the bar while the other hoof busted a keg. The redhead
lost her sheet and her wig. She actually had short gray hair.
She went sailing naked onto a bunch of drunken soldiers
from Fort D.A. Russell.

"You know what to do," Everett said as he pocketed his

gun, and pushed Johnnie over an already overturned table. Then Everett fell onto the floor and began crawling through the carnage, picking up coins and bills and U.S. script and stuffing them into his pockets as he moved through the bedlam.

Glass—chandeliers, bottles, glasses, windows, businessmen's eye spectacles—shattered all around Johnnie. Women screamed. Men cursed. The horse snorted and the hooves trampled whatever got in the white stallion's way. One of the soldiers from Fort D.A. Russell must have been a trumpeter because he started blasting the charge command with all his gusto.

A shotgun roared from behind the bar—like that could stop anyone.

Johnnie knew what he needed to do. He scooped up whatever money he could find on the floor, cutting his left palm on broken glass.

Some say it was how the Harris brothers became outlaws. They would start a fight in a saloon and make off with whatever they could. When they had been kids, they did it for tobacco and matches and maybe a bottle of beer or liquor that didn't get shattered. The money had been little, hardly worth the tanning they got from their pa when they got home because they had not done their chores. In a town like Cheyenne, Johnnie figured they could make off with a fair amount of money. But there was a catch.

Someone had to make it out of the saloon and not get arrested.

That's where Johnnie was headed. A woman stepped on his left hand—the cut one—and while she was too tiny to have broken any bones, he figured he'd be sporting a hurting bruise for a while. With his crippled right hand, Johnnie wasn't good for getting any money, but he had managed to pocket a double eagle. Maybe two.

He caught a white flash to his right and let out a mix of curse and scream, fell to the floor and covered his face with his right arm as the stallion leaped over him. More crashes followed. Then curses. Then a grunt or two, and the shattering of another one of those fancy windows as the white gelding exited the Royal Flush in style.

That led to commotion and curses on Cheyenne's main street.

Johnnie saw a ten-dollar bill, and made his left hand work to pick it up. He rose to his knees, got knocked flat on his back, rolled over, made sure nothing was busted up too badly, and sat up.

He saw a mass of brawlers. He could not find any of his brothers. A man wearing sleeve garters and a well-groomed, curled mustache stood atop the bar, waving a shotgun this way and that, yelling orders that could not be heard probably six inches in front of him.

Backing up, using his feet and his bruised and cut left hand and his wrapped-up ruin of a right hand, Johnnie hoped he was heading in the right direction. His head slammed into wood. Stars flashed briefly. Another window smashed, and he heard the *whump-whump-whump-whump-whump* to his left. He felt wind rush past his ear as other noises came to him.

Turning his head slightly, he spotted the swinging bat-wing door. After taking another look at the wild brawling mass of indistinguishable people, he tried to stand, but fell down. His eyes closed, then opened, and he saw the gray-headed old woman.

Stark naked, she was the redhead with a smile and a wig on the back of a white horse. She bent down, grabbed his forearms and jerked him to his feet, almost pulling his forearms loose from his upper arms. "Ye don't look ol' enough to be in here! Begone, ye yearlin' pup."

She actually kicked him, and he went through the swinging doors and onto a boardwalk covered with glass and bits of wood, and stained with all sorts of beverages and blood. Whistles blew. The police force, or maybe members of a vigilance committee, were running from one direction. Another trumpet wailed, and Johnnie saw soldiers riding hard, reining in a few yards in the middle of the street, dismounting, and running right toward him.

"Inside!" he yelled, pointing and quickly getting out of the way. "Your soldier boys have started a riot!"

The citizens and the soldiers went through those swinging doors, and Johnnie felt a horse's breath on his shoulder. He turned slowly. One horse remained tied to the hitch rail. Other rails had been jerked from their posts.

Cheyenne's firefighters and two or three doctors—one of them might have been a dentist—rushed down the center of the street carrying their black satchels.

Also coming was a tall man in a black frock coat and black hat. The tin star pinned to a black brocade vest glittered, and Johnnie knew he wanted to truck with this man. He turned, swallowed, and started moving across the street. He could find a spot to watch, and see if he would be able to meet up with any of his older brothers, or if it would be left up to him to bail out one, two, or all three—or leave them in jail and take off for . . . ? He wasn't sure where he would go, or where he *wanted* to go. Up to Montana Territory, join the Seventh Cavalry and fight the Sioux? Go west to California? Or back home?

He could be free of his brothers at last. He had already become more self-sufficient with his left hand, and he had seen many men with one arm, one hand, one leg—some with no legs—and a very few with no arms. The loss of a limb did not mean the end of a life.

A plate-glass window—on the upper story—shattered, and a figure in a plaid suit came flying out, hit the awning, which broke his fall, and sent the awning falling on top of the suckers who wanted to get a closer look at all that was going on inside.

Johnnie wondered if the man was dead, but he rolled

over, pushed himself to his knees, smiled at the lawman who stood over him and said, "Ever seen anythin' like that, Wilbur?"

Wilbur swung the barrel of his pistol against the man's head. The man went down, Wilbur stepped over him, and went through one of the busted windows. His revolver boomed once. Again. Then a third time.

He cut loose with a cacophony of curses and finished by saying, "Every one of you is under arrest. Soldiers will report to the guardhouse at Fort Russell. Civilians will gather at the empty corral at Mansfield's Livery Stable, where Judge Cohen will tell you what fine you are going to pay or how much time you'll spend in jail. Anyone who wants to argue with that, I shoot."

Six deputies suddenly appeared, carrying scatterguns.

Johnnie figured he was clear, but it would be smart to cross the street so he wasn't picked up and faced with a fine or thirty-day stretch in Cheyenne's jail.

That's when he saw the preacher across the street.

CHAPTER 33

The noise was nothing new to a man like Taylor Callahan. Why, back before he had seen the errors of his wicked ways, he had taken part in a fair amount of set-tos in gambling halls and sordid saloons and other places that reeked of greed and drunkenness and lust and other sins. The clerk at the land office had rushed outside, which he should not have done.

Callahan looked at the papers he held and figured they would be a lot more useful on his person than in some dusty box of files in a freewheeling town like Cheyenne, which, if the commotion outside was any indication, might be wiped out like Sodom at any second.

He turned in his chair, saw something smash through one of those massive windows across the street, heard shrieks and curses of humans echoed by the screams of cats, dogs, horses, donkeys, mules, and oxen. He paused and tried to recall if he had heard an ox make any noise other than chewing on its cud.

Outside, the clerk pointed at a riderless white horse galloping down the street, and a man with his coat over his shoulder said something. The clerk pointed again, and the man with the coat over his shoulder nodded, then pointed at something going on at the saloon. That turned the clerk's head, but Callahan could not see what they were looking at.

He took it as a sign from the Major General in the Heavens that his first thought was the right one. Sticking the papers in the inside of his Prince Albert, he returned the folder of files inside the open drawer, found his hat, and cleared his throat. He straightened his paper collar, finished the cup of coffee the clerk had generously offered, and stepped onto the boardwalk, closing the door. Stepping beside the man with the coat over his shoulder, he said, "Quite the ruckus."

"I am sorry you have to witness such outlawry, Reverend," the clerk said.

A soldier galloped up on a black mount and slid to a stop. He was off the horse in an instant, bellowing at a handful of troopers standing outside the perimeter of what was called the Royal Flush.

"Sergeant Baldwin!" the officer thundered. "You and your men arrest any soldier you see. If they resist, knock some sense into them. And knock them hard, Sergeant. As hard as you can!"

The sergeant did not seem enthused by the order, but he called out a few names and he and his men showed true dedication as they made their way into the melee.

"Stranger in town, Reverend?" the man with the coat over his shoulder asked.

"My first trip to Cheyenne, sir," Callahan said pleasantly, as he looked across the street.

Horses were tearing loose from their tethers as the Royal Flush seemed to shudder. Another window was smashed and sent glass sparkling like fireworks on the Fourth of July.

"I'm sorry this is what you see."

What Callahan saw were riderless horses, whose owners most likely would be arrested shortly, and he wondered if he might be able to borrow a horse, unnoticed of course. Two horses, actually. He needed to get back to Peaceful Valley as fast as possible. "All towns have growing pains, my good man."

He saw the officer moving in with his men, which made Callahan respect the bluecoat more. That reminded him he ought to get word to the commander of Fort D.A. Russell but wondered if the commander might not just laugh him out of Wyoming Territory after hearing his outrageous theory. Another possibility occurred to him. The commanding officer could be part of the nefarious plot.

Or . . . Taylor Callahan could be crazy as a hydrophoby raccoon.

"Are there any coaches or conveyances running to Poudre City?" Callahan asked the man with the coat now on his other shoulder. "That would go through Peaceful Valley?"

"Every other day," the man said, then offered a cheer to the saloon girl who turned and put a fist into a muleskinner's nose. "So . . . tomorrow."

"I see." Callahan turned and spat. "How about a place to let a horse or two?"

"Plenty of those. Pick any livery. Except O'Donnell's." He nodded across the street. "That's O'Donnell on the ground. The one the deputy marshal is dragging toward the jail."

"Jail's gonna be full," the land-office clerk said.

"They'll chain most of 'em inside O'Donnell's livery," said the man with the coat. "Maybe O'Donnell, too."

"Indian Tanner's got a fine selection of horses to let," the clerk said.

"How does Indian Tanner feel about leasing rental horses on credit?"

Both men guffawed.

"Well"—Callahan tipped his hat—"I appreciate this most excellent street theater and all your help. The files are back in the drawer, sir. And your coffee was as fine as any I have tasted in many a stop." He watched a blood bay horse trot down an alley.

It looked like it had a lot of bottom and obviously was smart enough to get away from the carnage.

Callahan walked down the boardwalk, squeezing through gawkers, stopped to help an elderly woman climb onto a bench so she could get a better view of the ruckus since none of the men or women lining the front of the boardwalk would let her through. He stepped off the wood, looked down the alley, and took three steps toward the gelding.

"Callahan?"

He stopped.

"Reverend Callahan?"

Callahan turned, saw the officer who had ordered the sergeant to make the arrests, then joined him. The officer was dragging an unconscious corporal toward the alley. He dropped the man's leg and kept walking.

"Does any verse in your Bible have an answer, a reason, for this?" The quote bounced through Callahan's memory, and he saw that face—though much younger, the eyes just beginning to register all the horrors human beings were capable of. He had been a captain then—or was it a major?—at New Jerusalem—or what was left of the Missouri town in 1864.

The captain had stopped, his face revealing the horrors of what he had seen—what they all had seen—at what became known as the New Jerusalem Massacre. From what Callahan had read in newspapers and magazines, or heard sometimes in cafes, at funerals, or among the gossips, New Jerusalem had been abandoned. He would like to picture it as verdant farmland, the houses—those that had not been reduced to ashes—gone. Nothing left but one giant graveyard, where wild roses and daffodils bloomed all the year long.

"It has been—" The officer could not finish.

Callahan nodded. "It has."

Something else smashed across the street, but neither soldier nor minister turned.

"Still wearing the blue, I see," Callahan said.

"Yes. Regular army now, though. Are you still . . . preaching?"

Callahan nodded with a slight smile. "I see why Catholic priests have those collars turned around. Easy to spot. Easy to say, 'Why, that man is a priest.' Though some people think my black coat and black hat and black pants point me out as a Protestant."

"Preaching here?"

"Circuit rider." Callahan frowned as he thought *And I need to be riding hard.*

The officer suddenly stared at his boots. His lips trembled, and he did not look up as he spoke softly, in words Callahan could just hear above the screams and punches and breaking glass and wood.

"Do you have nightmares about . . . that . . . day?"

Callahan waited till the officer looked up. "Not about that day," he answered, knowing why. *That day changed my life. That day set me on this route I travel.* He spoke with honesty. "I have my own nightmares."

"Twelve years," the captain said. "I still see . . . everything."

"You have a chaplain at the fort, I presume," Callahan said, wondering if he were wrong to wish this troubled soul would take the hint. Callahan needed to steal that horse in the alley.

The man's head nodded, and looked up with tears in his troubled eyes. His voice trembled as he said, "If only we could have gotten there earlier. If only we could have stopped that—"

"Butchery," Callahan answered for him.

The man nodded, and the first tear fell.

And then Callahan ran those words through him again. *If only we could have stopped that . . . butchery.*

"Captain." Callahan said, and stepped closer to the troubled officer. He drew in a breath, let it out, and shook his head. "It's too late to help all those slain at New Jerusalem. But I believe those men and women, old and young, and those poor, innocent children, that they all walk the Streets of Gold. I have to believe that. And I believe you are here for a reason. The same reason I have found myself right here. You might think I'm madder than anyone on the planet right now when you hear what I'm about to tell you. But I'm going to tell you anyway. And then maybe—with the blessing of someone higher up—just maybe . . . we can stop history from recording another barbaric act committed by vile, ignorant, greedy and just plain savage butchers."

The blood bay eyed Callahan with suspicion but little fear as the circuit rider walked up slowly, keeping his arms spread apart and humming a fine spiritual he had heard at a gathering a few months back in Colorado. The left rein dragged on the dirt, the right one a lot shorter, probably being broken when the animal had decided that being tied up in front of the Royal Flush was no place for him to be on that particular day.

He let the gelding sniff his left hand while his right caught the dangling shorter rein. *Cut off one of the dangling leather strips hanging from the back of the saddle, tie it to the cut rein, it will work good enough. It's not that far to Peaceful Valley.*

The horse snorted.

Callahan smiled. "That's Job you smell. I bet you run a lot harder than Job." He studied the horse's legs and chest, stared into the closest eye that appeared to be sizing him up. "Well, yes, I bet a horse like you wouldn't need another horse. I bet you could cover that distance all by yourself. Couldn't you?"

The head jerked up and down as though nodding, slipping the shortened rein out of Callahan's grasp, but he snatched up the other rein fast and firm—just in case the blood bay decided to see what the street on the other side of the alley looked like.

Callahan moved to the saddle, jerked the horn, and studied the brand on the gelding's hip. Not that he would recognize any outfit's brand in Wyoming Territory, but it was not one that belonged to the Thompson ranch.

"I just want to borrow you," Callahan whispered as though singing a song. "Just borrow you . . . for a ride down south to . . . Peaceful Valley . . . Peaceful Valley . . . Peaceful Valley . . . if you'd be so kind."

He moved around the horse, jerked the strap, repositioned the saddle so it sat straighter, and began to cinch it up.

"Hold it, Preacher."

The voice Callahan did not recognize. Not at first. But he certainly knew what a revolver being cocked sounded like.

When he rose and stared over the saddle and down the alley where all of Cheyenne's finest were busy still trying to stop the biggest saloon brawl in the history of the city, Callahan did not recognize the face or the voice or the outfit. But the right hand . . . well . . . that was a dead giveaway.

"Johnnie Harris. As I live and breathe." Callahan draped his left hand over the saddle, while his right, hidden by the gelding, dropped toward the heavy bulge in one pocket of his Prince Albert.

"You won't be breathin' fer long, mister."

His hand stopped, but he quickly read the kid's eyes. The boy was too nervous, too green, too much unlike Boss Harris, his big brother, to suspect all Callahan had to do was pull the pistol and cock it. With all the noise from the main street, Johnnie Harris wouldn't hear a thing, maybe not even the report of the pistol shot that would send him to meet Saint Peter. But Callahan then brought his right hand up, and laid it across the blood bay gelding's back.

"You ruined my hand." The boy's voice cracked.

"You ever think about the family of that deputy we buried in Nathan, Texas?" Callahan let his eyes harden. "You think his wife, his children, his ma and—"

"I didn't shoot that lawdog."

"I suppose you didn't rob that bank, either."

"I—" He was so nervous he spun around at some imagined noise and looked as the awning of the Royal Flush collapsed. His face jerked back and the gun rose a few inches. "I just . . . held the . . . horses."

Callahan nodded. "In Texas . . . actually in most places in our Western states and territories, that's enough to get you hanged—legal or not—and planted in some shallow grave."

"You made me a cripple."

"One way to look at it." Callahan nodded. "Here's another. I gave you a second chance. Or the Major General in the Heavens did. Maybe that's how you got out of that jail in Texas. I don't think your pards were that lucky. What were their names?"

To Callahan's surprise, the boy answered, his voice breaking. "Wolf . . . and . . . Bigham."

Callahan sighed. "I'll say a prayer for them. You might try that, too. For them . . . and you."

The eyes hardened and the gun came up. "That's my brother's horse you're stealing!"

Callahan smiled again. "Which brother?"

"Boss!"

"And what brand does Boss Harris ride for these days?"

The kid's lips trembled. He didn't even think to look at the horse's hip and read the brand.

"Son"—Callahan sighed and shook his head—"you got

troubles. I know what it's like. Not living up to brothers. But I sure had a passel of daddies I tried to live up to . . . and most of 'em really weren't worth two shakes in an empty sack with holes in the bottom."

That usually left the congregation trying to figure just what in Sam Hill that saying meant. But Johnnie Harris wasn't even paying attention.

"I can't . . . I can't let you . . . Boss has been chasin' you for more than a year now."

"I'm not that hard to catch." Callahan nodded at the revolver. "You caught me."

A long silence, that wasn't exactly quiet, passed.

Callahan figured if the boy was going to kill him, he'd be dead already. So he played his hand. "Johnnie, I'd love to help you sort out the wrong trails you've taken and how you can get back on the straight and narrow. But there are men and women and a whole tribe of innocent Arapaho Indians that are in straits much dire than yours. I'm guessing Boss and your other brothers are part of that melee at the Royal Flush. But I'm riding to Peaceful Valley."

The gun came level and straight. "I can't let you go."

"Then you'll have to kill me, kid. That's what Boss wants. Now's your chance. But it'll cost you. The streets are full, and Cheyenne ain't no small town. I'm ridin' out. I assume he is locked up by now or about to be, providing nobody recognizes him from any wanted posters. But I don't reckon Boss Harris's name has come up this far north and west. Anyway, if this really is your brother's horse, when he is freed on bail he can find his horse—stolen, borrowed, or owned with full deed of sale—in Peaceful Valley. I have my own horse there."

Callahan swung into the saddle, nodded at the kid, and turned the blood bay around. He swallowed, wondering if his last swallow would be of his own spit, and how that would surprise all the population of western Missouri who would have sworn Taylor Callahan's last swallow would have been of forty-rod rotgut.

The horse took six steps down the alley.

He heard the kid practically scream, "I got brothers, Callahan."

The preacher kicked the horse into a walk. He did not look back.

He just said, "Abel had a brother, too."

CHAPTER 34

"Ask me, Marshal," Absalom was saying, "that sky pilot . . . he ain't comin' back here. Only a dad-blasted fool would come back here. Like me. Ever'body in the ter'tory knows I ain't got a lick of sense. I be a fool. Drivin' mud wagons and pretendin' Peaceful Valley might amount to somethin'. I'm a fool. The Good Lord knows that. So do ever'body. Includin' you. But that Callahan feller . . . he ain't no ignorant fool. Gots brains, he does. And here's . . ."

Grant Lee's shoulder hurt. His head hurt. And now his ears hurt. He pushed himself out of the chair and moved past the still-talking stagecoach driver, opened the door to the cabin, and if he were lucky somebody might just shoot him dead.

No such luck.

Gone were those mornings when Grant Lee could step out of the cabin, breathe in the cool, crisp air of Wyoming Territory, and hear nothing but the wind. Now twelve hundred Mexican Churros seemed to be letting the world know they were there, they were hungry, and they were doing something about it.

Sighing, he stepped onto the ground. His first thought was to head over to the saloon, let Kit pour him a morning bracer, but that would be unbecoming and certainly not fitting a man with the reputation Grant Lee had. He looked up Peace Treaty Peak, and decided that would be a good place to look for—"For what?" he said aloud.

He started to think that Absalom might be crazy as a loon, but even crazy fools said intelligent things sometimes. Didn't they? *Why would the Reverend Taylor Callahan come back here?*

Lee started walking again, making a bee line for the hill.

Rams, lambs, and ewes got out of his way. The two Mexicans at the bottom of the slope stared at him, but decided the slow-moving lawman meant no harm to their precious four-legged loads of wool. No one budged from the sheepherders wagon, and no smoke poured from the chimney. While nobody would ever mistake Peace Treaty Peak for Pikes Peak, Grant Lee's chest started heaving, sweat started rolling down his forehead and into his eyes, stinging like blazes, while his armpits and sides turned damp. He was out of breath, thirsty, and could not imagine how he even reached the top of the slope.

For a moment, he wondered if he might pass out. Then he raised an aching arm and let his hand touch the bandaged bullet wound. Reluctantly, he pulled the fingers away and held them up. He couldn't see a blasted thing, his eyes burned so from sweat. Removing his kerchief, he wiped his face and blinked repeatedly, still breathing like he had been holding his head in a water trough forever.

Eventually, his vision cleared, and he looked at his fingers curiously, trying to remember why he was staring at them. Then he remembered. And he sucked in another lungful of pure Wyoming air and let it out. His fingertips were clean. He hadn't opened up the hole in his shoulder after all.

The sheep still got out of his way. Sheep were a lot more cooperative than most of Iron Hand Thompson's cowboys, or Old Iron Hand himself. Especially that hard-rock of a rancher. He found the grave. No cross. Just a boulder the Widow Audrey Eleanor Thompson had had brought up there from the rocky country due south and west.

"A big rock for a hard rock." He found himself smiling. How many times had he heard that saying?

From there, he looked back down on the miserable blight that was Peaceful Valley. He saw the campfires from the surveyors. He thought he could make out Iron Tom. He counted heads. One was missing, and that one was easy to figure out. *Missoula Milford.* So he counted horses. Sure enough, the assassin's horse was gone, which made Lee's shoulder hurt more. That caused him to look over toward the Thompson ranch—not that a man could see it from here. Well, the hired hands and that tough-as-nails widow would be diligent. Lee still wasn't certain Milford was the man who had grazed the older boy and shot the other serious enough to have him still in bed.

He gave up looking that way and stared down at the town again. He saw the Reverend Callahan's white gelding rolling over in the corral behind the marshal's office, stirring up more dust for the wind to blow. He saw sheep. A few clouds. The tall grass on the tops of other hills being blown flatter by the wind.

He looked back at his cabin. And dreaded the thought of making his way down. Then he recalled why he had walked up this hill to begin with, and he looked at the boulder.

A.R. Thompson
B: 1823
D: 1872

No sentiments. No scripture. Not much of anything.

Wondering what the *A* and the *R* stood for, he almost laughed. He could come up with something real quick. And likely appropriate. Depending on those within ear shot.

"I guess you ain't hurtin'."

The marshal spun around to see the sheepherder's girl, not five yards from him, holding a staff in her left hand, and the wind whipping her long, beautiful hair toward him. He tried to talk, but the wind pushed the words back down his throat. He had to look down as the wind began blowing hard.

Something zipped past his ears.

"What?" he called out, unable to hear what the girl had said.

"Are . . . you . . . all . . . right?"

He shielded his eyes and looked up. The wind almost blew him down the ridge. Something kept him upright. He reached down and gripped . . . wool . . . He turned his head and saw he was leaning against a big ram. He tried to find the girl.

"*Are you all right?*"

He heard her that time. "Yes!" he shouted, and thought the wind might have blown the word right back down his throat. He could see her, but the mouth was not moving.

Debating with herself, she finally looked back toward the sheepherder's wagon, then at Lee, and she took a fast step closer, propelled by the ferocity of the wind. She spaced her words. "Are . . . you a . . . real . . . law . . . man?"

He tried not to laugh. "I . . . reckon!"

"Can . . . I?"—she took a fast step closer—"talk . . . to . . . you?"

"Up here?"

She stopped. He thought he had insulted her.

But where else could they go? That strange wagon? Back down to his office where Absalom would either gawk or guffaw? Lee also wondered why she wanted to talk to him.

He realized he was holding his hat on his head, pulled it off, and held it tightly. The ram that had been keeping him upright moved down the hill, and Lee almost fell down—or flew down. He understood the sheep had more sense than he did.

Turning back to the young woman, he said, "Come on! Down a few feet!" He pointed.

"My . . . brothers!" she yelled. "My pa . . . they'll be . . . mad!"

He didn't understand.

"Might . . . think . . ."

He understood what she was saying, but he shook his head. "We can't . . . just stay . . . up here . . . shouting . . . at . . . each . . . other."

She looked at her feet.

Realizing it had been a fool idea to go up here anyway, he gave up, followed the ram down the hill, and felt the wind lose its force. He could breathe again, though he figured it would take an hour to comb the tangles out of his hair. Then he stopped and turned around. To his surprise, the girl stood where he had been standing, looking down, he supposed, at the grave marker. Then she began moving down the slope. Toward him.

Protected from the wind, he tried to remember the girl's name. To his surprise, it came to him without much effort. *Freya.* Freya MacLerie.

Lee attempted his best reassuring, comforting smile. The woman stopped, her hair strewn every which way from the wind but still radiating beauty, though she wasn't as beautiful as Kit.

At least to his way of thinking.

Suddenly he understood why he had never ridden out of Peaceful Valley. And maybe that was why Kit had stayed, too, and had worked relentlessly to keep him alive after he had taken that heavy slug through the shoulder.

Everything became clearer. Just like that.

Then the girl, young Freya, looked up.

And he saw her eyes. His mouth dropped. He even gasped.

Freya MacLerie stopped. Those eyes left him and focused on something off to the southwest. Marshal Grant Lee wanted the young girl to look back at him, just so he could make sure he wasn't seeing things. After all, that wind could have damaged his retinas, or driven him insane. Settlers in the West were driven mad by the wind all the time. But the girl wasn't interested in him anymore.

Her mouth moved. He heard the wind. Then he heard her voice.

"Oh . . . my . . . God."

He turned around quickly, and his eyes widened, too, but he did not invoke the name of the Almighty Lord. He said something that was inappropriate in polite company and would have had his grandmother fetching the soap to wash out his mouth.

CHAPTER 35

"It took you long enough," Boss Harris said after he led Digger and Everett out of the corral that had been turned into a temporary jail in Cheyenne.

"Ten dollar fine for each of you," Johnnie told his oldest brother. "That's thirty dollars."

"I can do my own cipherin'," Boss said.

"Where'd you come up with thirty bucks?" Digger asked.

Everett dropped by the water trough and dunked his head, then came up shaking like a wet dog.

"I had to sell a horse," Johnnie lied, enjoying the looks in all three of his brothers' eyes, each wondering who was going to be left afoot. He turned to Boss. "Yours got the best price." Then he prepared to be slapped to the ground.

To Johnnie's surprise, Boss Harris laughed. "You got thirty bucks for that hoss?"

Actually, Johnnie had collected much more than thirty dollars crawling across the floor of the Royal Flush.

"Pert' good profit," Everett said. "Seein' how we stole that hoss."

"We'll steal another one, too," Boss said. "After we get

some whiskey for our breakfast. Then we're all ridin' south."

"South?" Johnnie asked.

"To a flea trap of a town called Peaceful Valley," Boss Harris said. "One of the citizens caught up in that brawl said he heard there was a circuit-ridin' preachin' down in Peaceful Valley. And said his name, or the name he was usin', was Callahan."

Reining up at the top of a hill, Taylor Callahan let his borrowed horse catch its breath while he stood in the stirrup and tried to get his bearings. That wasn't easy. Those parts of Wyoming Territory all looked the same as he rode across the country at night. He could follow the road to Peaceful Valley, but he was pretty sure he was nearing the point where he had found the crazier than a loon major. The major who had given Callahan a death sentence.

After settling back into the saddle, he leaned forward and patted the horse's neck. The gelding was a good horse, and had covered a lot of territory.

"A few more miles, buddy," Callahan whispered. He turned off the trail, put the horse into a trot, and rode east. He'd have to cut a pretty wide circle, but everything should work out fine. Killer of Ten Crows had said three days. That would give Callahan a full day to get ready, providing he didn't run into one of that crazy major's patrols and wind up dead.

The morning had dawned cloudy, dark but not threatening, just making ranchers and everyone else hope maybe it might rain. Morning rains always seemed peaceful, unlike the afternoon thunderheads that made one remember Noah and the flood.

The Widow Audrey Eleanor Thompson had been sitting

by her youngest son's bed all night. Her back and neck ached. Her heart ached, too.

Yet at that moment, the young man's head turned on the pillow toward her, and his eyes fluttered, then opened. Oh, those eyes. Those eyes focused and locked and the Widow Audrey Eleanor Thompson saw the green dots swimming in the dark blue, and her heart fluttered.

Walker's lips trembled, and slowly turned upward into a smile. "Hey, Ma," he said in a ragged whisper. "I'm . . . alive."

Her heart fluttered and her leg no longer troubled her. He looked a lot like Knight. A lot like his father, too.

"Yes," she said. "You are, my son."

The front door opened, and she heard the chiming of spurs on the hardwood floor after the door slammed shut. *More trouble,* she thought, *but it is about time Knight returned home.* She did not want to think about him so she leaned forward and whispered to Walker, "Are you hungry?"

His lips moved, he swallowed, and his head shook. "Thirsty."

She forced herself up, found the pitcher, and began to fill an empty glass. The door was pushed open and she met the stare, almost dropping the pitcher and the glass.

Those weren't the eyes she'd expected to see. They were brown. It wasn't her oldest son. She should have been able to tell by the steps on the floor. Besides, Knight would have called out in his booming voice matching that of the man buried atop Peace Treaty Peak. Knight had not announced his arrival because Knight was still not home.

It was Jimmy Jack Fontaine, one of the hired men. The fear in his eyes and the way he wrung the hat in his hands made her steel herself for the worst of all news.

"Ma'am," Jimmy Jack said. He nodded at Walker and tried to smile. "How you feelin', kid?"

"Thirsty," Walker repeated.

The Widow Audrey Eleanor Thompson recovered and stepped between the cowboy and her son, lifted Walker's head, and let him drink.

He downed the water as though he were a sponge. "More?" he pleaded.

"Of course." She handed the glass to Jimmy Jack, who tossed his hat onto the empty chair and fetched Walker some more water, returning the glass to the ranch woman.

When she tried to lift her son's head again, he shook it, and began pushing himself up against the pillowed headboard. "Let me see if I can do this myself, Ma," he insisted.

Yes, there's that pride. The pride of his father.

Walker drank again, and sighed. His mother took the glass and turned to the cowboy. "Where is Knight?" she demanded.

Walker pushed himself up higher in the bed.

"He—" Jimmy Jack practically crushed his hat, and his spurs jingled constantly as he moved his legs back and forth as though he had to go to the privy. Then he stuttered. "G-g-g-got . . . hi-hi-his-his-his-self a-a-ar-r-rest-ed. I-i-in . . . P-p-p-peace—in town."

"Grant Lee arrested Knight?" She blinked. "For what?"

The stuttering returned. The Widow Audrey Eleanor Thompson could not understand anything he said until his final word. "S-ssh-shh-shh-sheep."

"What sheep?" she demanded. But deep down, the Widow Audrey Eleanor Thompson already knew the answer.

This stinks. Knight Thompson inched his way through the Mexican Churros, crawling on his belly, soiling his shirt, hands, britches, chaps, and forty-dollar boots in sheep urine, sheep droppings, and all kinds of sheep wretchedness.

Two men would have been one too many, so Knight had left the cowhand inside the crumbling stone jail, told that old buckaroo to make himself seen in the doorway a lot, and to step back inside and put on the hat Knight had left behind. If that darned fool and half-blind Absalom saw Knight's hat on somebody's head, and then saw the cowboy wearing his own hat, Knight figured the stagecoach driver would think both prisoners were still confined—and the sheep were doing a mighty fine job of standing guard.

Slithering slowly like a snake on a hot Wyoming afternoon, Knight moved underneath a big, fat Churro. The *baas* sounded like the buzzing of rattlesnakes, but that was just his imagination, or insanity, after spending a night in that dungeon. Yet the animals were so noisy, Knight figured no one would think anything of their mind-numbing unmelodiousness.

He kept moving, wishing he had come up with his plan before dark. But, no, that would not have worked. The sheep had been quiet during the night, except for occasional bleats. Knight expected the lawdog had also kept a good eye on the cell. And he didn't know what those railroad men were doing, but that Missoula Milford might not have any qualms about shooting an escaping prisoner. That cold-blooded murderer might figure the councilmen of Peaceful Valley would pay a reward for killing an escapee.

Knight blinked. He spit something out of his mouth and did not look over to see what it was. Most likely, he did not want to know. He moved across burned grass, no longer slithering like a snake but crawling like a cowboy trying to escape jail successfully to avenge the death of his father. The sheep moaned behind him as he moved through ash and charred timbers, ruined lumber, and stones. Covered in ash, he rolled to his side, and looked up at a hill of ash and ruins of the old stagecoach station.

The mercantile was next door, but Harry would not tip off the law. Harry had known his father, who had staked him for the store. Harry wasn't dumb enough to turn Knight in. From there, no one from the marshal's cabin could see him.

But anyone at Kit Van Dorn's saloon had a good view.

He studied the building. No one was out front or standing at the batwing doors, but he could see movement through the doorway and windows. He came to his feet and sprinted, leaping over some logs black with tar and soot, and then sat against the fireplace.

That was a mistake.

A chunk of stone landed with a thud, scaring the blazes out of him and landing just inches from smashing his right hand. He eased his way from the chimney. He had heard someone say the chimney was the only thing worth salvaging but knew that was a lie.

If he stayed low, no one in Grant Lee's cabin or Kit Van Dorn's saloon might notice him. He also had a view of Peace Treaty Peak, covered with more than a thousand of those grass-destroying Mexican Churros of the man who had murdered his father in Texas.

He saw the sheepman's wagon. He saw someone standing next to the girl.

If he had his Winchester, Knight could have shot the man dead. Gotten his revenge. Only . . . no . . . no, that wasn't Angus MacLerie. That looked like . . . Grant Lee.

The wind picked up.

"Oh . . . my . . . God!"

The wind carried the sheepman's daughter's words all the way down the peak, across the Poudreville-Cheyenne road, through the ash and lumber to Knight Thompson's ears. Thinking he'd heard an echo from Kit Van Dorn's saloon, Knight turned, found the saloon, and saw Kit Van Dorn standing in front of the batwing doors. She stepped out, holding one door open, for Tin Horne and Rude Frank. And she pointed. But not at Peace Treaty Peak. She pointed to the other hill, smaller, and a bit farther southwest.

"Oh, my God!" The sight shocked Kit so much she let go of the batwing door she had been holding open and the heavy wood slammed into the gambler.

He let out a curse. "Are you trying to kill me, Kit?" Tin

Horne pushed his way out of the Three O'd Saloon, quickly spotting what had caught her attention.

So did Rude Frank, but Kit would later come to understand, he was the only person in Peaceful Valley who kept his head on his shoulders and did what most frontier settlers would consider the proper course of action.

He let the batwing doors swing as he stepped onto the platform, then onto the grass, then made a beeline for the livery, where he quickly put his slick fork saddle on the best horse in the stables, which was not, legally, his horse, and lit a shuck for Laramie, where he caught the next eastbound Union Pacific to Omaha, and there returned to the loving spouse he had left behind five years earlier and became an alderman and outspoken critic of the evils of gambling and gunfighting.

"Eugene!" Tin Horne yelled. "Get my . . ." His last word came out as a whisper. "Winchester." Then he cleared his throat. "Never . . . mind," he concluded.

Kit told herself she must be dreaming. The hills were covered with—. It had to be a dream. She was hallucinating. But if she were, Tin Horne was seeing the same thing.

"That must be"—his voice cracked—"the whole Arapaho nation."

Second Lieutenant Claudius Mason, United States Military Academy, Class of 1876, focused his binoculars. He saw Indians—hundreds, maybe thousands for all he could tell—lining up the top of the hills. He dropped the binoculars, the leather cord biting into his neck and the heavy spyglasses pounding against his sternum as he saw First Sergeant Kranz already galloping toward the major. Kranz was a good soldier. Experienced. A green lieutenant could learn a lot from him.

As smart as the noncommissioned officer, Mason's horse was already turning down the slope, not bothering to work its way from walk to trot to canter to gallop. Mason had to quickly grab the reins or he would have been left in the tall prairie grass.

"Sergeant!" he yelled, but could not get control of his steed.

The sergeant turned his horse west, trying to lead the pursuing Indians away from the major's camp. But Mason had yet to master the demands of getting a horse to go where he wanted it to go. It appeared to be making a beeline for the hidden camp the major had chosen. He sure hoped that's where the horse was heading.

They went up and down a good many hills, or so it felt like, and twice Lieutenant Mason barely stayed in the saddle. As he came down another slope, he saw the major's command, that stalwart, gallant leader riding at the point, holding out his hand to stop the soldiers and civilian scouts behind him and saying something.

Above the pounding of Mason's mount it sounded like, "What in the name of heaven—?"

The horse did not stop, so Mason dived off. He felt iron vises on his shoulders, and saw two enlisted men squatting on his left and right, and then the major knelt and removed the cigar from his mouth.

"What the devil are you running from, Mister Mason?" the major yelled.

"Sir." Mason would have saluted but the men on either side of him would not let him go.

"The . . . Indians"—he thought he managed to say— "They are at Peaceful Valley." He would have pointed but could not move his arms.

The major smiled, straightened, and looked south toward the settlement. "Excellent," he whispered. "Here goes for a brevet . . . or a coffin."

CHAPTER 36

"The kid," Missoula Milford whispered, "is in the ruins of that stagecoach station."

Thomas "Iron Tom" Aldridge opened his eyes. He still hurt all over, but the mankiller's words eased some of the pain that preacher had given him. "Kid?" he asked. "You mean . . . ?"

"The Thompson boy. The older one."

"There are two we need dead." Slowly, Iron Tom pushed himself up, grimacing from the sharp pains in his side and shoulder.

"And they will be. This one will be easy, though. He just escaped jail."

Iron Tom turned his head and focused on the blackened wreck. Seeing no movement, he whispered, "Where is he?"

"Behind the fireplace," Missoula Milford replied. "He crawled from the jail. Left his hired hand inside. Pretty smart for a ranch kid. Though I don't know where he thought he'd go from there. Should have come this way. That woulda made things a whole lot easier. Or circled around the marshal's digs, kept going to the crick. Then tried to make his way back home. That woulda been better for us. Kill him away from this . . . *town*." He spat out the last word in disgust. "But in town will work. Can't have a convict escaping jail." He eared back the hammer of his Henry repeater.

One of the nearest surveyors stood, but he wasn't looking at the jail or the torched ruins.

Iron Tom thought the man might protest what Milford was suggesting, but the surveyor knew where his money came from— and he'd get a lot of cash if they could pull off this railroad deal.

"Why don't you work your way around this side?" Milford told his boss.

"And get shot?" Iron Tom protested.

"He ain't got no gun, you idiot. He's a prisoner, and Grant Lee isn't stupid."

Still, Iron Tom hesitated.

"Just work around a bit. Scare him off. When he pops up from behind those stones, I'll blow his head off. Then we just got to take care of his brother, though I figure I hit him hard enough he might be dead already, his po' mama bawling her sweet head off." Milford started to move around.

Then Iron Tom heard Kit Van Dorn say something.

And the surveyor who was still standing pointed at a hilltop. "You might want to save that bullet," he said in a high-pitched voice. "We're gonna need it."

"What is your problem?" the Widow Audrey Eleanor Thompson scolded her foreman. "Do you not remember how to hitch a team?"

She pointed it at the cowboy, showing him she wasn't crippled so bad she couldn't stand on her own two feet. "We must get to Peaceful Valley as soon as possible."

"Ma'am," the waddie protested, "it ain't safe—"

"I'll be the judge of that, mister."

The door to the big house opened, and she turned. "Get back inside, you idiot!" she bellowed. "You are not to leave Walker till I get back from town. And if something happens to my son before I get back, you will feel the wrath of this mahogany!"

The door slammed shut.

The Widow Audrey Eleanor Thompson turned back, and then looked at the cowhand bringing in the sorrel toward her buggy.

"Not that horse, you fool!" she yelled. "Get the chestnut. I want the fastest two horses we have. We must get to Peaceful Valley as soon as possible." She whirled back to the foreman. "If you want to protect me . . . and my sons . . . and your job, you idiot, you'll be saddling your own horse. We're riding hard and fast to Peaceful Valley. Take as many men as you can, but I want four to stay here. Armed to the teeth with orders to fight to the death should anyone come here who doesn't ride for our brand!"

Killer of Ten Crows looked down on the paleface settlement, then at the hill where Iron Hand slept the forever sleep and all those sheep covered the place where Stands Firm would leave this earth for the happy hunting ground.

Stinking Coyote, mounted on his pinto mare, turned and spat, then pointed his bow at the hill. "This is what the pale eyes think of their Iron Hand. And now they show you what they think of Stands Firm! They cover this sacred hill with those ugly, useless, strange-looking animals."

Behind him, Red Bear yelled, "We are not Navajo. We have no use for sheep."

"They laugh at us!" Stinking Coyote said. "They mock us! We should ride down and kill all the sheep, then kill all the palefaces that think so little of the great Stands Firm!"

"They think so little of all Arapaho!" Red Bear agreed,

and pointed to the Indians from the other tribes who had come to pay their respects to the Arapaho chief who had formed alliances with other great nations. "They think nothing of the Cheyennes . . . the Comanches . . . the Kiowas . . . the Utes . . . and the Shoshones, either!"

"You are all wrong!" Killer of Ten Crows silenced them. "You do not understand the palefaces. But I do. Have you not heard what the paleface holy men tell us? Do you not remember the drawings in their books about their God, their God's Son, their own heroes from long ago? Let us ride to where Stands Firm will rest beside the great Iron Hand!"

"They're coming."

Freya MacLerie's words barely reached Marshal Grant Lee. Not that he needed to hear what she had seen. He had pretty good eyesight. Good enough to see what had to be hundreds, maybe even a thousand or more, mounted warriors covering not just one hill, but three others. The citizens of Peaceful Valley were, the saying went, a wee bit overmatched. Again he looked down the hill at the settlement. Someone was riding out at a lope. Whoever it was showed good sense.

It wasn't one of the surveyors. He could see Iron Tom and caught the sunlight reflecting off Missoula Milford's Henry rifle. As long as no one went crazy and started shooting, Lee figured they might survive. After all, wasn't Killer of Ten Crows coming to bury his great chief? Or had that been a ruse? Were the Arapahos planning on wiping out the town?

Well, that made no sense to Lee. Who would want to wipe out a place that didn't amount to a hill of goober peas? If that's what the Arapaho people wanted to do, they could have brought a miniscule fraction of what they had brought . . . No, they weren't coming to harm anyone. He saw the women and the children. They were coming to bury Stands Firm. It had to be that. Indians didn't bring women and children to battle. *Did they?*

"Look!"

Lee turned away from the approaching Indians. Harry appeared to be pointing northeast. Lee turned to see a guidon rise above that hill, then several horses carrying blue-clad soldiers. A bugle sounded the charge. Sunlight reflected off a saber.

Lee heard the sheepherder girl whisper, "Oh . . . no."

He cursed the soldiers. They were charging against a force that would wipe them out in the blink of an eye. And likely take everyone in Peaceful Valley with them.

The saber fell out of the major's hand. And the blowhard used both hands to jerk hard on the reins and pull his horse to a sliding stop.

Lieutenant Mason was already stopping his. Twisting in the saddle, he yelled, "Hold your fire! No one is to discharge his weapon." Two soldiers turned their mounts and started to kick them into a run back to Fort Centennial.

"Do not run!" Mason screamed. "Turn those horses around. Turn them around, you two troopers, or so help me I will shoot you in the back. We are not deserting. We are—" He spun back and looked at the major, who looked petrified, pale, and could not stop shaking.

"Sir?" Mason asked. When no response came, he asked, "Major, sir, what are our orders?"

The major said nothing.

Mason bit his lip, then looked at First Sergeant Quincannon. "Sergeant, do you have a white handkerchief?"

"No, sir, Lieutenant. Mine's green plaid."

Somehow Mason moved his horse over and beside the sergeant's, reached inside his own tunic and withdrew a white piece of silk. "Spear this with the tip of your saber, Sergeant," Mason ordered. "Then we will ride up that hill." He exhaled. "Maybe we can work this all out peacefully." He looked back at the frightened and greatly outnumbered soldiers. "Sheath your sabers or carbines and holster your pistols. We are on a . . . peaceful . . . mission."

He looked at the major. "Major? Major? Major?"

The man appeared to be in complete shock.

"Corporal Shultz. Stay with the major."

"Gladly, sir."

Lieutenant Mason looked back at Sergeant Quincannon. "Ready, Sergeant?" he asked.

"Not particularly, sir."

Mason managed to laugh. "Neither am I. But"—he recalled the major's boastful words—"here goes for a brevet . . ."

The good sergeant changed the ending. "And not a coffin . . . Let's hope, sir."

The Reverend Taylor Callahan stopped Boss Harris's horse on the hill. The quarter horse danced around nervously while the preacher tried to figure out exactly what was going on.

About a million or maybe two million Indians covered the hills to the south. Well, that was a gross exaggeration, but there were more Indians than he had ever seen. A small band of bluecoats had stopped on the hills to the north. Sheep still covered much of Peace Treaty Peak, and the sheepherders were gathered beside the girl and, if his eyes weren't playing a trick on him, Marshal Grant Lee.

Most of the soldiers began riding easily toward the hill.

All of them had put away their weapons. And what looked to be a white flag had been affixed atop a saber.

Callahan looked down to Peaceful Valley. Absalom was walking from the marshal's office up the slope. A bunch of sheep still surrounded the jail, which meant Knight Thompson might still be a prisoner. A figure stood in the doorway of the crumbling stone building, but that man might be the cowhand from the Thompson ranch. Other people were joining Absalom. Kit Van Dorn reached the base of the hill first, with Tin Horne right behind her. Even the surveyors were walking away from their camp, all except one . . . Missoula Milford.

In the corral beside the marshal's cabin, Job whinnied.

"Well," Callahan managed to say. He breathed in, then exhaled, and rode Boss Harris's stolen horse to the top of Peace Treaty Peak. Reaching it first, he swung down, then patted the horse's bottom and watched the tired beast trot down the hill. Scattering the Mexican Churros, the horse weaved through the approaching residents and found the water trough in front of the Three O'd Saloon.

"Reverend," Grant Lee said, "you might should have kept riding for parts unknown."

Callahan had no response to that, but he removed his hat and bowed at Freya. "Ma'am."

She looked up and nodded slightly.

"What be this about, Preacher?" her father said.

He looked at Angus MacLerie. "You know what it's about," he told the Scotsman.

A buggy appeared on the Poudre River road.

"And so does she."

Killer of Ten Crows stopped his horse and nodded at Callahan, then he looked back at the approaching wagon. More sheep scattered.

"Let her through," Callahan said. He pointed to the stone marker. "She was the wife of Iron Hand."

The Indian's face changed, and he said something in his native tongue. Indians moved their horses away, creating a path that allowed the buggy to reach the top of Peace Treaty

Peak. By then, most of the residents had climbed the hill, though a few remained a good ways down, and some had stopped at the base of the ridge. Others seemed to have lost their will and were hurrying toward the livery stable.

The Widow Audrey Eleanor Thompson climbed out of the buggy, and walked toward Angus MacLerie.

The soldiers arrived, and the sergeant sheathed his scabbard and handed a pipsqueak of a lieutenant the white handkerchief with a hole in it.

Waiting until Iron Tom had made it up the hill, Callahan then looked back at Killer of Ten Crows. "I thought you said three days."

"My math"—the Arapaho shrugged—"not so good."

Callahan grinned. Well, if he were an Indian, he wouldn't trust a white man, either.

"What is going on here?" the young lieutenant asked.

"It's a long story, Lieutenant," Callahan said. "But with luck a troop of cavalry from Fort Russell should be coming in a few hours, maybe sooner, and I believe they will be here to arrest your commanding officer." He looked at Iron Tom. "And some surveyors."

A figure moved from what was going to be Callahan's pulpit, and then young Knight Thompson was running toward the hill. Missoula Milford started to bring the rifle to his shoulder, but immediately thought better of it.

Callahan let out a sigh of relief and turned back to the lieutenant. "Iron Tom here wanted to get a railroad track from Laramie to Denver. Well, not really. He wanted to start an Indian war. Putting a track over this hill—after he learned Stands Firm was dying and would want to be buried here—would be a good way to start a war. With a war and a railroad, he'd be quite rich. Problem is, this is deeded range." He turned to the widow. "Isn't it, ma'am?"

"That's right. When my late husband first came here, he had twenty cowboys. Twenty men filed claims. A hundred and sixty acres. Five years later, those men sold to my husband the land they had free title to. And so did you, right, Harry?"

The store owner nodded.

Unsteady on his feet and breathing hard, Knight stopped. "Ma . . . What's . . . ?"

Callahan faced Iron Tom. "You knew that. You had your hired killer try to cut down the two heirs." He shook his head. "Were you going to have the widow murdered as well?"

"Ma!" Knight started for Angus MacLerie. "This is the man who murdered my pa. What's he—?"

"Audrey." The Scotsman turned to the widow.

The boy stopped his questioning.

"Angus MacLerie did not kill your father, son. He wouldn't kill his own . . . brother."

Knight felt like he had been struck by lightning. He thought he even heard thunder.

Callahan looked up at the dark skies. It was thunder. He could smell rain.

Knight whipped back to face Angus MacLerie. "You're not—"

"Look into his eyes, son," Grant Lee whispered. "And look into your own. And look into Mr. MacLerie's daughter's eyes. That's all you need to see."

The boy just stood there.

"Ye papa and I were a lot alike, laddie," the Scotsman said. "Only he liked cattle and I liked sheep. When I got into a fracas with Texas cattlemen, he rode to help me. Sided with me. A Texan, and a cattleman at that: siding with a sheepman. That nary pleased Texas cattlemen, So he died. But he died knowing sheep might be a lot more profitable than cattle. Sheep give ye meat. And wool. And in Wyoming Territory, in winters particularly, wool is a fine thing to have."

"But everyone said he died in a sheep war," Kit Van Dorn said.

"He did," MacLerie said. "He was a cattleman killed fighting for a sheepman. I be that sheepman. He was a brother, fighting for his brother."

"The names?" Grant Lee asked. "MacLerie . . . Thompson."

"Well, A.R. MacLerie was a wanted man in Savannah, Georgia, so he changed his to Thompson. Isn't that right, Audrey?"

The Widow Audrey Eleanor Thompson nodded but did not speak.

"It took me years to get enough sheep, and I've brought them here. Left Texas for good. We will show this world sheep and cattle do mix. In Wyoming Territory."

Knight stared at his mother, trying to comprehend everything.

"Ye got yer papa's eyes, laddie. My eyes, too. Just like Freya got my eyes. MacLerie eyes. But ye should keep the Thompson name. It carries weight in this country."

Grant Lee changed the subject. "What about this murder plot? This scheme to start an Indian war?"

"You don't have a lick of evidence," Iron Tom said.

"Yes," Killer of Ten Crows said. "He does." He turned in the saddle. "Tell him, Red Bear."

The Arapaho pointed the tip of his bow down the hill. "I scout for meat. Think about stealing paleface beef. No elk to find. Paleface drive all elk into hiding. See that man. One with shiny fast-shooting long gun. He hide in trees. Shoot down at paleface who raise paleface beef. Then run away. Not even try to take scalp. No honor in shooting man that way. Him coward."

Iron Tom's face paled. "You—No one . . . will take . . . an Indian's . . . word."

"Won't they?" Callahan smiled, then looked at the widow and her oldest son. "Y'all have some sorting out to do. Don't rush it. It'll take time. Lots of time." He looked down the hill, said, "This won't take as much time," and walked down the hill toward Missoula Milford.

About fifty Arapaho and other Indians, and just about everyone from the town of Peaceful Valley followed down behind him, leaving the Thompson widow and her oldest son with some sheepherders from Texas.

Callahan pulled off his Prince Albert when he reached the bottom, let it fall to the grass, then removed his hat. Missoula Milford started to raise the Henry, but the sight of all those Indians, and troopers, and citizens stopped him. Callahan went right toward him.

Milford didn't even see the fist that knocked him to the ground. He started to rise, but Callahan punched him again.

"You better talk, Milford!" Callahan roared. "Your only chance to avoid a rope is to sing loud and clear as to who ordered you to start shooting and why."

The man came up with a hefty piece of timber in his hands. Callahan backed away, moving toward the ruins. He ducked the first swing, but the second caught his right upper arm. Callahan went down to his knees. Milford let out a roar and charged, Callahan dived, the man tripped, swinging wildly again. Both men fell into the ash and muck. Callahan came up. So did Milford, but the killer had a rock in his right hand which he tried to smash into the circuit rider's face.

But Callahan went down onto all fours, and the killer fell over him, smashing into the chimney.

Callahan heard the roar, and saw the rising, choking dust. Hands gripped him, pulled him over timbers and rocks and ash. He was coughing, then rolling over, shaking his head, trying not to scream.

Only . . . he wasn't screaming. Strong hands lifted him up, but he still heard the screams.

"Somebody fetch Harry!" he heard Tin Horne's voice calling.

He wiped his face, turned around, and saw Missoula Milford lying in front of the smoking wreck of a stagecoach station, saw the two hands, crushed by the stones that had made the chimney.

The preacher looked at Grant Lee and Kit Van Dorn, then knelt by the hired killer. "Listen to me."

Callahan coughed, shook his head, squinted his eyes. "Listen to me. Your hands are worthless now, Milford. You won't be able to lift a gun or even pull a trigger. So my advice to you is to get right with somebody. A lot of people—when they hear you're no good with a gun anymore—will be coming for you. You want some protection, you better start thinking about yourself . . . and not some greedy surveyor."

He turned to spit, then looked up, and felt the first drop of a cold, cleansing rain.

CHAPTER 37

The mud wagon carrying the body of Chief Stands Firm stood next to the grave of Iron Hand Thompson. (Buster had sold the Abbott & Downing coach for a string of fast horses.)

The Reverend Taylor Callahan stood on the top of Peace Treaty Peak and looked across and down the hills at the Indians of various tribes. He looked at the soldiers (except those who were guarding the major, still in shock). His eyes traveled to the surveyors and the crippled hired killer, next to the wrecked stagecoach station, and to the residents of Peaceful Valley (except Buster and Absalom, who'd already galloped off to resume their war for a stagecoach contract since no train was coming through).

Callahan began his talk. "There's a saying, about rain and funerals . . . that the rain is just the tears of joy of the millions of angels who are waiting for a great human being to join them in Heaven."

He had started quite a few funerals with that one. It always pleased. And he was happy to add an Indian funeral to his list of things he had done. Through the rain, he saw four riders on a distant hill. He smiled and thought *Well, brothers carry a hold, young Johnnie Harris. But you might want to break that hold before too long.*

The four riders stopped and looked around.

Others on the hilltop turned at the sound of galloping horses. The guidon was the first to appear over the hilltop. Then a troop of cavalry reined up. Four troopers rode down toward the Harris brothers. The officer from Fort D.A. Russell stood in his stirrups, probably counting the number of Indians.

Good thing, Callahan thought, *they are here on a peace-keeping mission. Unlike that crazy major from Fort Centennial.* He said, "It's all right. I know the officer leading that command."

Since it was unlikely the soldier boys would keep the Harris boys locked up, it was looking like Taylor Callahan wouldn't get to preach the funeral after all.

"Folks, I'm not the man to say any words about Stands Firm. I have to be riding on. My job here is done." He heard the gasp, and a few sighs, and an Arapaho or two grunt. That was all right. It made him feel like . . . well   he'd be missed.

"Your marshal here's the man to say these words. And"— he smiled at Kit Van Dorn—"and maybe his . . intended?"

Kit blushed.

Grant Lee walked slowly out of the crowd, his hat dripping rain. "What are you talkin' 'bout, Preacher?" the lawman whispered.

"Four men are coming," Callahan said softly, nodding his head toward the northeast. "I'd like to be gone before they get here."

Lee looked across the gray skies. "They won't come here. They see all these Indians. So does the cavalry."

Callahan grinned. "Yeah. But eventually someone will think to fly a flag of truce. And negotiations will start. And the major from Fort Centennial will be arrested. But you don't have anything to hold those four boys on, though I could tell you what to do. But that young kid down yonder with a crippled hand. He's a project of mine, and I'd like another chance to save his soul. So preach a nice long funeral for me, will ya?" He held out his hand.

"You could stay here, Preacher," Kit said.

His head shook. "It's my fight. Not yours. And, as I keep telling folks, I'm done fighting."

"Missoula Milford and Iron Tom might argue that point," the lawman said.

"All right." Callahan put his hat on his head. "I'm done killin'. And I've long had this hankering to see an ocean."

"If it doesn't stop raining," Kit said, "you might see one here."

He laughed.

"You think the Widow Audrey Eleanor Thompson and her boys will sort everything out?" the lawman asked.

"I'm starting to like sheep," Callahan said. "What will help everyone in this Wyoming Territory is good neighbors." He looked over the couple's shoulders. He whispered to Grant Lee that whispering wasn't polite at a funeral, and the Arapahos and the white folks were getting restless—and soaked—but his biggest, unspoken concern was what if Johnnie Harris was dumber than Callahan suspected?

"Where will you go?" Kit asked.

Callahan looked down the slope and found Job. The horse looked ready to ride, or at least, find a dryer place to wait out the storm.

"I'm like a thirty-a-month cowboy, ma'am." He pointed at the clouds. "I just ride for the brand."

Walking like he was in something of a hurry, he headed toward the white gelding in the corral below.

TURN THE PAGE FOR A HIGH-KICKIN' PREVIEW!

**National Bestselling Authors
William W. Johnstone and J.A. Johnstone**

FOREVER TEXAS
A Novel of the American Frontier

**"Superb from start to finish. An instant classic."
—*New York Times* Bestselling Author Marc Cameron**

No one knows better than the American masters of epic Western fiction that forging a new life on the frontier takes hope, drive, and plenty of ammunition.

**The war is over. But a new battle is on the horizon.
Based on true events.**

It's 1852. The wounds of the Mexican War are healing. Regis Royle, co-owner of a steamship fleet, has made it out alive, relatively unscarred and with enough profit and foolhardy ambition to envision a new life in south Texas. With the help of his crack-shot kid brother Shepley, his glud-hunding riverboat partner Cormac Delany, and his old friend, raw-edged former Texas Ranger Jarvis "Bone" McGraw, Regis is laying claim to the prime jewel in a magnificent rolling prairie: the Santa Calina range teeming with wild mustangs, cattle, and eighteen-thousand acres of lush promise.

But all dreams have a price. For Regis, it's hell to pay— and the fire is coming at him from all directions. On one side of the border, it's *banditos*. On the other side, the Apaches, slave traders, and outlaws have Santa Calina in their sights. And none of them are going to walk away from the bloody battle.

The brothers Royle and their partners have the most to lose—including their lives. They made a pledge to themselves to build the greatest ranch in America. To see it through to the end, they'll have to ride hard and learn the bitter necessity of violence and bloodshed.

Look for FOREVER TEXAS, on sale now!

CHAPTER 1

The first shot pinwheeled the tall man's hat off his head. The second sent him diving for cover, and the third spooked his mount and sent it crow-hopping and snorting into the puckerbrush.

He heard a harsh, barking laugh followed with shouts of "Die, gringo!" . . . then shots volleyed at him from all sides.

The tall man managed to crank off a shot of his own. He heard a groan and a curse drift up on the still, hot air as the gunfire echoed and tapered off. Regis Royle had enough time to suck in a sharp breath between his tight-set teeth before a fresh fusillade pinned him tight in a wedge of sun-warmed sandstone.

He counted what he thought might be several guns still blazing, or someone was good at reloading. He trailed his fingers to his gun belt and felt his sheathed knife. He had three shots left in his gun. Fresh ammunition rested snugly in his saddlebags on the ass end of the horse he'd likely never see again.

"What you want here, gringo?"

Regis Royle spun his gaze toward the voice and closed

his hand tighter on the walnut grips of his revolver. He saw nothing save for an anaqua tree. In the blue sky far beyond, a lone gray cloud teased apart on a breeze. A meadowlark bobbed on a spiny jag and warbled its morning song.

"Who's asking?"

Ragged laughter echoed off the slabs of sandstone chiseled by wind and time.

Not a man prone to twitching at imagined spooks, Royle nonetheless felt a shiver of ice ripple his backbone. He hunkered lower and eyed around the boulder, looking longingly toward the receding view of his squirrel-headed, bucking mount, and with it his shiny new rifle.

He held the pose as if he were part of the warming stone. The meadowlark rose into the air, trailing dewy notes, and in a series of short swoops landed on a jut of gnarled mesquite some distance to the west—two hundred, three hundred feet.

Could be the bird was a friendly sort. Could be if Regis were a betting man, and at times he was, that bird was looking for a handout, a morsel from a kindly stranger. Could be that bird found the curious laughing man for him. Could be now was the time to place a bet.

Regis almost shrugged, almost smiled at his fanciful notion. Then he didn't smile, for he noted a shifting of light, less than a shadow's worth, in a darkened gap in the stony declivity beyond and below the twitchy, curious little yellow-and-brown bird.

"Thanks, bird friend," he whispered, and licked away a slow drop of sweat from the corner of his mouth, unseen beneath his thick black moustache. Too early by half for this sort of tomfoolery. He had land to check on, friends to catch up with, and an appointment in Brownsville to keep.

Now he was more annoyed than afraid for himself. He'd known, of course, of the danger of brigands out here, and had even been reminded of the cautions he should take when friends at the docks learned he was riding inland alone, on his way to Corpus Christi to visit other friends.

"Why you want to do a thing like that, Cap?" Lockjaw Hames had said. "No sir, if I was you I'd stick to the water. Safer around here. No injuns or Mexicans out to lay a man low, steal his boots and his hair, then pillage what's left out of his middle."

Lockjaw, who earned the odd moniker because his lips rarely seemed to move when he spoke, a task he was unafraid to undertake, had shuddered then as if he'd had a vision of something horrific happening that was fated.

Lockjaw was as solid a seaman as they'd come. Reputedly a former slave and now self-proclaimed free man, he was also the biggest man Regis had ever met, and that was saying something, as Regis himself was north of six feet tall by several inches.

Lockjaw was a steady presence on the steamers and riverboats, turning his hand to whatever task Regis or his partner in the shipping trade, Cormac Delany, asked of him.

Didn't mean Regis was about to take his advice to heart. He'd chuckled and said, "I appreciate your concern on my behalf, Mr. Hames, and I will endeavor to remain on the good side of the soil with breath in my lungs."

The big black man had paused, sacks of quicklime balanced on each shoulder, his bulging arms steadying them, and said, "Ain't no call to get uppity about it, boss. But you don't come crawling back to the safety of the docks saying how come ol' Lockjaw didn't warn you!" He'd stomped off, loading the hold of the *Missy B.*, a recently acquired craft Cormac had christened after a younger sister long dead, or as Cormac had said, "called to her glory."

And now here Regis was, pinned down in the rocks and grasses of this pretty river valley by an outlaw, no doubt. "Looks like you were right, Lockjaw," Regis mumbled.

Another shot, this time slicing in from east of him, scored a fresh groove in the dusty rock above his head. "Okay, at least two outlaws."

As if in response to his thought, a third, then a fourth

shot, each from different directions, pinged and whined in ricochet harmlessly above him. For the moment he was safe, but if they—by his best guess that would make at least four scurvy-addled curs out for his blood—decided to close in, he'd be a dozing fawn to their pouncing lion.

His ire with himself almost outweighed any animosity he felt toward the would-be thieves. Almost. He'd save his full steam for dealing with the prairie scum. And he knew he would, in part because Regis Royle was a man who never failed at anything he attempted.

He had fought his way to his position as partner in a shipping business, co-owner of a growing fleet of riverboats plying the waters of the Rio Grande and up and down the coast. He and Cormac had worked like demons during the Mexican War, the wounds of which were slowly healing, though still bleeding aplenty, since 1846.

Here it was 1852 and he was still scrapping his way through life. He sighed and carefully extended a long leg and flexed it, massaging his knee. A bullet pinged a few inches below the heel of his stovepipe boot. He yanked it back and sucked in air through his teeth.

He needed a plan, because sitting here wasn't getting a damn thing done. What sort of plan could he hope for? Stand up and shout, "Hey, gents, how about we talk this over?" He grunted at the folly of his thoughts. No, best wait them out, keep alert, and take advantage of the relative safety of this rocky hidey-hole he'd managed to wedge himself into.

Then another thought came to him: What if he weren't the only critter in this hole? If it got cold at night, which it would surely do, would a pesky rattler slide out of that crevice behind him and try to get cozy with whatever warmth might exude from his cramped body?

The idea didn't do much for his mood. Regis cursed his horse again, a feather-headed thing with a balky streak a mile wide. When he got back to Brownsville, he was going to buy it from the hostler he'd rented it from and either train it right or shoot it in the head and start with a fresh beast.

A smile tugged a corner of his moustache upward. He was thinking of the very reason he'd ventured out on this fine jaunt in the first place. It had been three days since he'd left Brownsville and ridden northward to Corpus Christi. He'd intended to pay a call on friends who'd moved there, attend a fair he'd heard was to take place in that bustling town.

Really, it was little more than a convenient excuse to get away from his beloved steamers. He still enjoyed the work, but he'd been at it for years without letup. He was still a young man, but sometimes he felt like he was ninety and ready for a rocking chair by a fireplace.

He knew the itch, for it had never really left him. He wanted to—no, he needed to venture beyond the waterways. And a trip on horseback, even if only for a few days, would help scratch that pesky, restless feeling.

But a funny thing happened on his way north. He'd cut inland a bit, in a northwesterly fashion, and he'd found a distraction he'd not even known he had been seeking. In fact, it up and smacked him in the head before he knew what was happening.

Actually, it had been more of a slow saturation of his senses. The day had been hot, as were most days in April in southern Texas, and he found himself riding without care or hurry. In light of his current situation, he knew he'd been lucky to make the journey unmolested.

Even the balky buckskin had seemed lulled into peacefulness by the green rolling prairie Regis found himself in. The wind played over an ocean of long floss-tipped grass stems, as if they were the surface of an endless sea. A little farther on and the land sloped gently to his left. Soon he smelled it, the earthy richness of flowing water. And then he saw it at the same time he heard it.

Or rather, he heard a splash. His horse's ears perked, and he reined up and watched something he'd never before witnessed. The scene fascinated him and hooked him in all at once. A herd of wild mustangs, perhaps half a hundred, were wading into the river to his left, dipping their muzzles and sipping long of the cooling flow.

All of them, that is, but a magnificent dappled brute of a stallion with wide flexing nostrils and a near-black mane and tail. His gaze scanned the far bank and raked across the all-but-hidden presence of Regis and his horse. Then the stallion's gaze swung back and locked with Regis's eyes.

The mustang stallion stared for long moments, an unfelt breeze riffling his topknot. He flicked his ears, snorted once, and stomped a foreleg. The splashing alerted the other drinking horses, and the entire mass of them—brown, fawn, black, gray—swung their dripping muzzles upward and seemed to stare at him.

Regis felt at once awed, at home, and unnerved, a combination of feelings he'd not experienced since the war's battles. The herd wasted no time in stomping up and out of the river. In moments, there was little more to prove that their presence had been real but dissipating swirls of mud that soon the river carried away.

He guessed the water for what it was—the Santa Calina, a flowage of clear, cool water that fed live oaks and anaquas along its banks. Those trees gave way to the waist-high grasses of the prairie he'd been admiring.

He took the mustang herd's advice and guided his horse through the grasses until they broke through and emerged along the muddy creek's bank. He slid from the saddle but held the reins as the horse sipped long and deep, glancing often at the spot where the mustangs had been across the river but moments before.

When the horse had slaked its thirst, Regis squatted low upstream and lifted his hat free. He squinted—the sun had been given free rein to annoy his sight—and scooped the refreshing liquid onto his face, down the back of his neck, and finally over the top of his head.

It felt so good that he remained squatting at the edge of the water and let his eyes close as he breathed in the lush, verdant smells surrounding him. A kiskadee called out, and another answered, somewhere up in the high, blue sky.

With a sigh, he stood and mounted up and kept riding, spying turkeys, quail, antelope, and deer, all eyeing him with interest and perhaps a twinge of suspicion as the wayward breeze carried his strange scent to them. They would scatter in all directions, coyotes as much to blame as Regis's presence in this otherwise seemingly untouched place.

It wasn't so much a valley as a wide, endless sea or rolling green cut through by the Santa Calina. Rough, wild, vague thoughts formed in his mind, drifted out again, and reformed, telling him little more than one thing. He knew, somehow deep in his guts and bones, that he wanted to be here for longer than just the duration of this pleasant ride.

He surprised himself by realizing he wanted to live here, to possess it somehow. But how? And why? Did he not have a life, a thriving business, friends, several women—prominent young things themselves the daughters of men of society—who wished to impress him? Why here, then? What was it about the place, other than its obvious raw beauty?

In this manner, Regis's thoughts rumbled and ricocheted off one another as he rode, much of the time at little more than a leisurely walk, the horse in no hurry, either.

It wasn't until he heard a crashing and a stamping in a thicket to his left, between him and the river, from which he'd strayed, that something happened that would alter forever the course of his life, the lives of countless others, and the very land on which he rode.

For Regis Royle, steamship captain, saw cattle. A vast herd of them—feisty feral beasts little more than ornery goats with wide horns and blood-red eyes and burr-stickled hides. Cattle that fought and stomped one another and rubbed their rank hides raw against mesquite trees. But they were cattle. And in that moment an idea came to Regis Royle almost wholly formed. He would ranch this very land.

He knew instinctively that if it weren't him, someone would, for it teemed with life. And what gave life its very essence? Water, the tincture of life itself, for without it life will not last. But here in the midst of this hot-as-sin place known as South Texas, there was ample water and lush green grasses, and massive herds of wild mustangs, hundreds, perhaps thousands strong, barely outmatching herds of balky, crazy-eyed cattle. And that wasn't to mention the wild game.

Here a man could own land, good and valuable land—though he knew some might debate those descriptions—and never go hungry. And more than that, he could raise beasts, horses, and cattle and sell them to others for profits that one day might far exceed the solid earnings he'd made from plying the waters of the Rio Grande.

And here, here it all was. He might be no landman, but he, by golly, knew opportunity when he saw it. And this was it—prime ranching land, water and all.

That had been three days prior, and thoughts of the place throughout his long, slow trip had leeched into his mind, his heart, the marrow of his very bones, and would not let him be.

He'd been poor company, he knew, to his kind friends in Corpus Christi, but he'd been haunted by the place, and he had cut short his trip by a day in order to repeat the journey from north to south, half expecting the mystical place to have been little more than some fiendish trick of the brain, some devilish whim sent from on high to torment him, for what purpose he knew not.

But it had not been the case. Instead, he had been, if possible, even more impressed with the sights and smells and sounds and feel of the Santa Calina range. All of it had been repeated—the stretches of lush grasses, gamma near water, the ample game and stock roaming the hills, the very creek, the Santa Calina itself.

Only this time his thoughts of it were anything but vague. They were sharp and shrewd and calculating, all the things that had made him a solid businessman now came into play, and he knew he had made a decision. Or maybe some unseen hand had made it for him. No matter, he was a practical man and now was the time for action. He would have the Santa Calina range.

He knew he would be bullish, ruthless if need be, in his pursuit of it. He'd not intentionally cause anyone harm, but neither would he mince in his pursuit of his goal. To the devil with anyone or anything that might get in his way.

Regis knew there would be plenty who would dare to stop him. This region was famous for Apaches and Mexican and Texas outlaws, all eager to lay low newcomers with blind ambition and money to burn.

Regis snorted. They'd not have reckoned on Regis Royle, for once he set his mind to a task, let alone his heart and his wallet, it would take all the Indians, outlaws, and the US Army, too, to peel him from his dream.

He'd just have to convince his pard, Cormac Delany, to back his play in laying claim to the Santa Calina. Regis wasn't exactly sure how much this land was selling for, but he doubted a place like this would come too dear. On the other hand, what did he know? How much land had he bought? Exactly none. So it could well come hard, and his own coin purse, while healthy, wasn't what he'd call fat.

Yet somehow he knew that Cormac would be intrigued, too, and not just because he'd want to humor Regis. He'd been a father figure to young Royle when he had been little more than a skinny starving stowaway on one of Delany's steamers.

Delany could have tossed him overboard and been well

within his rights to do so. Instead, the seemingly surly Irishman had scowled at Regis, told him he was too thin to be of use to anyone, and fed him.

He'd plied him with more food than the kid had seen since the Christmas before, when his mother's family back in Maine had hosted dinner for her and her two young boys, a kind but charitable gesture given that Regis's philandering father had gambled away their savings some months earlier.

Cormac had then made Regis a cabin boy, and he'd worked his way up, year after year, with Delany teaching him to read and cipher at night by light of an oil lamp.

Yes, Delany would back his play because he'd trust Regis and his intuition, in part because it was his own teaching that guided Royle. And it had paid off handsomely in the past. It had landed them shipping contracts that had rewarded the pair well, allowing them to expand their holdings.

Regis also knew he had to have Cormac in on such a deal because the older man's cultured ways would more than compensate for Regis's own reputation for a distinct lack of tact when it come to protracted negotiations.

And so, wedged in his rocky nest, Regis had smiled and nodded, caught in his blissful dream of the future despite the grim situation in which he now found himself.

And that's when the bullets, which had trickled to a random but steady flecking on him with rock chips that stung and nicked, poured on him once more. Through the long hours, the bandits never seemed to gain any ground, nor did they seem to lose interest in him.

They'd lobbed insults and sneers and jeers and hoots, and twice he heard glass shatter. So they'd been drinking. That was a two-edged sword. Good because their senses might be dulled, but bad because they would be emboldened for even more of this fool's fight.

"Well, let's get to it," he mumbled. He had decided to shuffle to his knees and prairie-dog up to see if he could size up one of the rats, when a fresh voice shouted from afar, and it kept shouting.

It was a yip—no words, but it sounded an awful lot like a man trying to imitate a drunken coyote. Or maybe the other way around. But curiously, the awful yowling was accompanied with the increasing loud sound of pounding hooves and, most important, fresh shots. Sounded as if it was coming at him fast and from the northeast.

Regis bent low and risked a peek around the base of the rock, hoping he'd not get a third eyehole for his trouble.

It was definitely a crazy rider, barreling pell-mell into their midst. Puffs of blue smoke from three directions told him the rider was not one of his attackers. Whoever he was, he was still yipping and howling and cranking off shots with a revolver and what looked to be a shiny new rifle. And he was tugging along a second horse behind. Hmm.

The man seemed to be pounding at everything in sight, except at Regis. Maybe his luck had turned. He resumed his own firing, measuring his shot and taking his time. Regis heard a scream and saw the back of a man as he emerged from behind the rock pile he'd suspected the first shots came from, thanks to the bird. The man bolted for a ground-tied speckled horse and leapt on, one hand held to the side of his head.

Regis saw spatters of blood on the man's white tunic. He also saw that the man wore an unusually tall blue-banded sombrero and a bright red sash about his waist. Regis aimed for the man's back, raised his barrel to adjust for distance, and . . . he held his shot. He'd not fired at many men in his life, and he'd certainly not shoot one in the back, marauder or no.

That didn't seem to bother the man who'd apparently ridden to his rescue. Friend or foe, he'd yet to find out. But the man wasn't bothered by shooting at the retreating bandits.

Regis risked a wider peek and counted four, five of them.

He looked again at the man barreling on in. He was still smoking the blue blazes out of the pan-hot afternoon. And what he saw surprised him almost as much as the events of the previous hour. It was most definitely his own horse lined and trailing behind the newcomer.

Regis stood, visoring his eyes with his left hand and holding his cocked revolver on the slowing howler with his right. The man raised the rifle and butted the stock on his thigh as he trotted up.

The sun was in Regis's eyes, but he swore there was something familiar about this fellow. Then the newcomer spoke and removed doubt.

"That any way to treat kin, Mr. Royle?"

No, couldn't be, thought Regis. He goosed his neck forward and peered up at the mounted man now but three paces from him. "Shepley? That you?"

"The one and only, big brother!" The newcomer slid from the saddle and landed with a plunk, his boots raising dust.

If a full-bore circus troupe had wandered at him out of the shimmering landscape, Regis Royle could not have been more surprised. And yet, the impossible had just happened. Before him stood his very own little brother, his only sibling, one Shepley Royle, who until that moment Regis had assumed was still a student at that Quaker boarding school in Connecticut he'd been paying for.

"What . . . But how . . . What are you doing here?"

The younger man doubled over as if he were choking on a hunk of cheese, laughing and smacking his leg with a palm. "To think . . . Regis Royle at a loss for words! Hoo-boy, I never thought I'd see the day!"

Regis shook his head and strode forward and stuck out his hand. "Shepley, I . . . I don't know what to say!"

"Start with thank you, you big ninny! I come all this way, show up in time to save your sorry hide, and all you can do is shake my hand?"

Before Regis could react, the kid jumped up and locked

his free arm around Regis's neck. "Good to see you, big brother!"

They smacked each other's backs for a few dusty pats, then stood back, Regis holding the youth's shoulders. "Let me look you over." He saw little and yet everything of the youngster he'd last seen four, five years prior? "Still the whip-snap, hell-raisin', risk-taking kid brother, I see."

"And a good thing, too, from the looks of it. I'm not sure how you ever got along without me all these years."

"Oddly enough, I managed." Regis smoothed his moustaches. "Question is, What are you doing out here? And at just the right moment, too."

"Oh, I come looking for you, of course. I had your address in Brownsville from that last letter you sent a few months back. Talked with a huge man, funny name . . . Big Jaw? Something like that. Anyway, he said you'd ridden out this way, but he forbade me to go after you."

"That'd be Lockjaw. And how'd you get away from him? He's not an easy man to disobey."

"He made a big mistake when he told me not to do something. Cause then I just had to do it! It's as certain as the moon and stars coming out at night or the sun rising and baking our heads off out here in this cursed wasteland! It's just the way it is with me, Regis. Can't explain it."

"I believe you just did."

Shep shrugged and smiled. "So I hopped my horse and rode on out. And the rest, as they say"—the kid looked around him as he untied Regis's horse and led him over—"is now history."

"Or dumb luck on both our parts. No matter, I see you are as humble as ever," said Regis, still smiling. He didn't think he'd ever smiled so much all at once in all his days. "Funny thing. I promised Ma I'd look out for you."

"Well, looks like you got it backward, big brother."

Regis worked his jaw muscles. Nobody in the world could be as exasperating to him as Shepley, and that included a pile of annoying, ornery old businessmen of his acquaintance. By gaw'd, but he'd forgotten how the kid could set him off. And this, despite the fact he was mighty glad to see him.

"Won't happen again." He stabbed his left boot into the stirrup and paused, looked up, then over at his brother. "Thanks, Shep. Appreciate it."

The younger man nodded. "Of course, brother."

Regis scanned the distance where the banditos had ridden. He fancied he saw puffs of dust growing fainter with each passing second. Whoever they were, they were not interested in a second dose. "I best find my hat. Oh, by the way, I'm pleased to see my rifle worked for you."

The kid raised the long gun and nodded. "Yep, just fine, just fine." He admired the blued barrel and rich walnut stocks. "Course it's tricky to load and ride fast, so I switched to my revolver." He patted the gun on his belt.

Regis nodded and mounted up without asking for the rifle back. "Where'd you learn to shoot like that, anyway?"

"That fancy school you sent me to," said Shep as they rode eastward. "Best part about it was the riding and shooting lessons."

"I thought they were Quakers."

"Oh, they are, but that doesn't mean I didn't pursue the more practical arts on my own time."

"Uh-huh. So you still didn't tell me what you're doing here. South Texas is a long ol' way from Connecticut, unless I'm forgetting something about maps."

Shepley smiled and sighed. "Mighty thirsty work saving your hide."

Regis didn't say anything but slid from the saddle and retrieved his hat. He held it up and poked a finger through a fresh bullet hole angling from left to right across his top knot.

"Yep, mighty good to have me around, huh, big brother?"

Regis felt the twinge, the momentary urge to clout, playfully, the kid on the ear. Instead he nodded. "Doesn't mean I don't want answers from you, boy. But thanks again."

They rode in silence for a few moments, then Shep cleared his throat. "Course, this means you'll stand the first beer."

Regis, slightly ahead, cracked a smile. "Only if you beat me to it." He tucked low and spurred his horse into a hard gallop, knowing Shep's brown eyes were wide and a growl was already crawling up out of the kid's throat.

Regis glanced back and saw his younger brother jam heels into his buckskin. Then the kid's old beaver topper, more hole than hat, whipped off his head. He didn't slow a hair. Time for hats later. Regis grinned and looked forward again. He had a brother to beat—and a beer to drink. A free beer, or he wasn't fit to wear the name of Regis Royle.

CHAPTER 2

It was close to dark by the time they rode down the dusty main street of Brownsville. All about them, squares of light shone long across their path. Bawdy, bold shouts from men, laced with good-natured shrieks from their fair counterparts, filled the night air, still warm but with an edge of ease only night in the desert can bring.

Piano music, pounding and urgent, leaked from over and under a set of poorly hung, puckered batwing doors.

"How about that beer, brother?"

Regis looked over at the slouched youth riding beside him. "I guess one for celebratory purposes wouldn't hurt."

"One?"

The kid's bald disappointment made Regis smile. "Unless you'd rather have milk?"

"Oh no, anything but that. I ever have enough money I'm never going to drink milk again."

"Thought you liked growing up on the farm back in Maine."

"Ha!" Shepley shook his head. "You're confusing me with you."

"Wasn't me! Why do you think I made for the coast?"

"Yeah, and left me to . . ." The kid's words pinched out, and he looked ahead at nothing. Regis didn't question him.

"How about here?" said Shep.

Regis eyed the cantina. "The Lucky Dog? Nope, too rough for the likes of us."

"After what we've been through?" The kid angled his horse toward the hitch rail out front.

"Nope, Shep. I mean it. There's a decent place down the lane. You go in there, you'll come out poor and dead. Place is filled to brimming with card sharps and worse."

Regis noticed how the kid watched through the open doorway, his gaze lingering on the dimly lit action taking place at the games tables.

Shep pulled on his wide smile and said, "Okay then, lead on, oh fearless brother of mine."

A half-minute later, Regis stopped his horse before a quiet, well-lit establishment.

"Millie's?" said the kid, reading the sign. "This a . . . bordello?"

Regis chuckled. "Not that I'm aware of. And don't let Millie hear you say that. But they do make a sinful apple pie, and I'm about ready to indulge. Figured we could fill our bellies before that beer." He looked at Shep, who eyed him back with the same dark-eyed stare. "I'm sorry to disappoint you, little brother, but if I don't eat something soon, I'm not going to be fit company for man or beast."

Shepley climbed down out of the saddle and sighed, then clapped a hand to his waist and offered a short bow. "To err is human, to forgive divine."

Regis regarded Shepley. "Well, sounds like something from that school stuck."

"Yep," said the young man. "The sap from that pine I climbed down to make my escape from their dastardly clutches." He laughed as he looped his reins around the rail and strode toward the diner's front doors.

It was apparent to Shep that Regis was a regular customer at Millie's. A thick-waisted German woman a good decade beyond Shep's seventeen years batted her eyes at him and fanned her shining face as she took their order. Regis barely had to speak when she let loose with a giggle that seemed never to end.

"Good girl," said Regis after she'd left. "Can't understand a lick of English, but she manages to bring out something tasty every time I wander on in here."

"Mmm, I'll just bet she does," said Shep, looking everywhere but at his scowling big brother.

"Don't let Millie catch you talking like that," said Regis.

"That wasn't Millie?"

"Nope." He leaned over the table. "She's even bigger."

The youth's eyebrows rose, and he looked toward the closed swinging door that led to the kitchen.

The feed was true to Regis's words, and despite his initial hesitation, Shepley tucked in with a vigor only a Royle could muster. "Only person I have ever seen put away that much food at once," said Regis, wiping his ample moustache with his napkin and reaching for a last swallow of coffee, "is Lockjaw. Or maybe me."

"What about Pa?"

Regis's grin slid from his mouth. "I guess." The old man hadn't been the easiest critter to get along with and was much of the reason Regis left home. "I'm sorry I left you back there like I did all those years ago."

Shep shrugged. "I'm tough. I could take it. Besides, Ma kept the worst of it from me. Then the old man left us, and we were better off. Then we heard he up and died, but you knew that."

Regis nodded. *Good riddance*, he almost said, then cleared his throat. "How about that school, then? You on a break? Odd time of year for it."

Shep looked away, his face reddening. Then he looked back at Regis. "I haven't been going."

"What?"

Shep sighed. "I don't go there anymore."

"But . . . I've been sending the money. It's a good school, Shep. You'll get a good education there. More than I had. Ma wouldn't let you up and quit. What's she say about this?"

Shep looked away, then at Regis's eyes. "She doesn't have a thing to say about it."

"What do you mean?"

But even before Shep replied, Regis knew. He could tell by the misting of the kid's eyes, the tuck of the kid's bottom lip. "She's . . . dead. Ma's dead."

They didn't talk for long minutes. Finally Regis said, "How long since?" His voice sounded hollow and old to him.

"Four, five months now."

The air left him. "How?"

"Doctor said pneumonia. I . . . I was there. Got home in time. I was with her." The kid cried, shame reddening his face as he dragged the back of his hand across his eyes. He wadded his napkin and coughed into it, then scrunched his eyes and wiped them.

"I been meaning to write again." Regis clenched his own red-and-white cloth napkin in his big fist. "So busy these days."

Shep didn't say anything.

"I'm so sorry, Shepley. Truly. I'd always meant to get back home before this."

"I know. Didn't help, though, did it?"

"Why didn't you tell me? Someone could have sent for me."

"Tried. I sent a couple of letters but never heard back."

Regis sighed. "I've been busy. Shipping . . . new steamer." He couldn't finish. Anything he said was a pathetic excuse not worth uttering.

After he paid the bill, Regis clapped a hand on his brother's shoulder. "Okay, I'll get us a couple of rooms at the Brownsville Arms. Maybe grab that beer before we turn in. I'll meet you in an hour or two in the lobby, okay? I have business to tend to. You're welcome to come along."

"That's all right," said Shep, yawning.

"Okay, if you're as tuckered as I am, I imagine you'd like to make it an early night. We can catch up more later. Sound good?"

"You bet."

By then they were on the sidewalk. "Good." He handed his reins to the boy. "Then you can take these two nags to Bowdrie's yonder." He nodded at a livery stable diagonally across the street. "Tell Tom I'll catch up with him in the morning. We go way back, helped each other out in the war."

Regis would later question why he didn't take his brother's enthusiasms for taking on a chore in stride. Maybe he thought the boy was growing up. He was, after all, seventeen now. He'd come to regret his lack of scrutiny.

But for the moment, he was headed to the office of his and Cormac's shipping company. He intended to leave Cormac a letter explaining what he'd found and his intentions for the Santa Calina range. He didn't want to waste any time in getting the purchase in the works, but he also didn't want to roust Cormac at his house. The man worked hard, doubly so while Regis had been gone. No need to bother him at home, despite the sense of urgency Regis felt. He was confident Cormac would back his play on this. He'd find out for certain in the morning.

After he did that, Regis turned left from their office and made for Joplin's boarding house, where he suspected his friend, one Jarvis "Bone" McGraw, would be holed up in the kitchen, trying to finagle his way into Mrs. Joplin's good graces and, with any luck, out of her knickers.

He grinned and shook his head as he strode up the street

and two lanes over. As it turned out he didn't need to make the full journey to the boarding house. From somewhere inside Barnard's Tonsorial Parlor, all windows alight, he heard a boisterous, deep-throated braying he knew could come from only one man. He stepped up onto the boardwalk and opened the door.

A man looked up at him from over a checkerboard. "Regis Royle, as I live and breathe."

"Bone, Mr. Barnard, how are you both on this fine evening?"

"Fine?" said the proprietor of the barbershop, a squat, bald, fat man with huge ginger muttonchops and a Donegal brogue as thick as the drifts of hair piled up in the corners of the room.

The man did not like to tidy up much, Regis noted—not for the first time—with a suppressed grimace.

The barber mopped his sweating red face with a voluminous handkerchief. "The last time the weather in this hellish hole of hell was fine, the Good Lord himself was in knee pants and all was right with the world."

Bone was a tall, lanky, raw-boned man roughly Regis's age. He stood—still not wobbly, Regis noted—and shook Regis's proffered hand.

Royle prided himself on his solid handgrip when greeting folks, but Bone, without trying to, had a way of commanding a situation with that one grip and looking you square in the eye every time. It was one trait among many that Regis admired about his friend.

"What brings you into town on such a night, Regis?"

"Oh, this and that, that and this."

"Uh-huh," said Bone as if reading his mind. He stretched and yawned. "Well, Barnard. Much as I like your company, you ain't getting any prettier, and I suspect it will be a cold day well south of here before you're a comely woman, so I'm going to take my custom elsewhere. And besides"—he inclined his head toward the portly Irishman—"you told me an hour ago that Myrtle had supper on the stove. I don't want to take the blame for you missing a meal. Lord knows you can't stand that!"

He raised his eyebrows and reached for his hat—a mammoth, wide affair. He pinched the brim and walked out, ignoring the muttering Irishman. "He's just sore because I licked him at checkers. Again. Man will never learn."

"I heard that!"

Bone winked at Regis and said, "I know, you Irish devil. Now get on home!"

"Sure, this lousy Texas Ranger thinks he can throw his weight around my shop, tellin' me what to do. If I were a fightin' man, I'd . . ." Barnard's muttering drifted to silence behind them.

"Man never changes," said Regis. "Hey, how about a quick beer? I have a notion I'd like to float your way."

"Sounds serious," said Bone. He stopped and tapped his chin. "If a conversation's going to take place, then we best do it somewhere we can hear each other. How about Stump's place?"

Regis considered the suggestion, nodded, and led the way across the street. Once the two men found a table and seated themselves with glasses of warm beer before them, he leaned forward. The place wasn't as empty as he'd have liked, but it was better than the alternatives—loud bars with louder people getting louder as their evenings ground on.

He sized up Bone, one of his oldest friends, a swaggering, womanizing Texan through and through, and a Texas Ranger to boot. And, Regis knew, one hell of a cattleman.

"I just got back from a few days up Corpus Christi way."

Bone nodded. "Decent town, growing like a weed in a rainstorm."

"Yep, but it's not what impressed me most."

"Oh?"

"It was the Santa Calina range."

"Ah, should have known. She got to you, too, huh?"

"You know of it?"

"Who doesn't? Oh, there ain't much of this region I haven't ridden through. It's surprising what you'll find down there flanking the creek."

"That's what I want to tell you about. I aim to buy it."

"You don't say?"

Regis nodded, noticing Bone didn't seem overly surprised. "Yep, and run cattle all over it."

"What do you know about ranching?"

Regis smiled and shook his head. "What I know of it could fill this beer glass." He emptied it, then said, "But you, Bone, know more about such endeavors than any other fellow I know."

"If you're buttering me up for something, you'd have more success with whiskey."

Regis ordered a bottle of their finest and poured them each a shot. "What I have in mind is a partnership, Bone. I aim to buy that range. There's fine water, ample cattle, horses, game, all just waiting for someone to put shape to it."

"And that someone is going to be you?"

Regis shook his head. "Not just me. You too. That's what I meant by a partnership. You have the experience running a ranch. You know cattle and cowboying and the land better than anyone I know."

Regis's voice rose, then he looked around at the few patrons aside from themselves in the dark little hole of a place. "I have my commitments with the fleet, but I'll work with you as I can."

"That's just what we need—a greenhorn rancher with one foot in the water!" This struck Bone as humorous, though Regis could not see why, and the former Ranger guffawed.

Regis looked around. Any more of that and he'd have to tell him to keep it quiet. He didn't want to tip his hand, not when the plan was so fresh.

"What?" said Bone, seeing his chum scanning the room. "You think you're the first to have this harebrained idea, Regis Royle?"

"It's not harebrained, and no. Well, I don't know. Hadn't really thought on it." He leaned forward and poked the tabletop with a ramrod finger. "There's a big difference between dreaming and doing, Bone. I haven't failed at much I've turned my hand to. Why do you think Cormac partnered up with me?"

The Ranger lost his smile then and got that windburned crinkly look about his eyes as he studied his friend. "You're serious, ain't you?"

"Serious as a frigate full of gunpowder."

"By gaw'd." Bone nodded and drummed the tabletop with his fingertips. He was silent a few long ominous moments. "It'll take a pile of cash to get started, you know."

"I know it."

"I mean"—Bone drummed his chin with his fingertips—"got to build corrals, hire a passel of men, the works. Then there's a cookie for chuck and such, quarters for them to live in, can't expect them to hang their hats in the thin air!"

"Never thought I would."

"You saying you're serious? All in on this?"

"Yep." Regis nodded solemnly.

"Cormac in on it too?"

"He will be, soon as he reads the note I left him. The idea's solid. Just have to track the deed, find out who owns it, and make it happen."

"Hmm. That'll take some doing, if I know anything of it. I expect you'll be dallying with old Spanish land grants and such. But it's probably nothing that money can't handle."

Regis leaned back and shook his head when Bone offered him a second shot of whiskey. "That's for you. Paid for the bottle. Figured it might help you think this thing through. But I would like to introduce you to someone, if you have a few more minutes to spare."

Bone's bristly brown eyebrows rose, and the shot of whiskey stuttered in midair halfway to his face. "You get yourself hitched to a woman in Corpus Christi, Regis Royle?"

"God no!" Judging from Bone's reaction, Regis knew his face wore a mask of horror. Maybe one day, but marriage now? No, no, and no.

"Okay, then. I reckon whoever you're about to spring on me can't be all that bad."

Regis shook his head and shoved back from the table. He waited to rise while Bone gathered the bottle and tamped in the cork.

Behind him, at the far end of the bar, a thin man in a colorful serape that barely concealed a blood-spattered tunic slid off a barstool and turned toward the door.

Had Regis been looking, he would have seen that the man's dark hair bore thick wrappings of muslin, with a brown stain along one side of his head.

He also would have seen a red silk sash about the man's waist. And in his hand the man held the brim of a distinctive sombrero with a wide, bright blue band. He also wore a smile that lifted the corners of his wide, bristled mouth as if he had just overheard very interesting news. Because he had.

Had Regis been paying attention, he also might have heard the man chuckling softly as he left the cantina.

As they walked to the hotel where he'd told Shep they'd meet up, Regis wondered just what sort of person his younger brother had become. It wasn't as if Regis really knew the kid. When Regis had left home, Shepley was less than a shaver. Then they'd seen each other, what was it? Three, four times in all those years, not counting today.

Regis groaned to himself. What did the kid want with him now? Best to get him sorted out, then send him back to that school in Connecticut to finish his education. *I guess a little interruption—of a few months of traveling solo—never hurt anybody*, he mused. As valuable as sitting in a classroom, in its own way.

But Regis always regretted not having had more formal schooling. With Cormac's help he'd been able to get a leg up on reading, and within a couple of years of being taken under the man's wing, Regis was tallying accounts books like a professional money man.

As soon as Regis entered the lobby of the Brownsville Arms and didn't see his brother, he frowned. The woman at the desk, a perky young thing he knew to be the daughter of the owners, likewise wasn't helpful. She'd not seen anyone answering to Shepley's name or fitting his description.

"Your brother, huh?" said Bone, not working too hard to tamp down a smile. He cradled the half-filled jug as if it were a child. "Why not let him have the run of the town? Never did me any harm."

Regis said nothing, but his raised eyebrows told his opinion of that idea. "Kid's seventeen—a mighty young seventeen—and fresh off the trail. Or stage. Or boat or train. I don't know which he took to get himself out here. But he's my charge now, and I won't have him come to harm, nor cause it for others." A twinge of guilt stabbed him in the gut as he said it. Thoughts of his old mama dead these five months threatened to upset his apple cart.

"You okay?" said Bone.

"Yeah, yeah. I got an idea where the kid might be. Passed the Lucky Dog on the way in. He seemed keen to test it."

"If he has a half dime in his pocket, it'll go amiss in that rat hole." Bone took a pull on the bottle. "We best make certain he's not in there. That's not a place even I choose to frequent."

But Regis was already legging it back up the street toward the loudest spot ahead. "He's there."

"How do you know?" said Bone.

"That's my horse and his, tied out front. Likely half my gear'll be missing, too. Told him to take them to Bowdrie's, dammit." He ended his sentence with a growling, groaning sound that caused Bone to pop the cork on the bottle once more.

Regis glanced at Bone and suspected his friend was secretly thankful he wasn't Regis's kid brother at that moment. Regis knew enough about himself to know that when his back was up, he was one wild-haired mountain lion.

Visit our website at
KensingtonBooks.com
to sign up for our newsletters, read
more from your favorite authors, see
books by series, view reading group
guides, and more!

BOOK | CLUB
BETWEEN THE CHAPTERS

Become a Part of Our
Between the Chapters Book Club
Community and Join the Conversation

Betweenthechapters.net